For My Family

And for Goober, who was the youngest of us, but the best of us.

And for Gunner, a legend on the Railway who always made us laugh.

Both taken before their time.

G. E. Webb

THE BLOOD PRINCESS

For

The Silk Mill

G. E. Webb

AUSTIN MACAULEY PUBLISHERS™

LONDON * CAMBRIDGE * NEW YORK * SHARJAH

A CIP catalogue record for this title is available from the British Library.

ISBN 9781528990776 (Paperback)
ISBN 9781528990783 (ePub e-book)

www.austinmacauley.com

First Published (2021)
Austin Macauley Publishers Ltd
25 Canada Square
Canary Wharf
London
E14 5LQ

Many writers have inspired me over the years: Stephen King, Dean R Koontz, Ken Follett, Wilbur Smith, Bernard Cornwall, Conn Iggulden, but none more than the King of British Heroic Fantasy, David Gemmell. Greatly missed by his legion of fans worldwide and I am proud to consider myself among them.

I met the great man the in 2005. They say never meet your heroes for you will be disappointed. They are wrong, and I was not. In the moments when I wanted to give up the encouragement he gave me that day kept me going.

Table of Contents

Prologue

Danyard looked back at the carnage behind him, he had never seen such devastation on a battlefield before, the dead and dying lay on the field for at least a league, the cries of wounded men and the anguished whinnying of horses filled his ears and thumped in his head. Blood seeped from a dozen cuts upon his body, his knuckles red raw and bleeding and his long hair matted with the blood and gore from those he had slain. The coppery taste of blood in his mouth hardly noticed after so many hours of combat.

He had lost his helm after the first charge as he had led the mounted Dragoons from their hiding place in the forest and smashed into the flanks of the enemy, his horse had been cut from under him on the second charge and he had battled on foot for the last four hours.

He was mortally exhausted and only stood with the aid of his two-handed broadsword stuck in the earth, now that the adrenaline was wearing away from his shattered muscles. He had thought all was lost when he had seen the King go down with the spike of a war hammer through his breastplate, being sure that it must have pierced his heart he had rallied what remained of the Dragoons and fought his way to the King, thus giving the King's bodyguards a chance to drag him from the field and to safety. The Dragoons had then turned their rage against the attackers and slaughtered their way ahead, using a classic hammer and anvil move to force the enemy against the main Kino'le army.

What remained of the army of Mar'thak had fled the field and the remaining mounted dragoons had given chase intent on destroying their ability to ever make war again, which meant they would be hunted down and killed. Danyard had never had a taste for massacre and was glad his horse was lost to him so he would not have to partake in it.

As he sank to his knees he could feel the blood of the battlefield start to soak through his leggings, his vision blurred as an overwhelming tiredness started to take him, as he looked forward he made out the shape of a rider approaching from the castle. He pushed himself back to his feet, afraid to show weakness in front of anyone, even though pain and fatigue racked his every move.

He let the rider approach, he could see the man was a servant of the King and not a soldier, wearing a bright purple surcoat and looking ridiculous amongst the death and destruction of the battlefield.

"My Lord Danyard," shouted the rider "The King requires your presence," "The King lives?" enquired Danyard.

"At the moment Lord, but you must hurry, he may not make sunset."

"Give me your horse, now."

"I have orders to bring you back together with myself upon this horse Sire," "And I am countermanding those orders, now dismount or I will cut you down,"

The rider looked down at the carnage surrounding him and then back at Danyard and started to dismount reluctantly, trying to step gingerly around the blood and gore slowly sinking into the earth.

"And while you are here, see what you can do for our wounded, many fine men perished this day, while you hid in the castle with the maidens, if you are not covered in blood and shit by my return, I will kill you myself!" said Danyard, as he mounted the mare and turned her to thunder towards the castle.

One

The Sisters

The Princess Victarny gazed out upon her domain, Kino'le, 'The Kingdom of Light'. It was a cold winter night outside the dome of light cast by the magic that just seemed to emanate from the castle and palace walls, a magic that even she did not understand. It provided light at night and always warmed the air of the city proper, extending half a league or so, yet it was not a barrier for anyone who wished to enter or leave.

Even in high summer, the outside, as she referred to it, meaning outside the light, not the city, always felt cold to her. Not so her subjects, who would wander off for days at a time to swim in the lakes and climb the surrounding mountains. She was never comfortable outside the light and she believed that her place was firmly here, within the city to protect and nurture it. Physical protection of her Kingdom was not her concern that fell to the Lord Protector, Danyard. Despite his efforts, most military pursuits were beyond her, apart from horse riding of which she was a natural; the remaining martial arts were a subject she had no interest in.

Her parents, the King and Queen of Kino'le had been killed in the last invasion by the neighbouring state of Mar'thak, her father, driving the attack that had broken the back of the enemy but he had died from his wounds the same day. Her mother had been killed the day before by an assassin, which is what had driven her grief-stricken father to lead his suicidal charge into the massed ranks of the enemy infantry, the fearsome Imperial Guard with him.

With his dying breath, he had appointed Danyard, who was then Lord Dragoon, Lord Protector until Victarny and her younger sister Amyeen, came of age.

The Princess Amyeen had disappeared on her eighteenth birthday, after a quite raucous party, she had gathered a few belongings, including her most valued possession, her sword, and gone to the stables, ordering her beloved gelding, Buster, made ready. Then she had ridden from the castle never to be seen or heard from again. Danyard had sent Dragoon patrols after her, but it seemed that she had simply fallen from the face of the planet; no one had seen her, or anyone matching her description. It had seemed that Danyard had trained her too damn well.

Victarny stopped herself from thinking about her; it always brought a tear to her eye. Although, they were completely different in character, she missed her so much and they loved each other dearly. Although, it was a rare moment when Amyeen was serious enough to tell her that.

Victarny was twenty-nine, her sister twenty-eight, she had been six and Amyeen five when her parents had been buried together, side by side, in death as in life. Her memory of them was sketchy, and she remembered very little of their actual character, only images of their lives together in the Palace walls. Danyard had been their father figure for most of their lives, he had always been there to protect them and when older, offer them counsel.

They had been tutored by him and others in the ways of the court and diplomacy with other nations, and everything that they would ever have to know to run a Kingdom, although technically it was now a Principality, as it was run by a Princess. Even so, it is still officially titled The Kingdom of Light due to its magic cast of light that not even she understood. Most referred to it as Kino'le, the shortened version form the old language but it was not just the magic that gave it its name, the Kingdom was, and had been for decades the most prosperous of all the Kingdoms in the known world, trade flourished and was a shining example of commerce that no other state had ever managed to replicate.

One of the main reasons for this was the reputation that its military held. The Army of Kino'le was the best armed and trained of any, discipline was upheld but most soldiers did what they did out of duty to the Kingdom, morale was always high, and Danyard took a personal interest in all aspects of his military, he was the only man who could promote above Captain and so all officers had a fierce loyalty to him that was hard to displace, although the nobility actually ran the army.

The Army, being an infantry foot soldier force of approximately fifteen thousand would patrol the Kingdom in companies of one hundred men but only within a five-league range of the capital or of Kardon, which was the main sea port and through which the vast majority of trade came through.

The outer areas were patrolled by the cream of the Kino'le forces, the Dragoons, a mounted force that had yet to be beaten in any battle or skirmish. Each man rising up through the Army to be noticed by the commanders, who received considerable honour when one of their men was chosen for training, let alone passing it. The cities were patrolled by the Imperial Guard, an older force with an average age of forty-five, as the only way to get into the Imperials was to serve a minimum of twenty years as a Dragoon.

Danyard had served his twenty years as a Dragoon, although most of it was as Lord Protector and so when he had to don any kind of ceremonial uniform now it was the Imperial Guard uniform that he wore. He still went on patrol. Although more often now, he would ride out and catch up with a patrol after a few days and then leave it early, sometimes catching another to ride in with. He did not tolerate yes men or sycophants, if someone had something to say they were encouraged to speak out, as were his officers who were all encouraged to question his logic, if they disagreed with him.

He was a legend among not just the officers but all the men, he would regularly challenge groups to fights with wooden practice swords, most ending up laid out but those who managed to strike him were then offered a trial for the position of Royal Bodyguard, the most prestigious position within the Kingdom's military, all held the rank of Captain, apart from Buldor, who was their overall Commander, but there were only sixteen of them, so fearsome was their reputation, all exclusively trained by Danyard and no one else, the last four days of which was carried out with no sleep whatsoever. Only six from every hundred passed and that was exactly how Danyard wanted it.

Danyard stood there now, ten paces or so from the Princess so as to give her room, his sword on his hip as it always was and his thick bladed kukri in its sheath on the small of his back. The two on-duty bodyguards stood in the doorway from the castle to the battlements ready to relieve Danyard when he had finished his discussion with The Princess.

"Stay clear of the battlements Lady," he called to her as she walked to the edge.

"Do not worry yourself Danyard, I am a big girl now, I will not fall." she replied.

"It is not the drop that worries me, any assassin with a longbow could take you down from below and be gone and into the woods before we even saw him,"

"Who would possibly want to hurt me Danyard, you worry too much,"

"Worrying is my purpose in this life My Lady, and there are those, who see this Kingdom with envious eyes," *and there were enough of them* he thought to himself.

"We have no enemies, only friends on all sides."

And this was the problem thought Danyard, she could never see the evil in people, how am I supposed to protect her when she still sees the world through rose-coloured eyes. Not her fault of course, she has no memory of the terrible battles fought over this place years ago. Danyard also knew the biggest threat to Victarny's reign was not from a nation state, not on its own anyway, it was from one person, he knew this for he had trained her himself, before he had driven her from the castle on her eighteenth birthday.

Thirty leagues to the South, in an old disused wooden fort built by settlers from Kino'le, sat and brooded a warrior woman a year younger than Victarny, she knew this, as she knew most things that Victarny did not.

At first glance, if seen on horseback, of which she was a natural, you would not know that she was a woman, which suited her needs perfectly. She wore heavy leather leggings with good quality calf length boots, a buckskin undershirt with a black leather jerkin over the top. Above this was a coat of oil blued chainmail, this, more than anything else set her apart from most warriors for only the best paid could afford chainmail, let alone paying to have it oil blued which gave it a dull finish and added to its level of protection. The ensemble managed to cover her female form from the casual observer. Her black hair was tied back to reveal a large facial scar on her left cheek. It ran from inside her hairline down to her jaw, her eyes were so dark brown that they appeared black, which again suited her needs when staring down opponents.

The two most important items of her attire were both on her left side, her beloved sword, made especially for her, a matching one made for Danyard, two handed but ultra-light and razor sharp, about three foot long, again in a black scabbard on her hip, and on her left shoulder, a large vampire bat, clinging on upside down, her jerkin reinforced with an extra layer of leather to prevent his talons from piercing her skin. She had named him Blood. Her horse had panniers for food and other essentials, and also her Dragoon war bow. She was the only person alive in the known world other than a Dragoon to be in possession of one. She was an expert with all her weapons, as she was with all weapons that she had ever held.

Her name was Amyeen, and of the many things that she knew, she knew that The Kingdom of Light was, by right, half hers, for she was the sister of Princess Victarny.

She had always seen things differently from her sister, darkly the old wizard Lorgane had said, but she just saw things in a different way and had never been taken by the Princess like things that so obsessed her older sister. The ridiculous girl clothes they tried to make her wear, with silly things in her hair and strange powders to put on her face. So one day Danyard had taken her to the training ground and she had found her true home. The armourers had made her a tiny set of armour when she was six and she had rarely been out of it, as she grew they re-made it and added to her chainmail, Danyard forbade her from proper weapons until her twelfth birthday, and then the Master Armourer and presented her a full set of weapons for her size.

From this moment, as she entered puberty and grew, she also grew into the most fearsome warrior Danyard had ever seen, apart from himself. He taught Victarny the art of diplomacy and he taught Amyeen the art of war, from strategy and tactics of large-scale formation to logistics and supply right down to individual combat, and she excelled at it all.

She knew that her sister and herself had a certain amount of magic within themselves but she did not know how to harness it. But it expressed itself through Blood, her vampire bat, one of her most closely guarded secrets was her ability to see through his eyes, she could send him flying with just a thought and see the view of the world from him, the bat himself could see, albeit not very well, this had she remembered from her lessons as a child, bats used some kind of sound echo to see with, but this did not seen to apply to this particular bat, maybe, she thought, the magic that enabled her to see through his eyes enabled him to see normally as well. This ability had made her a legend among warriors and common folk alike, she had only been beaten once and very few people alive knew about that, and that defeat was here, in the dark forest of Dalstock where this old rotting fort still stood.

Two

The Dark Place

She knew not why she came to this dark forbidding forest, but every time she was within a day's ride, it seemed to call to her. The place of her only defeat and also the only time she had fought for a principle and not a purse. No bounty was offered, no reward for safe passage of the settlers, she had heard about them and joined their convoy on a whim, in the end to come within inches of death, only being spared by the savages' leader, Garvak, when she had awoken from the strike by the spear that had caused her now famous facial scar. To her amazement he had also spared her horse.

She had also found Blood here, him being a creature of the darkness well-suited to its reputation. When she had come to from the battle, she had opened her eyes, and she had sat up and then felt something pulling at the skin of her throat, although there was plenty of fresh blood spilt on the wooden floor and around the fort, he was sucking fresh blood from her neck, she had only felt him when she moved, as she remembered from her childhood lessons as vampire bats bit their fangs secreted a toxin that numbed the area being bitten so the poor creature under attack did not feel it. She had pulled him off in shock and thrown him to the ground, raising her foot to stamp on him when something stopped her, a sudden feeling of empathy with him.

She realised that like her, this creature was just trying to survive, like her it was feared and possibly loathed, so she bent down and scooped him up, noticing that she had broken one of his wing bones when she had thrown him off of her. She had then sat down and with her back against the wall and had put him back on her neck and let him drink his fill, and that's how Garvak had found her. When he walked up the steps to the now torn asunder gate, her sword was in his hand and the man behind him carried her dragoon war bow, so obviously he had already been through the fort while she was unconscious and taken these items from her. He stood and stared for a while and she stared back at him trying to muster hatred for him, but she could not, she was too tired. He had long blond hair tied back, dressed only in a knee length green tunic of rough cloth and was barefoot, the others that she could see all dressed identical, all with no expression on their ruggedly handsome faces. Each armed with only a tall spear that ended in a matt-black razor-sharp spear head.

"You live warrior, to fight another day, but not here, ever again. You swear by your gods to never again invade my homeland then you can ride from here with all your weapons, or I can kill you now," he had said. "It is a simple choice, live or die."

"I will ride from here, I will never want to return you murdering bastard." she spat back at him.

"My name is Garvak of the tree people, and this is my brother Geel, this is our home, our people have lived here for thousands of years and we did not invite you, you are not welcome, you dwellers of stone and rock come here and attack this place full of life and start to destroy it, cutting down these magnificent trees to make your homes, and construct this…monstrosity. Here is your sword, I must say the finest weapon I have ever seen a stone dweller wield, and also your bow, we have taken all of your remaining arrows, you will not kill another living thing in my forest, unless…it is one of them… The Others."

"What others?"

"You will either see on your way out or you will not, if you do see, then it may be the last thing you do ever see, if you do not then it matters not."

"What of the innocents you have slaughtered here, the families, when word gets out of what happened here…more may come, seeking vengeance."

"There are no innocents, and you yourself are responsible for the deaths of seven of my people, five by this bow of yours and two by this sword and yet, I am prepared to let you leave here alive, with these weapons, so do not lecture me."

"If they hadn't attacked peaceful people, then I would not have had to."

"And if you had not come here then you would not have had to. They caused their own deaths the minute they entered Dalstock, if not by us then by the Others…and the Others would have turned them, my people barely survive now, any increase in their number would prove the end of us, you are the only survivor, if you speak of what happened here then it will be on your head when more come and we kill those also. Now begone!"

She had stood and stared into his green eyes, then she had taken her sword from him, and her war bow and walked to where another of them held her horse. She slotted the bow into its harness and then mounted the gelding and turned to stare at him but he had already melted back into the foliage. As she sat upon her mount, she remembered the bat, she turned her head and looked at him, realising that he still had a broken bone in one wing. Once again, very gently, she took hold of him and folded his wings in, as she did, she felt a pain in her own arm and nearly dropped him, she stopped herself from crying out and reached to her belt, where a small black leather pouch hung, this held her sword cleaning cloth and spare strings for her bow, which she took and shook out, then carefully laid him inside it before reaching backwards and placing him gently at the bottom of one of her saddlebags. Now, what to do with him she wondered and was then struck by a piece of knowledge she had picked up on her travels, there was a well-known animal healer by the name of Morlen, less than a day's ride from where she was. She turned the horse towards the overgrown track and set off in the direction of the place that was known locally as 'The Glade'.

As she rode, she became aware of something, she tried to go faster but it was a dark and dingy place, only sporadic sunshine got through the triple canopy forest above and around her. Her horse, Buster, would not go faster, too many twisting and winding roots stuck out of the ground, ready to trip a fast horse and she could not risk him breaking a leg or throwing her, she knew it would take days to get out without him.

The feeling that something was watching and following her was getting more substantial, she could hear the noise that forests made, small animals in trees, birds taking flight but the thing that scared her more than anything was not this noise, it was the lack of it. Whatever was following her was literally scaring all the other livings things stiff. There was a sudden crash from above her, as if something huge had just landed in a tree, she pulled up and stood Buster stock still, listening for it, and then again another almighty crash but this time from just ahead of her, it's jumping from tree to tree now she thought, well if I'm going to fight this damn thing then it will be on my terms, not its terms, she thought to herself, but I need to get to a clearing. If whatever it is lands on me from a tree then it's all over, she suddenly and abruptly dug in her spurs and galloped Buster as fast as he would go, will just have to risk it at the moment, she thought as she searched ahead desperately for a clear area.

She edged Buster around the track, hearing the thundering of branches bending and snapping above her, she was now ahead of it again but she knew it could just wear her down, eventually she and the horse would take a fall. She entered a small clearing and pulled up suddenly and made her decision, whilst not ideal it would have to do, she would make her stand here she thought as she flung herself from the saddle and drew her sword. She could hear it in the trees above her, now more cautious, it being used to humans running from it not making a stand. She got her fear and her breathing under control and waited, sword in hand listening. She heard the branches just behind and above her rustle and then felt the presence of it, without wasting energy on looking at what she faced she spun in a wild two-handed attack just as the creature was rising from its crouch after falling, aiming for where she expected its head to be.

At full height it was over two and a half paces tall, covered in dark black matt fur that did not reflect any light, it's huge head was dominated by it's equally huge mouth, and lolling inside and then snaking out rapidly was its tongue. Nasty looking and large fangs protruded from this gaping maw and she could see rows of teeth inside. Her sword blade struck its ribcage, slicing through flesh, bone and lung but then becoming stuck, she pulled at the sword but it would not budge, the sliced open ribcage holding it fast, the creature screamed in pain and blood erupted from its mouth at the same time, covering her as she pulled and pulled on her sword and also making her retch violently. She saw his mighty arm come back and she knew it could easily claw her head clean off, the sinewy muscle more visible now, she had no choice although it hurt her to do so, she let go off her precious sword and ducked, bringing her kukri from its sheath as she did so and swung it up into the very top of its femur, again cleaving through solid muscle and causing an almost explosive spray of blood. This time because of the axe-like thickness of the kukri blade she managed to wiggle it free and she jumped backwards, trying to get some distance between them. Blood from the kukri ran down her hand and arm and she felt the black ooze thicken as she stood there. The creature still stood before her, it must bleed out soon she thought, how much fucking blood can it possibly have left inside it!

It looked at her hesitantly, then tried to back away, but the wound in its leg caused it to stumble and it fell, she was tempted to rush at it, but it might be a feint and so she stood her ground. As it fell backwards the blade of her sword protruding from its back hit the ground first and it was forced back through its ribcage, the beast screamed again and swung its opposite arm across its body and knocked it free where it clattered against a tree root as it fell to the forest floor.

She could see then that it was dying, the bright red colour from its mouth was fading as its lifeblood spilt from both wounds. She walked cautiously towards it; stopping to collect her sword, as she approached, she suddenly shuddered, knowing she looked into the face of evil incarnate. And then she slowly and surely wiped down her sword blade and replaced it in its scabbard. Then, using her kukri, hacked its head clean from its body, she did not know why but she just felt this was the right thing to do.

Three
The Healer

In the place known locally as The Glade, Morlen went about the business of caring for her animals, not really hers, there was no fence or corral, no barn, shed or enclosure, but animals came to her just knowing it to be a place of safety, especially being so close to the dark expanse of Dalstock Forest a few leagues away, most animals avoided the dark forbidding place unless they were desperate for a place to forage in the dead of winter.

She studied closely the wound on Sophie, her old nanny goat, it was on her right shoulder and still oozed a little blood, she pinched it together and concentrated on it as she felt the heat run through her fingers and the wound closed enough to stop any more loss of blood. She knew, it was from a vampire bat, again it must have come from Dalstock, maybe an older one who could not make it back with the colony. She hoped, it would move on, for although she could use her powers to prevent it from targeting Sophie again, she did not want to, all creatures to her were sacred and she could not show favouritism to any one in particular.

She had only ever seen a vampire bat up close once before and although wounded, it had been a prime example, she had not realised, just how big they were until the day the warrior woman had ridden into her clearing, looking like death itself, every bit as frightening to behold as the legends that now followed her said she was.

That day was still clear in her memory, she had known someone was coming and so had let herself be seen. When she was quiet, and at peace, and she stood stock still and could slow her heart rate she was simply not seen, animals could still see her but people, whose senses were not at in tune with the world around then just did not notice her, it was not an invisibility as such, she could just be still and seemed to melt into her surroundings, she found this very useful when she travelled to the nearest village once a moon, or even the nearest town once a season. One of her favourite things was to sit outside a tavern and watch the world go by, knowing she could not be seen.

The warrior woman had broken the tree line at the glade and ridden towards her cottage, she had been tempted to hide from her but had been fascinated by her appearance, leather and chainmail, covered in dark blood that had congealed and stuck to her, she could see it was not the blood of a normal creature and so her interest grew. She let her approach and stared up at her.

"I am in need of a healer, it is said you are such," she had spoken.

"I am a healer of animals, not of people. Although, you look as if you need help of some sort," Morlen had replied.

"I have an…animal…that requires help."

"Your horse looks perfectly healthy to me lady."

"Not my horse, the creature I refer to is in one of my saddlebags," and with that she had dismounted and retrieved the bat for her to see.

"I was in a small skirmish, I awoke later to find him drinking blood from my neck, I ripped him off of me and broke his wing, I think anyway, or one of the small bones in his wing."

Morlen took him and laid him on her picnic table, carefully unwrapping the soft leather that held him. "Yes, he has a broken wing, I can splint it, but when I am done, will see to you that cut needs stitching and cleaning and you need cleaning, thoroughly. The blood that covers you needs to be scrubbed from you, only one creature I know has blood that thick and I had always hoped that they never really existed, it appears you survived the 'Small skirmish' with it and it did not."

"The skirmish was not with him, that was after, on my way out."

"Then you fought the Tree People of Dalstock? Why? Why would you do such a thing?"

"I did not start this fight; they attacked my people."

"What were your people doing in their forest? Do you not know the legends of Dalstock!"

"Does it matter woman, are you going to help us or is your reputation as a healer just a charade?"

"Yes of course, I have never turned from a living being in need of my services and I shall not start now, even from a creature of darkness."

"I will assume you meant the bat by that remark."

"Yes, I did mean the bat," replied Morlen as she smiled and the tension left the air. "Please come to my cottage, strip off all of your outer garments then you may warm some water from my hearth to clean yourself with, by which time, I will be ready to stitch your face. This vampire bat, he has drunk of your blood hasn't he?"

"Yes, I had no choice, I am no expert but I am aware that they need to drink their own bodyweight in blood each day just to survive, and that is when they are fit and well. I could feel his need so I let him."

"You did a noble thing, but, there is a certain magic in the air in these lands, this act of kindness will manifest itself somehow."

"I think it already has. When I move him, touch him, I can feel the pain in him, not spiritually, but physically. My arm hurts where his wing is broken…"

"I have heard ancient legends of this, but never personally known of a case, all I can say is be careful, and do not let him feed from you again, it could…affect you."

"I will be careful with him, when will he be able to travel?"

"At least two days, that goes for you as well, you need to rest lady."

"I am no lady, as those who have faced me are aware."

"It is of no concern of mine, your heritage, but I have never seen a horse that fine beneath a commoner, or clothes that well-made, and chainmail gone to the expense of being blued…even the best warriors do not bother with the expense, but as I say, it is of no concern to me."

"Bounties pay well… I can afford these things, I live for days at a time outside and fight for a living, I only buy the best, so I can be comfortable and safe."

"If you say so, now my name is Morlen, and you are?"

"Neema, it is not my given name but it will do."

"Neema it is, you will have a scar on your face but not as bad as if it was to heal elsewhere, it will heal faster and better here, like I said, something in the air. When I have stitched you up there is another room in my cottage that you can stay in, only one rule. Although, you may keep your weapons with you, I know what you warriors are like about your precious weapons, you must not use them, no hunting. We do not eat meat here, I will draw some blood from your horse to feed the bat to help him heal but other than that, no flesh to be consumed."

"Your house, your rules, and thank you."

That had been eight years ago and although Neema had ridden away after five days with promises of visiting each year, she never had, but the reputation of the warrior woman now known as 'The Blood Huntress' was legendary, Most stories Morlen smiled at, but some made her shudder, her prediction about the dark influence of sharing a consciousness with a creature that lived from the blood of other creatures seemed to have come true.

Four

The Vision

Amyeen sat in her garden and enjoyed the last of the warm summer evenings, she owned a modest house with extensive grounds for horse riding and training in the city state of Ceredon. Ceredon was technically a city but it did not fall within the boundaries of any other Kingdom and was so large that most considered it a nation state within itself. Amyeen's house was on the western edge and surrounded by a high wall, it had once been owned by a minor noble that had a reputation for liking his privacy and a zero tolerance approach to trespassers. He had passed away some years ago and what remained of his family had sold it on. Amyeen had paid the asking price and a bonus if the family kept the rumour going that he was still alive and more cantankerous than ever, so as to not attract any unwanted business or visitors. The main gate to the property was always locked but she had had built into the wall a number of smaller and well-hidden entrances that she used when she needed to travel.

She had a small staff of two women who cooked and cleaned and an old man by the name of Samuel who looked after the stables and the garden, all of who occupied the upper floor and she used the whole of the downstairs which was where she also had her strong room were for her armour and weapons.

Samuel's teenage grandson Lemuel helped out three days a week and also delivered food and supplies from the nearest market, he was quickly becoming a fine archer under her supervision but she forbade him from entering any tournament for fear of attracting attention to himself. His main asset as far as she was concerned was that the boy could play stupid with remarkable ease.

Even before she had found her 'Blood Vision' as she referred to it, she had quickly gained a reputation as a tracker and hunter of men. So legendary now was her reputation that it was becoming a hindrance to her, she could not ride anywhere without being recognised and crowds tended to form around her. She no longer needed the money that her trade bought her, she was wealthy beyond what most bounty hunters could only dream of but sometimes she just needed to get away and hunt people, and then sometimes something happened that she felt she had to intervene. Her last hunt had been such a situation.

A small group of bandits, said to be four of them, had been attacking small convoys and single wagons on the road between Ceredon and Kino'le. Initially they had just stolen goods but the last two times and seen an escalation in their violence, and the last time and seen a family murdered, a six year old boy had survived by hiding in the woods but he had witnessed his parents and older brother and younger sister slaughtered.

Danyard had especially ordered a dragoon patrol, forty-eight men, to hunt them down but they had managed to escape the ambush set for them and fled across the border to Mar'thak. The Dragoon patrol sent a rider back to inform Danyard and set up a picket line across their side of the border to prevent them returning. The hope was that the Mar'thakians would flush them out through their side and into the waiting dragoons. But the Mar'thakian high command was dragging their feet and no solution was forthcoming, also the group had managed to avoid all the other bounty hunters from catching them.

Eventually Scallion, the man who ran the orphanage where the boy had been taken had been approached with an invitation for The Blood Huntress to assist in their apprehension. The orphanage was one of many ways in which contact could be made with her, for she no longer advertised her services on town notice boards as she did not have to. There was the orphanage, an armourer and a small market stall selling exotic goods. Once a fellow bounty hunter, who had wanted to try to try to kill her for the glory it would bring him had made an approach to the armourer and then followed his messenger. The bounty hunter was found a day later hanging from a tree in the main square. Nobody had ever tried to find her in person again.

She knew, they would be in the dense forests of Mar'thak, in late summer they were overgrown and navigation was near impossible, near impossible for a normal person that did not have the use of a high-flying vampire bat to scout for her. From what she knew of hunted men, which was extensive, she thought they would be holed up somewhere and hoping to hide out into the winter and then make an escape, but it would have to be somewhere secure but close to a river, two very good things about water helped the hunter, men could not live without water and water is heavy. So she headed for the base of the mountains following rivers through the dense thick foliage. Blood flew ahead of her and she could see through his eyes while she rode, then he would land to feed and she would release him to do so. The coppery taste of blood always came to her when he fed and made her retch so she would use this time to rest Buster and plan her next stage.

She tracked them for two days before Blood found a scent where she thought they would be, at the foothills of the mountains where there were plentiful caves and crevices to hide and take shelter in. The next day, Blood caught his first sight of them, a small but well used and well-made firepit just outside a cave, and four men sat around it. She made her camp and sat down to study their routine for a whole day and a night, putting all her concentration through Blood's eyes. Although, she had mastered her Blood vision whilst riding, she could not concentrate properly on either while doing both. As she watched, she saw one of the men constantly standing and pacing, and appeared to be very vocal with the other three. She could see all Blood could see through him but sounds came out as a garble, she was unable to understand what was said. But she did not need to hear them, she understood perfectly, they were arguing constantly which was a good sign, the last thing she wanted was a group with high moral that would stick together.

She slowly but surely went about her camp business, tending to Buster, making a fire, but all the time watching and studying their routine, she saw where each man slept, the fact that they did not bother with any of them taking guard, just the odd patrol around, usually alone, this would be their downfall.

Before sunrise she had struck her camp and was moving towards them, Blood was still there having fed on one of their horses that night, and flying overhead giving her a perfect top down view. As she approached, she dismounted and strung her dragoon war bow, selecting a broad head arrow she remounted Buster, nocked the arrow and held it loose across her lap as she approached. She wanted as much blood and chaos as she could create, hence the broad head, designed to cut clean through muscle and arteries so that the victim of the arrow would bleed out as a pose to die instantly, used mainly for large game like deer that it was hard to kill with a single arrow.

She stopped, when she had a clear view to the camp and cave mouth they were using. She lifted the war bow still with the nocked arrow, drew back on the string putting it dead centre of her face and waited for a count of five, then eased the pressure, she did this four times and just as she was about to ease again one of the men stepped into her line of sight. He was about seventy paces away, side on to her, and although she was mounted and in clear view, he had not seen her. She loosed the arrow, it rose and then started to fall at which point it hammered into the side of his neck, knocking him clean off his feet and spraying blood in a massive arc as he fell, trying to scream but not knowing what had happened to him or why, he suddenly had no voice, the edges of the broadhead having severed the base of his tongue.

She then dug in her spurs and charged, the second man heard and then saw her and already had his sword to hand, but she had perfectly anticipated his moves, as he stretched out to strike her she bought her own sword down in a singing act and cut through both of his wrists, taking the nearest hand off cleanly and the further one with part of his forearm, blood exploded from the stumps and he fell back screaming, staring in disbelief and horror at the mess his arms now were.

The third man turned and tried to run but he was no match for her mounted on Buster, she ran him down, kicking out from her high up position and striking him between the shoulder blades, he fell hard, tangled in his own sword belt as he fell and smashing his head hard on a rock.

She looked around for the fourth man but he was nowhere to be seen, so she dismounted after replacing her sword in its scabbard but picking up her war bow. The third man was struggling to stand after being kicked to the ground, he also seemed to have some kind of leg injury, as he was staggering away from where she had ridden past him, again she selected a broadhead, nocked it and brought the string to her face in one smooth movement, she loosed and followed its flight, taking him clean in the back exactly where she had kicked him, the force of the arrow knocked him to the ground but she could see half of it protruding from him and so left him, if he was not dead, he soon would be. She returned to Buster and put the war bow away in its holster once again and drew her sword as she took a slow steady walk to the cave mouth, where the fourth man stood waiting, sword in hand and wearing pieces of mismatched armour that he possessed. As she approached, he spoke.

"I never wanted to harm anybody, I knew we should not have hurt them, especially the little ones. Even if you risked taking me in alive, I would rot in a dungeon forever, but you do not do you? Risk taking people alive. I could not stand to be near then in the end, I slept away from them, savages all three of them, but it matters not to you what I say now."

"You had plenty of opportunity to surrender, you chose not to, you chose to run, now raise your sword and defend yourself for I am bored with this conversation and do not care about your feeble excuses." she replied.

He suddenly exploded into action taking two quick steps and bringing his sword in a vicious side swipe, she used a downward block and stepped back, absorbing the impact and turning it, she let herself be turned away then swung all the way around and cut cleanly under his breastplate and into his abdomen, her blade being stopped only when it hit his spine, she pulled it out forward and stepped back as he fell to his knees and then slowly toppled onto his front as his guts filled the air with their stench. She looked down, exulted at once again being the victor. She knelt down and pulled his head up by his hair, looked into his dying eyes and then stood up and walked towards where she had left Buster.

As she passed the fire, she saw the second man was still alive, he was laid by the fire and shivering through blood loss and shock, the air smelt of melted flesh and she saw he had tried to cauterise his stumps to stop the bleeding. He had stopped when the pain had become too great, they still seeped but were now black and sickening to behold. He looked up at her and spoke.

"Please…please…help me, you…can take me…with you…put me in the dungeons but please take the…pain away."

"There is only one way for the pain to end for you now, you know this," she replied as she knelt and pulled her skinning knife from its sheaf, she looked into his eyes as they started to glaze over and she cut through his leggings, then opened up his femoral artery.

"The pain will end soon now, close your eyes and it will all be over," with that she headed back to Buster to clean her weapons.

That had been a week ago now, and despite the euphoria that she had felt at the time she was now feeling an aching melancholy, Danyard had once told her it was the just the natural balance of things, she felt good then she would have to feel bad later.

She watched as the sun started its slow decent and then was suddenly struck by her blood vision, he had just emerged from his bat house to start his nightly feeds but what she was seeing was not directly from his eyes, she saw the Glade, and Morlen's cottage, and then about a dozen men running towards it, some strange kind of weapon in the hands of each one. Morlen could not be seen but that was to be expected, then she saw a mighty stag running as one of the men pointed his stick weapon at it and flame exploded from the smaller end, the stag fell, blood pumping from a massive hole in its neck. Even she, who lived a life of violence, was shocked by what she had seen.

"Samuel!" she shouted, as she launched herself from her seat and headed for her strong room "Saddle Buster, and enough supplies for three days, Now!"

She did not know what devilry was at work with these strange weapons but she did know that her friend Morlen was in grave danger.

Five

The Mission

She turned from the track she had been heading on and into the forest, it had been a long time since she was last here and much had changed, as all forest do, an area of living plants was constantly changing, paths overgrew and new ones formed, trees grew and changed shape, even the course of a river could change if the weather was extreme enough in winter, she did, however have an advantage over any other living person, a vampire bat that could fly high above her and show her the way.

Within an hour, she had found the path leading to the Glade, she dismounted and tied Buster to a tree a couple of hundred paces from where Blood had seen the sentry, his strange weapon was loose in his hand, not how the others had been carrying theirs when they had fired, he took no precautions to hide himself and was wandering about mumbling, clearly unhappy about something. She left her dragoon war bow on her back and drew her sword, taking very careful steps toward him, despite his lack of vigilance he had chosen his place well, on the far side of a small clearing about thirty paces wide, she would not be able to take him completely by surprise. She approached the clearing, and watched, he was suddenly spooked and picked up his weapon, putting it to his shoulder as would a crossbowman, then there was an audible click as he pulled back something metal on the mechanism at the rear of it.

She broke her cover and ran for him, covering the thirty paces as quickly as she could, at the last moment he caught sight of the movement and turned his body and the fearsome weapon towards her, she leapt to his side and brought the blade of her sword down in the centre of the weapon with every ounce of her strength behind it, it sliced clean through the metal tube along the top and smashed the wood underneath, he stepped back looking astonished at the two halves of it and then looked down at the blood quickly flooding the front of his jerkin through the huge gash that had opened up in his chest, he fell to his knees and looked up at her.

"Please…no… I…," he said.

"You are already dead, you just do not know it," she replied and then he fell forward onto his face. She looked down at him and then cleaned her sword blade before returning it to its scabbard, then she took her war bow from her back and pulled an arrow from her quiver.

Morlen sat against her small cottage and tried to relax, it was becoming harder to remain unseen now, all around the glade were corpses of her animals, hideous wounds upon them, and the men laughing as they strode amongst them, congratulating each other and started to gather fire wood, she sighed to herself, they were settling in for the night and she was not sure how long she could keep this up.

She had known they were coming; they were chasing a stag and the stag had run to The Glade, knowing it as a place of safety. She had seen a vision of its death throes an hour before it had charged through the brush, bleeding heavily and near death. She had sent the vision impulsively to the vampire bat of Neema, not knowing if it had been a success.

Before the arrival of the men she had prepared herself mentally to relax, she could not remain unseen if she was in a high emotional state. It had worked until she heard one of the weapons discharge its dreadful load, flame had roared out of the small end and the sound was deafening, each time she had jumped near out of her skin and she was sure that one of the younger men had seen her, he had looked right into her eyes, then as he shook his head and blinked she had taken her chance and vanished as smoke had momentarily obscured his view. He had shaken his head again and stared right at her, but she had known from his expression that he could not see her. This did not mean that she was calm now, it was starting to get dark and she forced her breathing under control, knowing that when it was fully dark, she would be able to move around at least.

She watched as the fire was lit and expertly managed, each man started to unpack his own cooking utensils and then the arguments started.

"Why the hell are we out here, when there is a perfectly good cottage just there?" asked one.

"I have explained this enough to you, you fucking idiot, out here we can see and hear anybody approaching, and be ready for them, in there we would be completely taken by surprise," replied a large bald man, who by his manner Morlen took to be the leader.

"But we could take it in turns in there, in a nice warm bed," said the first.

"I have had enough of you and your fucking whining Parkan, go to the path from the forest and watch for anyone approaching, and keep out of sight"

"Why me Cambor, it's always me."

"Yes, it is always you, and has anyone else here complained? No, they haven't, because they know what happens when they piss me off, now go or I will gut you where you stand," Parkan looked around at his colleagues, then picked up his weapon and moved off towards the tree line, once again feeling stupid as once again his mouth had got him into trouble.

"Also, we stay out here because it is said that the woman who dwells here is a witch, and I do not want to be turned into a toad by morning, I am ugly enough as a human," they all laughed as the tension left the air. "Now get some of that venison on the fire before we all starve and then get some rest, apart from you Callan, you can relieve your idiot friend in the small dark hours."

"Yes, Cambor no problem. I saw her, the witch woman, just as I fired at the stag, she was suddenly there and then just as suddenly, not there. I thought it may have been a trick of the light, with all the smoke and that, so I did not mention it, until now."

"Well, if she is here then she is no real threat to us, unlike her friend," Cambor said and realised his mistake immediately.

"What friend?" inquired Callan.

"You may as well know; you have earned that right. It is said that she is a friend of The Blood Huntress. Balstore told me to avoid this place at all costs, but we just got caught up in the chase for the stag, and it led us here, one of those things…"

"Surely you jest with us Cam," said a small wiry man, who had not yet spoken.

"I wish that I did Namtu, I really wish I did," he had known Namtu on and off the battlefield for twenty years now and had never seen a look off fear on his face like that before.

"So, even if we accomplish this mission, we may yet spend the rest of our lives being hunted by her, she has never failed to fulfil a mission, never. A personal vendetta does not even bear thinking about. I will continue, as I always do, but this, this is a bad omen for the start of this mission, no more stupid risks Cambor."

Even though the man named Cambor was the leader, he was still obviously very wary of the one named Namtu, *curious*, thought Morlen.

"We are sworn to protect you Nam, and we will, do not worry, I will get you to Kino'le and then it will fall, and she will have bigger problems to worry about, or so says Balstore, even I wonder, how he knows these things sometimes, but he is rarely wrong."

They all looked around at each other then and at the quickly darkening sky, Callan watched as a large bird flew overhead and then realised that it was not a bird but a really large bat, unusual, he thought, normally they fly in colonies, it was then that an arrow flew from the dark tree line and skewered his arm to his chest. And chaos reigned.

Cambor flung himself at Namtu, covering him with his body as the gigantic Edvar did the same to both of them. He lay there being squashed by Edvar's massive weight and he knew who had loosed that arrow, what he did not know was how the hell she had got here from wherever she had been and how she had known they were there. Callan was screaming, causing more chaos, one man had stood up too quickly and the staggered backwards into the fire with an arrow in his shoulder and he was also screaming. And as he looked up another man was hit in the leg, he fell, also screaming. She is doing this deliberately he thought, she could have killed them but she needs the shock that the screaming causes.

"For fucks sake Edvar get off of us, Nam is safe, we need to get away, get to the tree line, up the northern path, Parkan can cover us, if the fucking idiot is still alive." Edvar rolled off of them and stood, dragging Namtu to his feet, Cambor knelt up and pointed his weapon at the tree line, looking for movement, he saw a brief shadow flit across his vision but he could not track it, he did not want to waste his only shot as then, he would have to reload in the falling darkness, which he did not want to do. Namtu and his giant bodyguard Edvar ran to the wood edge and were waiting for him, in a kneeling position with their weapons pointed outwards towards him and the skirmish. He suddenly heard a sword clash and it made him jump, *she is in amongst us now, with that famous sword of hers, time to go,* he thought as he ran to join his two colleagues.

34

Amyeen withdrew her sword from the chest of the last man and wiped the blood and bits of bone from the blade, there was suddenly a shout as three men broke cover and ran for the tree line, she spun around, sword at the ready and prepared to go after them, but as she watched her instinct for danger suddenly stopped her, this was no run for their lives, this was an organised and careful withdrawal, the first man ran twenty paces and stopped and knelt, then the other two ran to him and did the same, then the first would repeat the move, this way they moved quickly but safely from her, she could pursue but she had seen the damage just one of those weapons had caused, and so she let them go, watching through Blood as she did so. The two men together held her fascination, even in the dying light she could see one was small of statue, very fast and light of foot, but the other man was the biggest person that she had ever seen, nearly twice the size of the first man and close to a pace taller and wider than the third, the word bodyguard screamed at her, but a bodyguard that the wealthiest Lords and Nobles would pay a small fortune for, what the hell was he doing here harassing her friend?

Speaking of which she had not yet seen her. "Morlen, are you here?" she shouted.

"Yes, I am," she replied, as she appeared from around the side of her cottage, "I did not know, if you would get the vision, but I knew you would come if you did get it."

"Lucky for you I was home in Ceredon, only half a day's hard ride, I could have been hundreds of leagues away, you look terrible by the way," and she did, tear stained, exhausted and still shaking through fear and adrenaline.

"I do not care how I look at the moment, my animals, they have all fled." "They will all return when the smell of death has dissipated."

"I am sure you are correct, let us get inside, I will get a fire going and some hot water, you can wash off that blood you are covered in."

"It is not mine; I assure you."

"I am well aware of that, never has so much blood been spilt on my land, I hope it does not affect the balance."

"I am sure it will not, in time the land will heal, besides, the worms have to eat as well."

Morlen shuddered at the comment and wondered, how anybody could be so nonchalant about the death and violence surrounding her, but she had come and if she had not then Morlen did not want to think what may have happened to her when she could no longer keep herself hidden.

They headed into the cottage, where Amyeen stripped off and cleaned her weapons and equipment, only when every item was spotless did, she bother to wash herself. By the time she had finished, Morlen had fallen into a deep sleep in the bed in the corner of the room, she watched her for a while and thought what a strange pair of friends they were, the hired killer and the healer. She closed her eyes and checked on Blood, he was on the hunt so she released her vision and control of him, she had only ever once stayed with him when he fed and she had vowed never again, the coppery taste of animal blood in her mouth had been there for days and the implications of this and her bond with him had, for the first time, frightened her. She redressed and left the cottage, heading into the woods to bring Buster in, she knew that she was perfectly safe as was Morlen for Blood would alert her to any danger.

Six

The Survivor

"Neema quick, this one is still alive!" was the shout that woke Amyeen with a start, she was slightly disorientated and shook her head as she rose quickly, grabbing her sword as she stepped out of the door. Morlen was kneeling down near the embers of the fire the men had built, and staring down at an unconscious man. To be fair he looked dead to Amyeen, pale skin and deathly look about him but his eyes were closed and when she looked carefully, she could see the slight rise and fall of his chest. He was the first man that she had loosed her arrow at and it was still there, pinning his arm to his chest.

"Not for long, he won't be," replied Amyeen as her right hand went for the hilt of her sword.

"NO! YOU WILL SPILL NO MORE BLOOD HERE! Besides, he is no threat to us anymore, he is just a wounded man in need of help."

"Suit yourself, but don't blame me when he slits your throat in the night."

"He will not, what kind of arrow did you use, a broad head or plain pointed head?"

"Luckily for him, I left my broad heads behind, it should just pull right out and then try to stop anymore bleeding that occurs."

"Should we move him to the cottage first, keep him warm?"

"No, the reason he is still alive now is that he has not moved, I remember this one, he sat right here, when I took sight and loosed my arrow, the move could still kill him. Put your weight on him and I will pull it out. Ready?"

"Yes, just be quick, I do not feel well."

Amyeen got a good grip on the arrow and pulled sharply, it came out with a squelch and a small quantity of blood oozed from the small hole in his arm. She lifted his arm up and looked at the wound on the side of his chest, it had also spilt some fresh blood around the dark brown blood stains on his tunic.

"Well that's good," she stated "His arm wounds will heal and it does not seem to have collapsed his lung."

"What shall we do with him now."

"Bring some hot water here, we will clean and stitch his wounds here and dress them, then carry him into the cottage, keep him warm, if he does survive the day then he should continue to recover until he is strong enough to kill us both!"

"He will not, I can tell, he has a kind face and he has been healed here, it has an effect on people, it did on you and your little dark friend."

"Yes it did."

They spent the rest of the day digging a large pit at the edge of The Glade and with the help of Buster they hauled the dead bodies into it, stripping them of armour and weapons first, which Amyeen told Morlen she could sell at the local town, except the new and mysterious weapons they all carried, and the equipment that she worked out went along with them. She had a strange feeling she knew how they worked and the implications frightened her, especially when she saw the markings on the hilt of all the swords that she collected, the mark of Balstore of Branvere, famous in the known world as the world's finest weapon smith, among other talents that he was notorious for. These strange weapons she put in a pile with everything she thought went with them and wrapped them all in a canvas sheet that she carried to use as a shelter.

On a whim, she picked one from the pile and took a close look at it, the wide end was similar to the stock of a crossbow which then tapered down towards the trigger area which also had some kind of metal mechanism, she kept her finger well away from the trigger, not knowing if any were loaded. From the mechanism down it continued to taper but now there was a long metal tube held in place against the wood by a series of metal bands and although, the banding was as tight against the tube as possible it did not bend or mis shape the tube in any way. Balstore was famous for his metal, his swords always strong but never brittle, never known to shatter in battle like some cheaper weapons did. She should know, for her own beloved sword carried the mark of Balstore. She hefted the weapon to her shoulder, heavy, she thought, but very well balanced, an average person could get used to this very easily, again, this concerned her greatly. She returned it to its pile and turned for the cottage, tomorrow, she thought to herself, we shall see what this weapon is and how it works, if this man makes it through the night.

Callan awoke with a start and looked around him, he blinked a few times to gain focus and looked at his surroundings, he was in some kind of small cottage but he could not remember for the life of him how he got here, he was in a bed against a wall in a small room, the door was slightly ajar and he could see some of the cottage through it. He started to sit up but pain suddenly racked through him and made him gasp, he let himself relax back into the soft blanket and although still in pain, he was soon asleep again.

He woke a few hours later, this time he was more careful, he gently lifted the bed clothes from himself and look down, his chest was so tightly bound that he had trouble breathing, his left arm was also bandaged, being as careful as he could, he sat up and swung his body around to sit on the edge of the bed, he let the pain swamp him for a while and then waited for it to subside. He suddenly knew, where he was, the witch's cottage and the whole thing suddenly came back to him, mainly memories of a pain he had never known before, an inability to breath and his arm that he could not seem to move from the side of his chest without causing more pain. He remembered screaming and even that had hurt. But he was alive, he wondered what had become of the rest of them, surely, if it was her, not even she could have killed them all, not Namtu and Edvar. He did not think any person could kill Edvar. Maybe a mountain falling on him might slow him down but kill him, he did not think so.

The door was opened from the other side and a young woman stood there, she did not look like any kind of witch that he had heard tale of but also she did not look like the known world's finest warrior, she was slim but not overly so, short hair and pretty, dressed in dark cotton leggings, good boots and a light wool spun top, all perfectly functional for someone who lived way out here.

"You are up then," she stated "And alive, that is good. Come outside into the fresh air, do you the world of good" she took him by his other arm and led him to a table outside, as he approached he saw her for the first time, the famed Blood Huntress, and he stopped dead, causing Morlen to stumble. Her hair was loose and hanging down, she was dressed in her leggings, boots and a white top with no sleeves, and she was sat at the table running a whet stone over the blade of her kukri.

"Do not be afraid," said Morlen "She won't hurt you."

"No, I will not, not yet anyway and if I wanted you dead you would be, so sit down and stop quivering man, even I have to look after my weapons."

"You need to eat something, build up your strength, you will heal quicker here than anywhere else but you still need to help it along. I will bring you some bread and broth, but drink this first, it will help you with your pain. Maybe my friend here will not kill you while I am gone…but before that, what is your name and why are you here?"

"My name is Callan, I…we, are from Branvere, on a task set for us by Lord Balstore, under orders from his Most Gracious Majesty Cathal the Silver."

"There is nothing gracious about that man, or his pet dog Balstore." snapped Amyeen.

"Please, Neema, let him speak."

"I thank you for letting me live and I do not disagree with you about Balstore. My…err…friends, they all…died?"

"Apart from three of them, in a group, a small lithe man and a big bald man and another the size of which I have never seen."

"I thought they might get away, the three of them, the small man is Namtu, a Captain of Light Infantry, the giant is Edvarius, answers to the name Edvar, not that he ever talks and he is the bodyguard of Namtu, and the last man is Cambor, he and his brother Carmak both command Infantry Battalions within the Branvere Army."

"And what of this weapon? This mysterious fire stick that can put down a fully grown stag instantly and at a distance?"

"It has many names, but Balstore has settled on the name Gunne, I have no idea why, I am starting to feel very weak again ladies, can I please rest again? Tomorrow, I will tell you all you wish to know and even show how the Gunne works, but now, I think I am about to pass…out…" He said, as he slipped from the bench and to the grass as Morlen grabbed at him to lower him gently down.

"You gave him a fucking potion, didn't you?" snapped Amyeen "That muck, you gave him to drink, some sleeping potion or some such?"

"Yes, I did, I knew you would interrogate him, make him show you the weapon Gunne thing, so I protected him, he needs to heal, even here in this place of healing it will not be instant, another night of good sleep will help him immensely."

"You are too soft and too compassionate, if they had found you yesterday, they would have shown you no mercy."

"They would not have hurt me, but not as I would wish it, out of compassion, they somehow knew that we were acquainted, the one he called Cambor told the rest of them that, I heard it."

"How the fuck do they know that? No one knows that."

"They did, must be this Balstore, I have heard the name before but in the last day more than ever."

"Some think, he is a wizard, warlock, mage or whatever the fuck they call them nowadays, but he is not, he is just a very clever man, but completely ruthless. Power mad."

"It is not important is it."

"It is to me, I have spent years with no one knowing anything about me, personal details anyway, to be told something only you and I know disturbs me."

"But there is nothing you can do about it."

"I can fucking kill Balstore for one."

"Is that your answer to everything? Kill it"

"Yes, it is the life that was forced upon me years ago, and I have no room for anything else," She stood up from the table and went over to the prostrate from of Callan, lying on the grass, she leant across and picked up her kukri from the table and stared down at him, then returned it to its sheaf in the small of her back. "We had better carry him back to bed then."

Seven

The Weapon

The next morning, the animals started to return to the Glade, much to the relief of Morlen who went fussing about them as she always had. Even Sophie the old goat came bounding back. Callan was up and feeling much better, he could not believe how quickly he seemed to be healing, the wounds already felt closed with new skin forming across them, just his muscles hurt but he could live with that. He looked across at the Huntress, she was handling an equipment belt stood by the table, the contents spread out upon it.

"Time to talk boy." she shouted over at him.

"Of course, what shall I call you? Not sure if you like being called Huntress."

"You can call me Neema, it is not my name but that is none of your business. Now what the fuck is all this?"

He picked up a small leather bag and emptied the contents on to the table, small metal balls about the size of a hazelnut ran everywhere, he picked one up.

"This is the lead ball, it is fired from the Gunne, pick one up and feel the weight of it, surprisingly heavy aren't they?"

"Yes, they are, from what I know of projectiles that can be an advantage, can give more stability in flight."

"Yes, that is correct. This sealed horn contains what is now known as Gunne Powder, it also had different names but again, Balstore now calls it that." He poured some out on the table, and then took out a tinder box which he struck into the small pile. The effect was instantaneous, the powder erupted into a flame and created a huge amount of smoke, which sent them both coughing from the bench. Amyeen came back to the table, her eyes stinging.

"Smells like pig dung." she said.

"One of the main ingredients, as you can see it is a flammable explosive, burns at an incredibly fast rate, this is what propels the ball from the Gunne. This goes in first, usually in a small measured paper wrapping so you get a consistency with each firing, but in an emergency you can just pour it in, there is a spike at the base of the tube that will pierce the wrapping." He picked up another leather bag and spilled out a load of what looked like small brass buttons "These are percussion caps, they fit on the Gunne like this, on this stud, they are filled with a small quantity of Gunne powder, when the trigger is pulled the cock hammer here flies forward under a simple spring mechanism which ignites the powder in the cap, the flame shoots down a tube within the stud into the base of the barrel, igniting the powder there, it burns fiercely in the confined space that is blocked by the ball and then when enough pressure is built up, the ball is pushed out with a huge explosive force, propelling the ball at incredible speed."

"Then what? It is useless, other than as a big stick."

"Then you reload it, with practice takes about twenty heartbeats, put in the powder, then the ball, bit of cloth wadding to keep the ball in place, ram it down with the rod kept underneath, pull back the hammer, put on a cap and aim again."

"I could loose three or four arrows in that time."

"Yes, you could, but you have never seen the damage of these can cause. The noise of them all going off at once is deafening, the effect on an army would be devastating. Do you want to try it for yourself?"

"Of course, I do, but not here, I do not want to frighten the animals, they have only just come back, bring enough of that stuff and one of them, we will go into the woods."

They walked a quarter league or so into the woods, far enough away that Morlen would not be able to hear the noise.

"Now place the wide end in your shoulder, and wrap your hand around the area here, your finger should naturally find the trigger, when you are ready look down the tube at the notch on the end, at one hundred paces put that on what you want to hit, and squeeze gentle pressure on the trigger." Callen instructed her she did and the Gunne almost leapt from her hands knocking her back a pace as smoke once again obscured them briefly from view. They both heard the sound of the ball ricocheting through the forest, the tree fifty paces to their front completely undamaged.

"You could have warned me about that kick, nearly broke my fucking shoulder."

"Yes, I could have, but now you will always remember it won't you? This time really hold it tight into your shoulder, then ride with it, let it take you back a little but brace for it." She reloaded and tried again, this time hitting just above and to the right of the mark Callen had scored into the bark. "See you are a natural at this."

"I am a natural at every weapon known to man and now one not known to man!" They stayed in the woods until she had used up all the powder and shot that he brought with him, then, smelling of smoke and pig shit they started a slow walk back. As they walked Amyeen spoke.

"I do not like this weapon, its implications, it is dangerous. In the wrong hands. A lot of them on a battlefield would be devastating, an entire army would be unstoppable, and they can only get better, more improvements, faster loading, more accuracy, and so you know, I do consider Balstore the wrong hands."

"This is the third generation of this weapon already, the first was a thread cord that had to burn down, very unreliable, you never knew just when it was going to ignite the powder and fire it. The second Balstore invented the mechanism with the trigger but still with the cord, but the trigger sent the lit end of the cord over, more reliable but not very good. Then, after many months he managed to invent the percussion cap, they are simply shaped then a very small amount of powder is sealed on the underside with wax, it works very well, in any weather too. You have obviously heard of Balstore, despite what you think of the man he is a legendary master of smithing ability, bakes his sword blades in clay to harden them but keep the metal supple, does the same with the tubes on this weapon, takes weeks to make one, so much precision is needed, and forged at just the right temperature."

Just then they came across a path junction and two halves of a Gunne, Callan bent down and picked them up, blood stained both parts.

"This was my friend's Gunne, Parkan, he was sent to look out for you, I guess you found him first."

"It was him or me, I make no apology."

"It was not a criticism, but he was my friend and I will miss him, you must carry a very good sword to slice clean through the metal of a Gunne."

"Yes, it is a very good sword, made by an armourer in Branvere, the blade baked in clay to harden it." The statement hung in the air between them. She changed the subject.

"How many of these weapons are there now?"

"Only the ten we carried, but Balstore was working on another one, a special one for Namtu, longer tube, and some different kind of loading mechanism, to help with the loss of compression that dropping a ball down the tube causes, ball does not fit exactly so power is lost when it comes out the other end, make it airtight and the power and accuracy would be incredible."

"The small man that escaped me, that is Namtu I assume, what is so special about him?"

"He can use this weapon with accuracy that is almost magical to watch, any one of us is good up to one hundred paces but beyond that, not much use at all. Namtu put a ball through a tin plate at two hundred and fifty paces before we left, Balstore thinks if he can get the Gunne right then Namtu could use it up to eight hundred paces. He is the ultimate professional soldier, whatever he does, he does with complete dedication and discipline. Makes all his own lead balls and polishes them to remove imperfections, weighs each one to make sure they are identical, reduces all the variables."

"Okay, but why? What did you all cross the sea for? Ten men is not an invasion army is it, even with this weapon."

"We did not cross the sea, we came around the long way with a convoy of wagons, which we then split from, they had another mission. We are not an invasion army; our mission is to escort Namtu to his firing position so he can make his one shot."

"Why? Why all this for one shot? Who could possibly be that important that ten men, sorry nine men, escort one man to make one kill?"

"The Princess of course."

"Princess? What Princess?"

"Princess Victarny of the Kingdom of Light."

Eight

The Kingdom

Cambor looked down on the port city of Kardon from high in the mountains, it was the main port for traders and travellers heading for Kino'le, because Kino'le City itself was inaccessible by sea due to its location built into a high cliff. Balstore had told him that the Palace and outer castle that protected the Palace had its rear wall on that very cliff and it was a thousand pace drop straight down into the sea. Again he had no idea how Balstore knew this.

All goods being traded in the Kingdom went through Kardon port and were then transported in almost never-ending convoys by horse and cart for the five day journey to Kino'le City. The road between was heavily patrolled by the Kino'le Army and by the fearsome mounted Dragoons, as well as local militias hired by the merchants.

The real wealth lay here in Kardon, many foreign traders dealt with the same Kardon merchant for generations instead of making the ten day round trip themselves. It had made merchants in both cities very wealthy and they paid their taxes to the crown for the road maintenance and the security the military provided. It was said that the road was the safest place to travel in the whole of the known world, and the few bandits that did attack were usually tracked down and made an example of very swiftly. It also gave an invading army a serious problem, the administrative heart and the financial one were in two separate places, five days apart, attack one and the other had time to prepare or launch a counter attack. The Army and Dragoons being of equal number in each city, and then there were the Imperial Guard, everyone an ex Dragoon and they patrolled the cities and were charged with each ones defence, he did not know the numbers exactly but there were at least five hundred Imperials alone in each city.

They had purchased a pack mule and travelled the high passes instead of the roads in case 'she' had followed them. Cambor still could not believe what had happened. He had not expected them all to make it, but to lose seven highly trained and experienced men in one go was almost too much for him to bear, and the fact that he had run like a frightened child had really shaken him. At least he had got Namtu out alive, the mission was still viable, and to be honest, with only three of them now, easier to manage. Even with the massive bulk of Edvar drawing attention to them, but Namtu would not go anywhere without him and for Edvar's part he would not let Namtu out of his sight. He had never seen such loyalty before. He stood there now, a pace taller and wider than any other man Cambor had ever known, his massive broadsword high on his waist, capable of cleaving more than one man in half with his formidable strength behind it. He smiled at the memory of the first time young Callan was introduced to him, he could not even lift Edvar's sword completely, the blade tip staying firmly on the ground. Callan had a way about him, people warmed to him, even Edvar had smiled at him and Namtu had appeared fond of him, as much as Nam would ever let his true feelings about anything or anyone show. Such a shame Callen had insisted on bringing that idiot Parkan with him, but they were both dead now. As long as there was nothing wrong with the weapon when they finally got hold of it, for they had lost their armourer amongst the seven men and even as good as Namtu was with a weapon, he was not a smith.

"We must travel into the city proper, find an inn for a few days until the boat and your precious cargo arrives." he told Namtu.

"I would rather camp out here in the mountains, where we are safe from prying eyes. Edvar and the Gunnes are quite conspicuous." he replied.

"We would attract more attention travelling in and out every day, we can cover the Gunnes in a blanket and once we have Edvar inside an inn he can stay in the room while I go and check the port every day. We can have food brought to the room, it will be the safest way, we descend tonight and find an innkeeper, who does not ask too many questions and likes a lot of coin to keep it that way."

"Okay Cam, it makes sense, but no more stupid risks."

A rare and unusual tear came to Amyeen's eye and she wiped it away quickly as she turned away from him. Although, she had left her life there behind her, she still loved her sister, even though they were so different and the kingdom itself for that matter.

"Why? Why Kino'le?" she asked as she turned back to face him.

"Balstore and therefore the King, believe that the magic of Kino'le, the light and such, comes from, or at least is manifested by the royal blood. The younger Princess vanished years ago, no one knows what became of her, although again, I think Balstore does, that leaves Victarny, he believes, if she is out of the way then Branvere could successfully invade. You are from Ceredon, why do you care? What difference does it make to you?"

"Because I have travelled, I lived in Kino'le for a while, years ago, it is a wonderful place, trade flourishes, people are well off and happy and it is well managed without being despotic, unlike Branvere. Your beloved Silver King with his pet dog Balstore, is a demonic dictator, the people are frightened all the time, any kind of dissent is punishable by death and the majority of people are deliberately kept in poverty. It is a terrible place, as you must know as you are from there, I would hate for that nasty bastard on the throne of Branvere to destroy what took generations of hard work to create, and he would destroy it, most aggressive nations want our resources, our trade routes. Cathal and Balstore want to rule the known world, and will destroy anyone or anything that could stop that, the Kingdom of Light would be razed to the ground, its people enslaved. You will tell me all you know of this plan."

"I will tell you everything, when you live in that environment you do not know it is not normal, it is only when you leave and go elsewhere you realise, I will give you all the assistance I can, but please, not here, I need to rest again, can we return to the cottage?"

"One thing, before we go back, why the Gunne? Why not a longbow, or a mercenary with a sword close up?"

"Nobody alive, apart from a few in Branvere, have ever seen a Gunne wound, nobody can understand the damage it causes With an arrow, they would have to be really accurate, to guarantee a kill, with a Gunne they do not, any chest shot, as the ball passes through the body at that speed it can destroy internal organs, makes a small entry wound but a massive exit wound, the size of a fist, bits of flesh and bone blown out and extreme bleeding, even the best surgeon would struggle to save her. The ball itself sucks in her clothing and if the surgeon does not get it all out it will slowly poison her and that is, if she survives the actual shot. It is truly awful."

"And why the Princess? What has she ever done to hurt anyone? What difference to the invasion would the light make?"

"Have you ever heard of the legends of Dalstock? The Dark Stalkers? Well, it is not a legend, they exist, but they cannot function in light, they are slow and sluggish, but in the darkness they are almost invincible, savagely strong, huge talons and about half the height of a man taller than a man. They are being collected from Dalstock by a convoy of wagons led by Cambor's brother, Carmak. We travelled with them up until the day before ending up in Morlen's Glade, then we headed north and they continued west. The plan is for them to sunder the gates and engage the Dragoons, keep them busy while the main army drives straight into the city."

"You underestimate the Dragoons, they will tear them apart, more fearsome warriors, you have not seen and the Dark Stalkers are not invincible, I killed one once and if I can then they can. How many Dark Stalkers?"

"All of them I believe."

"There is a plot against the Princess, Danyard." stated Lorgane the wizard "I see great pain coming and the return of the dark one."

"Do not call her that in my presence again wizard, she is the Princess Amyeen of the Kingdom of Light, not some malicious and plotting woman." he snapped back.

"Woman! Hardly and certainly not the child you raised, she is a callous and evil killer, if the gold is enough, she will kill anyone, no conscience or pity."

"She would not kill anyone who did not deserve it, I trained her too well."

"And who trained you Danyard? Still, we do not know this, arrived from nowhere as a child, beat the King's Champion, half to death and flew through the ranks in an almost magical speed and now, Lord Protector of the Realm, who are you really Danyard?"

"Are you questioning my loyalty to this Kingdom old man? I have given most of my life to its protection and seen it flourish, not to mention the Princesses."

"The least you could do after talking their father into that suicidal charge into the ranks of the Mar'thak Army and then where were you when he took that fatal blow."

"You know full well, I was Lord Dragoon, my place was with my Dragoons and I talked him into nothing, the assassin that killed the Queen the day before convinced him of that, you know all this, why are you trying to goad me again, still bitter that you were not given my position."

"This reign of this Kingdom has never been my desire, just to serve the bloodline, of which you are not."

"No, I am not, but never again question my dedication, my devotion, to this Kingdom. Let me know of any more of your 'visions', but do not waste my time unless you have specifics."

"As you wish My Lord"

Danyard walked away slowly, keeping his anger in check, he noticed his hand was involuntarily on his sword hilt and he forced himself to let go, what was it with that damn old man, he had always hated Danyard and the feeling was mutual, always they had been at each other's throats. Always the whispers in the King's ear, but the King was a sensible man and he had always taken both sides with a sense of humour, knowing he needed them both.

Danyard did not even know if the man was a wizard, he had never seen him do anything magical, not that Danyard did not believe in magic, the damn Kingdom of Light was living breathing proof of it, and he had seen men who could manipulate it, but other than Lorgane's knowledge of things he could only know by visions, and an almost inhuman ability to convince people he was right, he had never seen anything miraculous about the smelly old bastard.

He headed out through the training grounds towards the stables, stopping to watch what was being taught, advising and coaching as he saw fit. The newer recruits were in awe of him, but the trainers were used to him being around and on his instruction, made no acknowledgement of him as he either watched or took control of a small part of the lesson.

Finally, he made it to the stables and waited as his warhorse, Spike, was saddled for him. He rode out of the training ground and then out of the castle grounds and then the back way through the North Gate and into the woodland beyond, where he gave Spike his legs and galloped him along a riverbank. He eventually slowed him and dismounted near a shallow part of the river, walking him and cooling him before he let him drink, then he stripped off and flung himself against the current fifty paces up river, swimming until his head was clear of all thoughts of Lorgane and he felt clean again.

Afterwards he lay on the grass in view of Spike and let the sun dry him, before taking a leisurely ride back towards the city. As he rode through he noticed some of the ladies in waiting being trained on the finer points of archery by his senior Master at Arms, Mellor. He dismounted and walked over.

"Morning Mellor, how are the Ladies faring?" he enquired.

"On the short bow they are excellent, unlike men who all think they have a natural talent and most do not, these ladies actually listen to what is being taught to them, they struggle with a broadsword but again a lot of men do, but on the smaller swords again they are of a very high standard." he replied.

"Enjoying your training Ladies?" Danyard asked of them all.

"It can be hard Sire, but worth it, it will help us protect the Kingdom and the Princess," replied the Lady Sarah, who had blushed deeply as he had approached, as it was common knowledge, she was deeply attracted to him.

"And how is Her Majesty today Sarah?"

"She rose early and tended her horses and is now holding court, as you are aware My Lord, we have many visiting dignitaries with us."

"Yes, of course, I shall look in on the court later, good day to you all. Commander Mellor, please continue."

They all bowed, as he mounted Spike and turned him towards the stables, ahh Lady Sarah, he thought to himself, it always brought a smile to his face to see her, the sight of her in her tight riding britches and white corseted top doing a bad job of hiding her ample bosom. He would like to see more of her but knew he would find her too much of a distraction, especially after the warning from the wizard, and as much as he hated the man he had to admit he was rarely wrong. Maybe when all this had blown over, he could find time for her. Maybe.

Nine

The Pursuit

"What do you intend to do about it?" asked Morlen.

"You say this Gunne will be delivered by ship to Kardon, direct from Branvere," said Amyeen.

"Yes, Cambor and Namtu will have to collect it in person, the ship's Captain will have strict instructions to only hand it to Namtu personally. Unless, Balstore himself brings it, which he could do, the plans had not been formalised when we left," replied Callan.

"Then it is simple, I go to Kardon, wait for the ship and kill them. And maybe, I will even get to kill that bastard Balstore."

"But you do not know what they look like, yes you caught a glimpse of them here, but could you pick them out in a crowd of thousands on the streets of Kardon, or the port itself for that matter."

"I think even I could recognise Edvar, the man is a monster."

"He will not be on the streets, he creates a stir on the streets of Branvere, where everybody knows him, in a foreign city, he will be quite an attraction, not what they want at all. He will be in the room of an inn for the duration, and because he will not let Namtu out of his sight so will Namtu. Only Cambor will go out on the streets and only I can recognise him, so you will have to take me with you."

"And what if he recognises you? It will not take long to work out what has happened, he will kill you where you stand, especially in the state you are in at the moment, you will be hard pushed to even make the journey right now."

"I think I can help there, in fact, I already have. Callan remove your dressing." Callan stood and removed his shirt, then began to unwind the linen dressings wrapped around his chest, staring in amazement at the rate he had healed, just a tiny scar remained and when he flexed his chest there was no pain at all.

"Cambor said you were a witch." he said with a smile "But I think you are an angel."

"It is a two-day ride or less if I push Buster, but a five-day walk, by which time they may have moved on, it would still be better if I travelled alone."

"There is a farm near here, I have been healing their animals for years, they will lend us two horses."

"Damn you woman, do you have an answer for everything? And what the fuck do we need two horses for, have you forgotten, I have a perfectly good horse already?"

"Do you think you are leaving me out of this, now that is a fucking jest, I am coming along, you need Callan there to identify Cambor, Callan needs me to get him a horse, therefore you need us both and besides…"

"Besides what…" spoke Amyeen, as she looked around and blinked a few times, staring into the space where Morlen had been standing and was now gone and then just as suddenly as she vanished, she was there again.

"Besides, know anybody else who can do that?"

"No I do not, but I do not like it, I work alone, always, then nobody else gets hurt because of me, except those who need to get hurt, obviously."

"Yes we know, but you cannot do this one without us, so it's up to you, ride off and search the busiest port city in the known world on your own for days on end or let us and our unique talents help you, and you also know you cannot go riding into a city where you are a legend, you will be mobbed more than the giant Edvar would be."

"Yes, yes, I know, girl clothes." she said with a shudder.

Morlen sat on the wall by the inn and watched the docks, she was doing the thing she loved, watching the world go by in the safe knowledge that she could see but not be seen. She watched the ships on the horizon, she watched the whores walk the waterfront, and she watched merchant wagons come and go, but mainly she watched the Harbour Master's house for a large bald man who would be checking on what was expected to be docking. The port was so busy that every ship had to send a rowboat ahead with a cargo manifest for the Harbour Master to decide on what got priority, then the rowboat would return to its ship with a small flag with a symbol on it to be hoisted from its mast, and the symbols would have a queue system, any ship not obeying the system ran the risk of being destroyed at a distance of a quarter league by the massive trebuchet catapults each side on the harbour walls. This rarely happened but sometimes warning shots were loosed at errant vessels, always doing enough damage to cost the captains but not sink whatever valuable cargo they carried. It was a very effective system, the same captain never made the same mistake twice after limping into port and then facing an extortionate repair bill from the Master Shipbuilder whose workshop was the only one authorised to carry out work within the harbour itself. And so she waited for Cambor to show his face, Callan assured her he would be in the port by now, and he was walking the streets also on the lookout for him, or by some miracle, Namtu himself, but Callan did not think it likely.

She had a sudden urge to look skywards and as she did, she saw Blood flying overhead, Neema keeping an eye on her and she was grateful for it. Since she had sent her vision to him, she had made a small connection to them both and she could feel his whereabouts within a quarter league or so, that was fine with her as she did not want to have the connection that Neema had with him. The potential frightened her.

They had travelled to Kardon along the main pass after Amyeen had destroyed the remaining Gunnes at the Glade by burning them in a fire pit until the metal was bent and warped and the wood was no more, then she had buried them, apart from Callan's weapon which he had insisted on keeping, wrapping it in a blanket to hide its form.

The farmer had been as good as Morlen said he would be and had lent them a fine pair of horses with full tack and enough supplies for five days. His wife had also dug out some more feminine attire for Amyeen, which included a pale pink embroidered shirt which she hated but had been forced to wear. Despite their promises not to Callan and Morlen had both laughed.

They found an inn near the centre with a good stable, the inns near the dock itself were full, as to be expected. They were usually full of drunk sailors and dockers all looking for a fight or a fuck or both, the last thing they needed was Neema killing one of them because he could not keep his hands to himself and the inevitable investigation by the Imperial Guard.

As she watched Blood fly away her eye was drawn to the horizon, and the setting sun, she knew no more ships would be allowed to dock today and so Cambor would not show his face so she jumped deftly from the wall just as

Callan appeared through the dock gates. His sword was on his hip as was allowed by law but his Gunne was hidden in the room under his bed, with all of its associated equipment. He missed it, he had carried it for days and it had become an extension of him, as all weapons should become with all good warriors. The feeling of power when he pulled the trigger, the knowledge of what it was capable of at range excited him and made his pulse quicken like no other weapon he had ever known, despite the wishes of The Blood Huntress he knew he could never willingly give it up.

"Why Lady Morlen, can I escort you back to your lodgings?" he exclaimed. "Why thank you kind sir," she replied, "I take it she sent you?"

"Yes, she seems to think you need some degree of protection and as I am out looking for Cambor anyway, I thought I could detour this way."

"Well, let us go then, what has she been up to today?"

"She never tells me and if I do ask she lies to me, but I think she visits armourers and smiths, every time I go back, she seems to be examining another weapon that I have not seen before, unless she bought them all with her and they are hidden in various places on her body."

Just as she was about to reply, Callan grabbed her and flung her forcefully into an alley, forcing a hand over her mouth, as he did so. "Shhh…" he hissed "Be silent, Cambor has just passed in front of us."

The look of fear was instantly replaced by one of curiosity.

"Where? Which one?"

"There, the big man, walking passed that tavern, bald head."

"I see him, I had better follow him then."

"Not on your own, you can't. If he suspects he will kill you."

"Well, you cannot, he knows you and thinks you are dead, if he sees you walking around Kardon your chances with him will be no better than mine, and remember, I am a witch…"

He looked around at her but she had gone, he could still feel she was there, close to him, but he could not see her, he blinked a few times to clear his vision and there she was again, just where she had been.

"It only works, when I am still, but it does work and I am getting better at it…?"

"Yes, it does work and I suppose, I have no choice now do I?"

"Not really, because I am going to follow him anyway and you cannot stop me because to do so, you will have to follow me and then he will see you and kill us both, so you better get back to her and tell her what I am up to, and be quick, because if any harm comes to me I am sure Cambor will not have to kill you because she will." She replied laughing as she moved out into the gathering dusk of the streets.

Women, he thought to himself, what did I do in previous life to deserve these two!

Cambor could feel something was not right, like all old soldiers he had very finely tuned instincts, soldiers without a good instinct did not become old soldiers. He had the feeling that eyes were upon him, he made a few irregular and sudden stops to check behind him but could see nothing out of the ordinary. Then, just as he was about to look back to where he was heading a young woman just seemed to appear in a shop doorway and she was staring right at him, got you, you fucking witch, he thought with a smile.

He put on an exaggerated stagger, to make the pretence of being drunk, to try to lull her closer, he stopped by a few walls to lean on them for support, discreetly checking backwards when he could. She did seem to have some magic about her, she could vanish from sight at will, this did not faze him or make him gasp. He had travelled the known world and seen many wondrous and scary things, a simple manipulation of light did not even impress him, he had seen greater use of magic and seen it better done. He saw an alley coming up on his right and so he staggered for it, as he reached it he tripped and fell face first into it but was on his feet in an instant with his back flush against the wall, and just as he predicted she came running around the corner and straight into his massive fist.

Morlen did not know what hit her, it felt like she had ran into the wall itself, her eyes sagged open, as she stared into the man's face, his breath stank of ale and nasty stubble adorned his chin, he was sneering at her with his hand tight around her throat pinning her to the wall, she knew she had lost consciousness but did not know how long for, it could have only been for a few breaths but she could not be completely sure.

She strained her neck to look around but they were in a small side alley off of a small street with not many passers-by, he had laid the perfect ambush and now she felt stupid, she had thought this some silly game but it was suddenly very real and very dangerous.

"So pretty one, what does a little thing like you want with an ugly old fucker like me then?" he hissed at her.

"Nothing Sir" she managed to say, "I thought, I knew you, that's all, my friend's father sir, I was just going to ask after her sir."

"You had better do fucking better than that girlie, You been following me for most of my way from the fucking harbour, like you had been waiting for me, you have some friends interested in me do you, one friend in particular who would struggle to walk about anonymous so to speak…" As he spoke, he suddenly felt a blade at his throat and looked down, the short sword was being held by an arm covered in a tunic with purple edging, he knew what this meant, he had seen them patrolling, The Imperial Guard.

"You may want to consider your next actions very carefully; we Imperials do not take kindly to big scary men who need to prove their worth by hurting young women. Now, release this maiden and with your other hand release your sword belt." He reached down and released the buckle, feeling it fall to the ground, where it was quickly and efficiently collected by one of them. The pressure of the blade against his skin did not lessen. "Good, you understand simple instructions, where are you from and what is your business in Kardon?"

"Trader, from Branvere, this little…" he felt the blade draw a trickle of blood and changed his tack to a more honest approach "I thought, she was following me, I am not popular in Branvere and have many enemies, jealous enemies, I thought she must work for one of them, spying on me to discover my contacts."

"Anything to say Miss?" the officer asked Morlen.

"No sir, I did think he was someone I know, but I was mistaken, I do not want any fuss, I will just be on my way."

"This man can be put in the dungeon for two weeks for what he has already done to you, but it is your choice, but I will make sure he pays for your surgeon fees, that is a nasty graze on your face and I recommend seeing an apothecary so it does not go bad."

"I will be fine sir; I am a healer by trade."

"Very well Miss, it is your choice."

"I will be on my way now, but thank you very much for your assistance." She turned and walked away briskly.

"Well then merchant, your lucky day." Spoke the officer, as he took his short sword from the man's throat.

"Normally, we would take your sword as surety against your continued good behaviour, but we have just been informed that your King arrives here tomorrow. He must have sent a messenger bird to your trade commissioner in Kino'le as they have only just informed us by fast rider, so on this one occasion you may keep your weapon, but do not cross us again. We collate all our information from all our reports, so we will know, I will leave you to give your name and where you are staying to Atrop Commander Harkan here. He and his men will inform your Innkeeper of this and he will report to us any further problems."

"Thank you sir, there will be no further incidents."

"Any problems Cam?" Enquired Namtu as he entered the room he was sharing with Edvar.

"No Nam, no problems." He lied, Namtu was suspicious enough without the further worry that someone was watching them and now the Imperial Guard were also.

"Any news on the ship? I hate these four walls and Edvar needs to get out in the open."

"Well that I can help you with, how long since you last met the King?"

Ten
The Visit

Danyard rode at the head of the column of forty-eight Imperial Guardsmen, each one an ex Dragoon, the only way to get into the Imperial Guards, it was considered a semi-retirement for most Dragoons. They still drew Dragoon pay but did not have to be away from their families for long periods at a time on patrol. They patrolled the cities of the Kingdom but were occasionally called upon to perform a ceremonial duty, as this was, and Danyard was dreading it. The average age of most was forty-seven and all had served a minimum of twenty years as a Dragoon. All were expert horsemen and experienced warriors but they had a maturity that managed to settle most disputes without them having to resort to violence. And those drunk or stupid enough to pick a fight with them soon learnt a hard lesson.

Danyard, a true warrior, despised the ceremonial part of his role but sometimes duty had to be honoured as this one was. He much preferred his own battle scarred and dented armour to the purple and sliver livery of the Imperial Guard full dress uniform, with the ridiculous plumed helm and silly bits of coloured lanyard tied on. Her Majesty, the Princess, loved to see him in his ceremonial garb and had tried on numerous occasions to get him to discard his old dragoon light armour, to which he always replied, "It is battle damaged but it is also battle proven." and she always gave in.

The message had been delivered by the Branvere High Commissioner for trade two days ago, His Royal Highness, The Silver King, Cathal of Branvere, would visit the Kingdom of Light, arriving in the port city of Kardon in three days' time to pay his respects to The Princess Victarny. Danyard had been furious, sailing time from Branvere was five days plus all the planning that would accompany a Royal visit so this must have been planned weeks ago and yet only given three days' notice, forcing Danyard to push his men and horses hard to reach Kardon in time, for protocol demanded at least someone of Danyard's rank to welcome him. He had suggested that she refuse the visit but as she had pointed out they simply could not do this and he had reluctantly admitted that she was right. One thing she excelled in was diplomacy, as her sister excelled in war. She had stated laughing, that it was one of the rare opportunities to see him in his ceremonial dress.

He had handpicked the other forty-seven men with him from the ranks of Imperials at Kino'le, he could have just as easily ordered by carrier bird the Kardon Imperial guard to be ready but he wanted the same men who rode out with him to perform the escort back, that way they would know of anything that could give away an ambush had changed on the way back.

They were divided into six groups of eight named atrops, and each group of eight could easily be divided again into a half atrop of four men, it gave excellent command and control and each man was encouraged to think on his feet and not just simply follow orders. The system was a direct copy of the Dragoons as it worked so well and ensured that at least four men together went into any trouble whilst patrolling the cities.

He was dressed identically to every other man there and was on paper at only in command of Atrop six, although no man there would question any order given to them by him. Danyard never wore anything different to those around him, and he gave all his officers the same order, do not identify yourself to the enemy, your men know who is in command, the enemy do not need to know. He was only leading the column at that moment as it was the turn of Atrop six.

Danyard, like most of his men, despised the Silver King, as he liked to call himself, and accompanying his King would be the accursed wizard Balstore. Danyard had uncovered evidence that Balstore had been a driving influence in the failed invasion by Mar'thak all those years ago but, without starting another war could do nothing about it and it galled him that he was powerless, and even more so that Balstore knew this, he was now so close to the King of Branvere that no one could touch him.

He looked down at his two-handed sword and shuddered, as much as he despised the vile man he could not take from the man his skill as a smith. He had taken the young princess over the sea to Branvere as she had turned seventeen, on a diplomatic and trade mission, as Victarny never liked to leave the Kingdom. He had heard of the legendary armourer Balstore and had visited him in his workshop within the palace grounds. He explained that Amyeen required a sword, not a ceremonial one but a proper warrior's weapon, but it had to be light so she could wield it with strength and finely balanced for her smaller stature. Balstore had taken some measurements and informed Danyard that he could do what was requested but needed a month, Danyard had thought this an excessive amount to time but he was intrigued so had agreed, and they stayed as guests for a month.

On the day they were due to leave, he had taken Amyeen to the workshop. Balstore, with great ceremony, had presented the young Princess with her sword, it was truly a work of art, blade about a pace long, perfectly balanced, razor sharp but with a strength to the steel that Danyard had never seen before. And then Balstore had presented Danyard with the swords twin, slightly larger, but with the same balance and beauty to it. He had nearly gone weak at the knees when he had handled it, he gave it a few practice swings and the blade sung as it split the very air. Then Balstore had told him that both weapons had been forged from the same ore, the scabbards and handles come from the same tree, and the handle lining was skin from the same shark, that both weapons were truly as one and should be kept so. It was only a year later that he himself had purposely driven them apart.

He was one of the few people who knew the true identity of the one known as 'The Blood Huntress'. She had earned the name when she had successfully tracked and killed a man who was himself a skilled tracker, so knew how to confuse a trail. He had murdered a young inn maiden and ran from the scene; numerous hunting parties had gone after him but after a month there was still no news of him. She had tracked and killed him in three days and when asked how she had managed it she had been quoted as saying 'I could smell his foul blood' and had walked away laughing, with a bag of gold. From that moment people had actually believed that she could sense the blood of her enemies and track them down and so the legend was born.

Danyard had trained her in all forms of combat and had known no one better, but he had only ever given her the basics of tracking and stalking so even he did not know how she managed to be so successful, and successful she was, never yet failing to find her prey and collect the reward. He could not even imagine how wealthy she now was, yet no person seemed to know where she lived, except somewhere in Ceredon. Ceredon, or The Great City, to give it its old name, was the largest city in the known world, so large that it dwarfed some nations, and now in fact was becoming a nation state within itself. But even in Ceredon she would need a house with grounds, to practice, and stables for her horse, and staff to maintain it, but no one, and he had paid enough spies over the years to find out, could furnish him with any information.

He remembered the tale of her mission that had seen her settled in Ceredon, The Great City had been plagued by a band of bandits, robbing and then killing most of those that they robbed, each robbery worse than the last and the body count rising, with no apparent pattern to where they would strike next. The Baron who ran that quarter of Ceredon, a notoriously miserly man named Blake, had been forced to offer a reward for their capture or destruction. No one knew how she had found them but again the rumour of her smelling their blood surfaced and the morning after they raided again she walked into Baron Blake's stipend office and demanded her payment, which he obviously refused to pay as he claimed, there was no proof that she had done anything.

She had turned without bowing or speaking a word and walked away, asking when she should return with proof, Baron Blake flippantly told her later in my court, hoping that she would be too intimidated by his guards to show her face, but show her face she did, and dragging a large sack with her across his highly polished marble floor. Again, she asked for payment in front of the assembled nobles of the court and again he denied her, in the time it took him to blink she pulled her kukri and split the sack open, there were gasps, as eight heads rolled across the floor, one rolled right to the Baron's feet, and she then asked again for payment or whether he wished to join them. As he shouted for his guards, her sword was already in her hand and there was a moment where everybody held their breath, until suddenly, as seemingly as one, his guards threw their swords to the floor and stepped back, the clattering of them startling in the open but silent hall. Then she spoke, "I will not ask a third time…"

He paid her there and then but she had made a dangerous enemy, he later was heard saying that he would find someone to track and kill her, it is rumoured that she then decided to settle there, to show him that she was not intimidated by him, but he knew the truth and the basics of strategy, keep your friends close but your enemies closer.

"Lost in thought Sire?" asked Maston, the half Atrop leader to his right. "Just thinking of an old friend." he replied.

"Unusual to see you smile is all my Lord."

"Yes, I suppose it is, but the least we can do is smile when we think of those we have lost."

"Yes, my Lord, the city is not far, what are your orders?"

"Send atrop four ahead to prepare the Imperial Mess for our stay, make sure they have enough grooms for the horses and a steaming hot bath for us all, we must look pretty for the despot King tomorrow."

"Yes my Lord," he shouted as he turned his mount backwards to speak with Atrop four commanders.

Morlen thanked the Imperial Guardsman and looked on as he returned to his three companions watching as he purposely strode down the street, completing his half atrop. She had assumed that the other four men would be dealing with Cambor and deciding his fate, but she knew that for her the adventure was now over, for Cambor had seen her face and would not only remember it, but be actively looking out for it. Besides she needed to return to the Glade to heal her wounds without scarring. She was sure her nose was not broken but it was certainly swollen and she had a graze on her cheek where she had struck the wall and she could already feel her face start to bruise.

She headed back to the main street and followed it down, working her way back to the inn, as she passed a tavern doorway a man was flung through the doorway and landed near her feet, he tried to stand but there was something wrong with this arm, then she saw with horror that the bone was protruding through the skin, and then Amyeen appeared from the same doorway and said to the man, "I gave you two chances to get your hand off of my breast, you chose to have your arm broken," She looked up and saw Morlen staring at her "What the fuck happened to you, you look worse than him."

"It's a long story, but we need to get away from here, before the Imperial Guard come, they are quite vigilant…" she replied.

"Good for you my friend is more compassionate than me, your lucky day scum bucket." she spoke to the now pale and sweating man at her feet, then said to Morlen "You are right, come on, let's go."

When they got back to their inn Callan was beside himself with worry, over everything that had happened.

"How have you managed to maintain a life of secrecy for fucks sake, the pair of you, covert, discreet, unnoticed, these words mean anything too you! You picked a fight with the man we are following, and got the Imperial Guard involved, and you, you just picked a fight with a drunken idiot! And on top of this, the fucking Silver King himself will be delivering the cursed weapon himself, how the fuck we are supposed to get anywhere near him! This is a disaster." Morlen looked suitably chastised but no one who was alive now had spoked to Amyeen like that since she was a child and she did not like it.

"The King will not be stupid enough to be seen with the Gunne and to be honest Balstore will not let it out of his sight unless he hands it directly to Namtu or Cambor, so it is he, we will have to watch for and ambush." She replied to his rant.

"We will not get close to him, your bat may do but even you will not get close enough to take him and all his men on, there will be security within security, but, we can work out where he will sight it."

"What does that mean?" asked Morlen.

"Every weapon is different, every person is different, arm length, eyesight, chest size, all have an effect on how a body holds a weapon and therefore how its projectile will fall, to sight it, he will need a large flat area, preferably with little or no wind, up to eight hundred paces."

"There is a large cove on the way to Kino'le, a natural harbour, really well protected by high cliffs either side, it is known for its beach in the summer months, if I was sighting a long range weapon it is where I would go, this time of year nobody would be there, too far out of the way to attract a casual visitor."

"So, we do not even have to wait for the ship, just camp out at the beach and wait for them there?"

"I would be happier seeing that they are at least heading that way, the three of them. I may even be able to watch the transaction through Blood, then I can track the Gunne, we cannot gamble that they will visit the beach and then we miss them as they casually stroll past us a few leagues away, so we still need to await this ship and follow, at a safe distance. Tomorrow, I will be in the harbour and will watch that damn ship and its cursed cargo arrive, after we have set Morlen on her way home."

Eleven
The Two Convoys

The huge dark wagons rolled over the hillside, forty-four of them in all, the last four wagons for supply but the first forty painted black inside and out, with tar pitching on the cracks so no light could get in. The convoy leader, Carmak, brother of Cambor, sat on his horse and looked back at them, each wagon pulled by four heavy horses, they did not need four per wagon at the moment but they would, when they were loaded. He was the only man who knew the exact nature of the cargo, and even he was uneasy with it, but the orders had been given to him personally from King Cathal himself and he could not disobey a Royal Decree, a huge honour really.

He had refused to ride on a wagon himself so he had more control over the convoy and also had employed his eight most trusted men as outriders. They buzzed up and down the convoy line barking at the wagon drivers and trying to keep the whole thing together, two further men on horseback scouted the way, again the most trusted from his Legion.

Each wagon had two drivers, but to Carmak's dismay, not soldiers and unused to the military discipline he would expect from men working under his command. It irked him but he had to admit that he needed them, professional wagon drivers that could work a team of heavy horses over sometimes rough ground, military wagon drivers did not have the experience of large transport wagons, just the small fast ones used for the supply chain.

He wished his brother Cambor was still with them, they had been escorted by the group until they had had to go their separate ways, Cambor and his men towards Kardon and Carmak towards the dark brooding forest of Dalstock, where their dreaded cargo awaited.

Cambor and Carmak had joined the King's Legions together as boy soldiers after they had run away from their vicious father and his failing farm.

Cambor being fourteen at the time and Carmak a year younger, neither had ever known their mother. Both had risen quickly through the ranks with their inherited love of violence and unshaking loyalty to each other, the hardship of military life was easy compared to the life as dirt poor farmers they had been brought up into. The training officers and instructors had soon seen their ability as a pair instead of two individual soldiers. Both now commanded a legion each but they were unique within the command of Branvere's forces for they usually acted as one, and as such had never failed in a task set by the hierarchy. Also unusually for Branvere military, each man was expected to consider every other soldier his brother, both had studied the tactics employed by Danyard and both were admirers of him, although through necessity quiet about this admiration as any deviation from standard Branvere military indoctrination was considered treason. Only because of the double legion's constant success was it tolerated. Carmak wished he was with them now, instead of babysitting this bulky, unwieldy and largely un defendable convoy.

Each driver was armed with a crossbow and a sword, but even though he tried to run anti-ambush drills they were slow and unwilling to react to his commands, and each and every one of them knew, he needed them, if he didn't, he would have hung half a dozen of them from trees along the route so far.

One of his scouts was galloping towards him and he hailed him as he neared.

"The dark forest is in sight Lord, about two leagues away in the valley base, it looks every bit as imposing as they say, seems to have a permanent cloud over it. I am not happy about this place my Lord, the safety of the wagons in that dark and enclosed space, we would be defenceless if attacked on the narrow tracks inside, lots of cover for an attacking force, we would be wiped out."

"We will not be entering the forest proper Mernan, we just need to wait on the western edge tomorrow night, for now do you have somewhere for us to set up camp tonight?"

"There is an abandoned quarry cut into the hillside around the next bend, good hard ground for the horses and close to a stream, it will be tight but we should fit all the wagons inside it."

"Good work, get to the back and get the supply wagons brought forward and in first, I want fires around the entrance and hot food for everybody, a small rum ration also issued, but not much, any of those fucking idiot drivers end up drunk I will fucking hang him and burn his wagon to dust. Then when they are fed and a little bit merry, I will brief yourselves first and then them."

"It will be as you say Sire."

Amyeen allowed herself to be moved out of the dock by the Imperial Guardsman, it looked like they wanted to shut off the area while the ship docked, the Imperials were moving people out and getting ready to close the huge harbour gates to the crowd. She could see the ship carrying the Royal Party, and more importantly the Gunne, just moving around the headland now. She was not worried, for Blood was already hanging in the shadows of the eaves of the Harbour Masters cottage and she only had to concentrate for a second to get a view of the dock.

The Imperial Guard were forming up facing the dock. This was not the regular Imperial Guard based in Kardon, these would be from Kino'le proper. She wondered who would lead the parade, she had a vague hope it would be her sister but in her heart she knew it would not be, Victarny had never left the City boundary while they had been growing up and she had not heard that she had since. She also did not think that Danyard would be here, she knew he hated the ceremonial side of his position and would find an excuse to get himself out of it.

They had seen Morlen off the night before, Morlen and Callen had had a tearful goodbye, hugging each other for what seemed an eternity, before she had ridden off with the few belongings that she had come with and a bag of silver that Amyeen had appeared with to pay the farm for the horse that Callan still needed. Callan had wanted to go with her, to see her safe home in the Glade, but he knew he was needed with Amyeen. She would have let him go but for the first time she was glad that she had a companion. While she waited and watched the docks, he was back at the Inn packing their belongings and making sure that the horses were ready for a rapid departure if required.

They had paid for their lodgings to date and also slipped the inn keep an extra coin to leave later in the day, but they were glad to be getting out, a half atrop of Guardsmen had been making enquiries of local landlords over an incident where a woman had broken a man's arm and a description had been circulated. She could not afford to be questioned by the Guards, they were all ex Dragoons and she feared that one may recognise her and then she would be forced to run and may have to hurt one or more of them and that is something that she did not want to do. Danyard may have need of every single one of them soon.

She moved with the crowd, and picked a spot against a wall near to the dock gates, she leant against it and looked through her blood vision at the dock. The Imperial Guard were forming up in a Royal Reception Formation with an officer at the front, she could not see his face as he was facing the sea with his back to the building and she dare not move Blood now in broad daylight with so many people, soldiers at that, having their attention drawn to him. The huge ship was alongside now and ropes were being thrown across to the dock men who grappled with them to pull the ship in close and tie her up.

She watched as the gangway was lowered and the first of the Branvere Royal Guard marched off and formed up opposite the Imperial Guard formation. The officer of the Imperials raised his sword and saluted first as was custom to a visitor, the Branvere officer returned the salute and then turned himself and his men around in one smart movement to face the ship. King Cathal the Silver of Branvere appeared on the deck and walked towards the gangway, with his entourage following. Balstore was at the forefront of the group and Amyeen shuddered at the sight of the vile wizard, remembering him from when he made her sword, how could someone capable of creating such beauty, also be such a monster.

"Her Royal Highness the Princess Victarny welcomes his most Gracious Majesty King Cathal The Silver of Branvere to The Kingdom of Light, may your visit bring you joy," shouted Danyard so all could hear.

"Ah Lord Danyard, a pleasure to meet such a fine warrior, I trust you are well," spoke Cathal.

"I am well your Majesty, although merely a humble servant of my Kingdom," he replied.

"Yes of course, and as you should be, you remember my friend and counsellor Lord Balstore?"

"Of course, Lord Balstore, a pleasure to see you again, life would have appeared kinder to yourself than me, you have hardly aged."

"I try to keep active and healthy Lord Danyard, I see you still carry the sword I made for you."

"It is the finest weapon, made by a true master of his craft."

"And what of its twin? Do we know what became of it?"

"Sadly no, the sword is with its owner and no one knows the whereabouts of either."

"It is a shame, such a thing of beauty gone forever," the obvious reference to the Princess Amyeen grated on Danyard, whilst they had stayed in the Palace in Branvere during their visit all those years ago Balstore had not managed to hide his attraction to the young Princess and Danyard had made it his priority to make sure she was never alone with him, mainly through the fear that she would kill him if he tried anything. It had caused some considerable friction between the two men, which was why he had been so surprised when he had also been presented with a sword.

"The Harbour Master's residence has been made available to you if you would like to rest, whilst your carriage and horses are unloaded."

"That would be most pleasant, if you would lead the way Lord Danyard."

"This way then please, Your Majesty."

Amyeen watched, as the King and Balstore walked after the officer, and then she realised, he was no ordinary Imperial, it was Danyard. The man who had raised her and her sister, protected them and tutored them in how to rule a kingdom, and the man who had betrayed her and driven her away. Strangely she did not feel any anger at the sight of him, she felt no hatred, he was a decent man with a large degree of humanity for someone in his position, although he was a ruthless killer on the field of battle he was surprisingly compassionate off of it. And he had trained her in everything that now kept her alive, and what had made her a legend in a man's world.

She was still looking out for any one of the three, the man named Cambor, the small lithe Namtu and his giant bodyguard Edvar. If she could just get close to Namtu then it was all over, all the pain and suffering that a war would cause could be stopped by the death of one man. But she knew in her heart they would not be, could not be, seen anywhere near the King or Balstore, if they were caught, dead or alive then the King would be in too much of an awkward position. So, she reasoned, they would make contact on the road to Kino'le. Callan and she would have to follow the convoy and observe as much as they could, and if possible, intercept the Gunne.

Amyeen was about to leave when her Blood vision caught some movement on the dock, a carriage was being assembled, not just a normal carriage, a huge royal carriage, parts being brought up from the hold, and seeming to just fit together. This has Balstore all over it she thought to herself. Then the horses for the Royal Bodyguard were led up and she suddenly knew how this invasion would work. This one huge ship had carried about sixty men and horses and a huge carriage, with a fleet of these ships a massive army could be assembled and more importantly, kept supplied.

When the carriage was assembled the Royal party emerged from the Residence, she watched for a while, King Cathal stopped before stepping into his carriage and waved to his Guard, who were now mounted and formed up in the centre of two columns of Imperial Guardsmen and without any more fanfare set off as the massive harbour gates started to swing open. Amyeen suddenly realised that she had loitered too long and now the crowd was thickening, making progress away from the gates was slow and frustrating. They all wanted a sight of the Silver King, most had heard of him but few had ever seen him, and they were now pushing and shoving for a view, just to say they were there when he came to the kingdom.

As she moved back against the wall the first four atrops came through the gates, four abreast, then half the Branvere Guard, then the royal carriage followed by the other half of the Branvere Guard and then the remaining atrops of Imperial Guards. She watched with mild curiosity, looking at faces she may recognise from the Dragoons, whom she had spent a lot of her child and teenage years training with. She watched as the last atrop passed her and was about to try to move away again when one of the end men turned and looked directly into her eyes. It was Danyard.

Amyeen tried to look away but she knew it was too late, he had recognised her. He had been her guardian for too long, watched her grow from a child to a woman not to have known her face the instant he saw her. He stared at her, and as much as she tried to, she could not look away, he craned his neck to keep her in sight until she finally dragged her eyes from him. She knew she had a bit of time, he would not break rank yet, the crowds were too thick still, but soon he would send one of his men to close the city gates, he had no reason to arrest her, there were no bounties on her, but, she knew he would try, for her sister's sake he would try to get hold of her.

She was angry with herself now, how could she have forgotten his first rule, never stand out. He was at the back doing what he did, observing everything without being noticed, of course he would have been at the back. And he had done what the rear rank is trained to do, looked back to check the rear, but this time he had got the shock of his life.

The crowd was thinning now and she started to run back towards the inn, she hoped that Callan had the horses ready, don't let me down now Callan she thought as she ran. Just as she turned from the dock street, she saw the man next to Danyard break off and make his way through the crowds, he could not move quickly yet but he would soon. The man would order the city gates closed until the convoy got there and only be opened for them, trapping her inside, which she could not afford to happen.

She slowed and got control of Blood, she sent him straight to Callan, hoping he would get the message, or at least get the idea that she was on her way. She started to sprint now, she gambled that Danyard would not tell them why to close the gates but just to do it, therefore they would not be looking specifically for her. She rounded the last corner and ran for the stables at the rear of their inn just as Callan emerged with the horses.

"Mount and get moving," she shouted at him "They are closing the fucking gates!" She threw herself at Buster and leapt upon his back, heading him around to the direction of the nearest gates and sped off, leaving Callan to try to keep up.

As she approached the gates, she saw a full atrop of Imperial Guardsmen about to close the gates, she drew her sword and screamed until she was hoarse, the sudden screech making most of them startle out of her way, a few stumbling to shut the gates on her. She shot through with Callan hot on her heels, the Guardsmen looked on but were not mounted, so had no capability to give chase. Amyeen galloped Buster for half a league before she slowed him down and let Callan catch her, she looked back to check they were not being pursued and then slowed to a walking pace.

"That was a close one," she said, more to herself than to Callan.

"Yes…very close, but why, I don't understand why, why did they shut the gates?"

"Somebody recognised me," she replied tersely.

"Who recognised you? And why would it matter if they did? You are not wanted by any kingdom or nation, there is no bounty on you, no outstanding commissions and who could have recognised you that had enough authority to close the gates of the biggest trading port in the known world? Who the hell are you, who is the Blood Huntress?"

"Let this go Callan, please, just let this go."

"It must have been at least a Lord, the person who greeted the King, he recognised you and wanted you detained, someone from Kino'le, what have you done to harm Kino'le? You said you were welcome there, that you like the..." he froze in mid-sentence as he felt a blade at his throat.

"I SAID, LET IT GO! Just be fucking quiet, I do not want to kill you but I fucking well will..."

Callan carefully looked around at her dark eyes and realised that he had not seen this side of her, the dark angry killer he knew her to be, but there was something else as he watched, she discreetly wiped a single tear from her eye.

"It's okay, I am sorry, please just be calm." He said as he gently pushed the kukri away from his throat. "It is your business, not mine, and I am sorry."

"Just remember that in future Callan, my business. I am hoping you packed all of our equipment, I need to get back into my real clothes and out of the pretty girl shit."

"We will need to find out where the King and his party will be staying, they will need to hand over the Gunne soon, probably tonight."

"There are many Inns on this road, dozens in fact, but the biggest one is where the roads cross, has over fifty rooms and stables for over a hundred horses, it will be there, it is the only one large enough for all the King's horses and all the King's men. I will send Blood to scout just to be sure."

"I saw him, Blood, your bat, just before you hit me with your arrow, he flew over, doing your scouting for you I know now, I did think it suspicious at the time, a lone bat, but then it was chaos. All part of your plan I suppose?"

"Yes, I was outnumbered ten to one, I needed every advantage I could think of gaining. A panicking enemy makes stupid mistakes."

"We were panicked enough, Cambor knew you were friends with Morlen, he was very spooked by it."

"How did he know, nobody knows that?"

"He did not say how he knew, but it must have come from Balstore, all intelligence in Branvere comes from Balstore, the King has a spymaster but he is quite useless."

"Tell me more of Namtu, why is he so special?"

"He is only a Captain really, quite a low rank, but he has the respect and admiration of the whole kingdom, he is always chosen for 'Special' tasks. He has a particular skill with any projectile weapon, it is almost as if he can see where any projectile will land. Weather seems irrelevant to him, he just seems to know where to aim, be it bow, crossbow, sling, bolas, spear, literally anything, and now, the Gunne. His first time with it he missed, but that is because it is a completely different to any other weapon ever seen, by his fourth shot he was hitting targets at triple the range of anyone else, it is almost magical to watch."

"What about other weapons? How is he with sword and shield?"

"He is good, he has developed a small unit into a kind of light infantry, only forty-eight men, lightly armoured and only a short sword for protection up close, hardly any other equipment apart from their bows and quivers, they run everywhere, but silently. They can get close to an enemy and launch a quick attack for a short period, maybe a dozen arrows each then vanish away again, sometimes loosing blind over defences, it has a devastating effect on the moral of the enemy, because by the time they have got a patrol together to go after them they are long gone. And then, a few hours later they do the same thing.

"But the biggest problem, quite literally, in getting to Namtu is getting past Edvar. No one knows where he came from, he never speaks but I get the impression he can, just chooses not to, but he is utterly devoted to Namtu, I have never seen them apart. He has a special room in Namtu's house, as well as a specially sized bow, the only man in Branvere with anything like a longbow. His broadsword is as damn near as tall as me, he can put so much power behind it that he once cleaved three men clean in half with one swing, worse thing I ever saw"

"How did three men get together like that?"

"Tied together, criminals, sentenced to death, it was a test of his sword and of his strength, officially the King ordered it but we all knew Balstore wanted it done, show off his mastery at sword smithing."

"So, it is safe to say that at some stage I will have to fight Edvar, I have fought big men before, they do not worry me, the bigger they are the more arrogant, they are so used to getting their own way through intimidation. It shakes them straight away when you face them down, then they usually use their strength straight away, I use that against them to put them off balance. But this Edvar sounds different, more intelligent, I will be cautious."

"Once you are through Edvar then Namtu is no match for you with a sword, but then who is?"

"There is one, the one who trained me, but again that is my business. How old are you Callan, twenty-one?"

"I turned twenty the day we set off, why?"

"Something is bothering me, why you? You seem younger than the others, and to be honest, more intelligent and not as savage as the average infantryman."

"I was one of Balstore's apprentices, still am really, not that I could ever return to Branvere now. Balstore has ten apprentices at a time, aged from twelve to twenty-one, this was my last test, before becoming one of the King's armourers, it is then ten years' service to the King before being allowed to start on your own. I am the Gunne expert, I helped Balstore design and build it, and if there is a problem with it, I was to fix that problem."

"So, you are a master armourer too?"

"Yes I am, the trade that Balstore has taught me, I will be forever grateful for, but the man is a despicable pig, likes young girls, enjoys hurting them, I hated him being near me."

"I have heard of that before, you know he made my sword? When I was there, I never saw any apprentices."

"The palace workshop is just for show, I assume you visited him there, all wealthy clients do, the real work is done at his estate workshop, there is a dormitory there, where we all lived. The first year you are just a skivy, cleaning the dorm and the workshop, but then in the second year you start on the basics, working leather and wood, a lot of leather sewing to toughen the hands and create strength of arm, that kind of thing. Then, on your final year you get sent on a mission with some, or a lot, of soldiers. It is usually an operational mission, something real that has to be done, usually some poor soul Balstore has taken a dislike to and he has decided needs to be killed, so not just an exercise, there is a chance you could end up dead or wounded. If you return from the mission then you become a weapon maker for the Kingdom, indebted I think they call it, for ten years, until it is considered that you have paid your debt, but only if the new apprentice passes his mission to replace you, otherwise it's another year before you are allowed to leave service."

"So some do not return?"

"Some do not…only one since that I know of."

"Does Balstore expect you to deal the killing blow?"

"Not essential, but you have to play an active part, you cannot dodge the responsibility, Balstore's saying is that armourers are dealers in death, which we are really, so he thinks we should see the harm of what we create can do."

"Have you killed anybody?"

"No, I have not; I just hope that when the time comes, I will not shame myself."

"I do not regret any of the lives that I have taken, every one of them had a choice, and mostly it was them or me."

"My friends at the Glade did not."

"Yes, they did, they could have run, three of them did and three of them still live. Would they have shown mercy to Morlen had they found her?"

"I do not think that Cambor would have let them hurt her. He was aware of your friendship, somehow. Namtu was terrified when he heard, I have never seen him scared before."

"I wonder what else he knows about me that he should not, it matters not. The first person that I killed was a man that tried to rape me, he grabbed me from behind, I collapsed into him without struggling to give him a sense that I had given up, then threw him over my shoulder, he landed heavily on his back with the wind knocked from him, but that was the least of his troubles, as he went over my body I pulled my skinning knife and slashed his femoral artery, that's in the top of the leg, in the groin, he bled out right there, while I stared into his eyes, on the floor of a dirty trading post. I was eighteen at the time and trying to get away from…somewhere, I had stopped for supplies and the man was already there, trading. The man's brother swore vengeance on me, tried to track me through me the forest, not the first to make that mistake."

"What happened?"

"I let him track me, led him a trail that ended against a cliff face, no way back except the way I had led them in, but by the time they got in I was back out, they had literally walked straight over me. There were three of them, two stayed mounted but the brother walked in on foot, a lot smarter. As I rose from the undergrowth, my bow was already in hand and I smoothly nocked an arrow and pulled back, from about seventy paces the arrow took one of the horsemen clean through his back and out of his chest, the second horseman tried to turn around but I threw down my bow and charged him, his horse reared and threw him, he stood quickly, but he was off balance so my sword took his head and one shoulder and arm in a single swipe. The brother turned to me with a look of horror, contemplating whether to go for his sword, before he decided I said to him 'You do not have to die here, you can walk away."

"Did he, walk away?"

"Yes he did, just walked his horse out of there and rode away."

"And that was it?"

"No, apparently he was some kind of minor noble, wealthy family, went off with a sword master and trained for a year, tracked me down in a small town and challenged me to open combat."

"And you beat him, was he good, after a year's training?"

"He was all right, too confident of his own ability and the justness of his cause, kept ranting and raving about what he was going to do, I really couldn't be bothered with it and I did not want my sword blade to get damaged by his so I killed him in thirty heartbeats. Let him swing his big broadsword about and vent all his rage then stepped inside his swing and put my blade clean through his ribs on his left side, cut one of his lungs clean through. Arrogant prick had ripped his jerkin and undershirt off, flexing his muscles, left his ribs exposed, easy target. His blade never even touched mine, or me for that matter.

"Shame really, I liked that little town, but I thought I had better move on, before some other idiot with a grudge decided he needed to be killed by me. I had tracked and killed about a dozen men by that stage and was making a name for myself, but after that I needed to get my head down, slip away for a while, so I joined the convoy for Dalstock. I thought they were naive but I was between towns and jobs and so I let them persuade me, and if they did manage to settle in that dark and forbidding place then I have always found it handy to have friendly faces in strange towns."

"I heard of this, the settlers from the Kingdom of Light tried to build a settlement there, logging and such, to try to bring the Light of Kino'le to the darkness."

"Yes, they thought if enough of them went then a part of the light would follow, like I said, naive."

"They were massacred by the savages, weren't they? I did not know that anyone had survived, but you did, you were there?"

"Yes and yes, they were killed by the savages, but, the world condemns the Tree People of Dalstock, to give them their correct title, but who were we to march in there, start cutting down their trees for our own use. Trying to change the nature of the place, yes it is horrible and dark and dismal, but it is theirs and not ours, not ours to decide that it needed to be changed into something colourful and full of fucking badgers and frolicking foxes like some kind of fairy tale."

"But they killed them, surely they should have just warned them to leave."

"They did warn them, in their own way, sabotaging camps, setting fires, but you know what the bloody Priests of Light are like, stubborn, see everything as some kind of fucking trial."

"So you fought them?"

"Yes, once they decided that they would not leave then I had no choice, I had to help them fight, organise their defences. Give them a chance at least."

"But you survived?"

"To be fair to the Tree People again, they let me live, and I must have killed half a dozen of them in the final fight, but still they let me live. Damn they were quick, fastest reflexes I have ever seen, take aim with an arrow and by the time you loose it, they have vanished back into the undergrowth, same with a sword, they seem to be able to anticipate your moves. And their spears, like no other weapon I have ever seen, big black blade, narrow leaf shaped and razor sharp, it was one of them that sliced my face open, knocked me unconscious. When I came around, the leader, Garvak was standing a few paces away, and Blood was at my neck, drinking my blood, I jumped up and pulled him off, broke one of his wings, and all the time Garvak just stared impassively at me, like he had not a care in the world.

"He gave me a choice, live or die, ride away or try to kill some more of his men, strangely it was Blood, still in my hand that made my mind up. I could feel him squirming in my grasp and I had a sudden epiphany. Die in that dark place or live and try to get help for this wounded creature, I chose to live and I rode out towards Morlen's glade, she fixed him and me. I fought a Dark Stalker on my way out as well. That's how I came to know her. She set and fixed his wing and stitched up my face, stayed there a few days."

"When you came to her aid, how did you know, that she was in danger, you were not just passing."

"She sent a vision to Blood, the residual magic in Dalstock and the glade is vast, it manifests itself, it created a bond between the three of us, but stronger between myself and Blood. I saw you shoot the stag, I saw you all, looking for her, I saddled up and rode hard, and the rest…well you know."

"Yes, I know, we all got killed."

"Blood has settled in the eaves of a suitable inn, we should get moving quickly again and get settled before the King's convoy passes it, just beyond the large inn the road forks, one way to Kino'le and one way to the beach, we will be ready for them tomorrow."

Danyard strode around the inn and looked at the defences that he had in place, he had two full atrops on guard at a time, one atrop of which were archers, the remaining four atrops were resting but in full dress, ready to go at a moment's notice. The inn was huge, and took up a lot of ground which worried him, but he had ordered it commandeered by the Kardon Imperial Guard two days prior, not a single person who was not involved in the convoy was staying there. His second in command, a new Captain named Maston, was with him at that moment, listening and learning. He was trying to concentrate but he was still reeling from seeing Amyeen at the dock, why was she watching the Silver King, surely not even she would accept a commission to kill him, would she?

"So, Maston, the gates had not yet been fully closed when the woman and her companion rode through, and they charged with swords drawn at the Imperial Guardsmen?"

"Yes, but not them both, only her, she drew it and held it aloft and screamed at them, they had no time to do anything other than dive out of the way."

"And they did not give chase?"

"No Sire, I spoke with the commander, he had orders to shut the gates but not to stop anyone from leaving beforehand and he did not want to alarm the convoy that he was expecting any minute by organising a pursuit, and he had no horses close by anyway."

"A wise choice, was there any other news from the city log, specifically involving any women as attackers not victims?"

"Yes, a known drunkard had an arm broken by a young woman, a nasty piece of work who was well known to the Guard, apparently he was warned to get his hand from where it should not have been and when he did not, she snapped his arm clean through the elbow joint. Witnesses say she removed his arm and put him in an arm lock and that could have been it, but she then put her knee through his elbow with her bodyweight behind it the way it was not made to go. The same witnesses inform me that it makes a very sickening crack."

"Makes me wince just thinking about it, I do not think he got much sympathy from the Imperials though?"

"No, he did not. After that another young woman appeared and they walked away together, towards the southern quarter."

"Another woman, was this the same person who she crashed through the gate with?"

"No, that was definitely a young man."

"So, we have no idea who this man or woman are?"

"No Sire, if you do not mind me saying, you seem very interested in this group."

"Exactly, group is what worries me, I have never known her to work as part of a group."

"Her Sire, do you mean…?"

"Never mind, I do not want any of the Branvere soldiers to go anywhere alone outside of the inn, do not stop them from leaving but escort them everywhere, and if that means man on man then so be it, if we all have to stay awake all night then we will."

"Of course Sire."

"Good, now let us get inside and rested."

Amyeen and Callan had watched the convoy pass just as the sun had set, they stood back from the window and in shadow so as to not be seen. She had sent Blood to follow and they had stopped for the night at the trading post inn a quarter league ahead.

"The King is now settled into the inn." She said, "Where will the weapon be?"

"It will be in one of his or Balstore's personal chests, no one would dare search them, it could not have been passed to Namtu yet, there would not have been an opportunity. They, nor the King, can afford to be seen near each other, if they were captured in the attempt on the Princess then the connection would be made too easily. They will have to make the transfer tonight, somewhere near but not at the inn, which means that they will have to leave the inn without an escort, I assume Danyard would not allow this to happen."

"You assume correct."

"How would they know where to meet, you said you did not know when you left that the King was coming to Kino'le?"

"The Trade Commissioner, he would be the contact point for them, or his office at least."

"Then why not just let him hand it over?"

"Pride I think, Balstore again, he would not allow anyone else to handle this weapon except Namtu, and he would want a full report on the patrol so far, I would not want to be Cambor when he has to explain just how he managed to lose seven out of ten men including his latest apprentice."

"So, we go and watch the inn tonight, follow them and ambush Cambor and company on the way back."

"We cannot do that, we cannot alert Cambor to our presence, just think about it, we would need to get close and undetected, so that means on foot, but then how would we move fast if we had to? All three of them will have their Gunnes with them at the meeting, a few seconds is all it would take for one of them to fire at you, it just has too many unknowns and risks. But we know they will be on the beach tomorrow, alone, just the three of them. We can get there hours before them and set up an ambush, you have your war bow, I have my Gunne, take them down from a distance and that will be it."

"Okay, then that is what we will do, Blood needs to feed now so I will release him, but he can watch the meeting for us tonight."

"That is settled then, now I must clean and prepare my own Gunne, it has not been fired for a week and it needs to work perfectly tomorrow. I am no match for any of them with sword, and my archery is poor at best, it is this or nothing."

Twelve
The Assassin

Namtu looked down at the weapon he had been handed and a breath caught in his throat, never before had he seen such a fine example of craftsmanship. Even in the dull light provided by the moon he could see what a masterpiece he held. The dark mahogany wood ran the length from the butt to the fore end stock, the metal work engraved elaborately, glinting at him in the moonlight. The barrel was more substantial, the metal looking denser and perfectly blued, the whole thing was heavy and solid looking and the sighting system was already attached front and rear.

"This is a new concept in its modifications, this is the first one that will load from the rear end." spoke Balstore "Therefore, there is no loss of compression in the barrel, as the shot fits the barrel perfectly, we used your own shot mold to make a batch of balls and built the barrel around them. The barrel breaks open at the stock by pushing this lever here, the barrel rear end is exposed to allow you to place the lead ball in, it will sit half a thumb length in, enough room to place a packet of powder in behind it, then snap it shut. The powder packets are exact, and they will fit behind the ball. As you snap it shut a small spike pierces the powder packet so when the flame travels down it ignites, and you know the rest."

"Yes, I know the rest." he replied in a daze.

"Now, Cambor, do you want to explain to me again how you lost my best apprentice and six other good men?"

"The Blood Huntress is how, and as you, my Lord, seem to know everything, maybe you could have warned me that she would be there, close by."

"I could, but we do not have time for it, this area is surrounded by Imperial Guardsmen, including the Lord Danyard, it took all of my skill to get passed them and I have to get back in yet, and I sense…evil eyes upon us, someone, or thing, is watching us."

"They have the Gunne, I know nothing of these weapons but even to my ignorant eyes it looks a masterpiece. The three of them have just left Balstore who was on his own, he has headed back into the woodland, in a seemingly straight line towards the Inn, I am sending blood after the Gunne, although I am tempted to see how Balstore gets back into the damn place."

"There is no need, we will be on the beach before them tomorrow, Namtu will need to be in the open, we will get them there."

"What is so special about the sighting system?"

"Even though, this weapon was made for Namtu, with his exact measurements, it does not mean the ball will hit where he wants it too, the rear sight moves under a minute notch system left to right and the front sight moves up and down. He will fire a small number of shots and adjust in what direction he needs to, then test it for different ranges, it could be a long process."

"Why did he not just bring it with him, why all this subterfuge?"

"Firstly, he could not risk it being damaged on route, we were on the road for a long time, anything could have happened, we might have even been attacked by the Blood Huntress! Secondly, it was not ready, Balstore was experimenting with a rear, or breach, loading system when I left, he thought it would help with power as none of the explosive force would be wasted as the ball does not make a perfect seal on a fore end loader, but if the ball was to go into the rear of the Gunne where it is fired from then the barrel can be made narrower a small way down and therefore create an airtight seal. No waste of force, more power and hopefully more accurate too."

"Okay, so he really will be able to hit a target at six, seven maybe even eight hundred paces?"

"Yes, he will, I saw Namtu hit a target at two hundred and sixty paces with a standard Gunne, with a better barrel, breach loading and the sighting system, I would estimate him to be a maximum range of about eight hundred paces."

"That is an awful long way for us to search for him, we had better make sure we get him tomorrow."

"And with that in mind let us get some food and then we can turn in for the night, I am exhausted."

"Okay but have it sent up, I do not feel sociable tonight, and we cannot afford for some idiot to pick a fight with me."

"I agree, I will go down and talk with the landlord."

Thirteen

The Bodyguard

Namtu smiled as he looked down at the driftwood, it was perfect, about a pace and a half wide and two paces long, light in colour from being bleached by the sun and salt spray. They were just on the sea edge, the surf lapping at their feet. It was a cold winters day, bright sky but very little wind so perfect conditions for their task ahead.

They had ridden down from their camp in the woods earlier that day, passing the inn where the King had stayed, but giving it a wide berth, fearful of being stopped by an Imperial Guard patrol. The horses were a short distance away with their reins tied to an old fence post. They did not want them bolting from the noise of the Gunne.

"This will do Cam." Said Namtu "Can you mark a narrow cross on it with your knife, dig out the outer wood, it should be darker underneath, then dig it in the sand by half a pace, so it is solid in the ground. I will start one hundred paces away, I need you to mark where the strike is with your hand after each shot, I will adjust at one hundred and then move down in one hundred pace intervals raising the sight each time, and hopefully striking near the same place each time too."

"Okay I understand what we are doing, but surely, we need a lookout, what if someone comes?"

"Who is going to come here in the dead of winter, unless there is something that you are not telling me, is there Cam? Did something happen in Kardon that you forgot to mention?"

"No, I am just being cautious, it is why I am here, to keep you safe in strange lands."

"That's why Edvar is here, keeps me safe in any land, do you want to tell him he has to stand eight hundred paces from me?"

Edvar looked on impassively, not even acknowledging that they were speaking about him.

"If you put it like that then I have no choice, do I? Go to your first position and I will wave when it is dug in. Let us get this done and off this beach, I hate being exposed like this, no cover anywhere."

Namtu and Edvar walked off along the beach, counting paces as they went, Namtu suddenly stopped and cleared an area of sand and then laid out a blanket and other pieces of his equipment upon it. He carefully took the new leather pouch containing the small packets of powder and laid them out, then his own lead shot balls, which Balstore had promised him would fit this Gunne. He looked for the ramrod and then realised that he did not need one, for this weapon loaded from the rear, no need to ram it all to the back of the Gunne.

From the kneeling position he broke the Gunne open using the catch that he had been shown and exposed the rear of the barrel, he could see the area that the ball sat in and he placed one there, as promised it sat there, not rolling down the barrel as he had feared it would. He then placed a sachet of powder behind the ball and snapped it shut. He then placed a brass percussion cap on its stud and pulled back halfway on the hammer, the trigger stiffened at this and he lay down on the blanket and pulled back all the way to full cock on the hammer. He looked down the barrel through the sight.

He adjusted himself to a comfortable position and then slowed his breathing, he lined up the fore notch with the rear sight aperture and lined both up with the cross that Cambor had scratched out with his knife. He watched as the fore sight rose and fell in time with his breathing and at the right time, squeezed the trigger. Flame leapt from the muzzle as the ball shot away and smashed a hole in the driftwood. He waited while Cambor pointed to where it had hit, low and to the right, he adjusted the sight and repeated the process. This time the ball struck just above dead centre of the cross but too high, he adjusted and fired again, this time the ball struck the absolute centre, exactly where the lines met. He smiled and stood, he then started walking away down the beach, counting the whole time, as he did so he adjusted the rear sight on its elevation dial by one click. The system appeared to be as reliable as Balstore had promised, one click matched exactly one hundred paces and he was able to strike the driftwood within a hand space of the centre right out at seven hundred paces. He could hardly make out the driftwood at that range, but he just instinctively knew where to aim, it was like a hidden hand guided him.

He stood up from his last shot and looked down the beach, he could not quite see what had happened but he knew that something was seriously wrong, Cambor seemed to be laid on the sand, his blood ran cold and he started to run towards him, that was when he saw their horses and one other stampeding down the beach towards him. His heart almost seized with the realisation, he stopped dead and stared at the horses, sure enough, one of them had a rider, and as he stood dumbfounded, he saw the rider draw a sword and hold it aloft. There was only one person that it could be. Damn this woman, they did not even hurt that cursed witch, did not even fucking see her, why was she still pursuing them!

Namtu knew that one day this time would come, the day that Edvar would give his life to save the man who had saved him, the unfairness of it made his blood boil, tears of rage streamed down his face but his iron discipline was what had made him what he was today. Poor sweet Edvar, built like a monster with the heart of an angel, abused by those who had raised him, rescued by Namtu and now fiercely loyal to him, and now, the poor giant would have to face one of the greatest warriors the world had ever known, just so a greedy despot could take what was not his, but the sense of duty was strong in Namtu and he had to obey his King, despot or not.

"Edvarius of Mar'thak, the time has come my friend, you must make time for me, I must get away, I must…you know what you must do." Namtu spoke with a lump in his throat and a tear in his eye, he stepped forward and embraced the giant man, more tears flowed and snot ran from his nose, almost beside himself with grief and anger.

As usual Edvar remained silent, he gave a short nod to Namtu and turned to face the horses now only a few hundred paces away, Namtu wiped away his tears and turned and ran for his life, grabbing his equipment as he went.

Edvar calmly walked out towards where the horses would pass, not even drawing his sword he stood and waited for his fate. As she approached, she tried to swerve to one side but Edvar was too quick, he launched himself at her horse, grabbing it around the neck with his massive weight behind it, bringing horse and rider crashing into the sand.

Amyeen could not believe what had just happened, this man had literally head locked her horse and brought it down, she had managed to slip her feet out of the stirrups just before they all hit the sand and she rolled away from the massive crushing weight of the horse and giant but she had to release her sword at the same time. She tried to stand but as she did Edvar was there, easily lifting her clean from the ground with one huge hand around her throat, she panicked and tried to grab her kukri from the small of her back but before she could his other huge hand had drawn back and slapped her around the head. She felt like she had been hit by a tree but luckily for her, he released her as he struck and she was battered across the sand. She staggered, as she tried to stand once again but already Edvar was moving towards her, as he approached and grabbed for her she let the dizziness take her and she collapsed in on herself, Edvar's punch he had aimed at her sailed passed her face by a hairs breadth, and his unbalance forced him to turn sideways to her, she put all her remaining strength into a stamp to the side of his knee, the power behind this would have broken the leg of a normal man but Edvar was no normal man, he staggered and gave a shout of pain as he collapsed onto that knee, giving her enough time to dive for her sword.

She stood, sword in hand and faced the giant, her head was still spinning from the slap, the wind knocked out of her and her throat constricted, but at least she was now doing what she did best, and the sheer joy of holding her beloved sword again giving her strength. Edvar reached for his massive sword and it flew from its scabbard and again she swallowed hard, never before had she seen a man that fast with a sword, especially one the size of Edvar. He stood and stared at her, bringing himself to his full height, a pace taller than any other man that she had ever seen, and about a pace wider, he must have been three times her weight, his heavy muscles seeming to want to break free of his skin.

She knew that she would only get one chance at this, if he got hold of her again it would be all over, she took a deep breath and lunged for his legs, he moved with the easy grace of a cat, blocking her thrust and parrying her away and flinging her back into the sand, she landed heavily on her back near the surf. He instantly advanced on her and she only just rolled away as his blade hit the sand where she had been a heartbeat before, she jumped up and got behind him, slicing him across the back as he tried to stand, his jerkin split and blood sprayed out in an arc but it did not even slow him as he released one hand from his sword and back handed her across the sand and into the shallow surf of the sea.

She landed hard in the surf and struggled to a stand, staggering backwards from him as stars were bursting in her head and nausea washed over her, her vision started to dim and she knew, it was all over, she could make out him striding towards her and that damn massive broadsword being drawn back for the killing stroke, she remembered what Callan had said about cleaving people in two but she could do nothing now to avoid it as it came flashing towards her. As it did, Edvar suddenly staggered and his entire right shoulder exploded in a mass of flesh and bone, however his sword still struck her and she was lifted clean off her feet once again, she landed heavily in the sea and pain exploded through her chest. Before she lost consciousness, she thought to herself, how can being dead hurt this much?

Callan awoke from what seemed like an eternal sleep with the worst headache that he had ever known and someone was banging loudly on the door and shouting.

"Wait, wait, what is wrong for fucks sake?" he asked as he staggered to the door, opening it to find the inn keep there, red faced and angry.

"You have only paid for the night, you need to be off, others need this room." he replied.

"What, what time is it?"

"It is near midday, your companion has already left, saddled her horse and took off like her tail was on fire, now please do the same!"

"All right, all right, I will be gone soon, have someone saddle my horse."

Callan looked around the room and came to the sudden realisation of what had happened, she had used a potion on him, drugged him to stop him going with her, so she could fight them alone. Whether this was just her way or she did not trust him was of no importance now, what's important was that not even she could kill Edvar and Namtu, and that is assuming she could kill Cambor first. He went to his bed and looked under it, with relief he saw the blanket roll exactly as he had left it, he quickly unrolled it and gave it a cursory check, it all seemed okay.

He packed his few belongings but made sure he wore his equipment belt, as he walked down to the stables, he mounted his horse and flipped the stable boy a small copper, asking the fastest way to the beach as he did so.

He rode as fast as he could towards the beach track, pulling up and dismounting as soon as he saw the sea, he hobbled the horse to a nearby fence post and took his Gunne from the pannier, unrolling it and relishing in the feeling it gave him. He started to walk towards the sea, the dunes came into view and he started the loading process, he had made a point of learning to do this while he walked, knowing that one day he would have to do this on the move, satisfied with what he had done he pulled the hammer to half cock and last thing he did was place the brass percussion cap on its stud. When he was satisfied, he headed up into the dunes, he did not want to give himself away, or her if she had not made her presence known yet, as he crested a particularly large dune, he realised his covert approach did not matter, for she was charging towards Namtu and Edvar with three other horses alongside, she wants them for cover and distraction, he thought to himself, she thinks of bloody everything.

He quickly looked about to account for all three of them, a small figure was running away down the beach towards the far cliffs, that had to be Namtu, a very large man was standing facing the horses, had to be Edvar, he looked the other way, about two hundred paces in the other direction near the surf was a prone figure, he thought that he could make out at least two arrows protruding from the body, had to be what remained of Cambor, he could see what was about to happen and he started to run through the dunes, towards where she rode hard down on Edvar.

He lost sight of them as he ran down a dune, then scrambled up the next, he was closing on them fast but he was still too far to help her, even with his Gunne. As he crested the last dune, he watched as Edvar picked her up by her throat and slapped her across the sand and he winced, only imagining what it must have felt like, she fell across the sand like a rag doll, and then Callan started to run again as the ground levelled out onto fine sand, he ran watching this battle of titans until he was about one hundred and fifty paces from them, then he slowed to a walk and brought the Gunne up to his shoulder, pulling the hammer to full cock as he did so.

He tried to slow his breathing, he knew, he would not hit anyone or anything with his lungs pumping like they were. He saw what he thought would be the last move as Edvar backhanded her across the sand again and watched with despair in his heart as she tried to stand, he could see from where he was just how disorientated she was, hardly standing, her sword held weakly in front of her, it is now or never he said to himself. He made his decision, he brought the weapon to his shoulder and knelt in the sand in one fluid movement and took aim, very carefully and still trying to get his breathing under control, he raised the barrel to his eye and lined it up on Edvar's massive frame as Edvar bought his huge sword back for the killing stroke. The Gunne rocked in Callan's shoulder but he was ready for it and allowed his body to roll with it, how he had trained others to do, but he knew, he had missed as he fired, only to be shocked when the ball struck Edvar in the shoulder, bits of bone and blood exploded from the ghastly wound and Edvar lost grip on his sword, Callan saw it hit Amyeen in the chest but it had turned sideways as he had lost his grip on it, it had still sent her across the sand again but it had not cut her to pieces.

Callan shook his head to clear it and immediately started to reload, pouring powder and ball down the barrel as he stood and slowly walked towards the wounded giant. He placed the percussion cap on and gave the final pull back on the hammer as he approached Edvar and stopped about thirty paces away. Edvar's sword was on the floor and the man himself was on his knees blood streamed down his chest and Edvar just stared at the wound, trying to make sense of the incomprehensible mess his shoulder had become. Although, his face was now pale from blood loss no pain showed on his impassive features. Callan walked slowly forward, closing the gap to less than twenty paces. He raised the Gunne one more time and centred it on the giant man's chest, as he did so Edvar looked up from the mess that had once been his shoulder and stared right into his eyes, but Callan did not know this as tears were streaming from his own eyes, and he squeezed the trigger once more.

Amyeen's eyes flickered open and she looked around her from her supine position, she could feel blankets underneath her and on top of her, she tried to sit up but she felt nauseous and bile rose in her throat, she tried to fight it but in the end the pain in her ribs was too great. She knew, she was still on the beach as she could hear the surf, the edge of her vision caught sight of a fire. Every single breath hurt her and every muscle ached, and then, Callan was there, holding some foul tasting fluid to her mouth, she gagged on it and tried to spit it out but he pinched her nose and she could not fight him off, her head swam for a few seconds and then all was darkness once more.

"Neema," she heard from her darkness "Neema, how are you feeling?"
She looked around again, it was daylight and this time she managed to prop herself on one elbow, the pain had receded considerably and she had a vague memory of some fluid being forced into her throat. She looked at Callen, he looked distraught, the saddest look she had ever seen on anybody's face.
"What happened? Why do I live, his sword, Edvar's sword, it struck me, I should be in pieces on the sand?"

"I shot hm, with my Gunne, hit him in the shoulder as he swung, he lost his grip on the sword as it struck you, hit you on its flat side. Obviously, still enough strength to knock you through the air but it did not penetrate your skin. You do however have three broken ribs and terrible bruising on that side, I do not believe that you have any internal bleeding. There is no permanent damage to your face, but you will be ugly for a few days until the swelling goes down.

"Before Morlen left she gave me a number of remedies and other things to aid healing, they will help with healing and take away the pain. I have strapped up your chest, try to restrict its movement."

"And what of Edvar, you killed him?"

"No, you selfish fucking bitch, I executed him, shot him in the chest in cold blood, to stop him pursuing us later, and prevent him from aiding his master any further. Are you happy now that I have turned into the heartless killer that you are!" He replied with tears streaming down his young face.

"If you were the killer you think that I am you would not weep for the giant man, it is a credit to you and I really hope that you never get a taste for it, I would not wish my life on anybody, although many men would relish it, but, men are stupid. The compassion that is still within you is just something that I do not have room for, my instincts for survival are too strong."

"Then I am glad that I have chosen a different path."

"Do not judge me Callan, you choose to make the weapons that allow people like me to thrive, to become legends, and one weapon in particular that could change the way war is fought forever."

"I had no choice, I was apprenticed to Balstore at ten years old, I could not refuse him."

"Yet still you carry your Gunne, yet still you cannot let it go."

"And without it you would be dead! If you had not poisoned me then I would not have had to kill Edvar."

"No, not from as close as you did anyway. Would that have been better? From a hundred paces away, shooting Cambor in the back first, does that satisfy your misplaced sense of honour? Would you have felt like a hero then? I am sorry that the first life you took had to be that way, but it is the nature of death, despite what the stupid men think it is not glorious and it is not glamorous, it is hard and brutal and messy and I hope that you never get a taste for it."

"That would be my wish too, now rest, we must try to move tomorrow if you wish to catch Namtu, he is very light of foot and could be half way to Kino'le by now."

"Thank you, Callan, you saved my life, actually staring death in the face is a new experience for me and I did not enjoy it. Whether we catch Namtu or not Kino'le owes you a huge debt."

"And why is that exactly?"

"Because, I am the Princess Amyeen of the Kingdom of Light, who vanished years ago and I am the younger sister of Victarny. I am fighting to save my sister and I will not stop until Namtu is dead."

"You are who…?" The realisation suddenly dawning on him as he stared at her and knew that she spoke the truth, he could see the fear in her eyes, the fear of what could happen to her sister if they failed.

"You are the missing Princess, the famous mystery, how…what…what happened? What made you leave and why?"

"I was driven away, by the wizard Lorgane, he never liked me, I always sensed that he was a bit afraid of me. He convinced Danyard, I wanted the kingdom for myself, somehow convinced him that I would kill my sister. The wizard, unbeknown to Danyard sent three assassins to kill me, or her, I still do not know which, maybe both of us. Danyard killed all three of them but he got it into his head that I had sent them. He gave me a load of money and letters of credit with merchants in every city, some of which I still have, but as I said I was attacked in a trading post and the rest is history. I avoided the ceremonial and public duties that Victarny attended so my face was not very well known. Blood Huntress is a perfect life for me really, one legend hiding in another."

"It explains a lot and that you were trained by Danyard, explains even more. One of the Branvere Captains was a young mercenary for Mar'thak during the last invasion, he said that he had never seen anything like Danyard on a battlefield, so quick was he with a sword, barely engaging opponents' swords just moving through and around them and making one vital cut on each soldier.

"It was towards the end of the battle, just as the tide was starting to turn against Mar'thak. The King, your father, had just taken the wound that had eventually killed him and Mar'thak, seeing this, had thought they had won, when Danyard led a small party of Dragoons into the fray, he took the head of the man who had struck the King and three others in the first instant, then disembowelled a huge axe man and took the legs clean off at the knees of the

Mar'thak officer. The battle just seemed to stop around him, men, battle hardened men, just seemed to have no blood lust left in them after watching that, he put one foot on the dying officers body and spat at them, and still they backed off. I think they knew enough of them could overwhelm him but they also knew that the first men who did, would fall to that flashing blade of his.

"By all accounts, he looked terrifying, his long hair hanging down across his face, splattered with blood and he just stood there and laughed at them, and they knew they faced a madman. But then, suddenly four men found their courage and rushed him, he did not even move until they were upon him and then he moved with a speed no one had ever seen before. He took each of them down but without killing them, he took the sword arm of each man, what good is a man that makes a living through his sword without an arm. He knew this, as he watched them writhing around in the mud spraying blood. Then the rest really started to back away until one, then a few more and then all of them turned and ran and so began the rout.

"He always told that one man could turn the tide of a battle, to install fear in the enemy, but I did not know that he had actually done this, but it is of no surprise to me. My father effectively gave Danyard the Kingdom when he died, until Victarny and I came of age. A lot of the noble houses were not happy but what could they do, they needed to stick together to rebuild, they knew they could not afford a civil war, and the soldiers were all loyal to him, especially the Dragoons. The Kingdom was in a bad enough state. It did not take long for the Nobles to accept him, as he increased trade each family grew wealthier but he also made them train and patrol with the men they retained and so a great bond was made between them."

"Who trained Danyard?"

"Another big mystery, he arrived in the city one day, fifteen years old, joined the Kino'le army and after a while challenged and beat the King's champion, beat him with a stick while the champion used a sword. Immediately appointed as bodyguard and then soon became Lord Dragoon. The only people that he ever allowed to be close to him were Victarny and I, emotionally that is and he would not even tell us where he came from, I do believe that he told our father though."

"So, your Highness, how do you feel now?"

"Do not start that rubbish, I was never comfortable with all that, just call me Neema, it is nearly backwards for Amyeen which is why I use it. I feel a lot better; my ribs actually feel like they are mending already, I assume that goo you forced down me last night was from Morlen? I think she put her usual magic into it, broken ribs should take weeks to heal properly but I do feel almost well already."

"That is good, but I think we should still rest one more night, we can move to the rock face now and make a new camp there and then follow Namtu into Kino'le City, he will not rush his shot, he needs to reconnoitre a hide and make at least one practice shot against an aiming mark he knows the distance of, we will have time to find him, I promise."

"I have your word on this now Callan and you cannot lie to me, it is treason for I am a Princess."

Namtu stared into the flames of his fire and wept for Edvar, the gentle giant who had stood over him, quite literally, for the last ten years and in that time they had not been apart for even a single day. Namtu felt like a part of him had been ripped out. He had made it to the cliff edge and the beginnings of the long curling path up when he had heard the first shot and his heart had leapt as he reasoned that Edvar must have fired it, he had stopped running and stared as he saw Edvar fall to his knees in front of another man who had then slowly and methodically reloaded and shot him again in the chest at point blank range. He had screamed down at the beach but was then suddenly taken by a panic attack as he could not work out who could have possibly shot him. Who was the mysterious figure holding the smoking Gunne. He looked familiar with the weapon and confident in his handling and there was something familiar about his stance, this meant that someone not of Branvere not only knew how but was competent with this new technology. This could ruin everything he thought to himself as he stared down from the cliff path at the lifeless giant with tears of grief, rage and guilt streaming down his face.

Namtu had been leading a patrol on the Mar'thak border a little over ten years before, in the no man's land between border posts, when the two-man cart, the kind that some nations race with horses, carrying what was obviously a Mar'thakian nobleman, appeared over a small rise, just on the Mar'thak side. But it was not being pulled by a team of horses, or even a single horse, it was being pulled by a man. Even at the distance that they were, they could see he was huge, wearing nothing but a loincloth and a large leather harness that the reins and braces of the cart were attached to.

None of these battle-hardened men had ever seen anything so bizarre before and to a man they stopped and stared, not caring that they were no longer hidden by the foliage that they had been keeping themselves covert by. As they watched the nobleman suddenly sent a sharp crack of his whip to the giant's back and they all winced, but not a sound came from him as he struggled up the next rise.

Namtu flushed angrily at the sheer indignity of it, the humiliation that he must feel, of being treated worse than this man probably treated his horses. They watched angrily as the cart continued its journey, the whole time the nobleman cursing the poor man.

That night they had made camp and set sentries, and he called his second in command to him. "Toker, I must go and find the giant, I cannot leave him to that fate." he stated.

"Nam, I have served you for many years, and I have always stuck by you, but you cannot do this, this could be an act of war, a border incursion, we cannot simply march into Mar'thak and kidnap one of their citizens."

"I did not say we, I said I."

"But why? Why risk the King's commission? He will grant you your light archer unit soon, you know he will, you sold it to him on that last audience."

"I have to, I cannot leave that man, to be beaten and treated like that, it is simply not who I am."

"Please Nam, if anyone can do this it is you, but please do not do it, you, we, have too much to lose."

"I have to, I could not live with myself if I did not, I must at least try."

"Then please be careful, do not get caught, dead or alive, and leave no witnesses, especially noble ones that will be listened to."

That night, he had slipped away in the darkness and followed the track left by the cart, it was easy to follow, the narrow wheels and huge footprints marked it apart from the other tracks left, and Namtu was an expert tracker.

It did not take long for him to find the manor house; it was well lit inside as was the stable to the right hand side. The small racing cart was outside the stable, one side of the stable door left open spilling lantern light onto the lawns of the house. First thing I must locate him, then see if he will come with me he thought as he nocked an arrow to his bow.

He moved silently to the closed stable door, staying in the shadows, he peered around, there were horses in the three stalls on the left, and three empty stalls on the right, he was about to move when the door at the other end that led straight from the house banged open, and there stood the young noble, yet again with a nasty looking whip firmly grasped in his hand.

"On your feet scum," he demanded to one of the right-hand stalls "You will fucking speak, you will call me Sire yet."

The massive frame rose from the stall and stared with absolute contempt at the considerably smaller man, he pulled back his arm to strike with the whip, as he did Namtu made his decision and drew and loosed the arrow, striking him clean through his wrist. The whip flew from his hand and he let out an inhuman howl.

When the noise aided down to whimpering a soft voice emanated from the stable door. "Why do you scream? When you seem to so love pain?" Spoke Namtu.

"Who are you…? What do you want?" came the shocked reply.

"I am vengeance and I will be taking that man with me, so he can have a life, the life of a man."

"He is not a man…he is an animal, he cannot even speak, he understands nothing."

Another arrow flew from the darkness and struck the nobleman in his thigh as he tried to bring himself to his full height, blood sprayed out in a small arc and continued to pump as he collapsed to the stable floor.

"You have a big mouth for one so small," spoke Namtu as he walked forward, another arrow already nocked "Let me speak, while you slowly bleed to death, these arrows are barbed, they have already cut numerous veins and arteries inside you, but if you really want some pain I will let my big friend here pull them out, and by the smile on his face I think he understands perfectly what is happening."

Namtu looked across at him, Edvar had stood to his full height and dwarfed the pair of them, he knelt down and looked into the eyes of his tormentor and spoke.

"My name is Edvarius of Mar'thak and you, you are no more." And with those words he ripped the arrow from the nobleman's leg with such power that his femur muscle was ripped apart by the force of it, the large iron barb tearing flesh as it came free, blood oozed from the wound, the man's blood pressure already so low from loss of blood preventing it from spraying.

"Come then my friend, your future awaits." Namtu said to him.

G. E. WEBB
HE BLOOD
PRINCESS
USTIN MACAULEY PUBLISHERS™
NDON • CAMBRIDGE • NEW YORK • SHARJAH

The Blood Huntress, legendary hunter of men. It is said she can smell the blood of her enemies and has never failed to bring those to justice whom she hunts. Few know where she came from, but one man does for he is the one who trained her.

Danyard, Lord Protector of The Kingdom of Light, legendary warrior who once turned an entire battle and forced an army to flee.

The Kingdom of Light, a shining example of wealth and prosperity envied throughout the known world.

And there are nations who look upon this world with envious eyes, and one man who has a plan to take it with a weapon the likes of which no medieval land has ever seen, a weapon that will change the face of warfare forever.

AUSTIN MACAULEY PUBLISHERS
LONDON · CAMBRIDGE · NEW YORK · SHARJAH

"I knew you were coming for me; it is what kept me going." He replied to him. That was the first and last time that he had heard Edvar speak, but, as he soon discovered they did not need to talk, Edvar just seemed to know what he was thinking. Edvar had not left his side since and the pain he was feeling right now was beyond anything that he had ever felt, his breathing becoming ragged as his sobs become overwhelming but then it started to burn into a white hot rage and he screamed into the night.

"I will avenge you Edvarius, I swear that I will avenge your death and not rest until Callan is dead."

Callan! It hit him like a thunderbolt, the mysterious shooter, it was Callan, he had survived the arrow and now was working with her, which would also explain why they still pursued him. The Blood Huntress would not want harm to come to The Kingdom of Light, there was a rumour that she was a minor noble from Kino'le, but more importantly, Balstore's apprentice lives, and was actively hunting him with the known world's most famous hunter. He put out his fire, packed his meagre belongings and ran.

Fourteen

The Investigation

Danyard was troubled, not just by the sighting of Amyeen, but by something more elusive something on the edge of his reasoning, just beyond him. For the first time since the death of the King he felt the need to be away from the city. He had delivered King Cathal and his entourage safely to the castle and they were now comfortable in the guest wing, with a banquet planned for tonight, but Danyard had already decided that he would not be there. He had ordered an atrop of Dragoons to be prepared for at least a week away and they were down in the stables now, packing and preparing their horses. He picked his sword from it's stand and drew the blade It still mesmerized him, the perfect balance, the blade that never needed sharpening, it was truly a masterpiece. He returned it to its scabbard and secured it on his waist and strode to the stables where the eight men stood ready to mount. His own horse, Spike, was saddled and prepared.

The strop leader, DeWire, spoke. "Where to Sire?"

"Back to Kardon, I need to make some enquires on the road" he replied. "Yes Sire."

Amyeen struggled to the saddle of Buster with assistance from Callan. She was relieved to find him unharmed and all her equipment undamaged. They had done what they could for Edvar, Callan had dug a pit as deep as he was able, they had wrapped his body in a horse blanket and rolled him in with his mighty sword. She had left Callan alone for a few moments to gather his thoughts, although she had walked away, she had still seen tears streaming down his face and heard his sobs, she left him to his guilt and grief.

Namtu had two days head start on them now, so he would be in Kino'le, even on foot, if he was as fit as Callan said he was. He would find a quiet inn and lay up until he could find the Princess's public engagements, but even without them she could always be seen walking the battlements.

"We had better go then," She said, "You have their Gunnes?"

"Yes, as agreed, apart from Namtu's special one obviously, but I do have the one he brought with him. I will throw them into the sea from the high cliffs, I have kept all their powder and shot for myself, I may need it," he replied.

They left in a slow canter, each deep in their own thoughts, Amyeen assessing her injuries as she rode, indicated to her by the constant movement of her horse. Whatever muck Morlen had given to Callan and he had forced down her seemed to be doing wonders for her, even she could not believe how quickly she was healing. As they climbed away from the beach the path widened and they could ride side by side and far enough from the edge to prevent the horses becoming skittish. Finally Callan spoke.

"So why do you think Danyard forced you away from the Kingdom? After he saved you from the assassins."

"He must have believed what the bastard wizard told him, that I had sent the assassins, the old fucker was always having visions, a lot of which came to be so he could be very convincing, Danyard had no love for him but he was just too damn valuable to banish."

"In that case why not just let them kill you, save him some trouble."

"He could never have done that, he swore to protect us to our Father, he could not let anyone actually hurt us, even if he believed what Lorgane told him. I know he regretted it the next day for I had Dragoons looking for me, for months they tracked me but they never even came close to finding me. I think Danyard knew who had really sent the assassins, but he could not prove it, if he could then he would have already taken Lorgane's wretched head.

"The assassins were in the palace approaching the bed chambers when he first saw them, they had made their way through the servants' quarters and the kitchens, killing two maids and an apprentice cook on their way, he drew his sword and gave chase, shouting for the Palace Guard as he went. Two of them stopped to face him while one ran on, the story is that he did not even slow his stride as he went through them, leaving both dead in his wake.

"I remember waking from my drunken stupor in my sister's bed just as the third man flung the door open, I went for my sword on the floor as his eyes focused on me in the dark but just as I drew it the man's head just came away from his neck, and there, behind him, was Danyard. An icy glare on his face that was enough to still the blood of any man, never before had I seen him so angry. I think he felt insulted, he was always wary of the assassin, because that was what killed my mother. The single or small group of killers in the night, he could never really guard against it, and that night his worst fears had come to be.

"We both had two rooms that we used, on instructions of Danyard, so if an assassin did get in he would not be sure where we were, in our drunken state I had gone to Victarny's room with her and fallen asleep, while She had then gone to her other room, and only a few people would have known that. Danyard was convinced that I was in league with them, or had directly hired them. The bodies showed they were of the higher echelons of their trade, two had outstanding bounties on them from at least one other nation so they would have been expensive. He put it all together, incorrectly, and told me to be gone by morning, and I was."

"That is quite a story, would he have done it? Would he have killed you?"

"Normally, I would have said no, but this night, never seen him like that before, possessed of a rage I have yet to see again in a sane man. Anyway, enough of this, you have their Gunnes ready to throw from the cliff?"

"I do."

"Good, I do not want any more of those weapons in my Kingdom, it is bad enough that you still carry one."

"And if I did not, My Princess, you would be dead with Edvar standing over your body."

"Yes I would and I thank you for it, but I do not have to like it, now let's move, I want to make Kino'le by sunset."

"Lord Danyard, this man saw the people you seek, the man and the woman stayed at his inn for one night," said DeWire "It would appear the same night that the Silver King's convoy passed by."

The Inn Keeper looked down as Danyard approached, he looked scared.

"Tell me then Inn Keeper; do not be fearful for you have done nothing wrong, I just need to know about these people."

"The young man and woman, took a room the night that Branvere King and his procession passed, I took 'em for a courting couple, obviously well off though, horse each, stable lad said very fine ones too, paid up front but wanted separate beds, she insisted on it, bit odd I thought."

"Anything else you considered odd?"

"Well yes, everyone else came down to watch the King pass, but they did not, stayed in their room, mind you nothing would have got out of that room with her, a right beauty she was, oh I remember now, she left early in the morning, before him, quite a bit before and in a hurry, took all her stuff and left him sleeping. I had to wake him up when someone else wanted the room."

"And do you know where they went?"

"Well it so happens, another traveller told me he saw her galloping down the beach road, he thought she was that hunter woman, I told him he was being daft but she could have been now I think about it, damn good sword with her."

"Very good, you can go now, thank you for your time."

"Thank you Sire, I got plenty to be getting on with."

"DeWire, get the men mounted, fancy a day at the beach?"

They left the inn and followed the road to where it forked off to the beach, as they neared the dunes DeWire spoke: "What exactly are we looking for Sire?"

"I do not know myself, but she came this way and not the main road for a reason and that reason is what we are searching for, and you can start with what appears to be a body over there."

They all looked and saw the body, and as one they dismounted and walked towards it, it was immediately obvious it was the body of quite a large man, with two arrows protruding from it, Danyard approached and pulled one arrow from his neck, it came out clean.

"No barb, used by someone very sure of themselves, some who does not need the cutting edge of a broadhead arrow to slice open arteries but likes the punch of a narrow point, better penetration through the body."

"I agree Sire, but why two arrows, either one would have killed him."

"The neck one first, you can see the blood splatter around it, he still had blood pumping around him when it struck." Danyard cut open the man's jerkin and looked at the chest wound, "No splatter, or very little at least, she loosed the first one and got him in the neck then the second as he lay dying, just to be sure."

"She, Sire?"

"You know who I mean, but why would he be here, in the open, if she was hunting him how did she know he would be here and why for damnation would he think he was safe on a wide open fucking beach?"

"The dunes are about a hundred paces away, as we came in I noticed some leather strands tied to the fence there, thinking about it he, or they, must have hobbled their mounts there and later she just cut through the reins of each horse, probably on approach, make them panic, cover her movements."

"Yes, that makes sense, so we think the archer loosed from the dunes too?"

"Absolutely yes."

"So, you know there are only a few archers in the known world who could make that arrow do that, from one hundred paces."

"Yes Sire, but why? Why the interest from us? If she hunts this man or men what is it to do with us? If someone can afford her then I dare say they deserve what is coming to them, I have never heard of her killing innocents, even those who have challenged her she has always given them a chance to walk away, most are too stupid or prideful to do so but that is their choice."

"I do not know, but something is eating at me on this, something is not right."

"Sire!" Shouted another man further down the beach "There is a mound here, I think it is a burial mound."

"Do the Imperials at Kardon have a tracker?"

"Yes Sire, I believe Neelas is resident."

"Ah my old friend Commander Neelas, send a rider to Kardon, I want two atrops with a wagon to transport the bodies and Neelas, and some kind of apothecary or surgeon, a good one, not some lunatic tooth puller or idiot that is too quick with a bone saw."

"Yes, Sire."

Carmak, the leader of the convoy stood on the roof of one of the wagons and spoke to all his men, he was worried but he could not let them see this.

"Tomorrow we collect our cargo, our forty wagons will pull of the road near the Forest of Dalstock and be loaded, the wagon drivers must be off the wagons at this time and calming the horses, for they may get skittish."

"What is our cargo Lord?" enquired one.

"You have the right to know, our cargo is the creatures of darkness that inhabit the forest, some know them as the Dark Stalkers and each wagon will load five of them, then move away to the holding area for the next one to load. The creatures themselves will be subdued and will not attack you, but do not make eye contact with them and make sure your horses are blinkered."

There was a chorus of angry voices as the fear of what had been asked of them settled over them.

"Quiet, you will be silent…these orders come from the Silver King himself, do any of you wish to explain to the Royal Court why you disobeyed a direct royal instruction? Now we stay here tonight and most of the daylight tomorrow, then, as the sun falls, we move the half league to the forest, do any of you wish to discuss this further?"

No one spoke.

"Good, now go to your wagons and see to your horses and then rest."

"So, Master Apothecary, what killed him? I can see the wounds to his chest and shoulder, but what caused them?" Enquired Danyard.

They had dug up the remains of Edvar and cut away the horse blanket that had become his shroud, then they had laid him out with some dignity and awaited the wagons from Kardon. Then they had set up camp for the night and discussed the bizarre events of the day. But to a man, they agreed that the body belonged to the biggest man they had ever seen and had started to refer to him as the giant. Then the wagons had arrived and they waited for first light for the apothecary to examine him.

"I have not seen a wound of this type before Lord Danyard and I have fought in many battles and tended many wounds. Have you ever seen anything like this before?"

"No, I have not, not with this level of damage, the shoulder has been completely destroyed."

"I agree, now if we turn the body over we can see that he has an exit wound on his back from the chest wound, notice that the back wound is terrible, I can fit my fist inside it, parts of his ribcage are missing as well as it has completely destroyed one lung, and I am completely mystified as to what caused it. Something travelled through his body at a speed at which is completely impossible and caused this damage."

"Well, I need to know exactly what happened here and you have until sunset to tell me that. The Master Tracker Commander Neelas will help you with anything and these men are at your command, do whatever you need to do, scour this beach and dig up whatever you have to, the weather has been mild, hardly any wind so whatever was left behind from this skirmish should still be here, report back to me before sunset."

"Yes Sire, we will do our utmost."

Danyard walked over to the horses and mounted Spike, leaving the men and atrop leaders to their work he put Spike through his paces, galloping him through the low surf and along the cliff paths, he was glad of the distraction and the chance to be alone for a few hours.

Two hours before sunset, he returned to find all the men sat around a fire. They rose as he approached and Neelas spoke.

"We believe this is what happened, there were three of them at first, the giant, another much smaller man and a bigger than average man who we believe was the man with the two arrows in him. They hobbled their horses at the fence post by the dunes, then all three walked here, then the giant and the small man walked down the beach stopping every one hundred paces or so. At some stage the arrow man received his fatal arrows but not until the other two had reached about eight hundred paces down the beach. The archer, loosed one arrow then came in close for the second arrow to be sure he was dead, but came no closer than fifty paces, very sure of his work."

"Or her work, I know some excellent female archers."

"Yes, indeed her work, could have been, light of foot also. After the second arrow he or she, ran back to the horses, cut their reins and then riding the one she arrived on galloped them all down the beach towards the giant and the small man, I believe he or she did this to give herself a bit of cover. At first, the giant and the small man ran towards her but then they stopped and the small man ran the other way, towards the cliffs and the path to Kino'le.

"The giant and her, had some kind of sword fight, there is a huge gash on his back, went clean through his chainmail so no normal sword either, that wound alone would have killed a lesser man. During this fight, a fifth man arrived on the scene, from the same direction, but came on a more direct path over the dunes, because of the softer drier sand there we cannot track him exactly but we tracked where he entered the dunes and where he exited. We believe that he was the wielder of the weapon that killed the giant, he used it at a distance and struck his shoulder and then up close, a dozen paces away or so to hit him in the chest, by which time the giant had fallen to his knees, probably weak from blood loss so more like an execution.

"Near to the dunes we found the remains of a small fire and what remains of a pain relieving and healing potion, the Apothecary says it was probably started in a powder form and mixed here on the beach, he stated the dose was much higher than he would have ever safely used, so again we can assume that the archer, he or she, was injured but not killed in the fight. And as there is no body I fully agree with that conclusion. I have not yet checked the Kino'le cliff path for sign of the small man or the archer and the fifth man who I believe are hunting him. But if he went that way then Kino'le is the only destination. We dug this out of the giant's shoulder and this one from the sand."

He handed Danyard two heavy lead balls, both were distorted and out of shape, he took them in his hand and a shudder went through him.

"These are what killed that huge man? These little metal balls bought down that giant and did that much damage to him?"

"Yes Sire, the apothecary said that to do the damage that they did they would have been travelling at about twelve to fourteen hundred paces every heartbeat, smashed their way through his body and out of the other side. We do not know of such a weapon but it obviously exists. I have seen hunters that can use a catapult or sling to stun an animal, but nothing that can propel a ball that fast, with enough power to penetrate skin and smash bone. It scares me Danyard, that somewhere out there a man is carrying this weapon."

"You said that the man lay down every hundred paces, what distance was his last position to the first man with the two arrows?"

"Eight hundred paces Sire."

"Then that is the range of this weapon, the one the third man has anyway, the fifth man obviously has a more basic and less accurate version hence his need to get closer to the giant, so two of these weapons and two men, at least."

"It would appear so Sire."

"And it is also one-man portable, as only one man escaped and we have not found it."

"I would also agree."

The implications settled on Danyard and a terrible fear struck him.

"DeWire, get your atrop mounted and back to Kino'le as soon as is humanly possible. On my direct orders triple The Princess's personal bodyguard and double the palace guard and try, only try I presume, to cancel all of her public engagements. If there is a man on his way to Kino'le with this weapon then she is in grave danger."

Fifteen
The Cargo

Carmak stood at the edge of the dark brooding forest of Dalstock and shuddered, it was dusk and the wagons were in a line waiting for darkness to fall completely, the men were nervous and the horses skittish. One set had bolted in their traces and overturned their wagon, smashing it to pieces against the trees as they ran, he had wanted the two drivers hung but he knew he needed them to help with the other wagons, he could not afford to lose men as well as wagons. Again he inwardly cursed Balstore, whatever dark spell he had woven over these creatures why couldn't he have done the bloody same for the horses.

He could see the dark shapes moving through the trees, never fully revealing themselves, he had always hoped that they did not really exist but now he knew they did. Then, one of them loped into his line of sight and he gasped, he could just make out its shape in the darkness, the darkening background seeming to hide its outline. As it got closer he could make out it's huge muscled body, even in its crouched over position he could see how big it was, its vile red tongue lolling around the gaping maw that was its mouth, it looked over at him and for one awful moment he thought it would move towards him, but it then suddenly looked away and lopped into the back of the first wagon, then more appeared, and more. The wagon drivers showed their professionalism for once and moved in and out of the line as quickly as they could, just wanting the loading to be over and slamming the rear doors of their wagons shut with a haste he had not previously believed they were capable of.

They moved up a small rise and then started to form the convoy on the road, markers laid out for them earlier. Many things bothered Carmak but nothing more than the actual creatures themselves, he could feel their hunger emanating from the wagons and it grated on his soul. His brother and he had always been loyal officers of the King, but now, for the first time since being a youth he had doubts about his role. He was terrified himself of these creatures and the thought of letting them loose in a city made him sick to his stomach. And then there was the remaining journey to Kino'le itself, another three days of traveling to reach the valley woods where the creatures would be unloaded, without being stopped by a Dragoon patrol. Balstore had informed him that there were no patrols in that area, he had studied the patrol patterns with his network of spies and they would have no problems, but he had never liked or trusted spies.

Namtu's light archers were also supposed to be in the area with a dozen mounted lancers for support but he had not yet seen them. They were being led by Toker, Namtu's second in command, a rare man who was actually of noble birth but chose to take orders from a commoner, such was the reputation of Namtu, but just another sneaky bastard in Carmak's opinion. For all he knew they were already here and shadowing him but Toker would not let his and his men presence be known until he had to, so Carmak could not rely on their help. Why did I agree to this madness he thought to himself as he watched the convoy take shape.

"Yes Garvak, they have gone." spoke Geel, his younger brother.

"Where? Where have they gone?" He enquired.

"Wagons came, but big ones, more like the wooden houses they like to build but on wheels, pulled by four horses each and a lot of them. They got in the wagons and the wagons went away."

"Where were these wagons from? Kino'le?"

"No, but that is where they are heading."

"This is very odd, who would want these beasts, we have been fighting them so long now, who else even knows that they exist, most stone dwellers are too scared to even enter Dalstock."

"Perhaps it is she, perhaps she has a shaman who has put a spell on them, to drive them away, she did kill one remember."

"No, not her way, born warrior she is, would not like the dark magic that would be needed to achieve this thing. There is only one reason that someone who is powerful enough to put them under control would want to do so, and that is to use them, to destroy others; you know how the stone dwellers love power. We must follow and observe, we must know what becomes of them, gather the people my brother, we follow."

"Neelas, I need you to follow the man's trail to Kino'le, find out what you can about the man and woman from the sign they leave, and the man they pursue, he should be easier to track as he was in more of a hurry. Take whatever you need, but at least a half atrop and a wagon if you wish. I will be going back by the direct road, report to me immediately that you arrive."

"Yes my Lord," he replied.

Danyard walked slowly back along the beach, his head swimming. He reached the wagon holding the body of the giant, now once again shrouded for burial in Kardon, he reached up and took the man's sword and hefted it from where it had been placed next to the shroud. Even with both hands, he could not hold it out straight and he let the tip of the blade fall to the sand, as he did he caught the glimpse of an engraving just on the hilt and his blood went cold, for his own sword had the same marking. It was the mark of Balstore, not one from the workshop of Balstore but his own personal mark, only weapons made entirely by him carried the mark. He shuddered in the cool evening air.

Amyeen laid on the single bed of the room in the inn and soared above the city through the eyes of Blood. She knew the streets well, Danyard used to take her out in the city, in disguise, to show her how the common people lived and worked. Blood flew fast but low over the city so it would be hard to get a good look at him, it was exhilarating, still, even after all the times she had done this and it took her breath away. Callan stood by the window and watched her sharp sudden intakes of breath as Blood took a quick dive or tight turn around a building.

She let him have his wings for a while, then sent him to the Palace looking for her sister. She saw the open window and flew him straight through it. She immediately spotted Buldor, the Commander of the Royal Bodyguard, although short by Kino'le standards he was one of the stockiest men she had ever known and his nickname, 'The Bull' was well suited. He was the first to be selected and trained exclusively by Danyard and was fiercely loyal to him. She sent Blood into the rafters where he could not be seen and watched Buldor for a while as he checked the hallway he was walking along for signs of disturbance near the windows. *Good for me you only check for humans* she thought to herself.

He moved to a door and she sent Blood after him, sweeping through the door before Buldor could close it behind himself. He was now in the antichamber of the royal court and would use one of the many side entrances that only the bodyguards had keys for, well-hidden on the inside of the court by long drapes, the doors themselves were very well maintained and regularly oiled to make them silent. Many a visiting dignitary had been startled to suddenly find a Royal Bodyguard, or even the silent brooding hulk of Buldor, behind them. She waited for her moment and again slipped Blood in through the door as Buldor stepped through.

Once again, she flew Blood to the high vaulted ceiling to settle him and then concentrated on what was happening below. Her Sister was holding court with The Silver King, Cathal, next to her. The despicable Balstore was nowhere to be seen, but Lorgane was. He stood on the other side of Victarny to Cathal, with the usual smug grin on his face. What evil deed have you committed now she wondered. She concentrated her senses on her sister's face far below, to try and lip read the small talk between the three of them, but she could not for the distance was too great and she dare not move Blood to a lower place for fear of discovery.

Amyeen was familiar with the scene, it was petition day and any citizen could petition the Princess to grant them favours, as long as it benefitted the Kingdom as a whole, it worked very well as many businesses that petitioned for land or building permission also had to then promise to take on a certain number of apprentices without the cost to the young person's family. Therefore sons or daughters of farmers could become smiths or carpenters and then they in turn could choose who they wanted to train, not who could pay the most. It was a scheme set up by her father and continued by Danyard, who, although loyal to the point of death to her father had always harboured a hatred of the noble classes.

As Victarny addressed the hall, Amyeen realised that she would not find out anything here about her sister's movements for the coming week so she sent Blood out through the main door as it opened and she released him to feed. She had only ever once stayed connected to him while he did this and she swore never again, it had taken three days for the taste of animal blood to leave her but what frightened her the most was that she had wanted to do it again, in her darkest moments she found that she could easily crave, not just the taste of blood but the feeling of feeding on it.

She was still amazed by her connection with the bat, she could see perfectly clear through his eyes although one of her tutors when she was a child had told her that bats are virtually blind and used some kind of sound wave to see. His other senses affected her too but the main one was his hunger, he was nearly always wanting to feed, he had to drink his bodyweight in blood every single day just to keep himself alive, and more if he burned energy by flying the amount she demanded of him. When he was hungry, he become increasingly difficult to control and was constantly distracted by livestock, which he could sense from quite a distance, and if desperate, even cold spilt blood.

"Neema," Callan gently called to her "Are you awake?"

"Yes, I was with Blood, I have just released him. I was checking on my sister," she replied.

"And she is healthy still?"

"Yes, she is, looked well at least, where have you been?"

"Looking for Namtu, I do not believe that he will stay in the city, especially now that he knows that you hunt him, he is a skilled woodsman so he will have a well-hidden camp somewhere in the woods within a league or so. He will find out the Princess's public engagements and stake out a firing position, within eight hundred paces of where he believes that she will be. He will lie up the day before and then crawl into his prepared position during darkness and wait for her. So we have two choices, we try to find his camp and take him there, or we work out which of these places he will try to kill her at." Callan took a rolled-up poster from his jerkin and dropped it onto the table, it announced three public engagements that Victarny was expected at.

"The damn Merchants Guild has these things printed up each week; I had forgotten about them, the local merchants like to attract a crowd so they always proclaim a Royal visitor whether she intends to show up or not. Danyard has been trying to stop the practice for years but the Guild contributes too much to Victarny's good causes so she allows it. She has never taken seriously any threat against her, what are these places and events?"

"Supposedly opening a new theatre on the street of artisans in three days' time, early evening it says, attending an archery tournament tomorrow midday and is guest of honour at a wedding, one of her handmaidens it says, marrying a Dragoon officer."

"Not Sarah is it?"

"No, someone named Neosan, why do you ask?"

"Danyard always had a thing for the Lady Sarah, close to his age so he has known her for years and the most senior of her ladies, buxom wench, which he obviously likes. The only time you will ever see him nervous, big brave Danyard, hero of the Kingdom, put him in front of Sarah and he becomes a gibbering wreck, it's quite funny really, he should just marry the woman, or at least jump in the sack with her. She is as attracted to him as he is to her, she just hides it better, I asked him about it once, he told me to mind my own fucking business. Anyway when is it?"

"Two days' time, marriage at the Guild Hall and then a formal dance at the Dragoon Mess, I imagine that security will be tighter than a duck's arse for that."

"Yes, it will be but she will defiantly attend, she will not attend a military show, she has no interest in them, the street of the artisans is too narrow and overbuilt for Namtu to get a good shot at her so although she may be there Namtu will not be, but she will not shun those close to her, she will be at the wedding. We must reconnoitre the ground as soon as we can, the Dragoon Mess and the Guild Hall and the route, for she will be taken by carriage between them."

"So Neelas, what have you discovered about the man and the woman and man they pursue?" asked Danyard. They were in Danyard's private chambers, the only place that he relaxed and the only place his sword was not on his hip. Neelas stood near to the table that held the sword stand and sipped from the wine goblet that Danyard had passed him when he had first entered.

"The first man, as I said before, light of foot and small stature but immensely fit, his footprints lead me to believe that he ran all the way to Kino'le with only one stop, and that for food not sleep. The remains of a rabbit and small fire, very well hidden, his bushcraft is as good as any that I have seen or trained."

"Is he as good as you?"

"If he was a tracker no, but he is not a tracker, he is a hunter, pure and simple, a hunter of men."

"And the couple? How good were they?"

"No real way of telling, they rode all the way and made no attempt to hide their tracks, but unlike him they do not know that they are being pursued, they entered the city and the trail went cold. Our hunter did not, he went towards the river and entered it, but I could not find his exit tracks, it is my belief that he grabbed onto an overhanging branch of a tree and then went tree to tree for a few hundred paces, impossible to follow. So I lost him Sire. He did not enter the city directly, he lost himself in the woods surrounding."

"I did not expect an outcome any different to this, please stay and enjoy the hospitality of the Palace for a few days."

"I would love to Sire, but my son is expecting my first grandchild in a few days and I would not forgive myself if I missed the birth, so with your permission I will leave as soon as possible."

"A grandchild, but you are only a few years older than myself, how is such a thing possible?"

"You flatter me Sire, but my son is twenty-four now."

"Really, has it been that long since we fought together, without your skill, we would have never known of that border incursion, the Kingdom owes you a debt, may your journey be swift and trouble free my friend."

"Thank you Sire, I hope so too."

Danyard watched as Neelas bowed and left the room, a grandchild! It suddenly hit him then, how many missed opportunities there had been, all of his officers had married one by one, settled down with families. He had bedded a few maids when his needs arose, but never the same one more than twice, afraid of getting too close to anyone, in case they would be taken from him, as he had been taken from his father on his fifth birthday to begin his military training, as all five year old boys were in the land of his birth.

He had seen her today as well. Lady Sarah, they had passed each other in the corridor and his heart had missed a beat and she had blushed. She had spoken first.

"My Lord, I am glad to see that you returned to us safe and well."

"The pleasure is all mine Lady; it was only a small trip to Kardon. The Princess, she is well?"

"Yes Sire, the preparations for the wedding are continuing."

"Wedding?"

"Yes Sire, Neosan and Captain Nyston."

"Ah yes, I had completely forgotten, two days' time, I have had a lot on my mind, if you will excuse me Lady Sarah."

"Of course, My Lord."

She had bowed again and again he tried and failed not to stare at her ample cleavage as she did so, and then they had gone their opposite ways. He always felt so inadequate when he was near her, he could literally have any woman in the Kingdom and he had been fending them off for years now, but Sarah, there was just something there beyond his control. She was not even the prettiest of the Ladies in Waiting and considered a bit too chubby by most young officers, but to Danyard she was perfection.

He moved to the window and threw it open, breathing in the fresh winter air and looking out upon the Kingdom. I have made the Kingdom of Light what it is today, I have kept it safe and watched it prosper under my guidance, he thought, yet what light does it hold for me, none, until, right now. With that thought rattling around his head, he stormed from his quarters and went in search of Sarah.

Namtu lay and watched, perfectly still, under a pile of brushwood. The only movement from him was his regulated breathing and that of his eyes studying the land before him. He had found the poster the first day he was in the city, discarded in a street gutter, he had sat down with it for a while and considered his options, the street of artisans was too crowded and close with buildings, the archery field the opposite, too open and from what he could pick up just by listening he discovered that the Princess rarely attended military events. He concluded that she would attend the wedding of her Lady to the Dragoon Officer.

He had walked around the Guild Hall and studied it from all angles, but it was in the centre of the city and surrounded by other buildings, and he would have to get the Gunne there without being challenged. So he had then moved to the Dragoon Mess and his heart had leapt. It was on the edge of the city just inside the boundary wall, five hundred paces from the nearest tree line which was on slightly rising ground. Outside the mess there was a turning circle for wagons and carriages, she would have to stand to alight her carriage and then her head and torso would protrude over the boundary wall, from his elevated position in the woods he would have the perfect shot. He could not have asked for a better target area.

He walked the line from the wall counting paces as he did so, then counted paces into the woods, finding a spot fifty paces in that gave him a good view down onto the city and the mess, and here he built the hide he was now in. From the outside it looked just like the brushwood pile it was, but he had worked painstakingly to hollow it out from the inside, tying twigs together with thin strips of vine to secure it and pinning others to the ground to stabilise it. By the time he had finished he had enough room to lie there with his equipment next to him within easy reach. He had two days to wait it out now, and each day he would walk past this position to check on it. His main camp was a quarter league into the deep forest where few people ventured, but even there he took no chances, he went into the city each day to eat at a tavern so he did not have to light a fire and each night he returned and slept under the stars.

Sixteen
The Southern Patrol

Partis eased his aching frame from his horse and dismounted, signalling to the patrol that they could do the same. It had been a long border patrol and the horses had been unusually skittish through the land near to Dalstock Forest. He had intended to harbour up near to it but the horses just would not settle so he had been forced to continue for another league by which time night had fallen and no commander likes to camp in ground they had not seen in the light of day.

He was uncomfortable, something in the air was not quite right, but he could not put his finger on it, the horses were still nervous and that made the men nervous, each Dragoon having complete faith in the instincts of his horse. The patrol was a standard fighting formation of six atrops, forty-eight men and horses in total, in dragoon light armour, no heavy plate or lances, just shin and shoulder greaves, chainmail over jerkin with swords and the infamous dragoon war bow. They were patrolling the Kingdom edges and unclaimed territories to show a presence and dominate the land but were not expecting to have to fight, although each man was more than capable.

He looked around as he unpacked his kit, watching as the five other atrop commanders made their way to him, as they approached, he spoke.

"Is it just me or is there something evil in the air gentlemen?"

"It is not just you, Jeldin saw some odd tracks on his forward scouting, wagons he said, a lot of them."

"Did he say, why he thought them odd? These roads are used by many, it is no crime to travel in a convoy."

"No he did not, he is now sat quietly pondering. You know what he is like, goes all quiet and then suddenly announces to the world the solution to the problem only he knew existed."

"If Jeldin is worried then so am I, he has never been wrong before and he is the best tracker that I have ever known and I fought alongside Neelas once."

"I agree, what are your orders for the night?"

"Standard night routine, horses fed and watered and single sentries but with bows in hand and an arrow nocked. No fires. An hour before dawn, atrop three go with Jeldin and examine those tracks, I want him there with eyes on before the sun rises, I know how he likes to look at things in changing daylight. As soon as he is done catch us up on the Kino'le road and report, I want to know what has spooked our horses and more importantly what has spooked Jeldin!"

Danyard lay on his back and stared at the ceiling, he smiled, he could not stop smiling, he was naked and for the first time in his life he did not care that his sword was more than an arm's length from him, for it was under his heap of clothes across the room. But in his arms, lay the also naked Lady Sarah. She rested her head on his scarred and muscled chest and breathed deeply, the regular rhythm of sleep obvious. He stared at her beautiful face and was briefly overwhelmed as a moment of monumental happiness engulfed him.

He had gone in search of her asking various servants if they had seen her, It had seemed for a short while that fate was determined to keep them apart forever, as he went to her last sighting she had just left, he had started to run, barely in control of himself when she suddenly stepped form her quarters in front of him.

"Sire…you search for me…how can I be…" she never finished the sentence because he took her head in his hands and kissed her with a passion that he had not known he possessed, they had then forced their way back through her door and fell onto the bed. The rest had been a blur to him and he did not even remember removing his or her clothes. And now, he lay with her and was too sacred to move for fear of waking her and ruining the moment, a moment that he had not dreamed possible, a tear ran down his cheek and into her hair and again he smiled, the smile, it seemed to him, of a condemned man given a reprieve.

"So these wagons, at least thirty, maybe more, went to the edge of Dalstock, loaded something, or somethings and then moved towards the city?" asked Partis.

"Yes Captain." replied Jeldin.

"Anything else?"

"Living beings were loaded, not a cargo as such, whatever went into the wagons went in voluntarily, no force was used, no sign of a struggle. And the wagons themselves, huge. Half as big again as any of our own supply wagons, and four horses per wagon, not two."

"Care to hazard a guess at what?"

"I do not guess Commander, if it was not for the fact that we all know they do not exist then I know exactly what went inside those wagons, from the footprints."

"There is only one place that this road goes and if they are as big as you say then they will have to stay on the road, how afar ahead would you say they are?"

"Half a day at a gallop, but that puts us with them at night and we do not want to be approaching them at night, with no idea of numbers, weapons or outriders. Of which there are at least six and all expert horsemen."

"You are correct obviously, get the men mounted right away, we move as close as we can and shadow them through the night, then make our plan, but they are between us and home so one way or another we will encounter them. Commanders, make sure your men are aware of that, by tomorrow there will be blood."

"One other thing, another group already track them, about the same number as us but lightly armed and on foot, barefoot."

"Then we must assume who they are, if we assume what is in the wagons?"
"Yes, those who slaughtered the settlers all those years ago."

Partis turned away and mounted his horse, deeply troubled. For the first time in his life, he was truly scared, what a day for revelations, creatures that did not exist threaten his home and he may also have to fight the savages of Dalstock. *I know I may not make your wedding day my cousin, but I can damn well make sure that you have one* he thought as the six atrops of dragoons mounted their horses and thundered after the convoy.

"What will we do now my Lord?" asked Sarah.

"Stop calling me that for a start," replied Danyard as she stood naked from the bed and started to pick up her clothes.

"I mean, what does this mean, all of what happened today?"

"It means that you will be a real Lady, no longer in waiting, with a title, if you want that."

"Leave the service of the Princess you mean?"

"No, not that, you can still live here, within the Palace, but with me instead of the servants' wing, again if that is what you want."

"Yes Sire… I mean… Sir… Danyard. That is what I want, and always have."

"I love you Sarah, I always have, just too damn stubborn to admit it, but now I can, I am free and it feels fantastic."

"I love you also Danyard and also, I always have, but what do we do, how do we go about telling people?"

"We do not need to tell anyone, do you really believe that there are any secrets within these walls, with the amount of gossiping servants walking the halls, I would be surprised if Victarny does not already know. Besides, isn't there a public engagement soon, the marriage of the Lady Neosan to Captain Nyston. We will attend, hand in hand, give the masses something to gossip about and the Guild Masters a bit of cheer. Does this meet with your approval my Lady?"

"Yes, it does my Lord, yes it does." She replied, dropping the garments that she had just collected from the floor as she strolled back to the bed where he lay.

Namtu walked the tree line of the woods, where he would be making his shot; the city wall with the Dragoon Mess was six hundred paces away. He knew this for as he walked, he counted, such attention to detail was the mark of such a man, as little as possible left to chance. People were everywhere but he attracted no attention, they were too busy picnicking with their children and enjoying the warmth within the dome of light. He had heard of tale of it but never seen it before and it was truly the wonder of the known world. It spread into the woods where his hide was but did not extend as far as his lay-up position. At night, he was cold and then he walked through the woods into the light and the warmth enveloped him. Despite the amount of times he had walked through it still made him smile each time.

He smiled as he walked, an unusual sense of contentment settled on him, he had walked past his hide from different directions a number of times and it still was not obvious, just another pile of brushwood that the forest rangers had left and there were plenty of them. *Edvar would have loved it here*, he thought to himself and then suddenly his mood darkened as he thought of the gentle giant.

He looked around again with different eyes, his contentment gone and his rage building, you have no idea what is coming to you, you fools, my vengeance for my companion is coming your way, and it will destroy you all. Any regrets he had for the people and families before him now gone. He walked again towards the wall, tonight he would make his marking shot, he would shoot at the wall and then discreetly mark it, he had some rabbit blood in a small bottle that he had kept from the one he had hunted on his run from the beach, it would just look like a dark smear against the light sandstone that made up the wall but he would be able to see it from his hide and therefore know where his fall of shot would be, just a slight rise in his sight picture would put his aim on the Princess as she stood to alight her carriage. It was all perfect and now just a waiting game.

Commander Partis sat with his atrop commanders and listened to their counsel, it was dark and they had no fires lit as they harboured up in a wood. He spoke.

"What say you Jeldin, what do we face?"

"Forty-three wagons, I found the remains of another one, smashed to pieces, looks like its team bolted, each wagon has two drivers, not soldiers but still armed with crossbows, and outriders, at least six but maybe as many as ten. They are professional soldiers, cavalry sabres, short bows carried on each horse. So over ninety men, and even if the wagon drivers are not soldiers, which they are not because to control the size and weight of those wagons you would need men who have spent their whole lives doing such, it does not take much to get lucky with a crossbow, one can load and loose while the other drives. But at the moment they are harboured up as we are, standard defensive formation, all men dismounted and a quarter on constant patrol, crossbows strung and loaded, no fires, they are in enemy territory and they are fully aware of it. They are ready for trouble."

"I do not want to attack in darkness, for obvious reasons which means attacking when the convoy is moving, if I was that Commander I would move out whilst it is still dark, for the protection the creatures offer him so that is the assumption I am making, so first light, we attack the rear of the convoy. Where they are now could a man get past?"

"No, they have one of the creatures out and blocking the road, where they are the road narrows with high cliffs either side and they occupy the flat open ground before it, one man could get past the camp, if he were careful, but not passed that beast. I thought the damn thing smelt me and I was a hundred paces from it."

"Then we have no choice, attack from the rear, only be able to get the rear few wagons before they raise the alarm and then it is a proper fight. We need to try to panic the horses, get them to destroy the wagons for us, once it goes loud I want it really loud, fire and chaos. Now I say this in front of you all, once it starts I want you Tiplan and Jeldin, to take the remaining half atrop and get through the fight, you must raise the alarm in Kino'le."

"I understand but why us, why our atrop?"

"Because Jeldin is wasted in a fight like this, only he will be able to outwit the riders who will pursue him, He must get to the city, but you must give him that chance. You understand what I ask of you?"

"Yes, I understand."

"As I knew you would, the rest of you, we hold the future of the Kingdom of Light in our hands, we attack for one reason, we must slaughter every living thing in or around those wagons, and if we do not then we must at least slow them long enough for Jeldin to get through, that is all gentlemen, prepare your men, we move before sunrise."

The men rushed ashore in the darkness from the dozen row boats and spread out along the beach, they were dressed head to foot in dark clothing with bows to hand and arrows nocked. A low-pitched whistle sounded and they advanced as far as the dunes and took up defensive positions. They turned and watched as the ship that had brought them all this way beached itself on the sand behind, and from this craft poured tradesmen of all kinds who immediately set to work dismantling it.

The captain of the ship looked on with a mix of sadness and awe, sadness because the ship that had brought them across the treacherous seas was about to be destroyed, and no mariner likes to see that, but awe at the engineering marvel that it was, for it was about to be made into a floating jetty for all the other ships that were due to dock at. He, like most people of the Kingdom of Branvere, loathed and feared Balstore, but it could not be denied the man was a fucking genius. He had stood dumbfounded the first time he had seen it, the ship taken apart piece by piece and made into a dock that could support an entire laden supply wagon, not to mention a fully armoured horse and rider. Once assembled the arrival and unloading of the armies would begin in earnest.

Each company of one hundred soldiers or forty horsemen would disembark and then move to a staging area, the first platoon setting it up and providing a secure perimeter, then most would move off with their own supply wagon, it was a good system but he would be surprised if it remained as secret as it was supposed to do. He had escorted another ship most of the way which had carried the dower faced Captain Toker and his group of silent killers, they had been dropped in a cove too small for the main fleet some five leagues from where he now stood. He did not like to be in their company and was glad he was only the outer escort; he would not have wanted them on his ship.

He was not supposed to know the plan for this but sailors talked, and sailors listened in docks, and what he knew sent a chill through him. One thousand cavalry leading ten thousand infantry, but ahead of all of them two hundred Dark Stalkers to destroy the defences of the city. But even before them Toker and his silent sullen killers would lead the way and stop any word getting through, destroying villages and settlements that could raise the alarm. And then, they were tasked with killing Lord Danyard, one entire platoon of fifty men to kill one man. It would appear the Kingdom of Branvere would not be making the same mistakes as the Kingdom of Mar'thak.

The second invasion of the Kingdom of Light had begun.

Jeldin hid in the thick foliage, his heart hammered in his chest and he panted like a dog, he could see them moving around the low hanging trees that gave him refuge, it was still daylight and for once, he prayed it stayed that way. His sword was to hand and he slowly sheathed it, making as little noise as possible. The attack had started well and he had been sick to his stomach to not be part of it, but an iron code of discipline was the mark of men such as he and he had been ordered to hang back until he saw his chance to get through came, so he and Tiplan had held back with the Vanmere Brothers. They had watched as the dragoons had hammered into the rear of the convoy at full speed, causing panic and upturning the last four wagons before the defenders had a chance to get organised.

For a while, it went exactly as planned but bit by bit the outnumbered dragoons were slowly beaten back. Then, an ear-splitting scream had wrought the air as one of the creatures rose from the wreckage of its wagon. The dragoon nearest ran at it with his sabre held high, the creature swung one of its mighty arms at him and cleaved his sword arm from his body, as he collapsed to the forest floor the creature pulled him up by his head and ripped that clean from his body too. The dragoon's colleagues fell on the creature before it could do anymore damage to anyone and hacked it to pieces, but more and more rose as whatever stupor had enticed them into the wagons in the first place wore off and the dragoons battled for their lives. Crossbow bolts flew through the air, swords clashed and horses whinnied and died as did men.

"The time is nigh Jeldin, let us go, NOW!" cried Tiplan.

"What in hells name was that?" a battle horn had sounded and as they stared a company of horsemen had ridden into view, his spirits soared briefly until he saw the horsemen smash into the dragoons and he realised with horror that these men were enemy reinforcements, and they had come not from where the wagons had come, but from the sea, this was a full scale invasion.

"Now, we must go now!" screamed Jeldin as he spurred his horse forward, Tiplan and the Vanmeres in his wake, struggling to catch him. They skilfully skirted the main battle and rounded a bend in the road, as he caught up with Jeldin he turned to speak to him but then Jeldin suddenly pulled up, Tiplan looked forward as the one of the four lancers spread across the road took him straight through the chest, his chainmail shredding as it was no match for the sharp iron point that he had charged into. He fell from his horse with the lance skewering him as the lancer let it go and drew his sabre. The Vanmere brothers both suffered similar fates as Jeldin leapt from his horse and into the dark undergrowth, hitting the ground in a roll and skidding down a small incline.

He knew, he had some time, the forest was too overgrown for them to follow on horseback and they were in full plate armour which also ruled out immediate pursuit on foot, but he knew others would follow, and not far behind. The horsemen that had appeared had been dressed very similarly to themselves, a kind of light armour, and they had looked like hardened warriors. And now he was trapped by those very men, somehow they had got ahead of him, they must have sent a small force including the lancers to act as a cut off, and he in his haste to clear the area had leapt from his horse and run right into them, and more men were joining them with every passing minute.

He controlled his breathing and tried to think, he needed distance from here when darkness fell, for even he could not outsmart a Dark Stalker that tracked by scent, he may be able to lay a trap for one or two but no more than that. He looked through the undergrowth at the men who hunted him, they were very good. As he had observed earlier, they were in light armour, no chainmail, but leather reinforced jerkins and the classic 'Branvere Brown' leather trouser. One thing Branvere was known for was its ability to produce cheaply priced but good quality leather and the Branvere Brown was known throughout the world and trusted by warriors everywhere. They were armed with short hunting bows, perfect for a forest environment and arrows nocked, it would take but a second to draw and loose at him if they so much as got a suspicion of him. To his relief, they wore helms that would help with his plan.

He held his breath as one man came close to his hiding place, Jeldin slowly and silently drew his knife and waited, the man went down on his hands and knees to get level with the low foliage and discarding his bow, drew his own knife as he stuck his head through, his eyes widened in shock as he saw Jeldin and tried to shout but Jeldin was too quick, his knife went in under his jaw straight up into the man's brain, he wiggled it with all his strength to mash the front of his brain up and withdrew it, hardly a drop of blood came from the body as Jeldin gently dragged the man into the bush with him.

Several minutes later Jeldin emerged, wearing the clothes and carrying the weapons of the enemy, his helm was low on his head and he had an arrow nocked, he copied the movements of the men that were just ahead of him. He had to get past them so he quickened his stride slightly and started to move through them, still trying to keep his distance from each man. One man stopped and stared at him, he looked over at him and gave the man a nod, the man nodded back but still stared at him, Jeldin tried to not look back at him, he was ahead of most of them now, a hundred paces further or so and he could make his break, but he could feel the man's eyes on him, then he heard the man walking towards him quickly and without stealth through the undergrowth, he made his decision and pulled fully back on the string and turned and loosed the arrow at the man. He briefly saw the arrow strike the man's chest as he turned and for the second time that day, he ran for his life.

Amyeen and Callan walked through Kino'le City and Callan was struck by its beauty, fountains and statues adorned the public squares and it was the only city that Callan had ever visited that did not seem to have a poor quarter. Fearsome looking Imperial Guardsmen looked on and patrolled everywhere, and although he knew of their reputation they did not install a fear in him as most other city guards did. Each one of them seemed to exude an air of quiet confidence but with a generally friendly manner that was completely alien to him.

"I find it difficult to see how they maintain order when they appear so relaxed and friendly." he said.

"You have to remember that each and every one of them is an ex dragoon, with at least twenty years' service, which means they have survived battles and seen the consequence of war, it gives them a confidence but takes away their arrogance. Each one of them has probably lost a friend in conflict and nearly been killed themselves. Most city guards I have met have never seen real combat and think their power makes them immortal."

"That is the Branvere guard all over, nasty horrible men recruited for that exact reason, commonly referred to as The Bastard Watch, but that is how Cathal holds on to power, through fear."

"When I was there that is what I saw, people walking the streets frightened and afraid."

"It is a nation of fear, but when you are raised in that way you know no other way and think it normal, only when you travel do you realise that other people live in relative happiness. Anyway enough of this, your new look suits you, the blonde wig certainly, just how many cities do you have a safe house in?"

"None of your business, but most of the major ones, I keep disguises and weapons in each one, I never got round to the port city of Kardon. Anyway we must reconnoitre the Guild Hall and Dragoon Mess, somewhere in between he will make his shot, it is this way."

"How do you know the streets so well, when you grew up in the Palace?"

"Danyard used to take me on the streets at night, in disguise, said it was important that I knew how the common people lived, and that I knew my city. We even got into a fight once and were chased by the Imperial Guard, it was a close-run thing."

"A bit of a risk though, if you were recognised by the wrong people."

"Not really, Danyard was there, and there is no man alive that can take him, with or without weapons, he really is that good."

"Is he good enough, for what is coming?"

"He will have to be, and if he isn't, he will give them a fight that they will not forget, but if we can kill Namtu first it may yet be averted, they will certainly have a more difficult time of it without the Dark Stalkers to take the city."

"Maybe, but Cathal, or more precisely Balstore, will have a plan for Danyard, he has plans for everything, he will have men, a lot of men specifically targeting Danyard, and cavalry, remember that they have mounted horse as well, that is something that Mar'thak never had and it cost them dear."

"I am concerned about them, cavalry are one thing but cavalry and the creatures, as good as the Dragoons are they can only fight one at a time."

"Do you think the Kingdom will fall?"

"I do not know, for I do not know what we face?"

"What is this we? You could just ride from here and leave it to the gods?"

"And you forget, who the first casualty of this damn war will be, I cannot abandon my sister, or any of them. Just look around you Callan, look how happy they all are, could you walk away and leave this place to the rule of Cathal."

"You are right, if we survive this then I could make a good life here. Perhaps with a healer of animals that we know…"

"You are a bad woman, but yes, maybe. Do you think that she is all right?"

"Yes, I do, once she is back with her animals and the land does its magic she will be fine. Besides I would know if she was not, somehow she would have let me know. Now let us get some supper at that inn up ahead, then go hunting the hunter."

"My Lord Danyard, a pleasant surprise." Said the Princess Victarny, they were in her private quarters, Danyard being one of a handful of people with access to them.

"My Lady, how are things with the court today?" he replied.

"They are well, King Cathal is expected to leave us soon but as yet has not given me a day or time. I have not seen you on the training ground for some days now, the Army are missing your presence my Lord Protector. I also seem to have mislaid one of my Ladies, the Lady Sarah, have you seen anything of her?"

"Yes I errrr…have seen quite a lot of the Lady Sarah, as I am sure you are aware."

"Yes, I am and about time too, now come here and give me a hug you morose old sod, and please try to live your life a bit now. I do not expect Sarah back to her duties for a few days yet."

He gave the Princess a small embrace.

"I should really visit the training ground; I am sure that the army are missing me."

"Yes Danyard, go and play with your toys, I do not want you going soft on me and I have some special gossip to catch up on with one of my Ladies."

"Yes Princess."

Balstore bowed and spoke, "My King, the signal was given last night, a small row boat, towed out by a galley, and set ablaze with oil, a few miles from the cliff edge, it is time for us to leave."

"And how do you know it was our signal, not some unfortunate fisherman." replied the King.

"For I gave a green powder to mix with the oil, it gave the boat a green flame, it means that our ships have landed without opposition."

"Very well, send the trade commissioner to the court, let him give the notice, a quarter day should be sufficient. I assume that we are ready to leave."

"We are, the wagons have been packed for days now, and the stable boys put on notice to have the horses ready."

"What about the escort? Danyard will insist on it."

"I let it be known that the return journey would not require an escort, he argued, in the end we settled on twenty-four men, and they are Imperials, not Dragoons, we will dispose of them quite easily."

"And the place, in the wood, where we will wait out the battle, it is ready, your magic powder safely planted?"

"It is in place, secure in oiled sacks, no moisture can get into it, a few moments to prep it will be all it takes."

"And this northern patrol, you think they will find us?"

"I have planned for it, if they do they will not survive. Then we wait for word and ride back in, the conquering heroes, or if goes against us we ride hard for our harbour and sail home."

"Sail home to what? The noble families and the Council of Elders will have my head if this does not work, not to mention reprisals. Danyard near damn as ruined Mar'thak after that last fiasco."

"That was no fiasco, not for us, it taught us valuable lessons, lessons that another Kingdom paid the price for, and this time the Lord Danyard will not survive, Lord Toker has very specific orders on this matter."

Seventeen
The Tracker

Lord Toker was angry, angrier than he could ever remember being. After the landing of his separate force had gone like clockwork he had made his way forward in time to thwart the attack by the dragoon patrol, and now he hunted one of them, just one, but the man was a wily fox and so far had eluded him, and Toker was a man unused to failure. The bodies of two of his men lay before him, men he knew and had watched rise under his command, the first had a small knife wound under his jawline, hardly any blood but dead all the same. The second had one of their own arrows protruding from his chest.

"When he took our man's clothes, did he leave his own behind?" He enquired.

"Some Sire, we have his Jerkin," replied one of his men.

"Good, get a pair of them from the convoy, give them the Jerkin and release them, evade these you sneaky fucker."

"They do not function well in daylight My Lord."

"Yes I am aware of that, but they can still track him until it is dark enough for them to make their attack and the forest canopy will create enough dark shadow for them to follow, and follow is all we need at the moment, so we at least know we are trailing him in the right direction."

"What patrols are out at the moment?" enquired Danyard.

"The coastal patrol are not due back for a few weeks, the northern patrol and the southern patrol in a few days, I expected the southern patrol already to be honest although they are not overdue," replied Lord Gemmell, the Lord of Dragoons.

"Why the southern early?"

"Led by Partis, cousin of Nyston, getting married in a days' time. Less than really, it is near midnight now, so only one whole day of preparation for him after returning from a forty-day patrol, I would have been back before now."

"So would I, there is something still not right here, something I am not seeing."

"Same thing as before, with the Huntress?"

"Yes, she has something to do with it, but it is bigger than her, she hunts someone, her trail went cold, to be expected, but so did his. Other than that, they both came here. And she travels with another man who possesses a projectile weapon the likes I have never seen before or heard of. Normally if there is a bounty out there that she is chasing we hear about it, the Guild of Swords advertise them all openly."

"Maybe he just passed through here, that is why we have not heard any more of him."

"Maybe, I have been a bit distracted the last couple of days but that ends today, I have agreed only a half escort for the return of King Cathal to Kardon, but I want them fully armed, not ceremonial, battle armoured. Discuss it with Lord Jain. And if Partis has not returned by the morning of the wedding, send a small patrol down the southern road to meet them."

"Yes Danyard, I heard of your distraction and if I may say so, about bloody time."

"You may not say so, now fuck off and carry out your orders."

The next morning, Amyeen and Callan stared at the Dragoon Mess and once again Callan was stunned, it was a spectacular building on the edge of the city. It rose six stories high and elaborate windows adorned every level, but despite its beauty Callan could see the soldiers' eye in its design, easy to defend and hard to take. They had already been to the Guild Hall and followed the road joining them, looking out the whole time for anything unusual.

"Glass windows may look pretty but they can be moved up on a simple mechanism and steel shutters move into their place from the side, with arrow slits, the basements are full of arrows and I mean full, thousands and thousands of them. Every unmarried Dragoon has a room here and there is a dorm for others, who may choose to stay after a heavy night on the ale." She informed Callan.

"How many men can it hold?" he enquired.

"Not men, dragoons Callan, dragoons. Learn the difference, if you wish to stay in this city. The banqueting hall holds five hundred, no top table, everyone sits together, even Danyard when he is here. Although, he is technically an Imperial Guard now, but he has an open invitation to both messes, obviously."

"Both messes?"

"Yes, the Imperial Mess is on the North side, exact copy of this one. Each city in the Kingdom also has a Chapter House, smaller versions, enough for a standard patrol, with stables obviously. That is the only real difference other than size, no stables here, would take up too much valuable city space, five hundred horses. The dragoon horses are stabled at the training grounds. I have never been inside this or any of the chapter houses."

"Why not, surely as the ruler, or one of them, you can go anywhere."

"Only by invitation, it's not a sex thing, for dragoon wives go in all the time, it's a dragoon thing, have to be invited inside by a dragoon. According to that poster you got hold of the groom is a dragoon, so therefore each of the guests will be personally invited in. My sister will be just after the newlyweds, in the second carriage I would imagine, probably with Danyard or the current Lord of Dragoons."

"Danyard really seems to look after his soldiers, it makes a lot more sense to me, give them a sense of belonging, but it must cost a fortune."

"The Dragoons and Imperial Guard are the only soldiers directly employed by the Crown, the main army is made up of men at arms and officers who serve the noble houses, formed into regiments. If a man wants to join the dragoons, he applies directly to Danyard and if successful the crown compensates the noble for him, that way the nobles cannot complain that Danyard takes all their best men. Which he does do if I am honest. He also taxes the guilds heavily for the privilege of trading, they complain but in the last twenty years attacks on supply convoys have virtually stopped so they have come to realise that it is a worthwhile investment."

"Anyway, back to work, which way will she approach from?"

"Down the road we have just walked, her carriage will turn in this courtyard and stop close to the doors, then she will stand, wave and step down. That is her moment of vulnerability, and his best chance at her, but…we cannot be sure, he may know something we do not, he may be somewhere we have not thought of. If he is going to get her here then how long ahead will he lay up?"

"Half a day at least, he will want to be in position in the early hours, lay-up and prepare. He will have a main hide and at least two reserves. He will probably be in that tree line but it has a massive frontage and he could be as far back as two hundred paces, even up in a tree, we will have a job finding him."

"We start tomorrow, first light, hopefully catch him on the move, but now I need somewhere I will not be disturbed for the rest of the day, I need to send Blood out, get eyes on the rooftops for signs of a lay-up and the guild hall and the road between and the lines of sight, I will need all of my concentration so I am returning to the safe house, you have a key but when you come in do not disturb me, If I suddenly release Blood when he is flying fast it could hurt him, takes a few heartbeats for him to get control again."

"I understand, I will continue around the city, get my bearings and hopefully not get lost."

Commander Gromm the elder, of the Imperial Guard, looked along the road to where the Branvere Royal Guard forward scouts had just disappeared around the bend. He was hoping to meet the northern dragoon patrol on its way in, led by his younger brother, known as Gromm the Grim. Although, there was only two years between them his brother, still single at fifty-one years of age, had chosen to remain a dragoon. The life suited his brother, he was prone to fits of rage when cooped up too long and not many women could put up with him, he was a natural outdoorsman and got restless in the same place, hence his name and reputation, Grim.

He had been powerless to stop the Branvere scouts riding off and he was uncomfortable, it went against his orders but he could do nothing about it, forward scouts should be made up of both sides and no Branvere soldier was supposed to be left alone outside of the city gates. Although, he had suspicions that some had slipped out over the last few days. He had twenty-three men with him, making a total of twenty-four, all in half armour, giving a mix of protection and mobility. The Royal Guard were similarly attired as no man could ride a horse in full plate armour for more than a day, the exception to this were the two knights in command of the Guard, both riding the classic Branvere Destrier, huge muscled beasts that only the rider could approach so fierce were they. They stood about three or four hands bigger than any other horse he had even seen and were trained to stamp, kick and bite in battle, so the stories went, he had no trouble believing it. Both men and their horses were in full plate, and both men and their horses looked like they would kill you as soon as look at you.

As the royal carriage reached the bend one of the destrier knights slowed to lean into the carriage, from his position way back, he could not make out what was being said so he signalled to his atrop to follow and trotted his horse forward. As he reached the knight, he saw a sudden movement from him and went for his sword, but it was too late, as the man's mace swung around and hit him with full force across his chest, knocking him clean from his horse. He felt his breast plate buckle and heard most of his ribs break under the force of it, he was flung back from his horse and landed hard on his already broken ribs and would have screamed if he could have drawn breath, he rolled away to try and stand, but as he did he looked up and the last thing he saw was the massive iron shod hoof of the destrier coming down on his head.

Jeldin knew he was in trouble, all his life he had tracked and hunted, even as a small boy stealth had been his friend.

Always the smallest of his friends, he could not fight the bigger boys who would always single him out, but he could always outrun them, and so he did, running and hiding in the woods. Each time he did, he became more familiar with the environment, how trees grew, what bushes would hide him and what would not. Then he had learnt how to attack without being seen, those foolhardy enough to chase him into deep foliage would emerge missing a tooth or gaining a black eye. Soon enough nobody who knew of him would even raise their voice to him for fear he would be lying in wait for them one night.

His antics had caught the attention of the Imperial Guard many times and mostly the men who knew him laughed at the stories, appreciating the slight boy who scared the big oafs. But then one day it happened, one of the big oafs lost an eye to one of Jeldin's traps and the father, a wealthy merchant, had demanded retribution.

The Lord of Imperial Guard had appealed directly to Danyard on the young Jeldin's behalf for to see the boy punished for what most considered self-defence was something that the warrior instinct of the Imperials simply could not countenance. He and Danyard devised a solution. The Crown would pay compensation to the family and Jeldin would be apprenticed to Neelas the Tracker. For the first six months Jeldin had wished he was rotting in a dungeon, Neelas pushed the boy hard, forced marches in the dead of winter, living off the land for weeks at a time, but the close nature of the training created a bond in them that soon became unbreakable.

By Jeldin's sixteenth birthday, he and Neelas petitioned the Crown for funds for a tracker school, to select and train those like Jeldin who showed an early talent and Danyard signed off on it, both men being given the rank of Commander. Between them they became legends among men, soldiers sent on training missions would suddenly find an extra man among them, sitting at their fire and sharing their food, then the commander would be given a note stating, 'if this was real, you would all be dead' by the time he had read the note the man handing it to him had vanished back into the woodland.

After ten years, Neelas had retired to the Imperial Guard at Kardon and Jeldin had continued as Commander of Trackers until the call of the wild had grown too strong for him, and so he had left the school in the hands of the most capable instructors and returned to patrolling. Although of commander rank, he joined patrols as a dragoon and did not give orders, but all commanders listened to his advice and were always glad to have him. For the first time since leaving the school he regretted his decision, for now he was pinned to a tree by a spear through his left shoulder.

He had heard them from about half a league away the first time and it had sent shivers through him, the howl that had rent the cold night air. He had used every trick he knew to shake them off, running along streams, climbing trees and going branch to branch, but every time he stopped to listen, he could hear them getting closer. He did not know how many there were but he calculated at least a pair. He had long ago abandoned his tactical withdrawal and was trying to lose them, this was now a straight out run for his life, but he had known they were getting closer.

He had stumbled into a clearing and decided to make his stand, he still had his Dragoon Sabre but had lost the enemy bow a long time ago, it was just too unwieldy in the dense forest. There was a mighty oak on the other side of the clearing, he made his way to it and drew his sword with his back to the tree, at least he would see them coming now he thought. It was then that the spear had come out of the darkness and pinned him to the tree, just as the first one emerged from the undergrowth and stood its full and terrifying height.

Seconds later the other one appeared thirty paces to its right. Dizzy through blood loss, exhausted and in agonising pain, Jeldin looked at them and for the first time in his adult life he wept, he could not believe that it would end like this, ripped apart by a pair of creatures that a day ago he knew did not exist. He stared at them, they were hesitant, something was not right, they were sniffing the air and approaching very cautiously, the occasional growl went between them as if they were talking to each other. He tried to move his sword arm but a wave of nausea swept over him and it fell from his grasp. This seemed to signal something to them and they both suddenly launched themselves across the clearing, he looked on through tear stained eyes as they closed the gap and then, without warning, a dozen spears, identical to the one pinning him to the mighty oak flew from the darkness and impaled the creatures, at the same instant men rushed from the darkness and fell upon them. He watched in a combination of disbelief and relief. One of the men then walked towards him and grabbed hold of the spear haft pinning him to the tree and pulled it clean out of him. It was at that point that he passed out.

When he came around, he was laid out on the grass, strange looking men stared down at him, he sat up and to his surprise no pain wracked his every move as he had expected it would. He was bare chested and the spear wound was covered in some foul-smelling goo. Light was starting to show, so he knew it was near dawn. He focused his attention on the men surrounding him, they were all dressed the same, one-piece green tunics of rough cloth that came to their knees, long hair tied back and barefoot, and each with the nastiest looking spear he had ever seen. He stood and one of them spoke.

"I am Garvak, of the Tree People of Dalstock, it was I that speared you to that tree."

"I am Jeldin, of the Kingdom of Light and despite what you did to me I thank you for saving me, from them." He replied.

"We had to draw them out, get a clear aim at them, you were the bait, we give no apologies and expect no thanks. We hunt and kill these creatures; it is what we do."

"Then it was also you who killed the settlers, years ago?"

"If we had not then they would have, it would have been bad for our people, some of them would have been turned, they were not invited or welcome, again I give no apologies."

"Then it would appear that I am in no position to judge you, and you have saved my life, I thank you for that."

"Saved it for now, there is an army moving through here the like of which I have never seen, At least a thousand men on horses, big vicious horses at that, ten times that number on foot, and they are heading to your city of stone. They have an advance party, slaughtering all the smaller settlements on the route, and hunting those like you who would evade them and raise the alarm. From what we hear of their speech they come from a place named Branvere, across the sea. I do not know of it. It is dawn now, if you run and do not stop you will make it by dusk, your wound has been dressed and we have given you a plant leaf that will stop the pain and give you more energy than you knew you had, here are more of them, chew them when you need to but do not eat them, it will kill you. We will follow you, and watch this army, see what they do with the creatures that we hunt, and if, we feel it is right, we will strike."

"What of the army coming through here, will they not attack you?"

"You are a typical dweller of stone, despite your love for the woods which is obvious, you look but do not see. Did you see us during your run from this army? No you did not, and neither will they, now I suggest you run for your life and that of your city."

Eighteen
The Wedding

Danyard looked at Sarah and smiled, she was, to his eyes, absolutely stunning. They were both dressed for the wedding of Lady Neosan and Captain Nyston, he in his Imperial Guard full ceremonial regalia and her in a full corseted dress, which, once again, did nothing to hide her ample bosom. Her hair was tied back from her face but let loose at the back and showed her skin beautifully. He was amazed that someone as beautiful as her could possibly find a big ugly brute like him in any way attractive, let alone go to bed with him.

"Will Nyston be a good husband for my friend? I have known her since she was a small girl, watched her grow into the woman she has become." she asked.

"He will be away a lot, on his duties, but when he is there he will be, I do not let fools into my dragoons, and if the odd one did slip through, they do not get promoted to Captain." he replied.

"Surely they are Lord Gemmell's Dragoons now."

"Yes, they are, you are correct, but I will always be a dragoon here." He said as he thumped his chest, laughing. "Is there any room for me in there?"

"You know there is, and always has been."

"Yes, I know, so let us get to this wedding, shall we?"

"Yes, let us, I think we should walk with the dragoons, not take the official carriage, hold hands and give the masses something to gossip about."

"I like the sound of that."

As they turned to leave the room, he picked up his sword from its stand and placed it on his hip. "Do you think you will need that?" she asked.

"Have you ever seen me outside this room without it?"

"No, I have not."

"And that is why I still live, and those who wish to do me harm do not, and besides we don't want the gossiping masses to think I have gone soft do we?"

"Not yet I hope." She replied with a mischievous grin.

Toker's mission was not getting any better, he had been given one major task before the main battle, destroy any villages or settlements on the way and stop any survivors getting to Kino'le and raising the alarm. Up to a point it had worked well, each village was surrounded and a few fires set to get the stragglers out in the fields to come running back, then a few had been killed as a warning but Balstore had been specific, he still needed farmers to work the land after the invasion so most had been rounded up and held in barns and outbuildings by a few men and then they moved on. The exception was this damn rogue dragoon, who now, it appeared, had managed to kill the two Dark Stalkers that had been sent after him and removed their fucking heads!

"Well, any of you have any idea how the fuck a single exhausted dragoon managed this, kill two of these and have time to take their heads, whilst on the run!" he asked, they all looked away except one.

"He didn't, these are spear wounds, not from a sword, too jagged and too large for sword thrusts."

"And who the fuck are you, I do not know you, you are new."

"Chamley Sire, I don't know much about spears but I do know about wounds, I was apprenticed to an apothecary, I errrr…left his service."

"I remember now, he liked to beat you, then one day you beat him back and bit too hard, one strike kill wasn't it?"

"It was, but now I am here and I think we are hunted as we hunt, six wounds on each creature, in exactly the same place, one in each leg and four to the chest, all with similar blood splatter, so all simultaneous, no loss of blood pressure in any wound, this was an execution, not an ambush and a highly skilled one at that."

"And now you think they hunt us?"

"They killed these didn't they? Why not us too?"

"Okay, you make sense, but we still have a problem with that dragoon and we can only assume he is running for Kino'le now, what do you think we should do?"

"Get ahead of him, mounted, there is only one road into the city from here, lay a trap on that road."

The Blood Huntress and Callan rode from the stables of her safe house and headed for the woods surrounding Kino'le,

Amyeen was fully attired for battle, her hair tied back and her version of the dragoon light armour adorned. They cantered through the streets and people stared, not knowing if it was her or just someone pretending to be her, she paid them no attention.

"Do you not care if you are recognised now?" he enquired.

"What does it matter, this time tomorrow they may all be dead and I do not have a bounty on my head so I can ride here without fear of arrest." She replied.

"What if word reaches Danyard?"

"He will be making preparations for the wedding now, even if he does hear, he can do nothing to find me in such a short space of time. Besides, this is it, either way we will not be returning here, there is an army on its way. Today we do battle, have you brought your Gunne?"

"You know I have; I will need it."

"Blood is flying over the Mess right now; Imperials are clearing the route but I must release him to feed."

"Can we do this without him?"

"Please have some faith in my abilities, I am one of the world's best trackers without Blood and he will be done in an hour or so and I need him at full strength."

"Yes, of course, I am sorry."

Callan could not get used to the sight of Blood the Bat, he would return from his flights and cling upside down on her shoulder and she would stroke his furry face and make small noises to him. It was the only time she showed any compassion to any living thing, apart from her horse, Buster. Callan would not admit it to her but he had a fear of anything that fed solely on the blood of other living creatures. He changed the subject.

"What are our plans now?"

"We get into the woods and I start looking for sign, pick up his trail and see where it leads us, by that time Blood will be back hunting too, between us we should find something that will lead us to him. You will need to lead the horses, I need to be boots on the ground for this, the horses are only here if we need to make a fast escape, you may even have to hobble them somewhere if the undergrowth gets too thick."

"As usual you have thought of everything, apart from the one obvious thing, obvious to me anyway. Why don't you just walk up to the palace gates, knock on the door, and say. 'Hello I'm back, by the way you are about to get invaded."

"Because I do not know what Danyard would do, more importantly Lorgane, he could have me thrown in a dungeon claiming I am an imposter, what a present that would be for the conquering Balstore, me all locked up ready for him, and one thing I do know, that foul bastard wizard Lorgane is mixed up in this, at least this way I can fight and help."

"What makes you so sure he is part of it?"

"You said it yourself, Balstore likes to think he is a wizard, but he is not, he is very clever but knows no real magic, just parlour tricks. Lorgane is a wizard, sorcerer, fucking warlock or shaman, whatever they call themselves and whatever the difference is, he can manipulate the world around him and deal in things that are not explainable by other means. Who could control the mind, or minds in this case, of the Dark Stalkers? Not Balstore."

"But why? He is surely one of the powerful men in your Kingdom already, what more does he want?"

"He wants whatever power creates the light for the Kingdom of Light, it is something to do with my sister and I, but I do not know how. He always wanted to be rid of me, and when I first left I was convinced he was behind it, but the more I think about it now, the more it makes sense that he wants me alive, he wanted me out of the Kingdom because he knew when this day came Victarny would be sacrificed for the invasion. He could have killed me many times as a child and teenager, poisoned me or any other method of accident, but he did not. He forced me away. He needs me alive but not interfering with his plans."

Jeldin lent against the tree and got his breath back, although he was getting short of breath, he seemed to have unlimited energy, whatever magic was contained in the bitter tasting leaf was working, his muscles did not ache and his mind was fizzing with excitement. It was midday, he thought he could make it by dusk, but he did not know if he could make it ahead of the pursuing army by much. He suddenly heard horses galloping from his rear and without thinking dived headfirst into the undergrowth. He watched as a dozen horsemen thundered past him on the main road. They did not seem to be searching for him and he knew why, the road narrowed before opening up onto the plains before the city, he would have to get past them. He waited a few seconds and then ran on after them, he had to at least try, he would go as far as he could and see what opportunity arose for him.

From their position in the woods, Amyeen and Callan could hear the cheers of the crowd in the city, they must be at the Guild Hall she thought. She was concentrating on her current task too much to give it much thought though. Callan had twice disturbed her train of thought and now she had told him to follow fifty paces behind with the horses and not speak unless spoken to. She had found Namtu's main hide two hours ago and now she was tracking him back to his shooting position. He had got more careful the closer he got to it, and it was becoming difficult to track him as the paths he used more popular and had multiple footprints on them. She knew him small of stature but she had lost the prints she thought were his and was now studying branches of trees to find a place he may have climbed. Blood was no use to her at the time for the foliage was too thick for him to see through the tree canopy so she had him flying over the Dragoon Mess and then back along the woodland front continuously.

The outer grassed area was patrolled by what she had at first assumed to be Imperial Guardsmen, but as Blood overflew them, she saw they were in fact Dragoons, three atrops, twenty-four men and fully armed, sabres and war bows, at least Danyard was being careful about something she thought.

"We have to go deeper into the forest Callan." she spoke as loudly as she dared.

"Why deeper?"

"Because, I have lost his track, I have to restart from where I last had it, and there are dragoons out there, I have to be too careful when I am close to the edge."

"How do you know he left a trail; how do you know what you saw was him?"

"Because man cannot fly Callan, he moves, he disturbs things, he startles deer and rabbits who suddenly run, they leave the mark of that, he breaks the webs of spiders and even the most careful cannot help doing that, a freshly broken web tells me a huge amount, morning dew gets wiped away from paths, all of these things show me where he went, but I cannot do it quickly, hobble the horses here and we will work back on foot."

Namtu slowly let he is breath escape him, he ached all over from laying perfectly still while the Blood Huntress and the traitor Callen walked away from his perfectly camouflaged hide, she was good, he thought but at least one myth had been destroyed while he listened, she could not smell his blood and his

139

confidence in his own abilities rose. It had taken all of his willpower to not attack them, for the callous murder of Edvar. But he also knew that if he had done so then his mission was over, forever. Even if he killed them the soldiers out patrolling the tree line would hear and find him. He listened and waited while they walked away and waited further to ensure they were as far away as they would go before, he carefully and slowly eased his aching muscles into a more comfortable position. He listened as the crowds cheering died away, he now knew that his target was inside the Guild Hall, he laid out his powder packet and single ball and waited.

As the soon to be married couple said their vows, a dragoon atrop of eight men rode from the city's main stables and headed down the southern road, it was led by Captain Safreen, a ten-year veteran of the Dragoons. He had risen quickly through the ranks of infantry for the noble house he had been sworn to due to his swordsmanship, which even Danyard had been impressed with. He had been offered a place on the Royal Bodyguard and still stood today as the only man to turn the honour down, saying he would rather be out on patrol with his men where his skills would be needed more. He had been involved in many small skirmishes since then and had no regrets. He enjoyed the camaraderie of the Dragoons and led without fear.

This was supposed to be a standard meet and greet of a patrol but he got the feeling that Lord Gemmell was not telling him the whole truth. Normally a simple patrol as this nature would not require war bows to be carried but he had been ordered to take them, and also overnight equipment. He knew the patrol were a bit late but it was inconceivable that the whole patrol would not be coming back, occasionally one or two men did not return but never had an entire patrol not returned.

As they rode away, they passed through the dome of light and each of them shuddered as the temperature dropped. I will never get used to that he thought. There was something bothering him as they got further out from the city, and then it suddenly hit him, where were the people? There was absolutely no one coming into the city from the South, no people on foot, no horsemen, and most importantly, no wagons of goods, the southern road was always busy, always.

"What do you think Horton?" he asked of his second in command.

"The wedding, obviously, everyone has hurried into the city to get a glimpse of Her Majesty."

"How would they have known?"

"Those coming out would have passed word, it is the only explanation."

"It is the preferable explanation, but not the only explanation, let us get a move on, find out where this patrol is."

They went another half a league and rounded a bend, and they were confronted by a dozen armed horsemen set out across the road, they were about two hundred paces away and facing the opposite direction but he could see straight away, they were not Kino'le soldiers, but too disciplined to be a bandit group. He looked around at his men and all looked equally confused, one spoke.

"That is a Branvere uniform, not the Royal Guard that we have visiting, but the regular army, but how did they get here?"

"I do not know, but I really do not like this, we will ride closer, about fifty paces and then find out what they are doing, everyone draw your bows and nock arrows, at the first sign of hostile action, kill them all."

Danyard smiled at the picture-perfect couple and leant over to kiss Sarah, us soon, he thought. The wedding was complete and now they had the formal reception of the city dignitaries before the proper reception of the Dragoons, where Lady Neosan, now Lady Nyston, would be formally welcomed into the family of Dragoons. Danyard hated the first more formal reception, where he would be forced to be polite to the fat merchants that ran the guilds, especially this time as they were all eager to gossip about him and Sarah, which they were all glad about as they thought it may mellow him somewhat.

Young serving girls flirted about like sparrows, filling drinks and trying to catch the eye of any single dragoon, for it was widely accepted that if they married one, they would be set for life. Danyard did not drink often, only when he thought he could relax, and although he did not consider this as one of those times, he did partake of a glass of wine. He noticed the men and wives of the growers' guild and he wandered over to them, to introduce Sarah, although they all already knew who she was. As he approached, he caught a snatch of a conversation.

"So what of the late delivery of your vineyard then, any news?" one enquired.

"No, most odd, I was assured the dregs of the season were picked and ready loaded, expected yesterday latest but still nothing." replied another.

"What late delivery?" asked Danyard sternly.

"Ah Lord Danyard and Lady Sarah, a pleasure to see you both, and together at last."

"Forget your pleasantries, what late delivery, where from and how late?"

"My Lord, I am sure the wine business is not something that holds an interest to your good self."

Danyard lowered his voice. "If the next words from your mouth are not what I asked of you, your good lady wife here will be your good lady widow."

"I was expecting a small convoy from Parston, a small village four leagues south of here, they grow a hardy grape for me that makes an excellent fortified wine, I was assured of delivery yesterday, it did not arrive."

"I know where fucking Parston is, some of us actually get out into the wilds to make this place safe instead of sitting on our fat arses living off the labours of others. Is the Guild Master here?"

"He is in his office Sire."

"And you reported this to him, as required by your licence to trade?"

"I reported to my own Guild Master, it is his duty to report to the Master of Guilds." Sarah looked at Danyard and knew what he was thinking.

"Shall we pay our respects to the Master of Guilds Danyard?" she said as they turned and walked towards his door. The master was a slimy worm of a man named Oates, who always reminded Danyard of a weasel and he could never shake the image whenever he spoke with him. Unlike most merchants he was all skin and bone, but an expert politician, which is how he had managed to climb the greasy pole of the guild of Merchants. Danyard threw his door open and stormed into his office uninvited, just as a very embarrassed looking serving girl broke away from him and struggled to close her open blouse.

"Eeeeeee, my Lord!" he exclaimed "Such a pleasure to see you both, how can I assist my Lord Protector?" he stammered.

"You can fucking start by telling me why you did not report the late arrival of grape from Parston to the Imperial Guard, as is your duty under the office you hold and how many other deliveries are late and from what direction?" Danyard replied.

"But I did my Lord."

"Sarah, would you please find Lord of Dragoons for me, tell him I need to see him, alone, in this office." As she left Danyard's kukri flew from its scabbard and made a small nick on Oates's throat.

"Be very careful what your next words are, I have just had a very similar conversation with one of your colleagues, he was lucky, he was in a public place, you, are not."

"I… I… was going to, my Lord, tomorrow, I…er…did not want to spoil the wedding day with such trivial things."

"What else is late?"

"A stone convoy, for the new buildings in the northern quarter and a few spice wagons."

"All from the same direction, Parston, the southern road? And you did not find this strange then, all from the same direction?"

Just then Lord Gemmell walked in, took in the scene and very quickly shut the door behind him.

Danyard took his kukri from Oates's throat but then punched him as hard as he could on the side of his head, Oates crumpled to the floor.

"You and I cannot be absent from the reception, the Princess will notice and she cannot know about this yet for she thinks me paranoid as it is, and I cannot risk her countermanding my orders. But I think we have been invaded. Mobilise the army and prepare the Dragoons and the Imperial Guard. If we have an army coming this way then we know what direction at least and we can be ready for them, until we know for sure, then I can order Buldor to get her to a secure location. And have this slimy bastard thrown into the lower dungeon, strip him of all valuables first, I do not want him trying to bribe a guard. And find Commander Damerall, I have very specific orders for her. All her dreams may be about to come true."

"My pleasure Sire"

Captain Safreen rode towards the soldiers and swallowed hard, he had always faced whatever dragoon life had thrown at him with courage, but nearly all of those had been spontaneous events and he had always given a good account of himself, but he was now in a situation where he was outnumbered and at a complete loss to understand what was going on.

The twelve men had their backs to him and as a Dragoon Commander had every right to attack them without warning but he was curious. They could be part of King Cathal's party and then he would be in serious trouble, they could not be an advance party for an invasion, just twelve men, a normal advance party would be hundreds. He looked around at the increasingly darkening skies, not just from the onset of evening but from a mass of storm clouds rolling in from the South. His horse suddenly became nervous and started to whinny, shaking its head. He leant forward to sooth the beast and the first of the men turned his mount and faced him, all the others followed suit.

"What is your business in the Kingdom of Light?" he demanded.

"We do not answer to you Dragoon." one replied.

"You do in these lands foreigner; all answer to the Dragoons in the end."

"We may be foreigners at the moment, but soon these lands will be ours."

As he spoke, there was a sudden movement from the undergrowth and a man burst through, seeming to explode from the woodland and shouted RUN at the top of his voice. Safreen recognised the dishevelled form of Jeldin instantly and the sudden knowledge of what must have happened hit him like a thunderbolt, he went for his sword but suddenly felt weak, he looked at his hand on his sword hilt and saw blood, which was coming from three crossbow bolts that had suddenly appeared in his chest, he slipped from his horse as seven arrows from dragoons war bows flew over his supine form.

Jeldin had hidden in the same bush for an hour, he had suspected an ambush and therefore had not rushed immediately from the woods that hid him but had hidden so that he could study the area, this had been his only mistake for just as he was about to start his run up the last league to the city twelve men had ridden in and spaced themselves across the road. He daren't move as the closest was only a pace or so from him. He realised that he was stuck, he could not even move away from them, so close were they. Half were armed with powerful looking crossbows that would easily hit him through the undergrowth. He waited, trying to think what he could do, and then the patrol arrived with Captain Safreen in command.

He was now torn, he could see the men with crossbows but they were very discreet, the weapons themselves resting across the front of their saddles but pointing directly at the patrol, the patrol was far enough away that they may not even have seen them yet. He made a decision, he had to do it, he leapt up screaming as he did so and ran forward toward both groups of soldiers.

A number of things happened at once, the soldiers with crossbows raised their weapons and loosed their arrows and Safreen took three of them to the chest, the Dragoons loosed their arrows from their war bows and then charged, drawing their sabres as they did, Jeldin looked on as he ran, he wanted to join the fight, the Dragoons might win, but still someone had to warn the city, and he had already come this far, he saw Safreen's horse and ran for it, leaping over his body as he did, yet again with a heavy heart, he flung himself up into the saddle and turned the beast for the city, spurring it to the fastest gallop he could muster.

The crowds cheered as the procession moved towards the Dragoon Mess, no one seemed to notice that the Imperial Guard no longer lined the route. The crowds were good natured after so many years of abundance and prosperity and they did not notice just how many soldiers were missing from the city and the route, all they seemed to care about was the carriage of the Princess which also held the newlyweds and the fact that the Lord Danyard and the Lady Sarah were walking behind it holding hands.

One man paid a lot of attention, although he could not see what was happening, he listened and strained his ears to detect variations in the pitch and tone of the crowd, still he lay perfectly still, until he moved slowly and broke the Gunne open, he took the ball from its place on the leather pouch and silken cloth and placed it in the breach, then placed the small powder packet behind it and snapped it shut, wincing at the noise that could not be avoided. He had to ensure it closed properly, if it came open during firing then it would take his face off. He then pulled back on the hammer and waited for the click and the stiffening of the trigger and then put the percussion cap on its stud, then he laid the weapon to his front and said a small prayer for the soul of Edvar, before picking the weapon up again and sighting it on the dark blood stain he had smeared on the wall where he had estimated the carriage would stop. He had made his one ranging shot the night before, in the dead of night, but thanks to the light of Kino'le he could see perfectly well.

He had waited for an hour after for any patrol to investigate the noise but none had come and so he had very casually made his way forward and walked along the wall to check his fall of shot, he had been dead centre of the mark. Even if the carriage did not stop exactly by his mark it would be close enough for him to only need a micro adjustment of his aim. He controlled his breathing and watched the sighting system move up and down with his breath and he waited, his finger resting gently on the trigger.

Nineteen

The Last Chance

"For fucks sake Callen stay still and stop asking questions." She hissed at him from where she knelt on the path.

"I was only…" he stated before he saw her face scowling at him and decided to take her advice.

"I am trying to concentrate, Blood has picked up some scent towards the city and I am following a trail myself, I am doing two very difficult things at once and can do without you interfering."

They had already found Namtu's hide but not his shooting position, he had left behind most of his ball and shot so they knew for sure that it was his hide, Callen had reasoned that he would only get one shot so he did not need much more. Afterwards he would just need to walk into the arms of the invading army a hero.

The pressure was mounting on Amyeen by the second, she could hear the crowds and knew the procession was on the move, but the path was well used and had many footprints, and Namtu had been very careful, one of the best she had ever tracked and she still had not managed to identify his footfall, although she felt she was closing on him she could not see where he had left the trail.

She closed her eyes and sought Blood, she felt the familiar pull of his hunger but could not make out what troubled him, the smell of rotten blood was in him and she dry heaved as it washed through her, and then she saw what it was, a dark blood smear on the city wall near the Dragoon Mess and he was drawn to it. She moved him back from the wall, trying to break his scent trail and she saw her sister as the carriage drew into the courtyard, she was thrown into a panic, knowing she only had heartbeats to spare, she looked again at the stain on the wall and for the first time realised what it was, with a bone melting horror she saw it lined up perfectly with where her Sister's carriage would stop.

"Aiming mark," She said aloud "OH FUCK NO!"

She spun Blood around and flew him towards the wood line, she took complete control of his vision and scanned the trees for living blood, she rarely did this as once she did she could not stop him from feeding and then he was lost to her until he had fed and it became difficult to let go control of him again. She sensed the essence of Namtu, saw his image through the trees laying down pointing that damn weapon towards the wall, she turned and charged through the undergrowth towards his position running blind as she was still fully in control of Blood.

The ornate carriage carrying the newlyweds and the Princess entered the courtyard and started to make its slow circle towards the great doors of the Dragoon Mess, it slowed as it approached and Victarny prepared herself to stand, ready to alight, as the carriage came to a stop she stood and then turned and stared as a lone rider shouted as he tore up the track towards them.

Namtu stared at the sight picture, some kind of bird had briefly hovered around his aiming mark but now had gone, although it did seem to be flying straight towards his hide, he ignored it. He watched what he could see of the carriage make its turn and he smiled slightly as it stopped exactly where he had marked the wall. He heard some kind of shout but it was very faint and this too he ignored, he saw the Princess as she stood, turned and stared, something seemed to have gained her attention and it was the moment in time he needed. His breathing was already steadied and he let the sighting system rise on her frame and then fall with his breath and then rise again, as it did, he gently put more pressure on the trigger. The hammer flew down and struck the percussion cap which sent a flame down the narrow tube that it covered and explosively ignited the powder from the small packet in the rear of the breach. The powder burned with explosive force and it tried to expand but it could not as the barrel was blocked by the lead ball, it reached a point where it could no longer contain itself and the ball was forced under massive pressure down the barrel that was fractionally too small for it and it exploded out of the muzzle at a speed of around nine hundred paces per heartbeat and flew towards the princess followed by its own pressure wave caused by the air it disturbed at that speed. The Princess knew nothing of this as she stood and stared at the figure of Jeldin riding like a crazy person towards the city.

Blood flew straight for the hide, the hunger was on him and nothing could now stop him from feeding, he saw the flame. but did not deviate as nothing else mattered to him other than that all giving, warm life force that he needed to devour. He was suddenly hit by the pressure wave as the ball cracked past him and sent him into a spiral dive that he could not recover from, he hit the grass hard and rolled but still felt pain rip through him as the bones in his left wing broke in three places. He looked around at the sky and the wood line and tried to crawl but he could not, the pain was too great, and then it was dark.

Amyeen ran as if her life depended on it, it was so hard, concentrating on Blood, and trying to calculate Namtu's location from the point of view of Blood, then she saw the flame and she tried to steer Blood away but it was too late, the ball passed close to him and he fell from the air and landed hard, pain wracked through her and she screamed as she fell herself. she was in a complete blind panic as she tried to stand and in her moment of terror, she did the only thing she could, she sent all her thoughts to her sister, in the same way she controlled Blood, if she could just get her to move.

The Princess Victarny of the Kingdom of Light stood up in her carriage and turned to see who had shouted, she looked at the dishevelled dragoon riding for his life towards her and was confused as to the significance of it, she saw Danyard from the corner of her eye leave the arm of Lady Sarah and start running towards her, this also had some strange significance that was just beyond her reach, time seemed to slow down as she tried to make the mental connections, and then, just as she realised the danger she was in, an image of her sister flashed through her mind. Her missing sister was in the woods, she again turned and faced where her sister was just as an almighty pain shot through her body and punched her from the carriage.

The ball flew in a straight line towards her but rising at first and then starting to fall, as all projectiles do and struck her just above the left breast, it entered her body and ripped clean through flesh smashing her collar bone and utterly destroying her pectoral muscle. It exited from her back taking two broken ribs with its angle now altered downward it then embedded itself in the head of an onlooker, killing him instantly. The pressure wave caused by the passage of the ball at such high speed was sucked into the wound and exploded against her internal organs in the vacuum of her chest cavity, causing massive damage and temporarily stopping her heart.

Danyard heard the shout and did not stop to think what it could be, he ran for the Princess and started to leap up for the carriage, as he did she suddenly turned and faced the outer city wall, just as his foot reached the carriage, she was suddenly propelled backwards into his arms, blood spraying him as a hole in her back the size of a fist exploded from her. The force of her hitting him knocked them both from the carriage and she landed heavily on him as he landed on his back, the wind forced from him.

He shot out from underneath her and looked upon the wound in her chest, and then her now lifeless eyes. And then it hit him, what had happened to her, the mysterious weapon, from the beach. It had felled that giant man and he could not comprehend what damage it had done to her. He had been so distracted with Sarah that it had been put from his mind. The crowds were silent for a couple of heartbeats and then something happened that had never happened in the history of the Kingdom of Light, it went dark.

People screamed, panicked and ran, the few Dragoons and the Royal Bodyguard drew their swords and formed a cordon around the fallen Princess. Danyard looked up at Buldor and saw the despair in his face. The Princess suddenly gave a huge gasping breath and started to breathe again. It was dusk and Danyard realised just how dark it had become, the crowds were still screaming and running in all directions. He spoke.

"Buldor, get a table from the mess, lay her on it and get her inside, secure her in the strongroom and none of you are to leave her side, for anything."

"Yes Sire," he replied.

"Captain Nyston, get to the palace as fast as you can and get the Royal Surgeon and Apothecary here, use whatever force you deem appropriate to get past panicking citizens. Do not stop for anything there or back. If the Surgeon says she can be moved later then assist him."

"Yes Sire."

"Lady Neosan, I mean Lady Nyston, go with her and do what you can for her until the Surgeon arrives, assist where you can, you will not leave her side."

"Yes Sire."

"Sarah, would you go with them please."

"Yes Sire." She replied and looked at him with a mixture of longing and fear, not knowing what was happening but knowing that he would be at the forefront of it.

Danyard looked up as the dark storm clouds rolled in and the first flakes of snow fluttered to the ground, he and the Dragoons with him stood as an inhuman howl wrought the air, he was about to turn when Jeldin, spattered with mud and blood tore through the gates. He leapt from his horse and took in the scene before him.

"Oh no no no, I am too late…I…tried," he stammered, as tears fell from his face while the Princess was carried through the doors of the mess by her bodyguards, he fell to his knees and cried out in despair with his head in his hands. Danyard approached and put a hand on his shoulder.

"Jeldin." there was no response.

"JELDIN!" he shouted, "Look at me." Jeldin looked up at Danyard through the mud and tears "You are probably the only man I know who could have done what you have done, how long have you been on the run?"

"Days…two days I think, I can't remember."

"And what do we face?"

"Branvere, its Branvere, they have come by sea, thousands of them, with cavalry."

"I assume Safreen and his atrop are lost, and the Southern Patrol?"

"Yes, both, this is Safreen's horse, I had to take it."

"Yes, I know, you have done well, get inside the Mess and get cleaned and rested."

"That is not all Sire, have you ever heard of the Dark Stalkers of Dalstock Forest?"

"Surely that is just a tale to frighten children."

"I wish it was, I really wish it was."

Callan picked Amyeen up and lent her against a tree, she was deathly pale and tear streaked, she seemed to be in a trance-like state and would not respond to him, he tried to force water into her mouth but she just gagged on it, he shouted at her and eventually slapped her face but still could get no response. In the end he sat her down and tried to think. He knew what was coming, he knew who was coming and he hoped he could hide her until she regained full consciousness. But he also knew, they were now dangerously close to Namtu. He heard a horse whinny and looked around startled, with relief seeing it was their own mounts and they were nearly back to where they had started. He looked at Amyeen and decided that he might be able to get her mounted and then lead them from the forest, he started to walk towards the horses as something else happened that had never happened in the Kingdom of Light, it started to snow. Big fat snowflakes hit the forest canopy and then gently fluttered down to the forest floor.

As he saw the snow above, he suddenly noticed movement to one side of the path, something or someone was struggling out of a pile of brushwood, as he watched he saw the muzzle of a Gunne appear from the hide and his nightmare came true, he was going to have to face Namtu. His own Gunne was still secured to his horse and he did not think to draw his sword as the crouched figure of Namtu crawled out of the small space. Through fear and adrenaline, he ran at the crouched figure and aimed a kick at his head, Namtu saw it coming and just moved his head in time, Callan lost balance through his sheer momentum and slipped over, landing heavily on his back winded. Namtu jumped up and drew his short sword in the same fluid movement. Callan struggled to his feet and went for his own sword, but Namtu was quicker and punched him square on the nose. Blood exploded from his face and he staggered back, dizzy.

He looked at Namtu and realised who he was facing, one of the most feared warriors in the Kingdom of Branvere. He backed away, still thinking he could get his sword drawn at least, as he again went for it Namtu flew at him, slicing clean through his sword belt, only the chainmail hauberk she had insisted he wear saved him from being opened up from sternum to groin. He stepped back again in despair as he felt the sword and belt fall to the ground, he then realised that he was being toyed with, he would be dead already if Namtu wished it. In the time it took to blink Namtu's sword tip was at his throat.

"Traitor! Murderer!" he spat at Callan "You have anything to say before I take my revenge for Edvar? Or should I take you back to Branvere, let you rot in a dungeon for your treachery."

"I did not want to kill him Namtu, I had no choice, it was him or me." he replied, looking ashamed.

"No fucking choice, ah, we all have a choice, you chose to kill him, I watched you do it, from the cliff, you raised your Gunne and executed him in cold blood, an already wounded man. You are nothing but a coward and a traitor and now I shall slowly and painfully kill you." Namtu's head leant back in a maniac laugh as he spoke and then snapped forward, Callen braced himself and then watched in horror as Namtu's head fell to the floor and a fountain of blood sprayed out of the stump of his neck, and there stood Amyeen, bloodied sword still in both hands and the most frightening insane grin that he had ever seen upon her face. She was still deathly pale and breathing erratically, her face splattered with blood, snot and tears, her eyes wide with adrenaline and completely black, the whites vanished. She stepped over the just crumpled body and again raised her sword into a strike position. Callen looked into the eyes of madness and tried to back away, knowing her to be just as much a danger to him as Namtu had been.

"My sister is hanging onto life by the slimmest of threads and Blood is dead, and all because of you Callan, you and him and that cursed weapon, get the fuck away from me right now or I will skewer you to that fucking tree!" she screamed at him.

Callan knew she did not mean what she said and that shock and grief had taken hold of her but he also knew that she would actually kill him without a moment's thought at that moment. He edged away from her and as soon as he thought it safe, he turned and ran for the horses. As he mounted his horse and took the reins of Buster to lead him away, he took one last look back and wished he had not, for she had started to hack the body of Namtu into pieces.

While men rushed around to organise the defence of the city, and for that matter the Kingdom, the Princess Amyeen was going through her own personal hell. The madness was upon her and she wailed and cried and screamed and raged and then started the whole process again. All her life she had held a tight grip on the darkness within her but now she knew she was close to falling into insanity and never being able to find her way out again.

She had felt the full force of Blood crashing into the grass and then the unbelievable pain of her sister's wound, she had felt the lead ball rip through her, tearing muscle and breaking bone and the force of it punching her from the carriage, and her brain had shut down to cope with it. She had only been drawn out of it by the sound of Namtu's voice threatening Callan, almost in a trance she had stood, quietly drawn her sword and taken his head from behind so fast and cleanly that he had not even felt it.

She paced around the woods sobbing and for the first time on her whole life she felt truly lost, not even when she had left Kino'le did she feel this way, for in her young mind she knew she was embarking on the adventure that would make her. The heavy snow started to make its way through the forest canopy in earnest as the leaves above could no longer bear their weight and she realised that she was now soaked through and shivering, the pain of cold giving her some respite from her emotional pain. What remained of the assassin Namtu was on a mudded path and although she knew she had carried out the gruesome deed, she had no real memory of the mutilation of his body, just blurred images. Her rage was fading again so she tried to make contact with her sister, she could feel her weak and erratic heartbeat and soft voices around her but she could not make out what was being said. She released her sister and sank back against a tree, falling into her very own pit of despair.

Danyard looked on helplessly as the surgeon cut away the princess's upper garments, the surgeon, Lord Javin, poked his finger into the entry wound on her front and it came out sticky with blood.

"Her back Lord Javin, the wound on her back is large, I was sprayed by whatever went through her, I saw flesh come away as it came out. I have seen a wound similar to it before, caused by a lead ball, about the size of a hazelnut but propelled at massive speed, from what I do not yet know."

He and a few helpers gently rolled her onto her side and looked at the exit wound, he placed some clean wadding into the wound and laid her back down gently, picking up her discarded clothing as he did so.

"Before we do anything, we must get the cloth from this corset from inside her, see here, where the ball entered, it has taken a small piece of silk with it, if we do not get that out then the wound will fester."

"Are you going to operate on her?"

"Yes, I am, I do not have a choice, it may kill her but doing nothing will kill her. Your duty to the Princess is done Danyard, your duty to the Kingdom awaits you. You alone can organise the defence that we will need to win this war and you cannot do that from here, you need to be with the Dragoons."

"I cannot leave her, this place may be overrun, it is at the forefront of the city, where the enemy vanguard is marching to."

"It will be overrun whether you are here or not, she has her entire Royal Bodyguard here and I am sure my ugly friend here Commander Buldor is quite keen to break open some heads, if she dies, she dies and we can mourn her another day, if we lose her AND you then there will not be a tomorrow, now get to the palace."

"But I swore an oath to her father to protect her, I cannot leave her."

"AND YOU HAVE ALREADY FAILED HIM DANYARD." Lord Javin roared at him "Do not sacrifice the Kingdom as well because of your damn pride! I was there when the King died, I attended him in his dying hours, you also swore to protect the Kingdom. Now stop sulking like a petulant child and do your fucking duty!"

The words hit Danyard like a slap and he reeled from them but he knew the words to be true, he looked around and stared at the expectant faces, Buldor and the bodyguards, the Nyston newlyweds, various medical staff of Lord Javin and Lady Sarah. He knew what he must do.

"Captain Nyston, your men await their leader, go to them now."

"Yes Sire."

"Commander Buldor, as I have previously said, this place may be overrun, you know what you must do."

"I know that each and every one of us will die before any Branvere cunt gets near her, you need say no more."

"If, when the Surgeon has finished, he allows it, move her to the palace. I will have Imperial Guardsmen sent with a wagon."

He then looked at Sarah and felt a pain that he never thought he would have to feel again. He approached her. "Sarah, take my kukri, you may need it, I know, you know how to use it." He spoke as he unbuckled the belt that held it "And keep it hidden, on the small of your back, only use if you have to, let the bodyguards do what they do and do not get in their way, but if it comes to it, use it."

"But you may need it…yourself." She stammered in reply.

"No one will get close enough for me to need it, I promise." Sarah tried to speak again but could not, a lump came to her throat, he tried to speak but could not, he tried to stop the tears streaming down his face but he could not. Sarah looked at him and then turned away to save him anymore embarrassment, pretending to fiddle with the belt buckle in her hands. He turned and walked from the room.

Callan drove his horse as hard as he could, Buster was being led by his reins being tied to Callan's saddle at the rear. The snow was heavy and large flakes made their way through the trees to soak him. He knew he should stop and get his bearings, find his way to shelter but he was still too spooked by the image of Amyeen hacking Namtu's body up to stop.

He rode in the direction that he thought the city lay, but he was getting more disorientated by the minute, there was no light from the city and he was amazed just how quickly he had got used to the strange phenomenon and now he missed it when he needed it the most. He finally broke through the trees and found a path but he still had no idea where he was or what direction he was headed, until he passed a family on a cart heading in the opposite direction. He was too wet, cold and damn frightened to stop and converse with them, but at least he knew he was on the right track to find shelter, assuming they were running from the city.

The road started to get busy, as more and more families made the decision to flee, and it became more difficult for him to force his way through with two horses, only the fact that he was young and dressed as a soldier convinced most people to get out of his way as he struggled against the ever increasing flow. He grabbed one man as he went passed and spoke with him.

"Which way are you going? Which direction?"

"They say an army is coming in from the south, so we are going north, this is the North Road." he replied.

"So, if I keep going this way, I will reach the North Gate?"

"You will but why? Did you not fucking hear me? An army marching this way, and it isn't for no bloody state visit."

"I can't be bothered to explain myself to a coward like you, do what you are doing and run, some of us have bigger plans."

The North Gate, exactly what he was looking for, Amyeen's safehouse is in the Northern Quarter, if he could just get there, get himself and the horses dry, and, more importantly, check and dry his Gunne and collect the stash of shot and powder he had hidden there.

Twenty

The Defence

Danyard reached the Palace and strode to his quarters, shouting instructions as he went. He sent orders for all commanders to assemble in the Courtyard but first he sent for Lord Gemmell, who arrived promptly and spoke first.

"It would appear that you were correct Danyard."

"I wish I fucking wasn't."

"The Princess, she lives?"

"When I left her yes, the surgeon will be cutting her open about now, I have ordered a wagon and as many atrops of Imperials as Commander Jain can spare to escort her back if she is well enough. What is the status of the trebuchets, are the crews in place?"

"Commander Damerall is testing the beams and ropes as we speak, and wagons are ferrying load to them. I have never seen her so excited, using 'Her Babies' for the first time in action, but we are all scared, they have not been used in a long time, if they break under strain…men will die"

"More will die if we do not use them."

"I know. Other matters, many people are fleeing, we have advised them if they wish to leave to do so by the North Gate which remains open, I have sent riders to all outposts to warn the whole Kingdom. We have the staging posts for the big cities, replace the horses and riders every ten leagues, that way we think we can get word to Kardon in a day. they have their own invasion plan, until any other word comes from us, they will sink any non-Kino'le ship that approaches the harbour with their own trebuchets, good timing that Commander Damerall was here and not there, she would have died missing this opportunity."

"Good, we will need to carry on trading. But now tell me what do you know of the Dark Stalkers of Dalstock Forest?"

"That they do not exist."

"How much do you trust Jeldin?"

"With my life, the most straight-talking man I have ever met, for someone who has perfected the art of being a sneaky bastard, he is very honest."

"As you know, he was with the Southern Patrol, he is, at this moment, the only survivor. Captain Partis ordered him to get here and raise the alarm at any cost, not his fault but he was a few heartbeats late, but he has quite a tale to tell. Hunted by Dark Stalkers, a Branvere army the like of which has never been assembled before, rescued by the savages of Dalstock, with wounds to prove it. I have no reason to disbelieve him."

"Darkness, is what I have heard about them, they cannot function in light, like a lizard in the cold, they need darkness to function properly, and what do they have now?"

"They have darkness, are you suggesting that she was attacked just to put out the light of Kino'le?"

"That is exactly what I am saying, whoever planned this knew what we know, and there is only one person in this Kingdom, other than us two, that fucking Wizard."

"I never liked that cunt, and who of us three would be able to control these creatures, through blood magic or fucking voodoo or whatever they like to call it."

"Not you or I, he would."

"Send some Dragoons to his tower, and his basement, what is it with wizards, towers and fucking basements. Up high or down underground, or in his case, both."

"What do you want done with him?"

"If he will not come quietly do not try to arrest him, just kill him, he is too dangerous to try to take alive. But we have more important worries right now, like the defence of this Kingdom, let us join the men."

As they opened the door two stern faced atrops of dragoons stood there. "These are now your personal bodyguard Danyard, where you go, they go." "Sixteen dragoons, isn't that a bit excessive, the Princess has that many."

"The Princess will not be riding into battle at the head of an army, you will be."

"Fair one Lord Gemmell, fair one. Commander Grossman, glad to see you here, a bit of a return to bodyguarding for you then, I assume you are Commander of this little group?"

"That would be correct Sire."

"Good, these men to protect me will also have to act as my runners, you understand that?"

"Yes Sire."

"Good, is Spike ready?"

"Yes Sire, he is saddled and in his armour."

"Do the other dragoon mounts have armour?"

"No Sire, just the mail blanket, as per dragoon light armour orders."

"Then take Spike's off, I have no wish to become an arrow magnet, and as you and your men will be very close to me I think you will find that to be annoying too, big shiny ironclad horse to give the enemy archers something to aim at…no Commander, I have not survived this long by making myself obvious to my enemies, as well you know."

"Yes Sire."

Toker shuddered as the creatures loped through the lines of his men, he agreed with the sentiments of most of them that they did not see the need for such dark forces, the truth being that they scared them all, and each man was glad they did not have to fight them on a battlefield. He was sure, even against the Dragoons that the Branvere forces would prevail, but he did understand that they were needed to get inside the city wall. The creatures could climb almost sheer walls and leap huge distances which would eradicate the need for a long drawn out siege with ladders and towers and siege engines. The ships ferrying men and supplies had the components for them on board but he hoped they would not be needed; it would be seen as a failure of his new command.

He had reached the end of the woodland from the South some time ago and seen the result of the small skirmish of his men and the Dragoon patrol sent down to greet the larger patrol. All were dead apart from that one single Dragoon, he had escaped again, he knew this because everyone knew Dragoons worked in groups of eight, and eight bodies had been found but one horse was missing, only two of his men had survived the fight, both seriously wounded, and he was earning a grudging respect for the Dragoons who had fought.

The city knew they were coming now but it did not matter, just moments ago he had seen the famous light extinguished and he smiled when he thought of his friend and mentor Namtu succeeding. The Princess must be dead and nothing could stop Branvere taking the city. Kardon would be next and then the fleet could ferry reinforcements throughout the whole Kingdom instead of just the small bridgehead they had now. The mounted soldiers were coming through in dribs and drabs and forming up their lines, the first of the infantry were also arriving and forming lines behind. As soon as the first were ready the advance would begin, with a constant reinforcement coming from behind supplied by sea they could not lose. Within a day the city would be theirs and the famous Danyard's head would be put on a spike, by him.

The Blood Huntress, the most feared and respected warrior in the known world, sat against a tree and shivered, her clothing sodden, her chainmail wet and heavy, weighed her down. She was physically and mentally exhausted and drifted in and out of a fitful sleep, filled with dreams of death and destruction. From the depths of her consciousness she knew that she should move, get to shelter and out of her wet clothes, but she could not, she was overwhelmed and her mind was giving up and her body was following as her core temperature dropped.

She pictured Blood, all these years her sole companion, the times they had soared together over the woodland and the rooftops hunting their prey, she dreamt of him lying dead out in the field to her front, and then she saw the grass, from his point of view. Something stirred deep within her, a glimpse of reality tried to fight its way through her nightmares to her waking conscious, she was seeing through him, he could not be dead, BLOOD LIVED! Her eyes shot open and she flung herself to her feet, immediately falling again as her body sent waves of dizziness through her. Eventually, she stood upright and staggered towards the edge of the wood, the feeling coming back to her cold and aching body and the connection with Blood getting stronger as she staggered towards him through the trees.

She almost fell from the tree line onto the field and moved in his direction, not even having to look, going by the slow and painful beat of his tiny heart. She suddenly stopped walking forward and stood still without looking she knelt down and gently scooped him from the snow that had fallen on him, cupping him in her hands. His pain shot through her from his broken wing but she fought it down, she knew what she must do. She gently placed him on her shoulder and loosened the collar of her jerkin, then slowly started to walk towards the city wall as she felt his fangs sink into the flesh of her neck and her vital lifegiving blood was sucked from her.

Daskin did not know what was happening exactly, he was new to the Dragoons having only just passed his selection and training, not even been on his first patrol yet. His first duty had been guard of honour for the Princess, he had walked alongside her carriage through the streets and felt proud. He was twenty years old and his even prouder parents had brought all their neighbours out to see him in his Dragoon Ceremonial uniform. And then he had looked on in horror as the Lord Danyard had made a sudden dash for the carriage only to have the Princess's back explode in his face as he reached her, then the light had gone out and chaos had reigned. The crowds had screamed and run in all directions and he had drawn his sabre and instinctively helped form a cordon around her.

He had stood and watched in awe as the legendary tracker Jeldin had screamed through the gates on a bloodied horse and broke down in front of Danyard. A sense of unreality surrounded him, like some mad training exercise, he half expected a horn to blow and his training instructors to emerge and confirm they all did well. But no one did, instead there were words of dark creatures and tales of an army the size of which no one had ever seen. He had followed the Princess as she was carried on a table into the Dragoon Mess where upon he had been ordered into his Dragoon Light Battle Armour. There was officially a Heavy Battle Armour and he had been shown a set during his training, but in the years since Danyard had been Lord Protector it had fallen more and more into disuse, most Dragoons, including Danyard, preferred the mobility that came with light armour.

The last thing he picked up as he left his room was his dragoon war bow, and as he closed the door behind him, he was ordered to collect as many arrows as he could reasonably carry from the strongroom. As he looked out to the men already manning the wall, he saw the mess servants carrying barrels of arrows into position as well.

Now he stood on the battlement of the outer wall in the heavy snow near to the southern gate, which was being barricaded from behind with anything that could be put into place. He noticed a warrior walking towards the wall where he stood, and at first, he thought it was a fellow dragoon, so alike was he dressed, and then he realised it was not a he, but a she. Her armour was nearly an exact copy of his own, except that the chainmail was oil blued to a matt finish, the shoulder guard was a dull grey and not as ornate as his own and she wore no shin grieves. Also, the sword was different too, not a horseman's sabre but a two-handed broadsword but looked an excellent quality, he had seen a similar one before but could not remember where. The one thing that made him uneasy was in her hand, for she carried the one thing that only dragoons could possess, on pain of death, the dragoon war bow, there was no mistaking its shape. He drew back on the string of his own, his arrow already nocked, and took aim and spoke.

"State your business here warrior." She looked up at him with cold dark eyes and a chill went through him.

"I have a home here Dragoon, according to local ordnance three six one you cannot deny me entry to the city." She replied.

"I do not know of these laws you quote to me for I am merely a humble dragoon, not an imperial guardsman, and I have orders that these gates do not open, however, I also have orders that the North gate will be open to allow for fleeing citizens, you may make your way there, although no one is trying to get in, only out."

"So be it Dragoon, so be it." He watched her walk away and when she was out of effective range, he released the tension on his bow, for some reason that he could not fathom he had the feeling that he had just been spared a horrible death.

Callan stripped off his sodden clothes and then set about the fire, it had been made ready by Amyeen the day before, one of the standard things that she always did before leaving a safe house. The kindling took to flame of the first strike of the tinderbox and he fed it carefully, then rejoiced in the heat as it washed over his frozen body. Amyeen had given him his own key during their stay over the last few days, and he was thankful for that. The Imperial Guards at the North gate had questioned him as to his reason for wanting entry to the city but he had quoted the address of the safe house and they had been satisfied he was a citizen and allowed him entry. After a few wrong turns, caused by the lack of light, he had found the house and led the horses to the small but well-appointed stables at the rear. He had rubbed the pair of them down and covered each one with a fresh blanket before making his own way into the house. She would kill him if he let her beloved Buster go lame through being cold and wet. He sat in one of the big chairs by the fire in new undershirt and leggings with every intention of packing his meagre belongings and getting far away, but the combination of exhaustion and the warmth overcame his will and he fell into a deep sleep.

He awakened suddenly when he felt a razor-sharp blade at his throat, he opened his eyes and looked into the cold dead eyes of Amyeen. He was getting very bored with being scared for his life and so tried to act nonchalant as he spoke.

"You made it back then?"

"Yes, you made a fire, you are learning." She replied as she withdrew her kukri and sheathed it. He looked at her and saw the state she was in, exhaustion was etched into her face, she was wet through, pale and shivering. He stood up from the chair and walked towards her.

"I am truly sorry for what happened with your sister and you… Blood, your bat Blood." he said as he took her in his arms "I did everything in my power to try to stop it."

"I know you did Callan; I am sorry for what I said, I was not in full control of myself, it will not happen again."

"It does not matter, it is not a sign of weakness, you can let your emotional side out occasionally, even you are only human." She then broke down; huge wracking sobs tore through her as she finally let herself go and Callan held her as her wet body soaked his fresh dry clothing. Eventually she let him go and turned away from him as she stripped her wet outer wear from her body, not to hide herself from his eyes but so he would not see that she still wept. She had laid her weapons on the table but the remainder of her clothing she let fall to the floor, she stood in her undergarments close to the fire and let its warmth envelope her.

"What is that wound upon your neck?" Callan asked, "It is still bleeding."

"Blood, he is alive, I put him in his dark house before I woke you, but I let him feed from me, something in his saliva stops the blood from clotting, also numbs the area, I forgot about it because I cannot feel it. He has a broken wing which I have splinted and he will need to feed more than regularly to have the energy to mend."

"How much does he normally need?"

"His bodyweight every day, he seems to be getting bigger every year, I think because he is bonded with a human his normal growth cycle has gone wrong, he just seems to keep growing. I sought out an expert on them once and he is now bigger than all the large samples that the man showed me, so he needs a lot of blood to keep him alive."

"How will we feed him now?"

"I saw you got the horses back; I will put him on one now and he can drink his fill, but that will have to do him, and then I will put him in his bat house to rest. I cannot risk him losing consciousness and falling to the floor, it could kill him."

"I am no expert, but it seems the only option."

"You do not have to fight for Kino'le Callan, you could just ride away, or even ride into the arms of your people the returning hero."

"I could do, but I would forever be looking over my shoulder thinking that they would learn the truth, and then my life would be worse than over, for they like to let people literally rot to death in the dungeons of Branvere, at least this way I will earn the chance to settle here, if I do not die on the battlefield."

"In that case I do have a plan, and a plan that should keep you quite safe. As much as I hate to say this, is your powder dry?"

Commander Jain strode towards the town square in his full plate battle armour, it had been years since he had worn it and he felt good in it, the old feeling of fear, excitement and anticipation creeping over him. It had been years since he had been in a proper battle and he had missed it, never again believing that he would have the chance. But Lord Gemmell had pulled him from the reception and ordered him to, as quietly as possible, call out the full Imperial Guard in full battle armour. Then, as he was donning his own, there had been screams and the light had gone out, and he knew it was not a drill. It had only got worse as moments slipped by, runners carrying news kept him informed, the Princess attacked and near death, creatures that he knew did not exist massing at the head of an army with a thousand horsemen.

The mounted men did not worry him much, men on horseback needed space and were largely ineffective on cobbled streets, but they would still decide the battle on the field to the front of the city wall, and if they had a thousand as the latest intelligence suggested then they outnumbered the dragoons currently in the city by two to one.

What did worry him were the creatures, they would be used to breach the walls and the gate, they thrived in darkness and if they got beyond the walls they would wreak havoc among the citizens, Danyard asked if they had a store of torches, to which he had replied we have thousands of them, just nowhere to put them because the city had never had sconces built into its walls.

He turned the corner to the town square and the sign that met his eyes was the proudest of his days. Every single Imperial Guardsman was formed up, on parade and they all came smartly to attention as he walked forward. He stood and gave the Imperial salute back to them and then spoke.

"Today, once again my friends we join battle, not for glory, not for some ungrateful lord, but for ourselves and our homes and families. I know every one of you is a hardened battle veteran but this will be like no other fight any of us has ever fought. Commanders to me now, everyone else rest while you have the chance."

At the same time, Carmak finally relinquished control of the convoy and made his way to the joint infantry companies that he and his brother commanded. He was relieved to have arrived at all after surviving the attack by the Dragoon patrol, but he had lost all but one of his outriders which hurt him on a personal level as he had raised each one to their station himself and knew each man's family. He had also lost a dozen or so of the creatures as well as half of the wagon drivers but he could not bring himself to shed a tear over the useless fuckers, if they had listened to him, they would still be alive now. But damn the Dragoons were fierce fighters he thought to himself, disciplined and organised with a control on horseback he had rarely seen. If it was not for Lord Toker's sudden and unexpected arrival he was unsure whether he would have made it at all. He did not like the idea of facing the Dragoons on a battlefield, especially him being a foot soldier by nature. But he had been assured by the knights of Branvere that the Dragoons could not stand against the thousand Branvere Destriers that they would face.

But he had delivered over one hundred and seventy of the creatures and he had been told that was a success. Although he still had no word of his brother and Namtu. The light was out and so he knew that Namtu had been successful but he had hoped to find him and his brother waiting for them somewhere.

The plan that had been outlined to him was simple enough, the creatures would go forward first and scale the walls, while the cavalry formed a rear guard to engage the Dragoons if they showed themselves on the field of battle. Meanwhile the infantry would take the city on foot after the creatures had made entry to the city and caused widespread panic and spread the Imperial Guard too thin to deal with a real army.

Two unknowns bothered him, the warning and preparation that the city had gained from the escape of that single Dragoon that Lord Toker had briefed him on, and the status of the four massive trebuchet catapults that sat protected behind the city walls but with the ability to throw huge loads far beyond. With the first he assumed the worst and that was that Danyard had mobilised early and was fully prepared. But the trebuchets were another thing altogether and they scared him witless; he had been a young man when he had infiltrated the Mar'thak army on orders of Balstore during the failed invasion and he had seen them in action. He had been at the rear of a column when the first had loosed its load, a rock half the size of a house had landed just paces from him and had thrown him through the air like a rag doll, men and bits of men had been flung everywhere, causing more injury to those close by. That rock had embedded itself in the ground and not caused further damage but the next ones had been smaller and rounded so as they hit one column they kept bouncing to the next. And then all four had loosed heartbeats apart, the effect even on highly disciplined soldiers had been devastating and men had run from the field in utter terror, only to be caught in a flanking mounted charge by the Dragoons, most men run underfoot as they tried to flee. It had been a masterful use of strategy and timing and in his mind started the rout that Danyard was credited with.

The spymaster of Branvere, a nasty vindictive noble named Tromell had assured them all that the machines had not been used in over five years and they now sat rotting, the iron rusted and the wooden beams warped, but he did not trust spies or their masters but did trust that the Lord Danyard was a sly old bastard who would like the world to think that they were rotting away as part of his deception plan, and all good commanders had a deception plan.

That one time with the Mar'thak army had been the first time that the young Carmak had known true fear and he had stumbled dazed and wounded from the field of battle only to be confronted by a man possessed, it was the first time that he had ever seen Danyard and it was soon clear why he had risen through the ranks so rapidly. He was a blur as he cut and sliced his way through the battle, only lightly armoured he could move with a speed that was truly awe inspiring, his sword was lighter than those around him but just as strong so he could wield it with astonishing speed and accuracy.

He did not fight like any other swordsman that he had ever seen, he did not try to block he just was not in the space the enemy sword was aiming for by the time it got where it was going. He side stepped or ducked or leapt or dived and stepped through, his own sword cutting the man he had been facing, just enough to put him out of action. He wasted no energy finishing men, or even checking they were down, he just kept on moving forward, always going forward and cutting a swath that other men filled and followed. In the few heartbeats that he stood dumbfounded and watched twelve men fell to Danyard's sword and his eyes were filled with battle lust as blood flew from his long-matted hair. As he stood there his eyes met Danyard's and he saw the darkness there, he and those around him threw down their swords and ran for their life. He kept promising himself that this time it would be different, but the image of that day kept returning to him and made him shudder.

"They will attack tonight," Jeldin told the assembled Commanders of the Kino'le Army "The creatures they have cannot function in daylight but are ferocious in the dark. Each stands about the height of a man plus half again, heavily muscled and immensely strong. They are covered in matt black fur that does not reflect light. They have huge sharp talons and a mouth full of fangs, they kill by brute force and slashing and biting. They are incapable of simple thought enough to pick up and use a weapon, relying on their own strength and the fact that every living creature they see will generally freeze in terror on the spot or turn and run. They can track by sense of smell and do have some kind of mental communication between them, if a group attacks, they can co-ordinate the attack so one goes forward and the others wait, as happened to me."

"Did you kill one Jeldin?" asked Danyard "How do you know this? And how did you survive?"

"I did not kill any, the creatures share Dalstock forest with others, people. They have been known to us as Savages for the last decade after what happened to the settlers of light, all those years ago."

There was collective gasp as the assembled Commanders took in this news. One spoke. "So, the savage bastards who kill innocent settlers march on us also?"

"No Lord Terek, they do not. They are shadowing the creatures and waiting for an opportunity to destroy them once and for all. It is my belief that they will attack them when the time is right. I implore you to let these 'Savages' live if you see them, which you probably will not."

"And how will we know them?"

"They wear one-piece green tunics and are barefoot, most have long hair tied back and are armed only with spears, but they are spearmen of a skill the like of which I have never seen."

"I make you no promises Commander Jeldin, if my men are in danger and they are on the field of battle then they are a target like all others. However, I will take heed of what you have said."

"Thank you, my Lord. Any more questions?"

"What is your assessment of their capabilities, how will the Branvere commander use them?"

"I believe that they are a use-once throwaway weapon, they are to make it through the city walls for the main army to follow, probably try to destroy our gates, firstly and most obviously the southern gate. I do not see why the Branvere Army would want any of them to survive any more than we do, once they are inside the walls and the gate is down, other than spreading a little terror, they are of no real tactical use to anyone anymore."

"Then we must stop them Commander Jeldin, and I for one would like to say to you that no matter what the outcome of this, the Kingdom owes you a debt of gratitude for making your way back, you are a national hero and we salute you." Lord Terek stood and raised his sword in Jeldin's direction, and each and every officer and noble, including Danyard, did the same. Jeldin stood routed to the spot as tears streamed down his face.

The five hundred Imperial Guardsmen relieved the remaining Dragoons from the outer wall as Commander Jain took formal command of the Dragoon Mess, deploying his men at the now shuttered windows. He had overseen the movement of the Princess from the Mess back to the Palace strongroom with her ladies, the Royal Surgeon, his staff and her bodyguards in attendance. He looked on with a lump in his throat at the near lifeless form of her, still on the original table she had been laid upon. Although it had been cleaned, he could see where blood had dripped from it, where the wood had been permanently stained. How could she lose so much blood and still be alive he thought to himself?

He looked up and just caught an image of a hooded figure pass in front of him, he blinked and the figure was no longer there. He went to move forward and caught the sight of Buldor, he had never seen such a defeated and downhearted look on anyone's face before, but mixed with an anger behind his eyes that took his breath away, one hand carrying his lethal but beloved war hammer, as always.

"It is coming Buldor." he said.

"What is?" replied Buldor.

"Redemption, the enemy comes and so will your time."

"She lives, she dies, I will never redeem myself. Preventing this is what we are for, our sole purpose of existence, and we failed."

"Not yet my ugly friend, she lives and so do you, if they get as far as her then you will make them pay for it."

"I will, now fuck off and do your job Imperial."

"That is better you ugly bastard."

After that, he had walked on and checked the position of his men, one hundred were manning the windows of the Dragoons mess, to give them an elevated position to loose arrows down on the gate and wall, the remainder were on the southern wall, fires were being lit and oil barrels being moved up, fire arrows and burning oil would rain down on the attackers but he did not know what effect it would have on the creatures. Each man was fully armoured as they were the defenders they would not be running anywhere; mobility was not a priority to them. He wondered about his brothers, the Dragoons. Although lightly armoured their skill with sword and bow was beyond compare and their horsemanship excellent. They would be forming up now, lancers to the front, swordsmen behind, and the regular Army behind them, with the longbowmen in between.

Daskin had been relieved from the wall by a stern looking Imperial, the man had looked at his young face and he had seen the scorn on it. He had then gone with the other dragoons to the stables where his horse was ready for him and now, he sat upon it with the men he would fight, and maybe die with. He was frightened, but more for his parents than for himself, he had faced men before who wanted to kill him and he had killed them, on a border patrol with the Army. It was that action that had brought him to the attention of the dragoons and he had been invited to apply. His parents had come to his final parade when he and his fellow graduates had marched passed in rows and he had seen a tear not just in his mother's eye but his father's too. He was torn over his fears for his parents, he wanted them to be safe but he did not want them to flee, he did not think his father would run, he had been a soldier himself and although he never spoke of the battles he had fought in he knew that he had lost many friends and still had the odd nightmare.

"You all right brother?" the man next to him asked.

"Yes Sir, scared for my folks is all."

"Have you learnt nothing since you have been here? And I do not mean in the training school, you ain't in the fucking army now, you are a dragoon and we are all brothers. My name is Curan and you are Daskin from the northern quarter, two years with the Army and killed the bandit that killed your officer, ran him down after jumping onto your officer's horse and killed him with a broken sword. Quite a feat which is why you are now sat here on a fine horse and not marching in lines on foot."

"How do you know all this?"

"When you join an atrop we like to know everything about you, we ask questions, we find out. We like to know who we fight for."

"Surely we fight for the Kingdom?"

"Yes, we do. They pay us and our homes are here, but when it comes down to it, we fight for each other on the field of battle, dead or alive no Dragoon has ever been left behind. Every Dragoon here will kill and die for you, and you for him, regardless. It is what keeps us strong."

"What about Commander Jeldin? Did he not run from the battle that his men were dying in?"

"Yes, he did, he is the exception that proves the rule, and if he had not then this Kingdom would fall tonight, we would be drunk in the mess not on our mounts awaiting our destiny, not many men, not many Dragoons, could have done what he did."

"Was he really on the run for two days, no food or water?"

"Yes, all the way from Dalstock Forest."

"What about them, the ones they talk about?"

"I will not lie to you brother; it will be hard. These creatures are a pace taller than we are and about twice our weight, with claws and fangs and are immensely strong. They will scale the walls and try to break down the city gates for the main army to rush through. We will have to fight them out here on the open plain and stop as many as possible from reaching the walls, for once they are past us our brother Imperials will fight them inside the city alone."

"Can we not follow them inside the city?"

"And who would be left to fight the Branvere cavalry if we did?"

"No one, no one who is a match for them anyway, mounted soldiers will smash our army."

"You are learning fast, but you will have to learn much faster over the next few hours, but one thing I do know is that the best way to protect your family is to stop as many of those things as you can. Stick with our atrop and listen for our commander and do exactly what he says when he tells you to do it, give a good account of yourself and remember, you will never be alone."

"Thank you Curan, for re-assuring me."

"Do not mention it brother, it is what we do."

Callan lay down in the tower, protected from the snow and smiled. He tested and adjusted his position, the Gunne barrel lined up perfectly with the hole in front of him while he was in the prone position. The tower was on the other side of the gate to the Dragoon Mess but overlooked the plain to the front which would become the first battlefield. He was fifty paces from the wall but in an elevated position, looking down on it.

"How do you know of this place?" he asked.

"It was designed as a defensive position, for a lone crossbowman, but a normal crossbow was not powerful enough to reach much beyond the wall so we experimented with a powerful windlass but it was deemed too difficult to handle even with a two man team so it fell into disuse, the Imperials simply forgot about it. The aperture on the outside is masked by a gargoyle, you are firing that weapon through its mouth, I imagine there will be a bit of flame visible but not much, even in this darkness. Stay as far back as you can to reduce the amount that is seen but enough that you can get a good sight picture. Are you accurate enough at the range you will be firing at?"

"I will be, up to two hundred paces, I secretly modified a simple sight system for my own Gunne and I can easily attach it, it will at least give me variable range and adjustment if I miss."

"You must kill as many of the creatures as you can before they reach the wall, the Dragoons will fight them out there but then only the Imperials will be left to fight them inside the wall. They will be our last hope."

"And what will you do?"

"I am dressed almost identical to a Dragoon, I know how they fight and their command structure, in the chaos of battle they will not even notice me."

"I think they will."

"As long as you bloody well do, big hairy monster, kill the fucker. Sleek warrior princess killing everything in her path, do not kill!"

"Yes Your Highness."

"It will not be long now, I must go, I need to be on the field with my brothers. Do not waste time, energy and shot on wounded ones, if it hits the ground wounded leave it and aim for the next one, protect the wall, at all costs."

"I will, but I am not Namtu, my shots will not be hugely accurate."

"I know Callan, but I also know you will do your best."

She looked down at him and smiled.

"Callan, I want you to know, if we do not make it, I would not blame you if you went back a hero, just do what you can for my sister and me first." She then turned and walked from the small door before he had a chance to reply.

Danyard took one last forlorn look at the Princess and wiped away the tear that was trying to form on his stern face. He had raised her and her sister and now she was as close to death as she could be. The Royal Apothecary and the Royal Surgeon both saying that they did not understand how she was still drawing breath, as shallow as it was. The wound on her front was expertly stitched and tidy enough, but the wound on her back was monstrous, a gaping hole of damaged tissue and flaps of skin the size of Danyard's fingers.

The Surgeon had sent for the Master of Arms and Danyard had an idea why but did not voice his concerns of what he thought he was contemplating. He has also sent an atrop of Imperial Guardsmen to find the missing pieces of rib and they had done so, bringing their grizzly prize very quickly. Something else had been mentioned by the surgeon and a few of the bodyguards, a mysterious hooded figure had been seen in the strongroom, usually near to the Princess, but when anyone tried to focus on him, or her, the figure just seems to fade from view, not disappear exactly, just not be seen anymore. He had put it down to fatigue at first but too many had said they had seen the figure, but there was nothing he could do about it now so he put it from his mind. He had been told once already, quite forcefully, that he had other duties that day.

He stepped away and walked towards the door, his two atrops of dragoons waiting for him. He headed for the stables where Spike was waiting for him with his groom, as per his orders Spike was adorned identically to all the other horses. He mounted and waited while his bodyguards followed suit, and then, he led them out to the holding area.

He arrived to a massive cheer; the men once again glad to see him in his dragoon light battle armour. He signalled for silence and called his atrop commanders to him. He spoke.

"This will be the day we decide our destiny, we will, at the end of this day, be dead, alive and slaves, or once again victors, that choice we will all make when the time comes for us as individuals, but as a band of brothers that choice will be made by me alone. The creatures that we face will come first and they will come hard, however, only the lancers will engage them before they hit the city wall."

"But my Lord," Spoke one commander "We could destroy them all before they even get to the wall, if we all join battle straight away."

"Yes we could, we have intelligence that the enemy Mounted Cavalry number a thousand, we mounted Dragoons number less than half that, but if you were the enemy commander would you want a straight fight with us, or would you prefer to outflank us and while we are busy and drive your massive destriers through our infantry and then come back for us when we number even fewer and are in disarray? Our strength as mounted soldiers lies in our training on horseback and our formations and manoeuvres, which they know we practice. We ride small faster horses, they ride huge armoured destriers. We are manoeuvrable they are not. They fear us in formation so that is what we will give them. If the Branvere cavalry destroy us today then they have won, it is that simple, there is no other force we have that can stop them, not on those fucking giant savage beasts they ride. So, I hereby give this direct order, which you will pass to your atrops, and it goes against all that we believe in. Only the lancers will engage the creatures, we have to survive as a cohesive unit to stop the Branvere Mounted division, no man will break rank to help them, and I will know for I shall be with the lancers. And I say to the lancers, once the creatures are over the wall, they are no longer your problem, your brother Imperials will continue the fight. No Dragoon will enter the city... DO YOU HEAR ME DRAGOONS!" he shouted.

"YES SIRE!" they replied.

"MY NAME IS DANYARD AND I AM YOUR BROTHER, DO YOU HEAR ME MY BROTHERS!"

"YES DANYARD!" they replied. They were ready.

Twenty-One
The Advance

Carmak watched and shuddered as the creatures loped off towards the dark and silent city, the cavalry cantered behind them and behind them followed the infantry, his infantry now. He had just received a field commission to command the entire Branvere forces. A thousand horses, ten thousand men on foot, although at that moment only half the infantry had arrived. But he was now General Carmak, as far as he was aware the only common man in history of the Kingdom of Branvere to receive the honour. The infantry marched in columns of five deep, one hundred long. Ten columns of men marched towards the first city of The Kingdom of Light, protected by creatures of darkness.

It was planned that the infantry would arrive as the battle for the wall was over, for them to charge what was left of the gates and hopefully go straight through, then take the city and finally the palace, ensuring that the Princess and Danyard were dead at all costs. Lord Toker and his men had slipped away to wherever they thought would be able to carry out their primary task, to take Danyard's head, whatever the cost. Carmak was still unsure for he had seen Danyard in battle, Toker had not.

Other small groups had been sent on various mission as well, Carmak had no interest in whatever they were up to, the slimy bastard spymaster had been training small groups of men and Carmak despised him and so had avoided getting involved in any way.

The Imperial Guardsmen in the Dragoon Mess waited behind their shutters and looked through the arrow slits at the now heavy snow, another first on a night of them. Each man had a standard battle bow and about as many arrows as they could ever loose in barrels beside them. More of their colleagues manned the wall and so their aim was to be over the heads of their brothers, most wished they had their old Dragoon War bow still but Danyard was insistent of the fact they were for Dragoon patrols only. The Standard bows they carried had less power and accuracy but they would have to suffice. Stewards ran everywhere carrying more arrows and buckets of water along the wall and then there was a horn blast and a shout from the high tower.

"They are coming, be ready!"

The creatures could only be seen as shadows at first, fast moving shapes against the darkness and heavy snow, but as they grew near their terrifying forms could be made out. The Imperials loosed shaft after shaft at them from two hundred paces, trying to make good aim in the dismal light afforded them, and although they could make out the dark shapes against the now pure white field they were fast, some arrows found their mark but most thudded uselessly onto the soft earth, the few hitting only slowing them down as they loped on with the smell of flesh in their nostrils and a raging hatred in their dark and vile hearts.

As they closed to one hundred paces, the arrows started to make a difference, most now found their mark and caused damage that made some of them fall, with more arrows striking the fallen bodies. At the same time there was a horn blast and the first of the dragoon lancers thundered from their holding area on the left flank and charged into the creatures from the side.

Danyard, leading from the front, levelled his lance and picked his target, his two atrops guarding him following instinctively as the other lancers spread out and picked their own targets. Danyard's lance hit the creature in the side of the chest and punched through to the other side, he was forced to release his grip on the lance as he was lifted from his saddle, only his feet set firmly in his stirrups stopped him from being unhorsed, the creature fell, taking it's dying breath.

All around him similar skirmishes occurred, dragoon lancers finding their mark but some being unhorsed as they did so, but all the time creatures making it closer to the wall. Nearly every arrow struck a target now but the aim of the guardsmen was more considered and deliberate for fear of hitting the dragoons.

Daskin, freshly ripped from his saddle by the creature that he had killed looked at the creatures running from him and his brothers towards the wall, he looked around for his horse but could not see it, chaos surrounded him. He instinctively drew his sabre and fixed his eyes on a wounded creature staggering away from him and he ran after it, he caught up with it quickly and raised his sword to swing at it, when the top of its head suddenly exploded and its body crumpled before him, He stood and stared dumbfounded for a few heartbeats and then shook his head and ran on to find another target.

He could see a huge melee at the Southern Gate as the remaining creatures, about one hundred of them, scrambled for the top of the wall as Imperial guardsmen loosed arrow after arrow into the swirling mass of black fur from the battlements. He ran towards this fight, frightened but with the words of Curan still in his ear. 'Every dragoon will kill and die for you, and you for them.'

Callan reloaded with a speed and focus that he did not know he possessed; he was amazingly calm now. When Amyeen had left he had been very spooked, every sound and bump he heard had made him jump, thinking that the dragoons were about to kick down the small door and drag him away. But now it was different, an amazing sense of purpose and calm had settled over him. He had killed two outright with single shots and then the wounded one that had been about to be attacked by the Dragoon, he had fired just at the right time to drop the creature.

Then he had seen her as she thundered from the woodland with her sword raised high and took the head from a creature with such speed that its body ran on for another ten paces before collapsing on the blood-soaked ground.

He watched awestruck for a moment realising why the legends of her were so abundant, he now believed everything that he had ever heard. He shook himself from his stupor and picked another target. One of the still mounted dragoons was hacking and slashing at two of them just to give himself some room to manoeuvre his horse, but the poor beast was too terrified to obey his commands and just kept backing up. Callan could see his problem immediately, he could not dismount for he would have to turn his back to them but he could not get the horse to move forward to give himself the room he needed, it continued to back away, snorting and occasionally rearing up and each time it did one of the creatures took a swipe at its unprotected throat. Then one of them dived for the horse and sank its claws and fangs deep into its neck, the horse reared up again and kicked out madly but the creature was pulling him down to the ground, the dragoon had the sense to leap clear as his horse fell and Callan took aim on the other one as it rounded on the now standing dragoon, he fired just as it raised itself to its full frightening height to roar. The ball smashed through the back of its neck and out of its mouth, smashing its vertebrae and just missing the Dragoon's head as it cracked above him. The dragoon, not knowing what had happened but glad that it had, spun around and swung his sabre at the back of the one devouring his horse, cleaving a gaping hole in its ribcage.

As he scanned for more targets he realised that the battle for the plain was nearly over, dead and dying creatures littered the field as well as a few dragoons and their horses but nearly all that were still alive were now at the gate, he could do no more right now as he did not have the angle to fire on them. All he could do was load and try to kill the first one through. And then it happened, he watched in horror as one climbed onto the crenelated battlements and ripped the armoured arm from a startled Imperial, he tried to aim but he was laying at the wrong angle, another creature had managed to get a foothold fifty paces further up, he quickly adjusted his position and re aimed but it was moving too fast. Between the wall and the creature stood six Imperial Guardsmen spread out and they turned and faced it, but it had built up momentum and speed and easily knocked them aside, Two more creatures appeared in the same place and he aimed but fired too quickly, his shot going high, and then there were a dozen on the wall, all running hell bent for the gate, the few Imperials that had been there now slaughtered, a hail of arrows flew down from the Dragoon Mess but most were quickly aimed and did not find their mark.

The creatures now inside the city had one purpose only, to remove the gate and they went at it in a frenzy, the Imperials formed up inside charged as fast as their plate armour would allow and they hacked and slashed at them and the creatures started to fall, but they did not fall fast enough, with the massive strength the Dark Stalkers possessed they smashed the support beams and lifted the crossbar that four men had struggled to put in place and the gate burst open from the other side, creatures and Dragoons tumbled through in a hacking slashing and thrusting mass.

Danyard, pulled his sword from a dying creature and realised that he was inside the city gates, he had been unhorsed but knew that Spike was safe, he had seen one of his bodyguards leading him away and although he would have preferred the man fighting he was grateful for it, the bond between and a mounted soldier and his horse was a strong one. He looked around and stepped back from the fight, pulling his horn from its place on his hip he blew one long note and one by one every Dragoon joined him at the gate and they started to back away. There were about sixty creatures still alive and they seemed to be no longer controlled, their primal urges taking over as most suddenly ran into the city for easier prey, the few Imperials left trying to stop them but not being able to give chase in their heavy armour.

Callan heard Danyard's horn sound and wanted to shout NO! But he knew that he could not. Why were the Dragoons leaving the Imperials to fight alone, when they could not even give chase? And then he looked up at the field from which the creatures had come and he knew why.

The battle horn of Lord Danyard sounded and Curan turned to look, he had just withdrawn his sword from a creature's chest and although exhausted the bloodlust was on him and he did not want to leave the fight, he stared at Danyard and nodded his acquiescence. He had a few small wounds that were starting to sting but it hurt him to his core to turn his back on his brother Imperials and let them fight on alone. But his iron code of discipline was what made him a dragoon and he could not disobey. He noted with pride that Danyard was bleeding and only thirteen of his original sixteen bodyguards still stood, proving that, as always, their commander in chief had been at the forefront of the battle, no soldier could ask more of a leader. With relief, he also saw that young Daskin was still standing and now moving away from the fray, helping a fellow dragoon as he went.

Danyard was about to speak when their attention was drawn to a single dragoon still battling forward in the city. The dragoon had just cleaved clean through a creature's shoulder severing its arm and shoulder and then spun around and leapt to take another's head in a single swipe. Curan stared in fascination as the dragoon landed deftly and scanned for more targets. There was something almost magical about the way he moved, a sort of graceful dance more than a fight, every move perfectly timed and every follow through executed exactly. The only other person he had ever seen fight like that was Danyard himself. He was about to shout out to him when he realised that the creatures that remained had now dispersed throughout the city and no more could be seen. The lone dragoon chased after them and was soon lost to sight in the city streets as they all stared after him.

"My Lord." shouted Curan "MY LORD." Danyard stopped staring and snapped back to the present. "Yes, Curan, what is it?"

"Your orders Sire? Are you okay? Are you wounded; you look pale?"

"Yes, sorry, no I mean, I am not wounded. Back to the holding area, get all the wounded onto the remaining horses and get everyone back to the holding area, we should have spare mounts ready for us."

"Yes, Sire, who is he? I did not recognise him, the Dragoon, who is he?"

"Not he Curan, she."

"But there are no female Dragoons Sire."

"There was one…once."

Danyard was torn, he had given the most specific order of his life, no Dragoon, no matter what, was to enter the city. Yet here she was, at last, the Princess Amyeen, who may already be the rightful ruler, battling the creatures on her own, but he also knew that he was needed at the forefront of this battle. Without him the defence may crumble, not through any skill with a blade that he may possess but just by being there as a guiding light in their hour of darkness. He looked on as she ran for the palace and he smiled, he had been right all along, curse that damn wizard, she would never harm this Kingdom or her sister and now she had proven that, coming back and fighting with her dragoons for her Kingdom.

Amyeen ran after the Dark Stalkers, not really having any plan other than to get to her sister, she had dismounted from Buster as she had approached the gate, knowing the cowardly beast would probably make his way back to the safe house again, she had left the stable door open for that very reason. She ran from the edge of the Dragoon Mess and the shattered gate towards the palace, as she did so she heard an almighty voice boom out to her.

"DRAGOON!" she slid to a halt as Commander Jain and his bodyguard stepped from the rear of the Dragoon Mess. "Why do you abandon your brothers in their hour of need, you have a specific order to stay on the field of battle, not run into the city, no dragoon would ever disobey an order like this in my day."

"You do not command me Imperial." She replied with her sword drawn and the tip of the blade pointing at him, her arm fully extended.

"I command all in a uniform within the city walls, Imperial or Dragoon I have authority over them."

"Not all Commander Jain, not all." As she said this, she let her hair fall from its topknot and across her shoulders. Commander Jain staggered.

"Is that you Princess? Oh, in hells name is that really you?" he said as he sagged to his knees, his sword slipping from his grasp and clattering on the cobbled street as he did.

"Watch out!" she screamed as the creature that had been stalking him suddenly burst from the dark shadows of the building and leapt for him, ripping his head clean from his shoulders and backhanding his bodyguard across the street in one fluid movement. Amyeen ran towards them as the creature started to tear through his amour, quickly clawing through his breastplate and tearing his chest open. Her sword was held high as she approached and she swung down with all her might, at the last moment it felt her presence and raised its foul head to look at her, her sword blade went straight down onto the top of its head and cleaved it straight down the middle. Blood exploded from what remained of its head and sprayed her face which made her retch violently as she spat out the foul taste and wiped it from her.

There was nothing she could do for Jain, the man had no head, but she checked on his bodyguard, he lay on his back breathing but unconscious, she tried to wake him but could not rouse him so she reluctantly left him where he was, hoping he would wake before any more of the vile creatures found him.

She turned towards the Palace and stared at it, she could almost hear her sister calling to her, something was drawing her there, something that at the moment was subtle and weak but she knew would get stronger, now all she had to do was get inside the most fortified building in the kingdom during a war without having to kill anyone.

The remaining sixty or so creatures, now released from their mind control were in a frenzy of bloodlust, the scent of so many humans in one place was driving their senses wild. They ran through the streets battering down doors and savaging the citizens of Kino'le.

Daskin's father, Jaskin, sat at the table that he had made with his own hands and sharpened his broadsword, his wife, mother of Daskin, was lying dead on their bed on the upper floor, terrible wounds upon her, throat slashed open with such force it had damn near taken her head off. They had been with a group of neighbours in the little square that made up the daily market discussing what was happening when the first close howl tore them from their disbelief. The damn Priest of Light assured them that even though the light was gone they would still be protected, that no harm could come to them. He

179

had still wanted to go and fetch his broadsword but had been stayed by Mythra, his wife. That decision had been the last one she had made as it had effectively killed her. She had always followed the beliefs of the Way of the Light. Jaskin was an ex-soldier and had seen things which made him believe that if there was a god, he was a bastard that enjoyed making good people suffer.

The Dark Stalker had leapt from the roof of a house and taken the priests head in a single swipe that had caught Mythra as well, she had staggered back in shock, not really knowing what had happened and had died in his arms. The assembled people had scattered as the creature had dragged the priest's body away and he had fell to his knees with Mythra on his lap and she had died there, bleeding out in the street. Ha had carried her back to their modest house and cleaned her wounds, then slowly and carefully dressed her in her favourite dress and wept and wept and wept.

He had served in the main army during the last invasion and had risen through the ranks quickly, gaining a solid reputation. He had been credited with saving the life of the commanding nobleman during that final battle that had seen the King slain and with the very sword he now lovingly attended. It had cost him two months' salary but he considered it was worth every penny and had saved his life more than once, as well as the life of that stupid nobleman, whose own sword had shattered under an axe blow. He had killed that axeman and taken that axe as a prize, it was behind him on the wall, he had never used it for it was too heavy for him but he prized it anyway.

The proudest moment of his life was when his son Daskin had been presented with his Dragoon Sabre by Lord Danyard himself, his wife had hidden her tears but he had not and they had streamed down his face. After the war caused by the Mar'thak invasion he had been invited to join the dragoons himself but he had a fear of horses that he could not shake and so had been forced to quit the training after only two weeks. He had taken his pension from the army and settled into a life of carpentry which left him conformable but not rich. The riding lessons for young Daskin had nearly broken him but he was determined that his only son would not fail to be a dragoon for the same reason that he had.

He had heard the sounds of battle and he was well aware that his son maybe lying dead on a field, but still he had no regrets. He knew that he was with the lancers and so at the vanguard of any attack, but he also knew he was with the best trained soldiers in the known world with the best equipment money could buy, and a camaraderie that was envied by all other military forces of every nation.

A Dragoon patrol had repelled a border incursion a dozen years ago from one of the breakaway states of Mar'thak, during which a wounded Dragoon had been taken by the fleeing forces. The Dragoon commander had set up camp on the border and sent a rider back to report to Danyard. Danyard had immediately mobilised not only the Dragoons but the entire Army and marched them to the border. They took the High Commissioner for Mar'thak with them and sent him over the border with instructions that if the Dragoon was not returned within three days then he would consider a state of war existed between them and would commence hostilities. Mar'thak at the time had just recovered from the ill-fated invasion. It had taken years for the nation to rebuild its economy and could not even put together an army to face the might and wrath of the Kingdom of Light. The Dragoon was sent across the border within the day and also delivered were the heads of the men who had organised the incursion. All a soldier who risks his life for you wants to know is that you will come for him if he gets into trouble, and it was proved on that day. So, as strange as it sounded, he knew that his sons' best chance of survival was in the thick of that battle.

He had loved Mythra from the first moment that he had set his eyes on her and he had pursued her with a passion that he had not known that he possessed, and even to this day when they lay together it felt like the first time and they teenagers again. He knew that he could not live without her, so he ran the whetstone up the blade of his broadsword and waited for the door that he had carved with his own hands to be broken down and his sword would once again taste the blood of those who would take from him what was his. And he would kill as many of the damned creatures that he could before they killed him.

The five hundred longbowmen of the Kino'le army marched, each carried his massive stave bow, taller than the men who carried them. Each man also carried four fifty arrow quivers, a huge weight alone but they were the strongest men alive anywhere in the known world and they were not going far. Slung on their backs were their war hammers, a personal defence weapon for when they ran out of arrows. Danyard had commissioned the Longbow Regiment after the first year as Lord Protector, it had started with only a dozen men, young boys really, for training for the longbow had to be started not long after puberty or the muscles simply would not develop the incredible strength it took to draw one.

That first dozen had trained their younger brothers who had in turn recruited more until the regiment numbered the five hundred that Danyard wanted. It was a true family regiment, something that not even the dragoons could claim, the oldest man now had his son and one family of cousins numbered close to fifty. Now they marched towards their first real test, it would either make them or destroy them.

Because of the skill it took to use a longbow they were not trained in the finer points of combat, although each man carried a war hammer, a stout pole about the length of a sword which ended in a spike and boasted a hammer head on one side and an axe head on the other. They were not used often but were designed to prize open plate armour. The saying in the main army was that if you ever saw a longbowman with a war hammer in his hand then run away, for we have already lost.

After two years of the regiment reaching the number of five hundred that Danyard had wanted they had not even been sent on a border patrol so some of the nobles had made a formal complaint to Danyard, saying the cost could be better used on their other forces, not this expensive folly of his. Danyard had rejected their arguments for he had once seen the power a large group of longbowmen could wield on a battlefield and he had barely survived himself, something he did not share with them, but he did concede to prove his point to them.

Every year the annual autumn festival would require one hundred cattle to be slaughtered so the entire city could be fed at the expense of the city's guilds. On the preceding day he requested the presence of every nobleman outside the city wall. He ordered the gates locked and barred and spoke to them.

"You have asked for a demonstration of the stopping power of a well-trained longbowman, and this I now give to you." He blew a long note on his battle horn and waited, after a few moments the ground began to tremble the assorted nobility looked at each other nervously, then they heard the actual thundering of hooves and finally, through the early mist that had settled they saw the herd of cattle that was being driven towards them by a company of dragoons. While he could still be heard he shouted.

"If this was a mounted charge what could stop them?" The nobles started to panic and a few ran along the front of the wall trying to find an escape from the rampaging beasts but Danyard stood his ground and calmly blew another long note on his horn. The instant he did the sky darkened as five hundred arrows filled the air from inside the city, a few heartbeats later another five hundred did the same thing. The front line of cattle went down in a mass of bone, beef and arrows, those not killed outright fell and were hit by those charging behind, who in turn were peppered with pace long heavy bodkin headed arrows that smashed and tore their way into flesh and bone. Four more volleys flew and completely wiped out the charging herd. The remaining noblemen stood and stared at the scene of carnage before them, most horrified but also amazed at what they had witnessed. Not a single cow was moving, apart from the odd death twitch.

Danyard stepped forward to the beast lying not twenty paces from him and beckoned the now fraught nobles to him, they gathered around and stared at the massive beast that lay at his feet. It had about two dozen arrows protruding from its carcass but the one that Danyard was interested in was embedded in its head. He tried to pull it out but it would not budge.

"How thick and hard is the skull of cattle, harder than most armour? I think it probably is. If we are ever invaded again each and every one of you will face a mounted charge. Anyone who does not want to be protected by this regiment and face that charge alone then please let me know and I will make sure that the Kingdom does not waste any arrows saving you. And those who tried to run today please have a written explanation on my desk in the training grounds by tomorrow morning at the latest as to your actions in running in the face of an enemy, and then I will decide whether to make your lands forfeit and give command of your own regiments to someone who will not run in the face of an enemy. Good day to you My Lords."

At that same autumn feast he honoured the regiment by feasting with them, although he did admit the beef was a bit tough that year, but never again was the cost of the Longbow Regiment questioned.

And now the regiment marched from the training ground at the head of the main Kino'le army, the unit of five hundred longbowmen followed by the fifteen thousand men of the infantry. The lead longbowmen could see the mounted dragoons in their holding area and stopped fifty paces short of them. Danyard was waiting for them at the rear column, He gave a polite nod to them and they marched forward, the dragoons opening up and allowing them to move through their ranks, a column five deep protected the side view of them that was exposed to the wood line.

Sweat dripped from Morlen's nose as once again the dark shadows rose and closed around the Princess, she closed her eyes and once again threw them back. She staggered from the effort of it and sank to the floor, she had never felt as physically weak as she felt right now, the effort of keeping herself unseen and the Princess alive was draining her.

When she had returned to her cottage, she had healed herself and waited one day before heading straight back to Kino'le. She had taken a small room in a nice inn and spent the days walking the streets of the city, learning her way around, for when the day came that she knew that she would be needed.

She had gone out that afternoon knowing that today was the day so she had dressed in her hooded cloak and made her way with the crowds to the Dragoon Mess. Although she was expecting violence even she had been shocked at the damage done to the Princess, but she had pushed her power into her and restarted her heart when it had stopped and managed to get herself into the Mess with her unseen, and when they had moved her to the Palace strongroom she had simply jumped on the back of the cart and sat there, still unseen.

The Princess hung on now by the slimmest of threads and was only alive because they had moved her into the palace, for the palace walls positively pulsed magic, what was straining Morlen was the effort of channelling that magic, a force that she could harness and control in small amounts, it was like trying to fill a small cup from a waterfall, if she went to close it would overwhelm her, but if she did not get close enough she could not get any.

Suddenly the door flew open and in strode a large brutish man with two Imperial Guardsmen, the bodyguards tensed and hands went to sword hilts but they relaxed when they saw who it was.

"You have what I requested?" asked the Surgeon.

"We do," The two Guardsmen replied as they lay a small piece of cloth upon the table, they unwrapped it to expose two small rib bones.

"And you Master Armourer, you have made what I asked, in pure silver?"

"I have Master Surgeon," he replied and placed eight very fine screws and two pieces of silver plate on the table, next to the bones "And I have my tools if you require them."

"I never thought that the tools that make the instruments of death would one day save a life but it may be so, I thank you, please remain and assist where I need it. I have already reset her collar bone, the small plate will hold these two ribs back in place, the bigger plate will repair the hole in her back and we will have to stretch the skin over it and stitch it in place. I will need you to assist me with the more delicate work"

"Can she survive this?"

"To be honest, she should be dead already, I have seen lesser wounds kill healthy young soldiers, something else is keeping her alive, the power that lights the Kingdom perhaps, I do not know, but I do know we have nothing to lose, she will die if we do not, and we need to do this quickly, so we can close her up and leave her body to start healing itself. Are you with me Master Armourer?"

"Of course, I bloody well am man." He replied.

Amyeen ran towards the castle wall, from all around her came the screams of citizens as the remaining Dark Stalkers unleashed their furious bloodlust upon them. She had to get to the palace, some unseen force was drawing her toward her sister, even though her instincts were screaming at her to turn around to the streets and hunt down as many of the creatures as she could. She rounded a corner at a run and slipped on the wet cobblestones of the market square that fronted the castle wall and gate, the palace keep was within that wall. She could see Imperial Guardsmen manning the wall.

Although she could see them, she was confident that they could not see her, her chainmail was oil blued and dull, virtually black in colour, and the remainder of her clothing had been designed to not reflect light. Because of the light of Kino'le there were no wall sconces for street lighting and the only light came from the battlement's torches and windows with the drapes not drawn. All that could give her away was movement, and although she knew they would not leave their post to investigate her they might be reporting to Lorgane, for that reason alone she had to avoid them. But she was not worried, she knew the castle and the palace within like the back of her hand, she knew all the secret entrances for she had used them on her outings with Danyard many times, she even had a key on her for the one she would use tonight. There was a secret entrance that Danyard had had built into the barracks on the east side, and also knowing that every able-bodied man would be mobilised she knew the barracks would be empty, she turned west and stealthily headed for the barracks.

Kino'le city was built high on a cliff face so its outer wall did not actually encircle it, it just ran around the front. The barren cliff face was five hundred paces high and had never yet been scaled, the cliff face itself rarely catching sunlight so moss and lichen grew in abundance and ensured the rocks were always wet and slippery. The palace looked out over its northern side with a view of that wild sea and the castle spreading out around on its east, west and southern side. Danyard had loved this from the first moment he had set eyes upon it, knowing that they could never be attacked from the sea directly, all trade going through the port of Kardon, which all the previous Kings had built up from a little fishing hamlet during their reigns, all having the same thoughts of protection from sea invasion. Keeping the seat of power away from the ease of approach that was offered by the sea.

Twenty-Two
The Coastal Patrol

Captain Samuels of the coastal patrol rode like the wind with his six atrops, he had been told some very disturbing things from travellers on the coast road, a harbour, made in a few hours from a grounded ship, men and horses by the thousand being unloaded and marching in the direction of the city, ships by the dozen unloading quickly and then heading away again. He still could not bring himself to believe it but too many had said the same thing as they hurried away, he knew that this could mean only one thing, they had been invaded and by the sound of it his patrol were now located behind the invading forces. He could not attack an entire army but he could certainly disrupt their supply chain.

It had been dark for an hour or so when and he was worried that he may not see the harbour, for he did not know its exact location, but then they rounded a headland and his heart leapt, for in front of him were two huge fires, about one hundred paces apart. Markers, he thought to himself, to guide the ships in, he smiled. He was always happy when an enemy helped him like this.

From the light created by the blazes, he could see men milling about and another ship on approach, the harbour itself was an impressive thing, looked like it had been there for years, as he watched from the high ground a ship came closer and then ropes were thrown and men on the dock pulled her in. Despite himself he was very impressed, a very smooth and efficient operation, as soon as the ship touched the walkway men streamed off and formed up on the beach, officers shouting orders and the men forming up in groups of fifty, when four groups of fifty were ready they all marched off together. He moved back from the headland by thirty or so paces and spoke with his waiting atrop commanders, who had all seen what he had seen.

"It's time we pissed on someone's bonfire." he told them.

Jaskin heard them outside and knew the time had come, he had his sword ready on his hip and waited on the inside of his door. He looked around his modest house, the ground floor bedroom where young Daskin had been born and where he had grown to the man he had become. A tear flowed down his face as he remembered how they had spent hours just staring at his little pink face in awe and wonder. If his son was lying dead on a field then it was these fucking creatures that had caused it, and his anger rose as he heard them sniffing outside and scratching around the mighty oak door. It suddenly shuddered as one of them threw himself against it, he drew his broadsword and waited for his time to strike, one furry talon appeared through the door jamb as its immense weight pushed against it and he gulped and waited, the talon worked its way in forcing the door to bend as its wrist and forearm appeared, he leapt at the door and swung his mighty blade down, cleaving the wrist from the rest of the arm and then putting all his weight against the door, trapping its arm as its dark foul blood gushed from the stump. He did not know how much intelligence the creatures possessed but he did not want to let it escape and somehow stem the bleeding.

The creature howled and writhed on the other side of the door but he could not let it escape, every ounce of strength he had he put into trapping that bleeding stump, its blood was streaming down his side of the door, it was all over him and smelled like nothing he had ever known, but he kept the pressure on the door. Eventually the blood flow slowed and so did the pressure against the door and an almost pitiful whimpering started from the other side, he listened but felt no sympathy. He heard and felt the creature slide down the outside of the door and he stepped away. Every inch of his clothing was covered by the dark and stinking blood, he tried to wipe it away from his face but it made little difference. He was suddenly gripped by a rage beyond anything that he had ever known, almost to the point that he had no control over his actions, he threw the deadbolt open, grabbed the door handle and stepped into the street dripping the dark foul blood onto the wet cobbles of the street. He stared down at the near lifeless creature that was now missing one claw and without thinking thrust his sword into its guts, then wrenched the blade across the width of its abdomen, smiling like a madman as steaming entrails slopped onto the ground. He withdrew the blade and looked down his street, another two were trying to rip open the door of one of his neighbours. They stopped what they were doing and turned to face him.

Two of the guild masters of the Kingdom of Light, the Master Surgeon and Master Armourer, a very unusual pairing, were physically and mentally exhausted. It had taken less than an hour to do what they had to do but for the pair of them it had been the longest and most difficult hour of their lives. Three times during the operation the Princess had stopped breathing and the pair of them, had, on all three occasions, also stopped breathing. And each time after a few seconds, she would suddenly take a huge gasping breath and start to breathe again. They both agreed that it was almost as if someone was forcing air into her lungs. As the surgeon was making the last of his stitches on her back, sewing the armourers sliver plate into place he looked up into the face of a beautiful but exhausted young woman in a hooded cloak, she spoke.

"You have done well Master Surgeon, and I have done all I can as well, you just now rest and leave her to her fate, whatever will be will be, for many more will need your skills this day." He blinked and shook his head and she was no longer there, he looked around but no one else seemed to have noticed anything else amiss.

"What did you say Surgeon?" asked the armourer.

"Errr, nothing" he replied "But I think I need to rest, I will be needed later and I am seeing things."

Morlen looked back at the room as she slipped out behind a servant and smiled as the shadows that preceded the Grim Reaper gradually released their grip on the Princess. Right, she thought to herself, now go and find out what has happened to the other Princess. She knew where the safehouse was for she had followed Amyeen and Callan there a few days ago, unbeknown to them, she just had to get there without being seen and attacked by a Dark Stalker.

Although being as stealthy as she could be, she could not bring herself to draw her sword, if she was challenged then she would have to bluff her way through, she could not fight Kino'le soldiers, effectively her own soldiers, as her sister lay dying. She was moving through the barracks and as she expected they were empty, even those not fit for combat would have a role somewhere, helping the surgeons or even just fetching and carrying.

She had started to lose her stealth as the unseen force continued to grow stronger the nearer that she got to her sister, it seemed to want to drive her headlong and increasingly she could not resist it. The other thing she felt was the occasional twinge from Blood, her left arm hurt and she could feel his pain as sharp as he did, as well as his hunger, the pain of hunger that only a vampire bat could feel, or a human bonded with a vampire bat. The hunger pains seemed to come in waves and then one hit her suddenly that was so strong she fell to her knees, and was momentarily breathless. She forced herself up and further on and was about to pass from the barracks into the palace proper when a pain in her left arm exploded and she stumbled to the floor again. She suddenly felt light as if being lifted and it suddenly became clear, somebody was in her safehouse and they had found Blood.

Morlen made it to Amyeen's safehouse and rushed about to find Blood, anytime she pictured Amyeen she could feel her getting weaker and weaker, Blood's hunger was all consuming, no other thought entered either conscience. The link between her and Amyeen was becoming less frequent and weaker as the bond with blood started to take total control. But Morlen could feel someone was with her and that someone meant her harm, she had to hurry.

Where would a vampire bat be housed, somewhere dark, but secure, strongroom, where she kept her weapons, and the money she spent on the best weapons would mean it would be a secure room in the house, probably hidden. She rushed outside on a whim, looked at the house's outer wall and then started to pace it out, then rushed back inside and did the same. Sure enough, there was a two pace difference between the outside wall and the inner main wall, wood panelling covered the inside, again one more thing that most home owners could not afford, but Morlen had an idea that this was there for a reason. She picked up the lamp that she had lit when she had first arrived and moved it over the wall, looking for some kind of hidden switch, her finger brushed a knot in the wood and she brought the light to bear, she pushed her finger into the knot and there was an almost imperceptible click, and the door swung open on silent hinges, to reveal the strongroom beyond. Her lamp shone against the gleaming blades that adorned the walls but she had no interest in them, she looked at the single table and her eyes settled on a small structure that looked like a miniature hound kennel, the bat house. She quickly removed the roof of the house and looked down on Blood, his wing expertly splinted but hanging uselessly at his side; he looked up as he scented her and bared his fangs, his intention obvious.

"Oh no you don't, you crafty little bastard," she said as she covered him in a black cotton cloth she saw also on the table and scooped him up, as gently as she could.

"But I do know of a horse that will not object," she headed for the stable.

Jaskin was beyond fear, the rage was on him and he stared at the Dark Stalkers with pure hatred. They seemed unsure, small almost imperceptible sounds went between them and for the first time he knew what they were feeling, fear. Here was a puny human standing over the body of one of their own and covered in its blood, and it was not screaming and running away like all the others had. One of the creatures cocked his head in a confused way and looked at the other one, which was all the distraction that Jaskin needed, he raised his sword and flung himself at the creature like a rabid dog, bringing the blade down through its left shoulder, the creature screamed and tried to back away but was stopped by the wall behind it, Jaskin withdrew the sword and struck again in the exact same place once again putting every ounce of strength he could muster into the sword strike, this time the blade cleaved clean through its collar bone, shoulder blade and six of its ribs before becoming stuck in its chest cavity. He released his hold on the sword and staggered back as a sudden weariness took him and he looked around for the other creature, expecting a huge talon to take his head at any moment, but the other creature had decided that this particular puny human was not worth the trouble and had vanished up the street in search of easier prey.

He leant against the wall to recover some energy and get his thoughts together, he waited there a moment and then pushed himself away, his energy levels returned and a feeling of euphoria washed over him. He had expected to die horribly but he had not, he had triumphed over the creatures that he had been told could not be beaten. He was suddenly struck by a huge sense of duty, he had killed two of them, two! He could raise his own militia, him and his neighbours could take to the streets and hunt the fuckers down. He strode over to the one that still had his sword embedded in it, he put his foot on its body and pulled his sword from the hideous wound. Then he rapped the pommel of his broadsword against the door of his neighbour.

Amyeen stared at the figure before her, even though bleary eyes she could see who it was, it could only be one man, that cursed wizard Lorgane. She was on her knees and still felt pain and weakness in her left arm and a complete lack of strength all over. She knew this was her own fault, she had let Blood feed on her which made the bond an almost physical thing. She had only done this once before and had felt his sensations keenly for weeks after, his constant hunger, his need to be in darkness and his instinct for hunting fresh blood that overwhelmed all other senses. Now he was in a wounded and vulnerable state and instead of being a weaker bond it was a stronger one as he drew on her strength to help heal him. She hadn't left him that long ago but already he needed to feed again, to give him the energy to fight his wounds, it was like a living writhing thing inside her, constantly causing pain and waves of dizziness, and now, on her knees and weaker than she had ever been, she faced her mortal enemy.

She tried to bring her rage to bear, that had always worked but it weakened her more as pain shot through her head as her own blood pumped harder around her brain. She grabbed for her sword and tried to draw it but before she could he was there in front of her, and he kicked her over onto her back, smacking her head on the hard floor as she went over. He approached without a care in the world, and put his foot on her throat, and from his standing position, spat down into her face.

"So, my little dark souled friend," Stated the wizard Lorgane at the helpless form of the Princess beneath his boot. "It has been a long time, and you have been having some adventures, I always told Danyard that you would return and take the Kingdom for yourself, he never did believe me, except for that one time, but then I did poison him to make him more…amenable to my suggestions. I did also fail to mention the fact that you would inherit the Kingdom because your beloved sister would be dead, again at my instigation, but you know that too by now don't you."

Amyeen looked up through tear stained eyes at Lorgane and felt the hate flowing between them, it was an almost physical thing now, something strong inside her that was growing bigger and bigger, but still nothing compared for her hunger for blood, fresh, dark, bitter and lifegiving blood. She no longer had the strength to fight both the wizard and her hunger so she gave herself to the hunger, slowly releasing her consciousness to the vampire bat lying broken in her safehouse.

Although the pain of hunger was still there she no longer fought it, she closed her eyes and saw the heat emanating from the foul wizard, she slowed her breathing and could almost see his life blood pumping around his body, feeling the veins and arteries flowing with life, faster and faster it went as he became more excited, she knew he was still talking to her but she could not hear the words, only the torrent of dark red oxygenated life coursing through him. Her own heart no longer pumped hard as an overwhelming calm took her. She released her hands from the sole of his boot where she had been struggling to keep the pressure from her throat and her entire body went limp, and her left hand slowly went to her boot, searching and grappling, and then it flashed up towards Lorgane's groin.

Lorgane, Court Wizard to the Kingdom of Light, was still ranting at his captive when he suddenly jerked as if stung, he felt only a small amount of pain and was not sure what had happened but when he looked down the Princess Amyeen was suddenly covered in blood, he looked down at her confused for a few heartbeats and then he felt his strength leave him as the realisation hit him…he stared with growing comprehension at the small black bladed boot knife still grasped in her hand and he suddenly knew fear like he had never known before. In all his visions he had not seen this, all the deaths he had seen for himself did not include this one. She had reached up and slashed his femoral artery, and even if he was on the table of the best surgeon in the land he would still bleed to death. He had seen many people die in his time, but even he could not believe the rate at which his blood was pumping from him. With even more insight he suddenly knew what was happening to her, she lay at his feet still but now she was licking her fingers as a child would after a sweet pudding.

She suddenly found an immense strength and she stood, pushing Lorgane backwards as she did, he shot backwards and hit the wall, he tried to remain on his feet but his balance was completely gone and he slid down. She threw herself at him like a rabid wolf and an inhuman growl came from deep within her. He was dragged from his sitting position to his back and watched in absolute terror as her face neared his, her already dark eyes had an evil red tinge to them and thick saliva oozed from her open mouth and he thought she was going to rip his throat out, but she did not, she lowered her head to his groin and pulling his legs open she bit down on the wound her boot knife had made, ripping the soft flesh of his inner thighs and gorging on what was left to pump out of his now torn and shredded artery. He screamed like no human ever should do as she sucked with all her force at the now gaping wound in his leg.

Morlen, who was afraid of what she might see or feel did not want to do it but she knew she had no choice, she had to know if Amyeen lived. The bat had drunk deep from the horse and looked better for it but she knew she had to fix his wing or stay with him for the foreseeable future, but to do so she would have to join with him, and she did not want to. She gently lifted him from his rear end and ran her index finger up in the underside of his body to his head, gently trying to prize away his fangs from the horse's rump, he resisted but was in no state to fight her off. She took him in both hands and gently folded his wings in, cradling him, slowly closing her eyes as she did. The coppery taste of blood hit her throat hard and she retched violently, struggling to keep a firm hold of him at the same time as he struggled against her.

The vision of Amyeen hit her harder than the taste of blood had and she reeled away back into the wall, she saw Lorgane's near lifeless body slumped on the floor, she felt every slurp and gurgle from Amyeen as each mouthful went down her throat, getting less and less each time but the rage within her friend was what frightened her most, almost beyond human at that moment, dark, savage and primal urges possessed her and she knew she must stop her before she could not bring her back. STOP PRINCESS, YOU MUST STOP NOW… CALM YOURSELF, YOU ARE SAFE NOW, STOP… STOP… STOP…she pulsed over and over again, all the time holding back the rising bile as she felt every drop of blood that Amyeen consumed.

Captain Samuels watched as the last group of infantry marched away and he studied the dark horizon, trying to block the light from the fires from his vision as he did so. There was one ship out there and he estimated he had about an hour. The dock workers, as he suspected, when not being watched by military officers and noblemen on fine horses reverted to type and stood around one of the fires telling tall tales of past derring do, while they waited for the next ship.

The Harbour Master, he noted was exactly that, a balding fat man with a huge voice, more used to taking bribes than commanding men in enemy territory. He had put out no sentries, and in fact had no security whatsoever, even the cooks from the food tents had come and joined the men at the fire, all standing round it and letting the bright light ruin their night vision. Samuels almost felt sorry for what he was about to do but then he thought to himself, fuck them, they are invaders, not guests.

Every one of his forty-seven dragoons had his war bow in his hand and strung, an arrow nocked, and as they silently approached each man pulled back on the string, each dragoon marking a different man, he pulled back his own string and took aim on the bulging neck of the harbour master. He loosed his arrow and let his breath out into his whistle as he did so, instantly all the other arrows were also loosed. Samuels lowered his head as a pitiful few handful of screams were heard and the handful of men who had not been aimed at stood in a sudden daze from wherever they had been sitting and froze, not knowing whether to run or hide. Every dragoon had already re nocked and drawn their bows and he shouted to the remaining men.

"Stay where you are and drop any weapon you carry. Step into the light close to the fire and you will live, try to run and you will die!" One man made a foolish attempt to scramble away and four arrows struck him within a heartbeat, no one else moved.

"Now, who is in command here, or at very least, will speak for you all?"

Something nagged at Amyeen, something beyond her consciousness, she knew what she was doing but could not seem to stop herself, like she was in a trance, but something was pushing her out of it. She felt the life force finally leaving the vile wizard and then suddenly her own consciousness kicked in and she threw herself back from him, scooting on her backside along the bloody floor until she struck the opposite wall. She looked around in horror at the carnage before her.

Her face was covered in blood, she could feel it dripping from her lips and running down her neck, finding its way into her under garments and making her shudder. The floor was covered in Lorgane's blood, which had at first sprayed out from his femoral artery and continued after as she had not been able to swallow it fast enough, puddles adorned the floor and splashes of it slipped from the walls. Her own clothing was sticky with it, her blackened mail had glops of blood dripping from it and her leather leggings had soaked through to her skin.

She looked at Lorgane, and saw with disbelief the slight rise and fall of his chest, how could he still be alive for fucks sake! She knew she had to finish him, he was far too dangerous to leave alive, she had to be sure. But before she did she had to get one thing out of her system, quite literally. She crawled to the latrine room at the far end at vomited like her life depended on it. She vomited for what seemed like hours, her head thumped with the force of it and she thought she would pass out from the pain of it but she did not stop. What seemed like gallons of blood came from within her in a constant stream, the taste of it and the thought of what she had done pushing her to vomit more and more, and yet more and more came forth. Finally, when she though she may actually pass out she tasted stomach bile and knew she had finally purged herself. What kind of shit situation are you in when you look forward to the taste of stomach bile, she thought to herself as she finally collapsed exhausted to the floor.

She rested and then stood and walked to the wash station, she washed her face and ran water through her matted hair and scrubbed the blood from it and rinsed her mouth a dozen times. Then she walked to where he lay, still breathing, something else is keeping him alive she thought, he can't have hardly any fucking blood left. She looked down at him, pale, sweating and delirious, she had thought she may have felt some pity but she did not, she reached behind her for her kukri and pulled it from its sheath.

"Whoever or whatever is keeping you alive, survive this you fucker." she said as she swung the heavy blade down into his throat, it sank half way down with that one stroke and she pushed it further until she felt it crunch through his spine and sever his head from his body, just to be sure she picked his head up by the hair and threw it across the room. She turned and walked from the barrack dorm, knowing that no life force emanated from him now, as if she was still seeing through the eyes of Blood. One more final thought struck her, what the fuck have I done to myself, I may have gone too far with Blood.

"My name is Captain Samuels and I command this coastal patrol." Samuels stated to the shocked looking man in front of him. "What is your name and what is your role here?"

"Westa, Sire, I ain't no soldier though, just a common sailor, got tasked with helping with the harbour and the ships, I am the senior man left alive. So, I suppose, I'll be speaking for the men." He looked over at the half dozen men sat in a circle near the fire, guarded by four dragoons. "I guide 'em in and help tie em up, tell the soldiers where to form up."

"That is all very well, I have no desire for any more bloodshed, but neither do I have the time and luxury of a long cosy chat. There is a ship out there and it will be here very soon, I need to know what is on it. Now you have a choice, you can be a dead hero and join the rest of the dead heroes in that pile of dead heroes over there or you can tell me what is on that ship."

"Collaborating with an enemy carries a sentence of death in Branvere Sire."

"Unfortunately, for you and your men, right now, so does not collaborating. So, do we have an understanding, die today, or do not die today. But remember, Branvere may not win, strange things happen in war and fortunes turn quickly, and if Branvere loses the Lord Danyard will pardon you and your men for any war crimes and allow you citizenship, but only if someone like me speaks for you."

"Will he really Sire; how do I know that you speak the truth?"

"Because I am the son of a Mar'thakian traitor, not only a Dragoon, but a Captain of Dragoons. My father did not like what he was expected to do in the last invasion, the murder of children, the rape of women, so he deserted and handed himself into the next patrol he came across. He always said that despite being branded traitor he never was never ashamed of what he did, but he would have been ashamed of some of the things he may have been forced to do serving the army of Mar'thak. He was questioned by Danyard himself and what he told him allowed him to plan the final battle that forced them from the field. Lord Danyard is fiercely loyal to those who are loyal to him."

"Infantry Sire, foot soldiers. All the cavalry are now here, it'll be another two hundred soldiers, maybe with one nobleman and his horse and a pack mule, not even sure your good archers can fight that many off, once they are off the bloody boat they'll be on you like rabid dogs."

"Then we will have to make sure that they do not get of the bloody boat won't we. You must have plenty of oil here for the cooks and the marker fires."

"Oh yes Sire, got barrels of bloody oil sire."

"Good."

General Carmak watched as best he could from the small hillock, he had his spyglass from his trunk that had been brought by the first supply wagon, it was one of his most precious possessions and he treasured it. It had cost him more than his sword but he still swore that it had saved his life more than his sword, allowing him to plan better than the other officers of Branvere could. Despite the advantage it gave him he still did not know what was happening inside the city and it frustrated him. He had been tempted to commit his horsemen to follow the creatures inside but then he would have had to have the infantry follow them, therefore committing his entire forces to the battle quicker than he was prepared to do. And although, he was convinced of his victory, he still had his old soldiers caution that meant he wanted as many soldiers as possible to commit as he could. He waited for the rider from Toker's unit, which had managed, unseen, to get themselves into the woods facing the southern gate. The man drew his mount up close to his and spoke in a low tone.

"General," he spoke "Word from my Lord Toker, the main gate is down, the creatures are causing havoc in the city, from our place in the woodland we can hear their screams as they do their dark deed. The Imperial Guard still man the walls and are trying to erect some kind of temporary gate. Some of them have taken to the streets to hunt down the creatures but at least two hundred man that wall and seem to have an unlimited supply of arrows, we can see barrels and barrels of them on the wall. Get within one hundred paces of that wall and it will be an arrow storm. Even after it is overrun, they can fall back to the Dragoon Mess that seems to have some kind of metal shutter with arrows slits now instead of windows. The Dragoons have reformed and have placed themselves down the flanks of the main Kino'le army, which does not make sense to myself or Lord Toker. Unless they have something to hide at the front of the army, something that would be hidden from the flanks by the height of a man on a horse. The other side is against the wall so no need to hide anything, we cannot see there."

"When the dragoons arrived did you not see what was in the fore of it?"

"We did not arrive in time Sire, snow and rough close packed woodland, we could not risk a horse, or many horses going lame. As far as we can see they have no horse drawn wagon at the fore, so no horse drawn catapult or scorpion type weapon."

"What does Toker think? Or yourself for that matter, I have not seen you before, what is your name and why do I not know you as Toker seems to trust you as he obviously does."

"Chamley Sire, field commission, there seems to be a lot of it about at the moment, if you want my opinion, but Lord Toker disagrees with me on this, I reckon there are archers at the front of that formation, and not normal archers, Longbowmen. The only weapon that would be of any use to them at the range and power they would need to stop a charge by our heavy horse, and you simply cannot disguise a longbowman as a normal infantryman. The stave of the bow is at least the height of a man, it simply cannot be hidden and then used at speed, unless you hid it behind ranks of horsemen."

"Very well thought out, although you are an impertinent fucker, why does Toker disagree?"

"He says we would have known about it, Kino'le training foot archers, our spies would have told us, and they have never used foot archers before, famous for their mounted archers. Wrote the damn scroll on that, routed Mar'thak with the clever use of horse mounted archers, but foot soldiers as archers, they have never used them and do not send them on patrol with their army, why would they not? Unless they wanted as few people as possible to know about them. That is Lord Toker's opinion Sire."

"You both make a valid argument; you still think they have archers, longbow archers, there?"

"I think it would be safe to hope for the best but plan for the worst Sire?"

"I like the way you think Chamley, now return to your master and if you get even a glimpse of what they hide, I want to know immediately."

"Yes Sire."

Twenty-Three
The Militia

Jaskin stood with his friends and neighbours, about three dozen of them. Most of which had served at one time with the army and a few ex dragoons who had decided to not become Imperials, those few stood in their Dragoon Light Armour and had their cavalry sabres at their waists. There were even a pair of brothers who had recently retired from the Dragoon Mounted Archers and stood with their war bows to hand and a quiver stuffed with arrows. He had recruited these two first. They stood around him in disbelieving awe as he explained to them how he had killed two of these supposedly unstoppable creatures while their dark foul blood still dripped from him and the blade of his broadsword. He continued.

"And now, I say to you, where do you think you are safest, barricaded behind your doors waiting to be ripped asunder as you try to run as individuals, or our here with the rest of your friends, where we can take the fight to these fucking evil bastard creatures. Kane brothers, you are both renowned for your skill at archery, and you both have your bows to hand and I have seen the power you can put into an arrow, I will need you both at the fore, slow the fuckers down for us to finish, are you with me?"

"Aye, we are." they replied.

"Good, let us go hunt some evil."

Commander Damerall paced around and said a silent prayer as the mighty winch wound back the coiled ropes. Her crew of winch men straining their massive muscles as they wound back Trebuchet South, the ratchet giving a loud click every quarter turn as the cog found its seat. Despite their size and macho nature each man was looking as scared as she, for they knew if the rope snapped under this much pressure it had the power to rip a man in half. The only

200

safe place was in the trigger seat as the master carpenter had built it into a safety cage, protected by thick cut timber designed to protect the one who released the trigger. No one spoke or interrupted her, for although she was known as a good and caring commander, when it came to her babies, the trebuchets, she was single minded and did not tolerate any nonsense.

The Master Carpenter and Master Smith were also in attendance and they looked on in a frightened way, cringing at every creak that emanated from the wood or rusty looking ironwork. The basket was loaded and in place, filled with about fifty rocks that were about a pace across. The basket crews were standing now at a safe distance, each watching and praying that nothing broke, for all their sakes.

Trebuchet Commander was an unusual job for a woman, but she was the daughter of the original Master Engineer who designed and built them. When she was a small girl, she had gone to work with him most days and played in his workshop. In the moments when she had grown bored of playing, she would look at his drawings and ask questions and he would explain the principles behind them and the forces at play that allowed them to sling a load many times the weight of the actual machine through the air with such power. He had encouraged her to draw her own plans as she grew and to explain why she thought each part would behave like it did and if it did not work what she would do to rectify it. After many years she had become the Kingdom's leading authority on large projectile weapons and she studied with the Armourers and the Engineers Guild.

No one alive had a better intimate working knowledge of the Kingdom's Trebuchets, not even her father who passed away just before her eighteenth birthday, the day that Danyard appointed her Commander Trebuchet, the title previously held by her father. She was in overall command of the machines here and at Kardon, and although she regularly got to use the smaller machines at the port city, she had never used the ones in Kino'le, for they were being left to rot, or so Danyard had let the world believe.

The massive machines were covered by oiled tarpaulins and left to the elements, but, once a month the tarpaulins came off and secret inspections by the three of them, Masters Carpenter, Smith and Trebuchet, took place. She spent the bulk of her time at Kardon, supervising the maintenance and repair of the trebuchets that protected the harbour and training the crews, her and the Kingdom were lucky that she had been in Kino'le City for monthly secret inspections just as the invasion had occurred. There were four machines, East and North, still under canvas for they sat at the other end of the city, and South and West, which faced where the enemy would approach from.

She watched on as her crews wound them to capacity and then she counted out one hundred as the machine sat at maximum pressure, creaks and moans coming from the ancient timbers and strained ropes, the two Masters walking around studying various places under the light of a torch before moving away. Then she gave the order to release the pressure slowly and under control.

"You are happy Masters, both of you?"

"Yes, we are," both replied at once "As happy as we can be after these weapons standing idle for so long."

"Good, I have left orders for her to remain loaded but not under strain, it should not take long for her to be wound up again if she is required, now let us get to West and do the same, and then, when we are completely happy they will not disintegrate in the heat of battle, I will brief the crews."

Captain Jonoak stood on the rolling deck of the ship and fought to hold down the vomit that kept promising to rise. He was new to his command of two hundred infantry that he was to supervise to march on Kino'le and being a young man of noble birth, he had much to prove. The first and most pressing at that exact moment was to prove he could make the entire journey without being seasick, something which was becoming increasingly difficult the closer they got to landfall. His feet were placed apart as he stood at the prow but the rolling and pitching deck was doing its best to throw him from his feet. He was twenty-one and the son of a Duke, his father owned a harbour town which he would one day inherit, but first he had to survive his eight-year tenure in the Branvere military, of which, so far, only six long slow months had passed. His days in the officers' mess were a joy, where, because of his noble birth, he enjoyed the finest that the mess could provide, the envy of the poorer officers who came up through the ranks or even the lower nobles whose peasants scratched a living in the poor soil of Branvere. The ports, even small ones, being where the money was abundant.

But the days he spent in the field with his men annoyed him, living in a field, sometimes with nothing but a rough horse blanket to cover him drove him mad. Half the time he was also expected to march on foot like a common soldier, and not just that but to have to lead the men from the front, the indignity of it! All the pointless mock battles and running around in armour, it was very draining. He wanted to get this damn mission over and done with, get these men into battle and maybe even win the Kings favour.

He could see the ship's Captain and Helmsman, when he looked back, the Captain had the wheel at that time and they were both laughing at him, he was sure the man was steering into the biggest waves deliberately, the bastards probably had a bet on whether they could get him to lose his lunch or his footing. One day, he thought to himself, you will bring this cursed ship into my harbour and I will burn it and you to bloody ashes.

He had just let go of the handrail when shouts started all around the ship, the ship slowed as sails were furled and men shouted out the depth from each side of the ship and they made the turn towards the massive floating harbour. The signal fires were huge and threw light on the beach and jetty, men walked about and waited for the ship to dock, he was looking forward to getting some stable ground underneath his feet and a decent hot meal inside him.

All his men were collecting weapons and strapping on armour, he was lucky enough to be allowed a pack horse for his own armour, for he did not intend the wear the bloody stuff all the way to the city, it was full plate and weighed for too much for him to wear constantly. As a noble he was expected to stand out from his men, who, if they were lucky, had only chainmail over a jerkin with the odd piece of armour they may have scavenged from a body in a previous battle, and they had to wear it wherever they went so very few possessed even a single piece of plate armour, it just being too damn heavy to carry.

At last the ship approached the jetty and he saw six men standing along it at regular intervals, each man had a small barrel at his feet, odd, he thought. Maybe they will be giving us a tot of rum as we disembark, he thought with a smile.

As the commander of the infantry it was his privilege to be first down the gangplank, an opportunity that he fully intended to exploit and get off the cursed vessel. As the Captain shouted for the remaining sails to be furled, he felt the shudder as the mighty vessel ran along the jetty and he watched in confusion as the six men on the jetty suddenly threw their barrels in a high arc onto the ships deck. The barrels shattered on impact and what he had assumed was rum, but was actually oil, splashed all over the wooden deck. He looked back to the men on the dock but they were running hell bent for the beach and a sudden feeling of dread enveloped him. The Captain, always on the lookout for anything that could harm his precious ship, was way ahead of him and was screaming for his sailors to push off but they all knew it was too late as dozens of fire arrows were launched from the shore and started their deadly arc high into the sky but where they would soon rain down onto the oil soaked ship. He turned to run but to where, everywhere he stepped he slipped on oil-soaked wood, he looked at the jetty but it was already aflame, and then he saw the shallow trench they had dug from the beach and had filled with oil. Jonoak looked up in horror as the arrows began their slow arc down towards the ship, the first one hit the deck and it exploded into flame, instinct took over as everyman aboard thought the same thing, fuck King, fuck country, this one's for me, and they dived over the side of the burning ship and away from the flaming harbour.

Master at Arms Shapley of Branvere held his breath, as the palace guard walked past his hiding place, he was hidden in a small alcove in the main kitchens of the Palace. Having followed detailed instructions his eighteen men and he had been met by the Wizard Lorgane and they had been delivered to the kitchens by a subterranean passage that had completely lost and confused him and his men. The passage had been in an absolute dark that he had not believed could exist, not that it had slowed the damn wizard, who had constantly hissed at them as they stumbled after him in the blackness. At last they had come to the kitchens and he had placed them behind a heavy curtain in a back storeroom, as uncomfortable as they were jammed in together at least they had some ambient light.

"Only kill if you are discovered." Lorgane had told them numerous times. "Danyard has many plans for scenarios of war and most of them, in fact all of them, include regular searches of the palace and its grounds. The man who had killed the Queen during the invasion by Mar'thak had hidden in the palace for half a day, and Danyard never forgot that, if you kill anybody they will be missed and more will come looking for them."

"We are aware of that Wizard." He had replied "When the time is right, we will seek out and destroy Victarny if she still lives and then slaughter the household staff, we will be ready when the battle is fully joined."

"And remember to use the kitchen walkways, not the main corridors, you will only be able to go single file as they are narrow and only used to get food around the building quickly but they have short cuts to most rooms and are a handy rat run, and what works for and against you works for and against the patrols too, they will only be able to patrol them in single file, so they do them only intermittently."

"How many to a patrol?"

"Four, Danyard only does things in four or eight, did you study nothing of the intelligence I sent you?"

"Four could be a problem in single file, we would only be able to get the first two, the others could raise the alarm."

"Then be really fucking careful that you are not seen. One other thing, I want the Lady Sarah taken alive, bring her to me when you have her, she and Danyard have just started a relationship, I may need a bargaining chip if things go awry."

"And how will we know the Lady Sarah?"

"She is plump, very large breasts, and likely to be near to the Princess, are you sure you can take out the Royal Bodyguards?"

"I am a damn Master at Arms, are the Royal Bodyguards?"

"No, but they are personally selected and trained by Danyard, and despite the fact that I wish to see his body bent and broken in front of me I cannot take from him that he is an almost magical warrior."

"They are just men, made of blood and bone; they will bleed and die like all men do."

"Very well then, I must go now, I have an appointment to keep, someone very important is coming to see me."

That had been an hour before and now he knew, his time was coming, he looked at his handpicked men and gave the signal to follow, he silently moved the curtain aside and stepped into the kitchen proper. He unfolded the map Lorgane had given him and moved towards the first door that led to the narrow kitchen passageways.

For the many things that Jonoak cursed his father for, his insistence that his children learned to swim was not one of them, for that was the reason he was still breathing, albeit hard and fast as he lay upon his back trying to get his breath back. He had gone over the side of the ship with the rest of the men, but owing to his noble blood he had not been in his armour when he had, and so therefore had not been dragged to the bottom by the weight of it. Even a mail surcoat in water would make it virtually impossible to swim, and that was for the few who could swim, most soldiers thought it was a skill they did not need and so wasted no time on it, even a lot of the sailors he knew thought it better to drown quickly than spend hours trying to swim only to drown later. But swim Jonoak could and he had done so, and for his life, as fast and far as he could. Under the keel of the ship and jetty and away from the harbour, coming up for a few breaths of air when he had to before going straight back down again.

He had seen men under the water still struck by arrows near the surface and could see more arrows sinking to the bottom as the men above loosed volley after volley into his men. He had been tempted to undo his sword belt and let it go as it was slowing him but that would be a fate worse than death to him, or any Branvere noble. Family swords did not get surrendered under any circumstance, to the enemy or to the sea. It must be the bloody dragoons, he thought, it had to be, there had been some kind of warning about a coastal patrol but he had not been paying attention, it must be them. Who else but dragoons could have found the harbour, attacked and taken it, laid the trap and then proceeded to slaughter every man they could. He knew he would not get any quarter if caught, his sword would identify him as a noble and Danyard had no respect for the tradition of ransoming nobility back to their families. And these men were fighting for their lives and the lives of their families, King Cathal did not make a benevolent overlord to those he conquered, men and boys of fighting age were conscripted into his own forces or sent to be worked to death in the silver mines.

He swam as far as he was able before heading to the shore, and then he struggled through the surf before collapsing to get his breath where he now lay. But he knew he could not stay there for long; the dragoons would start to patrol soon. He knelt up and scanned along the beach, and sure enough there were two groups of four men fanning out, one group walking feet wet in the surf and the other about fifty paces farther up the beach towards the dunes, the very dunes that were his only hope.

He remembered some of his lessons from the military masters about the dragoon system of atrop, a group of eight men worked as a unit and could be instantly divided into two fours, it gave good all-round coverage and excellent command and control, and was secretly admired by those who understood war. Branvere military policy differed greatly, units of men could be made up of up to twenty which was virtually impossible to control and prevented individuals from thinking on their feet, they just tended to follow the group.

He dropped back down to his belly and slid himself back into the surf as quickly as he would allow himself to, knowing the only thing that would give him away at that moment was his own movement. From there he let the flow take him further down the beach, away from his pursuers. When he was as far as he thought he could reasonably get he again crawled through the surf and onto the sand, keeping a close eye out he made a mad dash for the dunes, running as fast as his sodden clothing would allow. As he reached the first tufts of long grass, he flung himself bodily into the dunes, hitting the ground hard as he rolled down the first one and needles of pain shot through his body. He found himself near a large tuft and he crawled to it, grateful that the soft dry sand here would not show his footprints. He stopped and listened, staying absolutely still, while still trying to control his heavy and erratic breathing. He could hear the slow careful movement of the dragoons near to him, and he tensed, then there was a shout from what seemed far away, but he reasoned it must be the men in the surf, they must have seen his clear footprints in the wet sand, there was a short whistle and he heard the four in the dunes run over to the surf. He knew this would be his only chance, he stood and ran, once again, for his life, towards the track that the army had used, towards Kino'le City.

"We have a runner Captain," said Atrop Commander Pixton. "Do you want us to pursue? He must have jumped from the ship, found his footprints in the surf but no idea where he went in the dry sand, definitely a man running but not weighed down, footprints too far apart for him to be laden, and would not have been able to swim as far as he did in any kind of armour, even mail for that matter, I would assume he also dumped his weapons when he went over, pursuit will not be a major problem."

"And since when did we assume the best-case Pixy, we always assume the worse, take your own atrop with arrows nocked and atrop two with sabres drawn, so in pairs, the swordsman guarding the bowman. Look for patches of trodden or flattened down grass, he would have gone to the nearest cover and then try to get to the woods, but you will only go as far as the dunes, do not follow the path to the city, I do not want you catching up with an army of thousands and then drawing them back here. If they get word that their supply chain is gone, they may try to retake this beachhead but we have some time before that, he can do no real harm to us at the moment. But while you are here, I need some local knowledge and you lived here as child, didn't you?"

"Yeah, brought up here, played on these sands most days, why?"

"I need an area where there are hidden rocks, just under the sea enough to be out of sight, I will be extinguishing these two fires and building some more, preferably where the ships will have their hulls torn out if they tried to follow them in to dock."

"I know just the place."

General Carmak watched with professional concern as his army spread out in front of him and formed its lines, the cavalry at the vanguard at that moment but could be moved so much quicker than the masses of infantry. He was troubled by many things, the trebuchet catapults that his spies assured him could not be used, whatever was hidden in the lines of dragoons and again what his spies could not seem to tell him. He should have the advantage, the Princess was dead, the famous light was extinguished and they had managed total surprise and the gates were down. Yet something nagged him, that soldier's instinct itched and itched and he just could not seem to scratch it. But he had to go forward now, whilst he still had the momentum, while his enemy was still reeling from the death of the Princess, to stall the attack now was to invite failure, every moment spent in the formation of his lines was a moment the enemy had to prepare. He turned to his horn blowers. "Sound the damn advance." He said to them "Let us get this fucking thing done."

Toker and Chamley lay on the edge of the wood, the fifty soldiers they had with them were to their rear hidden well within the wood, from the prying eyes of the lines of dragoons formed up to their front.

"It has to be archers Lord Toker, longbowmen, it must be, what else would they move their most important troops into position for? They need the height of the horses to hide the longbows from anybody who would be watching from here, like us." whispered Chamley.

"And how do they know we are watching them?" Toker hissed back.

"They do not, they are just being careful."

"Careful, no one is that careful."

"Danyard is."

"Not for much longer, remember it is our job to make sure he does not make it to the field of battle, and without him the whole army will crumble."

"If you say so, but I think you underestimate the man."

"And I think the whole fucking world overestimates him, no one is that good, just in reality no one is. And it sounds like you admire him."

"I do, he is the greatest warrior in the known world, never been beaten in battle, not even close to being beaten."

"That is treason back in Branvere Chamley, watch your tongue."

"Oh, just bury my head in the sand, shall I? Ignore the fact that us fifty are supposed to do what the entire nation of Mar'thak failed to do."

"Damn it, you are an insubordinate bastard, no wonder that bloody apothecary beat you, I am tempted myself. It is a great honour to be given this chance, imagine when we return to Branvere, heroes, the men who killed your finest warrior in the known bloody world, I promoted you from nothing Chamley, if you do not want it then fuck off back to the lines and I will find another, one who is not a constant buzzing wasp in my fucking ear."

"I do want this, I am just urging you to a bit of caution, that is all." They both turned their heads at the sudden sound of battle horns from the Branvere lines.

"Well it is all irrelevant now, we need to identify the man and take him, shouldn't be too hard, a man leading a charge has to give orders at some stage."

"You have just proven how little you know your enemy, he never identifies himself in battle, no special armour, no golden horse, no huge banner. It is one of the reasons he so damn hard to kill."

Twenty-Four
The Battle Joined

The buglers put their lives into that one long note, it sounded up and down the lines of cavalry who at that point all held their lances in their saddle stirrup, their swords safely in their scabbards for now. The huge Branvere destriers, trained to respond with absolute aggression to that one note, stamped their feet and snorted gulps of air, building up the energy they would soon need. Their riders knew they had to control them for now kept them on a close rein, holding them back to a walk so the infantry could keep up. Every man, mounted or on foot, had a dry mouth and butterflies raging in their guts, even those used to combat knew that this would be different, that the casualties on both sides would be horrific.

The Branvere army had a few archers, but not the longbows of Kino'le, only short range low power weapons that were not much use beyond fifty paces. They were at the vanguard of the Branvere infantry, in a vain attempt to stop any charge by the Dragoons, but each man knew that the speed of the oncoming horses and the short effective range of their bows would not stop, or even slow down, the dragoons, so each man hoped that their own horsemen would engage and destroy the dragoons first.

General Carmak let his horse go forward with the Branvere cavalry, but would not charge with them, he would hold back with his buglers who also doubled as his personal bodyguard, to control the main attack. He spied a rider from his right flank and felt a quick stab of fear, such was the tension in the air, until he realised it was one of Toker's men. I have to calm down, he thought to himself as the rider reached him.

"General!" he spoke "The Lord Toker is of the opinion that there must be archers with longbows hidden within the ranks of the dragoons, he says, he cannot explain what else they are doing in that formation."

"Has he actually seen them?" he enquired in reply.

"No general, but he is of the opinion that the archers must be longbowmen, so the height of a man on horseback would hide the height of the bow staves, if they had standard battle bows, they would not have to be hidden in this manner,"

"Go back to Toker, tell him I have understood what he says and he is now released to continue his primary mission, but this time go behind our damn lines to enter the woods, half that fucking army facing us probably saw you leave the woods and now know we have men spying on them, I would have you flayed where you stand now if I didn't need you to return to your master with my message, you fucking buffoon."

"Yes general," he said as he saluted and rode away as fast as his horse would carry him.

'Longbows' he thought with a shudder, three or four times the range at least of his own men's bows, and twice the power, maybe even more, the shock energy of one even striking an armoured man could throw him from his feet, even if it did not penetrate his armour. But he had also seen the bodkin heads some blacksmiths made, designed to cut clean through thin plate and chainmail.

He had seen the longbow demonstrated by a troop of travelling arms men once, the entire Branvere military had shown up for the demonstration, with Balstore and Cathal as the honoured guests. A huge marquee had been set up for it with a feast, so confident had the sellers been. The package had included two trainers that would start the training of the young boys, and all the bows and equipment they would need as well as the techniques required by bowyers and fletchers to continue to make them.

First the finest archer in the kingdom was asked to hit a target at his maximum range, which he did at seventy paces, then he was asked to loose again at a set of armour, and obviously the arrow just bounced off. Then a man previously unseen had stepped from the seller's tent and the crowd had gasped, so large across the chest and shoulders was he, he had then ripped off his jerkin to reveal a body the like of which no one in the Kingdom had ever seen, muscles rippled under his skin like writhing snakes, huge monstrous neck and shoulders gave the man a slightly deformed and stooped gait as he strolled to his place on the field, another man walked out to him and handed him a bow as tall as he was. He took it and nocked an arrow, the arrow itself a pace long with a heavy diamond shaped head. He drew the bow and the crowd gasped again as his muscles changed shape before everyone's eyes, the short squat man straitened up as his muscles elongated and stretched out, and then, in a whisper of quiet the arrow was gone. They heard the strike as it cut clean through the armour and embedded itself into the post underneath. A neat clean hole in one of Balstore's finest breastplates. And the crowd of military commanders went berserk, shouting and screaming their applause.

The man quietly nocked another and loosed it in a single fluid movement, this time it flew over the post with the armour and embedded itself in a tree another one hundred and fifty paces away, again the crowd roared their approval, each man thinking the same, with a company of men armed as such I would be unstoppable. And then the King stood, and the crowd fell silent as Balstore also stood and they walked towards the archer and the arms men, who stood smiling knowing they had made a very impressive display. But then they did not know of the silver King and his too proud advisor. Carmak had a terrible feeling in his stomach at what was about to happen. Armourers and Smiths were a proud lot, and the masters of them, as Balstore was, did not like to be humiliated. Balstore spoke first.

"A very impressive display gentlemen, one of my finest breastplates, one that I sell all over the known world, to many nations, and one you have just rendered ineffective, you have taught me a valuable lesson today." At this point the men knew they were in trouble. "Maybe our good King would like to try one of these magic bows, see what he can achieve, surely being a King, he should be quite resplendent at this form of archery."

"But my Lord, as we have already discussed, one has to be trained from childhood for such an undertaking." Stammered the leader "As you can see from Alden here, since puberty he has been doing this, it is the skill of a lifetime, look at his shoulders, even his bones deformed by the massive pressure he has endured, to be able to do what he can now do."

"Are you saying that our King, our beloved King Cathal the Silver, cannot achieve what a child can?"

"Not at all my Lord it is just…well…look at him yourself, he is no child now."

"I will hear no more of your insults, your Majesty." Spoke Balstore, as he took the bow from the startled hands of Alden, "Please show these fellows what a King is capable of?"

"I think I will, I shall punch an arrow straight through that breastplate as well." He said as he took the proffered bow and arrow from Balstore. He took up his position on the line and nocked the arrow, then stood his full height and started to draw back the string, it moved a hands width before it stopped, the King's face started to go red as he pulled and pulled at it, but it would not move another finger width, his face went purple and he suddenly staggered to one knee, taking huge gasping breaths as he flung the bow far from him. His bodyguards rushed to him but he shook them off.

"CURSE THIS DAMN WEAPON!" he suddenly shouted and Balstore smiled inwardly, all the while maintaining look of frightened concern for his King.

"Seize these fraudsters." Shouted Balstore as men stood and rushed towards him, but the three men were nowhere to be seen. A day later, the two salesmen had been found but the damn archer, Alden, had just seemed to vanish. Both men died under torture swearing they did not know the location of the archer.

That had been years ago, and he still shuddered at the power of that weapon, the weapon that could change the course of this battle and may now be in the hands of the enemy. All because of the pride of a man who was effectively just a fucking smith and another who was easily manipulated by him.

The bugle note was heard by the waiting Kino'le armies and the dragoons slowly walked their horses forward. Riding at the vanguard Danyard had no need to brief his officers and men, he had simply told them all formation six, movement four. Dragoons not on patrol regularly practiced mounted manoeuvres and plan six was the hiding of the longbowmen and movement four was to separate at the given command exposing the front ranks of the longbowmen so they could take accurate aim on their targets. The first volley may be over the heads of the dragoons but they would still make good ranging arrows.

The Kino'le army was made up mostly of infantry and they had their own plans and would respond to the ebb and flow of the battle as long as the dragoons kept them safe from the enemy cavalry that outnumbered the dragoons by at least two to one. Danyard looked forward, scanning the mounted formations coming his way, once again identical to every man around him. He knew their horsemen would try to draw him into a fight, but with his number disadvantage he also knew that if he engaged fully then his infantry would be vulnerable to a flanking attack by horsemen, and no matter how good an infantry company, it would never stand against a mounted charge by heavy horse, especially the Branvere Destrier, the largest horses in the known world, bred for one purpose, war.

The bloodlines were famous, the stud's being huge beasts that passed their size down through generations, small or weak fowls put to death at birth to keep the line pure, each generation seeming larger than the last as massive stallions mated with the largest mares. Each fowl trained to be a weapon in its own right from birth. They were known to stamp men underfoot into the earth and bite and kick anyone that came too close, usually only the horses master and one groom could approach any of them. If a large force of the beasts hit his infantry then it was all over, he was gambling on this one throw of the dice, and he had to do as much damage in that one throw as possible.

The infantry practiced against mounted attacks regularly as well, the line giving way to allow the horseman into the formation and then surrounding him, but it was only so effective, if the frontage of the attack was large enough it would swamp the infantry. He had to reduce the number of horsemen he was facing, so he could then keep what remained engaged and away from the infantry.

He had two ways to achieve this, the first involved using the trebuchets against them, but it was an awful risk. when he first took the role of Lord Protector, he had crews practice with the catapults every year, lobbing huge rocks into the fields around the city, but then he realised, if an enemy spent that much time planning an invasion they would not ignore them, for they were a contributing factor of the defeat of Mar'thak, and they would make a plan that either destroyed them first or somehow worked around them. When Master Engineer Forster had died, it was the perfect excuse to cease their use, or so he let the city believe. But in secret, he commissioned the man's Daughter, now Commander of Trebuchets Damerall, to take charge of their secret maintenance. It was one of his greatest coups against Lorgane, and the rest of the nobility for that matter, keeping the young woman from court and out of the spotlight. She spent most of her time supervising the trebuchets in Kardon and the trebuchets here spent most of their time under heavy canopies and when they were exposed he ensured they looked neglected, he even had the entire area cordoned off and patrolled claiming that they were not safe and could collapse at any time, which of course they never did. But despite all the secret attention they got, the machines had stood idle for five years now, and their crews the same. Each man had also been secretly paid for five years and they would have answered the call when it came, but five years was a long time, although most did spend some time at Kardon with Commander Damerall for practice shooting into the sea. He was thankful that she had been here when the attack had started and he knew that he did not need to tell her to prepare, she had a set of written orders for such an eventuality.

But, if they did not work properly then the load could fall short, killing his own men, or worse, the machine could disintegrate during the cycle, killing the crews. It was too terrible a risk. Added to that Commander Damerall would have to hit a fast-moving target, and that was what had swung it for him, so the fate on Kino'le remained on the shoulders of five hundred longbowmen and the gamble that it would be a surprise.

"Danyard." spoke one of his bodyguards.

"What?" he replied.

"A single rider broke the tree line and rode to the front of the formation, looked like he was delivering a message."

"Did he go back to the tree line?"

"No Sire, he rode like his arse was on fire to the rear of the formation, but he may have entered the trees from there."

"So, what do you think, watchers in the tree line to our left flank?"

"I would think it safe to assume Sire."

"Yes, me too, send two atrops to loose arrows into the trees, see if we can draw them out into a fight, but they are not to enter the trees."

"As you wish Sire."

"And take Jeldin with you, I swear that man has a better nose than a fucking bloodhound."

Callan lay in his tower, his Gunne to his front but no longer in his hands, it was loaded and the hammer at full cock. The remaining Imperial Guardsmen were just below him doing their damn best to reinforce the gate, carpenters sawed and hammered and shouted at apprentices but they knew it would not be enough, if the dragoons and the army fell then so would the gate once again and followed by the city, even a brand new gate would not stop that. He did not know where Amyeen was, but he knew where the army of his homeland was, for it was marching towards him right now, the mighty destriers at the vanguard itching to get into the battle to do what they did best.

Against the snow filled field, with the help of the moonlight, he had a clear, almost daylight view of the forthcoming battle. He could see most of the dragoons to his front, both sides marching towards each other at such a low pace it seems they would never meet, though he was dreading it when they did. From his high vantage point he could count columns and ranks and to his reckoning the Branvere horses outnumbered the dragoons just over two to one, I hope they have a trick up their sleeve he thought to himself.

Amyeen had told him that there were about one thousand dragoons in the city but between a third and a half were on patrol at any one time and Danyard liked a minimum of five hundred in the city at any one time, but if he started with five hundred he had lost some to Dark Stalkers, so he was now below that. The dragoons had standard patrols, Southern, Eastern, Western and Northern, as well as Coastal Patrol. But Danyard also sent out random patrols, sometimes for a couple of nights and sometimes for a month, it was these patrols that saw the most action for they were always unexpected, bandit groups avoided the patrol routes for obvious reasons and lived in fear of one of the random patrols. Once a bandit group had been identified the patrol absolutely did not stop until they caught and engaged them. Callan knew exactly how many Branvere cavalry there were for he had spent the last few years of his life making their damn swords and lance heads.

He did not know what to do at that moment, she had left no instruction after the attack by the Stalkers but he could not leave the building yet, Imperials were everywhere and soldiers in time of war did not have time to listen to excuses given by strangers wearing clothes made in the country that had just invaded them. He just had to wait and see what happened, and if any Branvere soldier got close enough he would do what he could.

Commander 'The Bull' Buldor of the Royal Bodyguard also known as 'The Hammer of Kino'le' stared down at the frail figure of the Princess that he had been sworn to protect, the fifteen others stood a respectful distance away, knowing his mood to be dark and foul, as was theirs for failure hung heavy upon them, although no person in the Kingdom would ever blame them. She looked dead, but for a faint rise and fall of her chest.

His sword was sheathed but as usual his weapon of choice, his Warhammer, was being held in his right hand near the head, at its point of balance. He had been asked many times why he preferred it and he usually stated the same thing, cut a man with a sword, he can still cut you, shatter his hip bone with a big fucking hammer and he becomes a man with no use of his legs, probably ever again, and he is not going to be hurting anyone in a hurry. Not many could argue that point and not many could handle a Warhammer like Buldor either.

He had once been a smith, apprenticed to a man named Gordos. The blue-eyed god was how he was known by nearly every maiden in the kingdom, long flowing blond hair, the bluest eyes anyone had ever seen and the body of a man who spent ten hours a day at a forge. He had been forced to bring his workshop forge inside the building for crowds of women would congregate to watch him work up a sweat each day preventing genuine customers from viewing his wares. The young Buldor had been chosen by him at a summer fair when he had won a competition to fell a tree by axe the quickest and at first he had thought the man an arrogant prick, but he had soon learnt the man was actually quite humble and grateful for the gifts bestowed upon him. They had formed a great friendship during his years of apprenticeship. The smiths craft taught to him by Gordos also forged his already impressive frame and bestowed upon him his love of the hammer, it being the first and last tool of any smith.

His life had changed forever when, on the way home from a tavern one night he had stumbled past the workshop and seen light inside. He had approached hoping to see his mentor and friend working late, and although he did see his master, he was not prepared for the sight that greeted him when he pushed the door fully open.

There were four of them, led by a minor nobleman named Tammlin, who had commissioned a sword and matching breastplate from Gordos and agreed on a price of one hundred silver pieces for each, but when the time came Tammlin refused payment, claiming they had agreed on one hundred for the pair and besides the workmanship did not warrant two hundred silver. That had been the start of the problem between them, for one thing you never ever do is tell a smith his work is shoddy in his own workshop. The situation was aggravated when Tammlin had tried to intimidate Gordos into submission, which ended in Tammlin being physically lifted from his feet and thrown through the double doors of the workshop and halfway down the street.

This had resulted in a complaint of assault being made to the Imperial Guard, who, reluctantly, were forced to act. Gordos was fined six silver pieces for the act which he promptly paid, three to the city and three to the victim. This added insult to injury for Tammlin, who had hoped that Commander Jain would have seen his point of view and fined the smith the cost of the sword, therefore still enabling him to purchase the pair for only one hundred pieces. But the days of a noble's word over that of a commoner were over, thanks to Danyard. It had escalated further when Gordos had borrowed the outside forge of a friend and in front of a huge crowd, melted down the pair of items that he had spent days crafting the family crest of Tammlin into.

To a proud noble this was too much, the man had gone too far, and so on that night he and his three friends had broken into his workshop and lain in wait for Gordos, deliberately leaving the workshop door ajar, knowing he would investigate rather than go looking for an Imperial Guardsman. As he stepped into the darkness of his workshop, he was struck on the head by his own tools that had been banded together and place above the door, the resulting blow to the head giving the four men the chance to lay into him with clubs.

They had originally only planned to rob the workshop but such is the way with the very proud and very drunk men, by the time they had stepped away from Gordos he was near death. So, a new plan was called for, one which required an accident to befall the workshop, so they started to fire up the forge, hoping a fire would destroy all the evidence of a beating.

It was at this point that Buldor had walked passed and seen the light flicker from within, wondering what Gordos could be up to he had investigated. The sight that met him when he pushed the door open still haunted him to this day, in their drunken stupor they had burnt parts of Gordos, hoping to disguise the beating he had taken and the only reason he recognised the man was one blue eye hanging out of its socket, the other had been burnt shut, his blond hair was gone, revealing a burnt and still smouldering skull, cuts, bruises and burn marks covered what remained of him.

The four men swung around to face him as he pushed the door open, the three under orders raising their clubs as they did so.

"Leave, right fucking now apprentice, you did not see anything, and you will be a rich man, but you need to leave right now!" shouted Tammlin. Buldor knew he should have, even if it was to run for a guardsman, but he could not, he looked at what remained of his friend and mentor and the anger grew. In one swift move he reached up with his right hand and grabbed a hammer from the rack at the same time kicked the door closed behind him with his left foot and quietly but firmly said, "Fuck you Tammlin."

Two of Tammlin's men went to swing their clubs but they were hindered by the small space they occupied, Buldor's hammer hit the first in the side of his head, low on the cheek, teeth and blood sprayed out as he went down losing consciousness, the second man connected his club on Buldor's back but he had not enough room to swing it so it was a weak strike, before he knew what had happened a pain shot through him that he had not previously known could exist as Buldor's hammer came from below and hit the man with full force and accuracy in the groin, he continued the hammer swing upwards and lifted the man clear of the floor and threw him onto the forge, now alight and burning hot, the man scrambled off screaming and spread hot coals with him as he did so, most hitting Tammlin as he scrabbled backwards away from the enraged apprentice. The third man had seen what little effect his comrades club had had on Buldor and was struggling to draw his sword. Builders hammer smashed through his elbow and ribcage, shattering both in the process. His screams of pain joined the others so Buldor put the hammer through his skull as he dropped to the floor.

Tammlin was backed against the far wall by this stage, he had burn marks on him from the coals and was pale and sweating, his hand was on his sword hilt but he had not yet drawn it, groans of pain came from his two men that were still alive but nothing from the third. Buldor looked down at them, the one with the head wound was in a semi-conscious state, dribbling and coughing up blood, the other seemed to be in his own personal hell, he was laid on his side curled up and occasionally squirmed around, the sounds coming from him pitiful. But Buldor had no pity, as he looked at Tammlin, blood still dripping from his hammer.

"You will hang for this apprentice, you fucking peasants, you can't tell me what I pay for armour and weapons, we tell you…there are laws, you can't just strike a nobleman, I… I will make you pay for this." stammered Tammlin.

"But I did not strike a nobleman, I struck these three cunts, and look what a sad state they are in now, but if I am going to hang anyway, I may as well finish the job and go to the noose a happy man."

Replied Buldor, and then a voice spoke from behind.

"Put the hammer down smithy, no one else gets hurt here." And he felt the point of a sword in his back, as he turned, he saw the purple livery of an Imperial Guard sleeve behind him. The hammer clattered to the floor.

The Noble families of the Kingdom were originally up in arms about what had happened and there were calls for Buldor to indeed be hanged. But then the two surviving men, who had been deliberately kept away from Tammlin, from their beds in the hospital, told Danyard and Lord Calstan the truth of what had happened. When the truth was known, what had actually happened to Gordos, the Blue Eyed God, there was a complete reversal and the Imperial Guard had had to deploy nearly all of its men to the Tammlin estate to prevent raging mobs from tearing it down brick by brick, it led to calls from even some of the nobles for Tammlin to be hanged.

Danyard had been put in an awful predicament, Tammlin should have been hanged for the murder of Gordos, but Buldor, too honest for his own good, had killed one of his men in cold blood, after his arm was already shattered and so he should face trial for that crime as well. But Danyard had plans for a man who could take on four armed men in an enclosed space and prevail. He discussed it on a daily basis with Lord Gemmell, who finally found the solution after studying the ancient laws of the Kingdom. Trial by combat, and to save time and money it would be easier and simpler all round if they fought each other.

Both were called to court, and Danyard asked if they both agreed, Buldor jumped at the chance but Lord Tammlin was a bit more reluctant, for the first time in a month he was in the same room as Buldor and he was clearly terrified of the man, but in front of the assembled Nobility he could not lose further face and so conceded, asking what weapons and armour would be allowed. He got the answer he wanted when Danyard replied with one word, Anything. And the time until the trial. One month for training. Tammlin's confidence began to grow.

Tammlin was seen every day in the training arena, the finest sword masters in the Kingdom flocked to him, hoping to earn excessive coin. He trained every day, sometimes stripped to the waste but other times in full plate armour. His confidence grew and grew as sparring partners were sent out of the ring flat out where a wooden sword had cracked into them hard. Of Buldor there was no sign, he had locked himself inside Gordos's workshop and would see no one. Noise of work came from the workshop and light from the forge could be seen through the windows but no one actually saw the young man. Word started against him, yet another swing of fortunes in the whole sorry saga as men and women thought him a coward who would run rather than avenge his master.

And then the big day came, those who could get to the arena did so, the streets were deserted and the shops closed as Lord Tammlin rode a silver mare through the streets adorned in his new armour that fully encased him, the breastplate a thumb width of pure thick steel plate, the shoulders a finger width and the leg armour the same. The best quality chain mail expertly welded into every join and possible gap, his new silver helm in his spare hand as he rode to the arena with his retinue. He waved to the crowd, who despite themselves and the hatred they had harboured for him, cheered. He dismounted in the arena with the help of two squires, such was the weight of his armour, and he placed his helm upon his head and drew his brand-new broad sword in a flourish, proceeding to make some practice cuts and thrusts to gasps of delight from the waiting crowd.

He looked towards the other entrance and in walked Buldor, simple cloth leggings, leather sandals and an old leather smock, and carrying a very large sack. Tammlin smiled, how the hell is he going to cut me when I have all this armour on, and he, is bloody defence-less. Maybe the poor man has realised he has been outclassed and just wants it over quickly. Buldor took off his smock to reveal his bulging muscles and he flexed them a bit, and started to stretch his massive frame before he picked up the sack and drew out what had taken a month of work at a forge. A Warhammer, the like of which the world had never seen. The whole thing was over a pace and a half long, beautiful wooden handle that was wrapped in leather strips and sharkskin for grip, the neck forming seamlessly to metal about two thirds up and the head, in beautiful shining steel, one side a traditional hammer head about the size of a fist, the other forming into a wickedly sharp axe blade, the crowd was awed by the sight of it, and despite himself Lord Tammlin took an involuntary breath.

The two men approached each other, Tammlin walked forward, he had considered a visor but had decided against it as it would restrict his vision, his sword swinging easily in his hand as he moved towards the younger man. He looked into the steely eyes of Buldor and knew the man had not come here to die, although he looked ill prepared at a distance, he looked frightening close up. His neck, shoulder and arm muscles were huge, almost deformed in their size and he appeared to have no neck, such was the hard slabs of flesh that covered him. Buldor walked with an ease as if he was out for a summer stroll, no tension showing in him as he took a few quick practice swings with that mighty hammer. The crowd once again made small gasping sounds as they saw the man's control of that weapon, like a swift dance he suddenly made a few leaps swinging it as he went, always perfectly under control. And then he stopped as suddenly as he started and he planted his feet and waited.

Lord Tammlin stopped three paces from him, and despite himself he gulped, suddenly nervous at the thought of facing this man. He gave a small nod and raised his sword, Buldor did not budge or acknowledge the start of the contest in any way, just continued to fix him with those steely eyes. They stood staring for a moment and then Tammlin attacked with a sudden explosive speed, bringing his sword high to bear the full weight of it down onto Buldor's head, but Buldor was expecting a flamboyant move as such and easily sidestepped past Tammlin, bringing his hammer straight onto Tammlin's knee from the side as he did so, Tammlin screamed with agony as his knee joint shattered and he collapsed into the dirt, landing on his front. Before he could even think what had happened Buldor twisted the hammer around and sent the axe blade clean through the prone man's back piece. The mighty hammer had all of its own weight and the full strength of Buldor behind it, it easily pierced the thinner armour of the back piece and smashed through his ribs, splitting the man's heart clean in two and killing him instantly. The crowd fell silent as Buldor let go of the hammer and he stood and looked around, he then wrenched it from the man's back and walked from the arena without a backward glance.

Danyard had been waiting for him as he walked away.

"How would you like to serve in a position where you would never have to bow to a noble again?" spoke Danyard.

"Tell me more," replied Buldor.

Sarah, the newly married Lady Nyston and the other ladies in waiting were still in attendance, as were Lord Javin and the Master Armourer, Lord Bastion. The Ladies had wanted to take the Princess to her chambers but Buldor had refused and as Commander of the Royal Bodyguard he had overall command, second only to Danyard with anything to do with the Princess's safety. So, he had the servants bring her bed to the strongroom, with anything else the Ladies wanted to make her more comfortable. They flustered around her and mopped her brow, and at the Surgeons instruction put sips of water to her mouth.

"Buldor, I can do no more for her." He stated "I will be needed at the battle aid station, as will the Master Apothecary, in fact all of us will. Keep her warm and hydrated, her fate is with the gods now, all we can do is wait."

"I understand, get yourselves where you will be of use, no further harm will come to her."

"I know that, no one blames you Buldor, no one at all, this was a failure of intelligence, not of loyalty or dedication, it took us all by surprise. But one thing you may not beware of, Guild Master Oates is currently being held in the lower dungeon, I do not know for sure but I believe that he knew about and maybe even assisted with the invasion, and is therefore a traitor. And it follows that he must have known of the plot on her life. I am sure that the Lord Danyard was meant to pass this information to you but was so busy it slipped his mind, or maybe he wanted something left of the slimy worm to question himself."

"Thank you for that information, I am sure that the worm may have some information that will help me with my enquiries, now fuck off and leave us alone."

Jonoak looked back at the fires, he was still wet and very cold and those fires looked very inviting, his hopes suddenly soared, thinking the army must have backtracked and engaged and destroyed the dragoons but then he realised there was something wrong with them, they were no longer at the harbour, or what was left of the harbour, they had started them elsewhere. The dragoons must have moved them, to draw the ships onto the rocks under shallow waters, damn these men were callous. He felt himself sink into a pit of despair as his situation sank in and the initial adrenaline was wearing off, he was in a foreign land, now an enemy foreign country, the sea and the enemy to his back, no food or water and his only weapon his family sword, which he would have to surrender if captured. He did not even have his tinder box for all his belongings were on his pack horse, which being in the hold of the ship was either drowned or burnt to death, along with most of his men, of which he could not bear to think about.

He sank further down into his despair until he suddenly snapped and jumped up. Fuck them all, he thought to himself, I will not sit here and watch the enemy destroy more ships and men while I slowly freeze to death, I will catch up with the army, if I am quick I may even get a ride on a wagon, it was a well-trodden path and the rear most company can't be too far ahead. The thought of capture gave him speed as he walked, the shame of it, his father would rather see him dead than captured especially if the family sword was taken from him, the sword that had been handed down through generations. But then an enemy patrol would probably not give him the chance to surrender anyway, an enemy nobleman alone walking away from a battle, he did not think he had much of a chance.

Garvak and Geel knelt by a mighty oak, they spoke in a dialect and low whisper commonly used by the Dalstock Tree People, to give them their correct title, although the legend of the Dalstock Savages had served them well in keeping out any further unwanted guests. They were a few hundred paces from where Toker's Light Archers were also laid up, which was the subject of their current discussion.

They had followed the road to Kino'le albeit through the forest that ran parallel, they had seen and passed many groups of soldiers and supply wagons, none of which had seen them. They had moved at speed through the woods, a speed that only a lifetime of living in the dark murky atmosphere of Dalstock could bring. They had come across where Jeldin had been stopped by those who hunted him and watched as the dragoons arrived. They had been impressed by how the smaller force had acquitted themselves in the small skirmish that followed and despite themselves, had been happy when yet again Jeldin Stone Dweller had escaped.

"Why did we not intervene my Brother?" asked Geel.

"Why would we, explain your thinking Brother?" he replied.

"We could have helped him, those soldiers from Kino'le would be alive, and those from Branvere would still be dead, it would have helped Kino'le."

"And why would we want to help this city of stone? What concern is it of ours who rules over the Kingdom of Light? They would not dare again to try to settle and conquer our dark home. I do not argue with you but just wish to understand how you see this thing?"

"This Danyard, it is said he is a decent man, a strong warrior, but above all he has no interest in the Light, never tried to harness its power for his own ends. This other, the One of Silver from the other place, he is manipulated by a darker force, and that darker force will try to use the power, why else send so many to do this thing."

"You speak the truth of it Brother, they would be bad for the balance of light and dark, which would affect our home too, the light here and the dark of Dalstock would forever be changed, but we cannot interfere in the affairs of stone dwellers, it is forbidden, we must just accept our fate and continue to fight the Dark Stalkers."

"If it is forbidden, why did we feel so happy when Jeldin Stone Dweller escaped again, was this because we had already saved him once, albeit for our own ends, and therefore we had already invested our time in him. Maybe being away from Dalstock has started to affect us, maybe our humanity is returning to us. The darkness that keeps our emotions in check cannot surface here, so close to what is still at the moment, The Kingdom of Light."

"I will think on what you have spoken my brother."

Danyard watched as the enemy drew nearer, he was still torn as to the decisions that he would have to make, the mounted charge of the enemy would have to start soon, while they were close enough to not tire the horses but not too close, they could not get up sufficient speed. He would then tell his buglers what order to give.

The dragoons were in their standard Light Battle Armour and on standard War Horses, a mix of mares and geldings but they were up against a cavalry of massive Stallion Destriers, bred for one reason from birth, to carry a fully armoured man into battle whilst wearing as much armour themselves as possible. The Branvere Destrier was the one thing that Danyard had total respect for in the Branvere army. On a field of battle, they would charge into a formation of men no matter how deep and absolutely did not know fear, once amongst men they would kick and bite and stamp on any that got in their way as well as carry their Knight. Danyard knew he could outrun the armoured horses but not outfight them, his men could literally run rings around them but eventually they would have to fight them, and nothing could stand against the fully armoured attack of the Branvere Heavy Horse.

The only thing that had come close to working once was the pike, a pole five paces long with a metal spear tip, one end in the ground and the other raised to the height of a horses chest, but there was no surprise with them, they could not be hidden on a battlefield and used in surprise so if an enemy commander saw them he would simply avoid them, or plan around them, for example using a wedge formation to split up the pikemen, then only a few front horse and men would be lost but the attack could still split a formation clean down the middle. Not only for this reason had Danyard discarded the idea, when he had been on his official state visit to Branvere he had witnessed the speed and power of the Branvere Destrier in a demonstration, the horses had leapt a huge distance and were the only horses he had seen that had chest armour, only a direct pike to the chest would stop them and if armoured, the pikes may just glance off.

So, he pinned all his plans on the longbowmen, even their heavy bodkin heads may not penetrate the expensive plate armour of the knights but he should be able to stop their horses, the entire future of the Kingdom rested on his decision and timing and the skill of those five hundred men he had trained.

He had complete faith in his infantry and the Kino'le nobles who commanded it, they would fight largely autonomously from the dragoons. He imagined what he would be doing now if he were commanding the enemy as he looked up at the enemy formations moving steadily towards him, any moment now he thought and just as he did another blast from the enemy buglers rent the air and the ground beneath Spike's hooves began to shake as the Branvere Heavy Horse moved into a charge.

Buldor backhanded Oates across the filthy stinking cell, he slammed face first into the wall knocking out two teeth on the stone brickwork. He had with him only one other bodyguard, not wanting to leave the Princess with less than a full complement of guards. The man's name was Nartan, known as Swiftblade for he was the fastest swordsman Buldor had ever met, apart from Danyard. Heavily tattooed but of slim build he had been a Royal Bodyguard for longer than Buldor but had constantly refused to take the second in command position that Buldor kept trying to force on him.

They were firm but unlikely friends, the exact opposite in size, Buldor only a few inches taller but twice the weight and breadth of shoulder. They had found they shared a dry ironic sense of humour and a hatred of the noble class that knew no bounds, in fact Nartan often stated that he only joined the Bodyguard so he would not have to bow to the bloody bastards. He was also the most unfriendly man Buldor had ever known, he did not speak to anyone that he did not have to which included any newcomer to the guard and Buldor when he had first arrived, but gradually Buldor had ground him down and their friendship had grown. Nartan addressed Buldor as Baldy and Buldor addressed Nartan as Ugly. There only other mutual friend was Grossman, currently commanding Danyard's bodyguard, who was known to both of them as Pretty Boy, due to his soft wavy hair and boyish charm. The name Pretty Boy had followed him back to the dragoons when he had returned to them an atrop commander a year ago.

Buldor, although Commander Royal Bodyguard, always appreciated the advice of Nartan, for he knew the man had no ambition and would never want to curry favour by being a yes man, if he thought Buldor wrong he told him straight 'you are wrong you bald bastard' to which he would reply 'thanks, now fuck off you ugly cunt'. Of all the men currently serving and previously served in the Bodyguard he trusted the words of Nartan the most, the man had no guile or tact and did not play games of politics like most others within the palace.

"We cannot stay too long Baldy." stated Nartan. "We cannot leave her for too long, if something happened…"

"This will not take too long will it you slimy piece of shit. Now, before you lose anymore teeth, is there anything else you want to tell me?"

"I… I…know nothing my Lord." he stammered just before Buldor's massive fist slammed into his jaw. "DO I LOOK LIKE A FUCKING LORD YOU CUNT." he screamed at him.

"No…no my er… Commander," He looked up into Buldor's eyes and saw the darkness there, he could see that he was as close to cracking under the pressure as any man he had ever seen before, sweat dripped from his round head and ran down his stubbled face and he was barely controlling the shakes caused by the adrenaline coursing through his veins now that he had a target for his wrath.

Oates knew he had few choices, if he told Buldor of his knowledge of the plan then he may stay alive for a few more days but he would not be able to deny he was a traitor in later days, and Danyard would hang him anyway. If he held out and was tried he may be able to clear his name but he just did not think he could hold out against Buldor at that moment, the man had always scared him witless and he had always been a coward in the first place, just being near him was usually enough to make him sweat, and the other with him, the one they called Swiftblade was worse, never speaking, even when spoken to, with a permanent scowl on his face and those ink marking all over his skin. His only hope was to hold out and hope that Branvere prevailed, but even then, he now had doubts.

When the trade commissioner had quietly visited him in the dead of night, he had been made an offer, just to keep quiet about missing convoys for which he would be made a Lord with titles in the new regime, but the more he thought about it now he realised they had been playing on his laziness and vanity. When he asked the scholars about the nobility of Branvere, he had found out they were a closed group, no new Lordships and been made in hundreds of years, the same families keeping a puppet King in power that they could manipulate and the realisation had slowly struck him, but by this stage the first late convoy report had arrived on his desk and it was too late, and once again his cowardice had shone through. He stared at the pair of them and was struck by one single thought, how can Branvere be victorious against men such as these.

He had a decision to make, if he was found a traitor all his wealth and possessions would be forfeit to the crown, his family shamed and turned out on the streets, but if he died in this filthy cell, suspected but not proven, then although shamed, they would still have enough wealth to move away and start again. For the first time in his life he made a decision not for himself, but for his family.

"Tell me Commander Buldor, Hammer of Kino'le and the most senior of those charged with the protection of the Princess, how did it feel, when she fell, the one thing that you have prepared your whole fucking life for and you failed in that one thing. The complete and utter failure of you and all your big tough men to stop her from being killed and you failed, you are a fucking joke." He closed his eyes and waited for the hammer blow; he knew was coming.

Callan felt the charge before he saw it, even from the height of his tower the massive destriers of Branvere shook the ground as they started their charge from four hundred paces from the front line of dragoons, who just sat upon their mounts and waited passively for them. He suddenly had serious doubts about the capabilities of these fabled warriors. One thousand men fully armoured and on the finest war horses known to man, also armoured, trained from a foal for one purpose, facing less than five hundred lightly armoured dragoons. Even from where he lay four stories up, it felt like an earthquake, the very ground seeming to shake and the thundering vibrations working their way through solid stone. He could make out the short lances of the front two rows and knew they would punch their way clean through the still unmoving dragoons. Don't just fucking sit there, he wanted to shout. He picked up his Gunne and pulled back on the hammer, it was already loaded and he felt with some satisfaction the click as the trigger mechanism fully engaged. He put the weapon to his shoulder in his prone position and tried to focus on one of the lead riders, he could not make out any one in particular because of the distance but he hoped to hit the front rank as they came on, while his stomach tied itself in knots and a cold dread settled in his heart.

He lay transfixed as the oncoming horsemen closed through three hundred paces, the noise and vibration becoming unbearable as the tension mounted, every person in the city must now know that the battle had started. He noticed a slight ripple in the ranks of the dragoons, then, suddenly without a word of command or sound of bugle the sky darkened as five hundred arrows took flight from inside the Kino'le formations, simultaneously, the dragoons parted, exactly down the centre of their ranks as if on a parade ground not a battlefield and another five hundred arrows took flight as the dragoons spread themselves down the sides of the flanks of the now revealed longbowmen, at the vanguard of the Kino'le forces.

A few arrows from the first volley fell short but the remainder found targets in the cramped front ranks of the galloping horses, arrows with heavy bodkin heads bounced from tough plate armour but punched clean through weaker arm and leg armour and chainmail of horses and men, and then the second volley hit, and then the third.

The effect on the leading formations of horsemen was absolute carnage, the front ranks of horses went down and the ones behind ran into them and then into the arrow storm that they could not turn from in time. Horses fell trapping the heavily armoured men who rode them, they tried to wriggle from under their fallen mounts but were then hit by more arrows as they did so.

The next few ranks tried to jump the chaos to their fronts and a few made it but then they were picked off by small groups of specialist target archers, none got within one hundred paces of the front line of longbowmen, who continued to loose shaft after shaft into the masses of horsemen to their front. The rear rows of horsemen could not see what was happening and continued to gallop forward forcing the ranks to their front into the lethal rain. The archers adjusted their aim higher and arrows started to fall on the ranks further back, causing more and more chaos as more men and horses fell and could not rise in the wet snowy field. And still the arrows punched into men and horses, splitting chainmail and smashing through joints at elbows and knees and groins and necks.

A few men rose from the chaos, stumbling to their feet in over a hundred pounds of heavy armour, disorientated and stunned, not knowing which way to turn in the bloodbath, surrounded by screaming men and dying horses and trying to find their way back by looking through the narrow slits of their visors. One brave man threw his helm from his head and stood looking around him before starting a staggered run towards his own lines, he went about twenty paces before an arrow struck him in the back of the head knocking him into the bloody quagmire of the once snow white field, but it gave the others a direction to turn towards and they did, they tried to run but their armour weighed them down, and their feet stuck in the soft snow and blood soaked earth, no more daring to remove their helms. The specialist archers at the flanks continued to target these men and again none made it back, the flatter trajectory arrows striking them in the back and even though most arrows shattered on their armour the force behind each one still knocked them down or at very least threw them off balance, and as they struggled to stand again yet more death rained down from above on them from the main body of archers.

The last ranks of horsemen finally managed to pull up and turn from the killing ground, and they turned their mounts and ran for the safety of their own lines of infantry, which had stopped short of the obvious arrow range. At the same time the dragoons suddenly advanced around the killing ground, flanking it on both sides and then closing it up to the front as the surviving Branvere horsemen galloped away. And then as suddenly as it started the arrow storm stopped.

Only about two hundred horsemen made it back to the lines of Branvere which left about eight hundred fully enclosed in the killing ground. Danyard had given another of his very specific orders, and one that did not sit well with him but he felt he had no choice, for the men and their horses in that field were too dangerous to leave alive.

The longbowmen slung their bows and pulled out their short pole war hammers and they advanced into the carnage ahead of them. Every horseman had his armour prized open and was checked for life, those alive were killed where they lay, usually by a quick knife thrust to the throat if they could get under the man's gorget, as was every horse, throat cut and left to bleed out on the field, all the while the sound of the slaughter was heard by the waiting Branvere Army. Screams for mercy were ignored, as the bulk of the young nobility of Branvere were systematically slaughtered.

The dragoons in the vanguard once again heard the screams as the sound washed over them, they did not like what was happening to their rear but they understood the need, each man glad he did not have to take part in it, especially the killing of the horses, something no horseman is ever glad to see, for the bond between a mounted soldier and his horse was truly sacred. But they also knew, these beasts of war could never be rehabilitated, even wounded they were still trying to kick and bite those who came near to them. And the sound of the war hammers striking steel continued as the massively muscled men who wielded them carried out their grizzly task.

Callan watched from his tower and was absolutely elated; the trap had been set and sprung by a master of warfare. He jumped up into the air pumping his fist up and down and shouting, he should have known, after all he had heard about Danyard, he would not simply let them overrun their lines. The pride of Branvere decimated right in front of his eyes. The discipline and cunning of the dragoons knew no bounds, they had sat and stared straight ahead as the Branvere destriers had come charging at them, they must have felt the immense weight and strength of those beasts through the ground and yet they had stayed, stock still, despite the tremors that must have travelled up through their own mounts, and with a signal not even noticed by him they had performed a perfect battlefield manoeuvre and led the enemy right into their trap.

He suddenly felt a weakness through his elation, he put his hand to his abdomen and felt a dampness, he took his hand away and looked incomprehensibly at the blood there, then he looked at the floor where his Gunne lay, a lazy tendril of smoke rising from the muzzle. It had fired when he jumped up and the ball had ricocheted in the enclosed space of the small room. He had not noticed in the excitement and adrenaline rush that had accompanied it, he suddenly felt very weak and pain erupted from the wound, he fell to his knees and then collapsed unconscious forward onto the floor smashing again his already broken nose.

General Carmak had never known a rage so intense, so much that he could hardly see, the blood pumping through his head so it fast it had given him tunnel vision. The three remaining cavalry commanders stood in his command area a respectful and necessary distance away, there had been a fourth, but he was currently on his back twitching in his death throes with Carmak's dagger protruding from his right eye.

"So, explain to me again, why didn't you evade, pull up or otherwise outmanoeuvre this relatively small band of archers?" He spoke with difficulty trying to keep control of his anger and emotions.

"We did General, that is why the four…three of us are here and the front lines are not." Spoke the bravest of them, a Nobleman named Kathreel.

"And how many horses do I have left to me?" He replied while vigorously rubbing his head, wishing the pounding would stop.

"Between two hundred and two hundred and twenty my Lord."

"And the attack itself, not one man, or horse, reached the enemy lines?"

"No, General"

"And who was it that ordered the withdrawal?"

"That was me General; I thought, it is better to regroup and count our losses than continue the attack. Our infantry is not as well armoured as our cavalry and would not have withstood the onslaught of those longbows, I too was there at that demonstration General, all those years ago and the damn things have always frightened…ummm…let's just say, I have a healthy respect for their capabilities."

"Why didn't you ride around the blockage, attack them from the flanks?"

"The dragoons split exactly down the middle, protecting those flanks, and we would have had to get out from the carnage first, which we did, by which time the momentum was lost to us. And then they moved as one toward us, but all they did was encircle our fallen, to prevent them escaping I assume, they know no other man can ride one of our horses, kill the man then the horse is now non effective as a weapon, so even the horses that did escape are of no use to us. Danyard is one cunning fucker."

"So, the damn archers had their front fully exposed, but you, on a Branvere destrier, finest warhorses known to man, fully armoured, could not, or would not, charge to them."

"No General, the speed at which they loosed at us, the first arrows not landed when the second one is on its way and the third leaving the bow, we could not see the sky for them, a storm of arrows, an arrow storm."

"So now The Lord Danyard has destroyed my cavalry, stalled our attack and our momentum, destroyed the moral of our men and moved the frontline of this battle five hundred paces away from his precious fucking city, without even a scratch on one of his own men. IS THAT FUCKING CORRECT!"

"Yes, General it is."

"Then you... Kathreel...probably saved us from total slaughter, you did the right thing in the circumstances that faced you. Now get to your men, reassure them, take command of what remains, I want three active companies of equal number from what remains, when you have done this get back to me, quickly, we finish this fucking thing today."

"As you command General."

"Don't say a fucking word Chamley," hissed Toker. "Yes, you were right all along, cursed longbowmen, and now the battle line has shifted five hundred paces from the city. We will have to move down with them, prepare the men, and quietly, not a charge, just like we moved in. And you Chamley, have a task, as you are such a follower of his moves and tactics, find Danyard in that lot, identify him for me, take one other man with you and sneak to the edge of the wood line, as soon as you think you have him send the other man back to me and he can guide us in. Then we can take the bastard. We will need to do this as soon as battle is joined properly. As we have already seen, he is too damn dangerous to leave alive to command this army."

Grossman sat mounted and stared at the enemy lines, he was in command of the two atrops that were appointed to the protection of Danyard, he had been given the task by Lord Dragoon Gemmell personally owing to his years in the Royal Bodyguard, all of which by necessity had to be expert horsemen, for the Princess loved to ride her horses. He had absolute authority to replace fallen men with others as and when he needed to, which he had done after the skirmish with the Dark Stalkers. He had been clawed along one arm but his chainmail had taken the brunt of it and the pain was receding now. He had secretly wished for just a small cut to his face to give him a battle scar and then Nartan and Buldor would stop calling him Pretty Boy. Despite all his scrapes in the dragoons he had never even come close to being injured in the face, he wondered why he was so jealous of the two ugliest men in Kino'le.

The two atrops were either side of him now, about two rows back, as usual Danyard not identifying himself to the enemy. Grossman was amazed at how calm he seemed; he had just won a huge victory but there he sat as if out for a summer ride in the woods. The commands he did give, he simply spoke to Grossman who relayed them for a bugler.

There was a suspicion that the wood line to their left flank was hiding a small number of enemies that were spying on the formations, that would be of no surprise, any decent commander would treasure such intelligence, what worried Grossman was that they could be there to identify Danyard. Buldor had virtually beaten it into him that the enemy would probably have a special group to target Danyard and it also made perfect sense to him, in fact the more he thought about it, the more he became convinced of it. It was well documented that Danyard had been the driving force that had routed Mar'thak in the last invasion so why take the risk that he would do it again.

Two atrops had been sent to the edge of the wood to send some arrows in but nothing had been heard, no answering arrows and no cries of wounded men so they had returned with nothing to report, apart from the fact that Jeldin had been with them and now he was not. This also came as no surprise to either of them, once Jeldin got a sniff of something, he would pursue it to the bitter end, and something obviously had tweaked his senses.

"Commander Grossman, get the commanders to me now, send a runner," stated Danyard.

"Yes Sire," he replied.

Jeldin lay in the undergrowth and studied the forty or so men, each was dismounted from their horse and steadying them to keep them quiet, they were very good, he thought. They were very familiar, he had the feeling that these were the same men who had hunted him earlier, a strange sense of deja vu kept washing over him. Their bows were all identical, that was to be expected but they were not the bows of the regular Branvere army, smaller, lighter but looked more powerful and he was sure he had used that exact same bow to escape before.

He continued to watch as two men crawled out from under a bush and they made their way very stealthily to the wood edge, he was intrigued and so followed.

Jonoak looked at the company before him, about two hundred paces ahead, he could see they were of Branvere but only about a hundred of them, he knew this for every twentieth man carried a torch, standard Branvere procedure, and he could see five torches. They were all dressed identically and marched in a very disciplined column, very unusual that they would have maintained that discipline away from the main army.

He had, by his own reckoning a miracle, found a horse, it was a dragoon horse for he could tell by the legend embossed into the saddle. It had been at a stream nibbling at tufts of grass and looked over to him as he had approached showing no outward signs of aggression. He had always been good with horses and had soon befriended the beast, unlike his own destrier, no man alive would have got near the bloody thing and even he still bore scars from its aggressive tendency.

There was dried blood splashed across the leather saddle and flank of the horse and he reasoned that the dragoon rider had chanced upon one of the advance parties of the attack. It gave him some hope as it was obvious that the dragoon had not survived. The tack seemed in perfect condition; things certainly looked up from that point. He had his family sword and now a bloody horse, he could start to look and feel like a real nobleman again.

He had mounted the horse and ridden as fast as he dared in the darkness along the tracks, he had passed two infantry companies already and he knew he should have stopped and introduced himself to the officers but he was just too damn elated to have escaped and found the horse to have to stop constantly and explain himself, he wanted to get ahead to the battle and prove himself, try to make his father proud of him at last.

And then he had seen this company and had been intrigued, so he slowed his mount as he went alongside them, curious as to why they were so different from a normal infantry company. He saw the officer ahead had hailed him.

"Say there, what land do you belong and who are you?" He spoke as he drew level.

"I am Huxton, Commander Gunne Company, we are not aligned to any land or any lord, we answer to the King directly, who are you?" he replied.

"I am Lord Jonoak, of Shamir Port, and you would do well to remember your manners when addressing a Lord, even if what you say is true and you are all Kingsmen. My ship was sunk as we arrived, damn dragoons attacked us and burnt it and the harbour to ashes, I may not be the sole survivor, I am sure they took a few prisoners of my men, but I am the sole escapee. What the fuck is a Gunne anyway, is that what you said, Gunne?"

"Yes, that is what I said and if you do not know then that is by design and I am not authorised to tell you. You have information on the supply chain though and General Carmak will need to know. If we have no rear logistics as you say then you need to get to the frontline and tell him."

"Since when was Carmak a fucking General, just some dirt-poor farmer that got lucky in a few skirmishes last I heard."

"Well it seems being under direct control of the Silver King himself has its advantages when it comes to information, he was to be promoted upon arrival, and as there is no light coming from ahead it would seem he was successful in his mission and now leads this war."

"Any news of the King and Balstore, did they make it out of the city before the invasion?"

"What am I, some kind of fucking seer? How would I know?"

"You seem to know everything else about this war that no one else knows. Being a guest in a country while planning to invade it, Balstore is a genius really, or if it goes wrong an arrogant prick, only time and fate will tell. But as you say I need to get to the battle lines; this horse is fresh but I could do with food and water."

"Supply wagon to our front, tell him I sent you but do not question him or what else he carries, if you do not know what a Gunne is then you are not supposed to know."

"Huxton you said? I shall remember the name." Just make sure you do nobleman thought Huxton because soon all your plate armour and fancy swords will be obsolete, when the Gunne rules the world, and then the noble class will be obsolete too. He did not really care who won, as long as he survived, for if the battle started to go against Branvere he fully intended to surrender to Kino'le and teach them the way of the Gunne. They would make him a Lord and equip their entire army with them. Being a Lord would be a lot better than an armourers apprentice with at least one more year to go for that fucking maniac Balstore.

For such an intelligent man, Balstore had proven himself to be very short sighted, they were guaranteed victory if they just waited a year or two, arm the entire force with Gunnes, they would conquer the entire fucking world, but even Balstore feared the power the weapon wielded. How there would be a massacre every time it was used in war and battles would escalate when the other side learnt its secrets. So, his orders, ratified by the King himself had been very specific, special missions like the assassination of the Princess and emergencies only, so his company of one hundred Gunne men would only be used if the battle turned against them, otherwise they would not even be shown to the enemy. What a fucking waste he thought.

Morlen lay in a semi fugue state on Amyeen's bed in her safehouse, she was exhausted beyond anything she had ever felt, she knew she had to sleep but she had one more task to complete, and that task was held tight in her hands. She once again pushed her consciousness into him and this time she did not gag on the taste of blood. She saw Amyeen on her feet and released that part of Blood to concentrate on his wounds, she let her mind wander over his bones, where the pain was greatest and she cried out as she found it, then she put her life force into him and felt him grow warm as his bones started to knit together, she was suddenly hotter than she could bear and she struggled to hold onto him as he wriggled in her hands and then suddenly she lost consciousness as he slipped from her cupped hands and flew up and around the room, finding the small window she had opened earlier to facilitate his escape.

Princess Amyeen of the Kingdom of Light, also known as the Blood Huntress, heir to the Kingdom of Light and legendary hunter of men strode through the empty barracks. They were completely deserted and as Danyard had planned for every person employed in the Palace walls had a job to do in time of war, whether that was helping with the wounded or ferrying supplies everyone had something to do, even Victarny's ladies in waiting. Although she was sure Danyard would have left them with her at this time, she knew she was still alive for she could feel her weak but regular heartbeat.

She stumbled as a vision suddenly hit her, a darkened room, an unbearable heat, a silent near dead form laid upon a bed and then suddenly freedom and the cold night air, flight and speed, soaring above the palace and castle and city.

"BLOOOOOOOOOOD" she screamed as tears of joy and relief ran down her cheeks. 'Oh you are healed, for fucks sake how is this possible' and then her thoughts went back to the vision, the prostate from on the bed 'Oh Morlen what have you done my friend, what have you sacrificed to bring him back, and my sister, for that must have been you for she could not have survived that wound without you'

She concentrated on Blood and got control of him and sent him back to the northern quarter to the safe house, to at least find out what state Morlen was in. He flew low over the rooftops at a speed she had not known he was capable of, the sheer joy of it for them both making her catch her breath. He flew over a group of armed civilians on the safehouse street, who were walking towards a group of about two dozen Dark Stalkers, must be the last of them she thought, grouping together for safety. The Imperial Guard and even the civilians must have given them a good fight if they felt the need to congregate again. She felt something else nag at her, something about them when they group together that she was told as a child but she could not concentrate on it while controlling Blood so she let it go from her thoughts.

Her immediate worry was Morlen, they would soon be passing the safe house and she saw through Blood that a window was open, it must have been opened by Morlen to let Blood escape after she had healed him and she had been too weak to close it after, or as she had seen in her vision, unconscious. But the creatures hunted by scent, they would know she was in there and would have an opening for them to force their way in.

They seemed to be approaching each dwelling and scouting around it, if they detected life they would start to try to get in, usually by the roof, they seemed to have discovered that was a weak spot of Kino'le houses, a few tiles ripped off and flimsy wood underneath. With the amount of them it was not taking long to gain entry into each house, with screams emanating from each one as they did so. She was torn, her almost unbearable driving need was to get to her sister in the Palace strongroom but she could not leave Morlen to be ripped to shreds in her safehouse, if it was not for Morlen then her sister and Blood would both be dead. She had to do something but what could she do, even she could not fight that many of them, she had barely survived against one. But she knew people who could, and did, for their whole lives they had fought them, and they were there in the woodland. The Dalstock Tree People and Blood shared a home and he could sense them, watching and waiting. She just had to think of a way of getting to where they were needed.

Twenty-Five
The City of Darkness

Jaskin stood proud over the Dark Stalker bodies, another three that will not be murdering my friends he thought to himself. Their dark almost black blood startling against the white snow now covering the streets. His small militia was growing, at first, they had discussed their plans but then they had heard a blood curdling scream that had wrought the cold night air and made their planning irrelevant as they had run towards the noise. They had found a pair of creatures ripping a hole in the roof of a house, the Kane brothers had loosed arrow after arrow at them, every one finding its mark and making them howl, the creatures screamed at them form above but as he had already seen they knew when they were outnumbered and would not jump down to the street, eventually they weakened so much through blood loss that they fell from the roof, landing with a dull thud on the snowy cobbles. The militia had fell upon them like a wolf pack with axes, swords and maces and the creatures had not stood a chance. The Kane brothers then retrieved what arrows they could use again.

This had become a regular pattern, they patrolled and found some of them, usually a pair and sometimes three, they engaged them with arrows and then charged them and each time they were successful, leaving broken bleeding bodies behind and the moral and confidence of the militia rose. Two things were starting to bother Jaskin, firstly how could they eat this much, from what they had seen they were not just killing through rage and hatred, they were feeding hugely each time they killed a human, and secondly, they seemed to be all heading in one direction. Whatever way the militia turned, whatever street they went into the creatures were heading north, and to a specific point north, like something was calling to them, something that needed a lot of human flesh to survive. He did not have time to ponder this as they rounded a street corner and were confronted by a large group of them, by his guess about twenty to thirty that were systematically searching a street and ripping asunder anything that stood in their way.

Jaskin froze, for the first time since he had drawn their blood, he was unsure of his next action, the burden of command suddenly felt very heavy on him. He had no doubt that his militia, which now numbered about fifty could fight this group, but how many of these good men would perish in the act, only about a third of them had any military experience and he just did not know how many bakers, stone masons and carpenters would stand with him if they charged at them. His mind was suddenly made up for him as a few of the brasher men charged around the corner, not knowing what they faced, shouting loudly and waving their weapons around. He tried to shout at them as they hurtled down the cobbled street to suddenly come to face what awaited them The first man, a boisterous shop owner named Hergg, came to a sudden stop as he looked up, his blood soaked mace fell from his hand, the sound of it clattering on the cobbles the only sound in the whole street. The creatures, as one, looked in his direction and then as one they howled as a Dark Stalker nearly twice the height of the others rose from a crouched position to its full and terrifying height.

Hergg stared at the tremendous monster rising before him, it dwarfed all the other Dark Stalkers as they dwarfed the humans, it did not howl, it did not make a sound as the other Stalkers around it fell into silence, as if in awe themselves. It stared with malevolence at the group of humans rounding the corner, it could smell the fear coming off of them in waves.

"Stand your ground." shouted Jaskin "Do not run, if we run, they will chase us down, stand your fucking ground."

"Fuck you Jaskin," said Hergg, and he turned and ran.

Lord Kathreel of the Branvere cavalry sat upon his massive destrier and leant forward to stroke the beast's ears.

"Soon my friend, soon, your sire and your brother perished at the hand of them bastard archers as did my own dear brother, but soon you will be trampling them under foot, biting and kicking your way through them, paying them back for your blood kin with their blood, this time we will have them."

General Carmak had placed him in overall command of all mounted men in the field and he knew this was his one true chance for glory, his one chance to return a hero, the man who had turned the battle back for Branvere. After a few

240

stragglers had made it from the harbour and a re-organisation he had two hundred and forty-seven men and horses plus himself which he had organised into three companies of eighty plus two commanders for each company.

He had watched from his high mounted position above the carnage as the dragoons had performed their split, on their smaller faster horses they had a kind of liquid fluidity that the Branvere destrier simply could not replicate, especially under the heavy plate armour they were adorned with. The destriers immense size and strength just did not lend itself to fast and agile manoeuvring. So, he had taken the smallest horses and ordered them stripped down to basic tack, including the riders who now only wore jerkin over chainmail, similar to the dragoons. These mounted soldiers were now in the rear, hidden from the Kino'le front line behind the other two companies, each man now only carried his personal weapon, usually a sword, and a lance. This time I will show you some fancy horse work Danyard, this time you will pay dearly for my brother and his men.

The dragoons that they faced were about four hundred paces from them, they had watched in absolute horror as the dragoons had surrounded their fallen friends and closed the gap, performing yet another perfect parade ground manoeuvre, and then listened with disgust as the men and horses had been put to death. An eerie silence had settled over the field as the archers had moved forward and carried out their morbid task, protected by the Dragoons. The odd scream and begging of men accompanied by the smashing and prizing open of plate armour had sent shivers through every man there, no matter what side of the battle they stood on. It had not taken long, the screams became fewer as did the horrid sound of steel headed war hammer on armour and the odd frightened whinny of a wounded horse. Every man there trying not to picture the blood that would be seeping from already broken and bleeding bodies.

It was said and accepted by all that Danyard did not relish slaughter, in fact he made it no secret that in battle he would always accept a surrender, this played upon the minds of enemy soldiers, them knowing they always had the option made it harder for them to stand when the battle turned against them, but that had not stopped him ordering the deaths of these men. He could not bring himself to hate Danyard for it though, it was the only realistic option and he would have done the same thing, but his heart ached for the bloodlines of the horses. Some of those slaughtered were the stud horses of long bloodlines, bloodlines that were now severed. When the order had come from the Royal

Court he and the other nobles had sent a deposition to be allowed to keep some horses back, to preserve the bloodline but Balstore had refused, stating that every horse in the Kingdom would be needed to outnumber the dragoons, he had of course been right but now those horses were dead and their precious blood sinking into the soil of a foreign land. He was riding the last sire from the bloodline that had made his own family wealthy, he and it had to survive for his family's entire future depended on it. He nudged his horse towards General Carmak and saluted.

"You are ready then Kathreel?"

"Yes General."

"Then you may begin, I do not need to remind you of the cost of failure here, if this does not work but you survive, I will have your family estate forfeit to the crown."

"I am sitting on my family's future already General, my elder brother led the last charge, he was riding the main stud of the bloodline, if I do not make it out still mounted then we are ruined anyway."

"Good, at least there is one man I know I can rely on, go and deal some death."

"Yes General"

"Our army is moving up Danyard." spoke Commander Loak "They cannot get directly behind us for protection because there are about seven hundred dead men and horses in the way, do you want them cleared?" They were in a command huddle, still mounted, ten commanders taking whatever men they had.

"No, we do not have the time or the manpower for it, you have seen the size of those destriers, each one would take a dozen men to drag it clear, and if there is another mounted charge then maybe we can lure them into that area, as they reach the bodies it may slow them enough to hit them with the archers again. Send a runner, tell the army to avoid the area, we will have to move forward to give them room, get them across quickly, I do not want them trapped if there is another charge.

"As soon as the army are behind us, we will advance, slowly at first, so the army and archers can keep with us, then when I order the charge, the longbowmen can loose over our heads. My plan is to open a gap in their lines for the army to pour unto, then again, we disengage and do the same again. I do not want a standing fight on horseback, we are made for speed and we must keep mobile. Remember they still have horseman and the Branvere destrier is a fearsome beast, do not try to take one on, it would be like riding into a wall and about as much use. Grossman, send more runners to the army and longbowmen, relay what I have said to all the commanders. I want to know the instant the army are in place."

"Yes Danyard" they replied in unison.

"I have him," said Chamley "There was some sort of huddle, I saw from up a tree, ten men around one. I can identify him, tan coloured horse, one of only a few men with long hair spilling from under his helm, seems to have a two-handed sword as well, not the usual Dragoon sabre, it must be him."

"Where is he now?" replied Toker.

"He is almost directly to our front, if we stick to the front of this formation, we will find him, wherever that front goes we must also."

"Good work let the men know."

"Something strange in the air brother," said Garvak "I sense something or someone, she is there in the city of stone, she is changed, darker. I think she has let too much of that creature of hers take her blood. Dark thoughts of blood and hunger swarm in her hidden mind." They were at the northern end of the wood, they had followed Garvak as they had for the last thirty or so years, and he had followed the enemy of his people north.

"She is trying to communicate with me, she has a greater understanding of the link between dark and light than her sister, even if she does not know it."

"What is she trying to tell you brother?" asked Geel.

"Images of them, they are in the city, all that remains of them, but it has happened, some have merged into the great one, they feed and feed upon human flesh to be able to do this, what we stopped with the settlers has now happened here. There is a group of stone dwellers there, they killed a few but they cannot stand against the one, the others will not let them near her. They are scattering now; she wants us to help them."

"Should we brother?"

"You have already advised that we do brother, do you now doubt your own argument for helping these dwellers of stone?"

"I do not brother, but I follow you, always, if you say we walk away and return from whence we came then so be it, but, this could be the prophecy fulfilled and the only time in our history that we have the chance, in ten generations our people have not had this chance to destroy them, is this not what we have always strived for, to rid this world of them?"

"We have, but do we have the right of this thing, yes we fight them for control of our home, and to protect our people, but they do the same, we kill them, they kill us. Do we have the right to destroy an entire race of beings, forever? The extinction of an entire race of living breathing creatures, do we do what we think is right just because we fight over the same piece of land?"

"This is your burden brother, we will do whatever you say, but will our children's children forgive us if we do not. The time we have been away from Dalstock has lightened you already brother. Our normal human emotions are dampened by the dark place we dwell, and our hard existence, but that is wearing away from you now, if this had happened in Dalstock then we would not be having this conversation."

"There is truth in what you say, but what of the balance, of light and dark, if we destroy the darkness, they represent then it will appear elsewhere, other innocents will suffer somewhere."

"They will anyway, man is too susceptible to the pull of evil to prevent it, this Kingdom of Light is only the shining example of humanity because of its location, there will still be balance brother, in the whole of the known world a little off balance here will make no difference,"

"I fear you are right; this burden is mine and mine alone, how do you suppose we enter a city under siege in the middle of a war?"

Danyard looked up with surprise as he heard the single bugle note break the still night air and instantly felt the ground shake as the remainder of the Branvere horseman hurtled towards him. From three hundred paces he could see the two separate formations and had to stifle a stab of fear. He had to meet them head on, they had reorganised in a fraction of the time he had expected and he was not ready, his infantry still not in the position he wanted. He stood up in his stirrups and turned to see how far across the killing ground the army had got, about halfway he saw. The formations were becoming ragged as they wandered across the carnage, some trying not to look down and some trying to look down.

While other were replacing their own weapons with the superior quality weapons of the Branvere nobility.

"Grossman, my lance NOW! And sound for wedge formation."

"Yes Sire." He replied as he leant across and handed the weapon over. He instructed the buglers and drew his sabre, he did not have a lance himself for he had to carry Danyard's but he reasoned he did not need one for all he had to do was stick as close as possible to Danyard and protect his right side.

He knew Danyard would be at the forefront of this charge and there was nothing he could do to stop that, it was Danyard's way, he looked over at him and waited for him to start the charge. Danyard's eyes met his.

"You may not be as pretty after this, but at least that ugly fucker Buldor will have to think of something else to call you, ready? Good, let's kill these bastards." He said as he dug his spurs into Spike's flanks and tore off into the oncoming lines of enemy.

The hours and days and practicing manoeuvres on the training ground again paid off as Danyard surged forward, his bodyguard a fraction of a heartbeat behind and either side of him, the next row set off a heartbeat after that and so forth, each man knowing his place in the formation and closing into a tight wedge, the rear men filling gaps as they saw fit and straining their horses so as not to be left behind, no man wanting to let down his brothers. The two sides of the previous formation now working again as one to form a massive wedge into the ranks of the enemy. And as always, their leader was leading.

You must wake up.

You must wake up. You must wake up.

WAKE UP…over and over inside his head Callan heard a voice telling him to wake up and wake up now. But I do not know how to wake up he replied to the voice, I do not even know who I am, how can I wake up when I cannot even remember who I am?

Wake up wake up wake up wake up wake up… NOW! …the voice in his head said and started to drag him upwards, up and up he went until he suddenly screamed as he was thrown into consciousness, gasping for breath with the vile taste of vomit in his mouth, he gagged and retched as he spat out the remnants of what had been in his stomach and that now also adorned the side of his face. Although he had re-broken his nose when he fell forward, he had at least ended up on his front so he had not choked to death when he had vomited.

Some things he understood, some things he did not. He knew he that he must have vomited, it was obvious but he did not know why. He could see his Gunne on the floor, but he had no idea why or how he came to be in this small room, he also knew Namtu and Edvar were dead but he did not know how he knew this, just a sad feeling in the pit of his stomach when he thought of the giant, silent, and surly Edvar.

He knew there was or had been a battle, vague images of strange creatures flashed through his mind but he could not pin them down to a time and a place. He had no concept of time, no idea how long he had been in that room or what he was doing there. And last of all he knew he was badly wounded, for his blood shared the floor with his vomit and he could feel it still leaking from his side, and the pain of it was making him weak. One thought crossed his mind, if there was a battle there would be people who could help him, he did not know if they would think him an enemy but he did know that if he stayed where he was then he would bleed out and die. He turned and crouched, wincing the whole time, to get through the small door.

Lord Toker could not stop himself from smiling as he watched from the safety of the woods, he had no doubt now that the man Chamley had identified was indeed Danyard, it could not be anyone else, leading the charge on a tan gelding, long hair flying behind, in a wedge formation so he could be seen and those either side but slightly behind of him with sabres not lances so they had to be bodyguards, so much for not identifying yourself you fucking idiot, you may as well worn a flaming helm. His men were ready and mounted, just waiting for him to move and they would follow, and the time to move was now, if he could hit Danyard's flank then he could disrupt the entire charge, he drew his sword and spurred his mount forward.

Twenty-Six

Cry Havoc

Danyard was in a panic, a feeling he did not like and was uncomfortable to him, as he led the charge, he knew he had been drawn into a trap. His Longbowmen were no use to him now as he was leading his men into what would be their impact area. Even if his men loosed at maximum height and pull, they risked hitting their own men. It was a risk they would not take; he hoped their commanders had the sense to pull them back to protect the main army.

He looked up from the view he had of Spike's head bobbing up and down, and studied the formations approaching, two straight formations, three deep about thirty long with a gap in-between of about twenty paces, he knew the enemy expected him to aim for that gap and that was the sensible thing to do, but he also knew the risk of being surrounded was too great, if he hit that gap yes he could ride into and decimate the ranks of infantry beyond it, but then his one advantage of smaller and faster horses would be lost to him, for he would not be able to disengage for another charge, and charges were what won a battle like this, not getting tied up in hand to hand fighting. He nudged Spike over to his left and turned the point of the wedge to the opposing ranks of Branvere cavalry, as he did so his eye caught a flash of movement from his left, a group of horsemen had erupted from the Woodline and were charging directly towards him.

The feeling of panic was in him and for the first time in his entire life, he was lost for an answer as to what to do. He could not disengage from the charge now, not with the momentum they had built up, to do so was to invite disaster as the two ranks of horsemen facing him would simply have to ride his dragoons down as they scattered in disarray. The horsemen from his left flank must have only one purpose, a purpose he had always known he would have to face one day, they had been sent to kill him, a special force, highly trained and highly motivated, with one purpose, to make sure he did not make it into this battle, let alone out of it.

He looked forward again, he was heartbeats away from the initial clash, he steadied his breathing, tucked his lance up into his arm and fixed his sight on one horseman who had fixed his sight on him and prepared himself, but then, to his absolute horror, a company of about one hundred horsemen, previously hidden from his view, broke cover from one of the formations and charged in a curve around their own formation and that of his dragoons. He stared at them with dread in his heart, lightly armoured, smaller horses, moving around the trap that he now knew for certainty not only that he had fallen into but he had led his men into. A trap that if it did not kill him then it would at least keep him engaged long enough for them to hit his infantry and open up a gap big enough for the Branvere infantry to pour into.

He sensed rather than saw, how close he now was to the opposing horsemen and he swung his head back to his front just in time to see his enemies lance driving for him, he dodged left in his saddle and thrust his own lance into the man's chest as he swerved, but he had put himself off balance and the force of his own lance hitting the fully armoured knight on his massive destrier threw him back in his saddle, held in by only his stirrups he flailed about trying get himself upright as Spike drove headlong into the enemy ranks, and then he felt a hand grab the mail covering his chest as Grossman pulled him upright again. He mouthed his thanks and pulled his sword from its scabbard as he looked in horror at the mess surrounding him.

His charge had led him through the three columns of horseman and into the massed ranks of infantry, he swung his sword left and right just trying to survive but he was also trying to make sort of sense of the maelstrom of battle going on around him. He could see the pikemen trying to get forward to use their long spears to try and unhorse the dragoons, and then he saw the men from the earlier flanking manoeuvre, off to his left charging through their own men and not caring if they got trampled underfoot on their way. And then he knew for sure, these men had one purpose, regardless of losses to their own side they were coming for his head.

Grossman was still at his side as were the rest of his bodyguards, but every time he opened a gap to swing at an enemy one of them filled it, and he nearly struck them as they put themselves and their mount in the way, he was becoming angry, feeling inhibited and hemmed in as he could not fight in the way he was used to.

"For fucks sake, give me some fucking room!" he screamed above the cacophony.

"Orders from Lord Gemmell, we are not to let anyone within a pace of you." replied Grossman.

"Well look over there, at that fucking group, hacking through their own men, they are coming here for me, now do what you have to but make me some FUCKING SPACE!"

Grossman snapped his head around towards Toker's company tearing through their own ranks, shoving aside any that were too slow or too stupid to get out of their way and the realisation hit him, a group sent with a single purpose and they were coming his way, he shouted for his two atrops and turned to rush headlong at the approaching horsemen, leaving Danyard without protection but at least with enough room to do what he did best, kill his enemies.

While Danyard and the dragoons battled through the ranks of Branvere infantry the men and horses of the recently formed Branvere Light Cavalry tore through the Kino'le infantry, shortly followed by the surviving armoured cavalry. The Kino'le longbowmen had been as surprised as the dragoons at the sudden attack and were not ready in their formations to provide much protection as the rapid horsemen had galloped around them. A few lucky shots had found their marks but the horsemen had hit the Kino'le lines virtually intact, utterly destroying the disciplined formations the commanders prided themselves on. The fully armoured destriers flowed through the gap made and wrought havoc on the lightly armoured foot soldiers. Commanders tried to scream orders that were not heard or blatantly disobeyed as men fell beneath the fearsome beasts.

The few Kino'le pikemen tried in vain to get to where they were needed but the horsemen were still moving too quickly for them to be effective. The longbowmen stood and tried to form into lines where they would be most useful but they could not shoot as men from both sides were everywhere. Their commanders were also in a panic and undecided as to what action to take, move forward and help the dragoons or move back to assist the infantry. Either way the longbows would be of little use in the close confines of battle, one by one they painfully dropped their precious bows and heavy quivers and pulled out their already bloodied war hammers, and they looked around them as they made their choice of which way to go, which in the end came down to blood, more men had relatives in the infantry than the dragoons, they turned and started to run back towards them.

Lord Kathreel, although carrying a wound in his right leg, laughed like a man possessed as he sat upon his destrier, it had worked, he had tricked that bloody fool Danyard and led the dragoons into his trap, a trap that even Danyard would struggle to free himself of. The army of Branvere had new orders, the rear not yet engaged formations were to make their way around the battle immediately to their front and engage the Kino'le army, whereas the fore units already engaged in battle with the dragoons and Danyard were to keep them engaged, to prevent them from joining the main battle and fighting with their infantry. All he had to do was keep this gap open for the infantry currently speed marching towards him now.

When he had first joined battle he had used his chain mace but he soon realised that without armour the bloody thing was as much a danger to him as it was to others, when he swung it and missed it came back to him with a speed that was startling so he had dropped it and drew his sword, swinging it with abandon at the enemy heads around him, even those in decent helms had been felled by the power he could put behind his mighty broadsword from his mounted position, a few arrows still flew by but he knew they were a largely ineffective force now, they would have to aim carefully now and taking out the odd soldier was all they could manage, no longer an area effective weapon. He continued to smile and hack at the foot soldiers around him.

Kathreel was not the only smiling madman, Toker could see his prize, his men were still with him and they forged a path ahead to Danyard, heedless of the damage they caused to their own men, Toker reasoning that the end would justify the means. He could see the man that had created a legend but he felt no fear, only exhilaration, he could not for the life of him see what was so special about the man. He was quite big but not huge, only the bulk most soldiers gained in later life, and he could take a peasant's head with a bit of flair, but all he was fighting at the moment were peasants, and that was all he was to him, a peasant. No family name full of honours, no ancient lineage, just an upstart peasant who was rumoured to be pretty good with a blade.

He identified Danyard's bodyguards who stood out like a war hounds bollocks as they stuck to Danyard's flanks and looked inwards more than outward at the threats as they should be doing. He identified their commander who seemed to be too damn pretty to be any kind of effective soldier and he signalled to two of his men to take him. He had given strict instructions that he alone would be the one to kill Danyard, their job was to get him to Danyard, and they could do whatever they wanted to achieve that goal.

The bodyguard commander suddenly screamed and his sixteen men turned their horses and charged at Toker's men, taking him completely by surprise, bodyguards simply did not behave in this way, they did not leave their protected one unguarded, especially when they knew they were outnumbered three to one, maybe he had underestimated Danyard after all, maybe the reason he was a legend among men was because he was actually a legend, he felt a quick stab of fear but quickly pushed it aside, no one could be that good. Surely?

Grossman screamed an order at his men and they spun their mounts on a penny and charged at the oncoming threat. He had already briefed his men on his suspicions so they were ready for the order, they knew they were outnumbered but each and every one of them was a volunteer who understood the risks involved in sticking close to a commander who chose to lead from the front. Toker's men were also highly motivated and renowned for their skill at arms, having been selected and trained almost exclusively by Namtu, and their armour was similar to the Dragoons in style, a form of light armour made of mail and small light pieces of plate over sections of boiled and shaped leather.

Toker himself held back and let twenty of his men to the front, to engage those bodyguards and keep them out of his way, he had his eyes on one man only and that man was still trying to make sense of the battle raging around him, not fighting as much as surviving, not looking for targets but more looking to orientate himself, only engaging those who were an immediate threat to him. Toker, who had never commanded a formation of more than one hundred took this as a sign of the folly of the man, not seeing the big picture and trying to make sense of it as Danyard was.

His men hit the bodyguards hard and punched a hole through their line which he shot through while he had the chance, aiming for Danyard, his sword held high ready for a sweeping cut to try and take the man's head, just as he did Spike suddenly reared up in response on his hindquarters to the threat and

Toker was carried onwards by his own momentum unable to stop himself as his sword came down into the flank of Spike's unprotected neck, blood exploded from the wound in a huge bright arc as the pressure that had been built up in the horse from its recent exertions suddenly found an outlet, it sprayed across Tokers face as he shot past, pulling his sword blade from the wounded animal as he went by.

Spike came down from his reared-up position and realized, he no longer had the strength to stand on all four legs and collapsed forward onto his knees and then his back legs gave out. The arterial spray of blood lessened from its high arc to a regular pumping trickle as Spike just sat there, legs folded beneath him and head down. Danyard slipped off of his saddle sideways as if in a stable and not a battle for his life and took a step backwards as Spike slowly fell to his side, dying with every slow beat of his heart.

Danyard stood quietly for a moment staring at him as the battle raged around him, looking on unbelieving as Spike took his last breath, he returned his sword to its scabbard and took off his helm shaking out his long hair, the battle continued around him oblivious, he bent down and placed his helm by Spike's head, he then looked up and turned, staring directly into the eyes of Toker, who had now turned his mount to face him once again, Spike's blood still dripping from his sword, mail and breastplate. The man smiled at him, a big fat smile, as if to say you are mine, you do not even have a weapon drawn you over rated piece of shit, then he dug in his spurs and charged at the waiting Danyard.

"How the fuck did you not kill him then Baldy. I would've done it myself 'cept there was a big bald bastard in my way."

"I made a big mistake once, as well you know, didn't want to put Danyard in an awkward position again. That slimy fucker has information that he needs to be questioned over, like who else was involved, and we don't have the time now, when this is over my time will come, right now we need to get back to her."

They were heading to the strong room, Buldor still shaking from the adrenaline coursing around his body and wanting to find an outlet for it when they heard a scream from one of the upper hallways, near to where the Princess's chambers were, followed by a dull thud, which to them both sounded like a body hitting the floor. They looked at each other, both thinking the same, the bodyguard's paradox, someone somewhere is in trouble, but it is not our priority, protecting the Princess is.

"What d'ya wanna do Baldy?" asked Nartan.

"The strong room door is locked, from the inside, it would take a week with a dozen men and hammers better than this to break the fucker down, she has fourteen of the best trained men in the known world guarding her behind that locked door, I am glad, I refused to let her be moved back to her quarters for that is where that scream came from, let's get up there Ugly."

Buldor ran up the stairs followed by Nartan who drew his sword as he did so, Buldor's mighty hammer was in his hands, as always. As he ran, he shouted for the Palace guard, he heard feet approaching and the rattle of light armour and weapons as a four-man patrol met them at the first landing.

"I believe assassins have entered the palace," he said to them "There was a scream and the sound of a body hitting the floor towards the quarters, follow me," pleased that each man had already drawn his sword.

"Yes Commander." they replied as one, all used to taking orders from him, although they had their own command structure Buldor technically outranked everyone except Danyard in respect of the security of the Princess so each new man to the Palace Guard soon learnt who really commanded, few having the courage to openly disobey him. They ran upstairs just in time to see an armed man run around a corner.

"You, run for more men, sound the alarm, I want all patrols here as soon as possible, you three prepare yourselves, this is it, this is for real, we do not know how many there are but I know we will probably be outnumbered, it is time to earn your pay."

Toker sat on his horse and stared at Danyard, the man just stood there, like he did not have a care in the world, Toker could not stop the grin from spreading across his face. There was the legendary Danyard, Lord Protector of the Kingdom of Light, Commander in Chief of its armed forces and fabled to be the most feared person to ever walk the field of battle and he did not even have his famous sword in his hand. He could see it clearly, very distinctive, two handed broadsword on his hip and his hands not even reaching for it, well this was a dream come true, how could he fail to kill this man, all he had to do was charge at him and so that is what he did, his men already clearing a path for him, holding back the foot soldiers that milled around looking for an enemy to fight. Another small stab of fear brushed his mind quickly as he dug in his spurs and charged, still the man did not move, paces away and still he stood unmoving, unblinking, waiting and…and…calculating, too late Toker realised that he was the one in the trap, too late he realised that Danyard had not been staring off into the distance but calculating the exact spot where he would pass him, but he had built up too much momentum to pull up and suddenly Danyard was a blur of movement and Toker shot passed him wondering what had happened. He was sure that something had happened and he felt weak and off balance, he gripped his reins tighter but could not seem to balance himself, he looked down to see why and screamed in shock, for his right leg was missing below the knee, a huge slash on his horses flank marked where Danyard's sword had struck, his and his horses blood was pouring from the wounds and he fell sideways from the beast and onto the bloody mess of the field.

He lay there on the wet ground as dizziness and tiredness swept over him in huge waves, he was so damn tired, just close his eyes for a while and doze then feel better to fight on, before his heavy eyelids closed, he saw another blur of movement and realised this was Danyard, the bloodlust upon him, he was going through the Branvere soldiers like they were made of water, none lasted more than a few heartbeats before him. He was whirl of long matted hair, flashing steel and sprays of blood. This was not the man he thought he had faced, this was a whole different man, this was the man Chamley had warned him about, the man who had turned the tide of a battle and forced an entire army to flee.

He let his eyes close and the darkness take him and he found a contentment in that solid darkness that he had never known, I saw something today, something that will be spoken of for generations to come. His heart stopped pumping what remained of his blood out of the stump of his leg and he thought no more.

Chamley stared in horror at the scene before him, Toker had lost a leg in a charge against a man that did not even have a weapon drawn, it had happened so fast, he did not even know how it had happened. Toker had charged and then in the blink of an eye Danyard's sword was not only in his hand but raised high and had struck down through Toker's leg, but the movement had not stopped there as Danyard did not stop to check what damage he had done, he did not have to, knowing the man would probably suffer immediate and fatal bloodless, and in the same moment he had swept through four foot soldiers who had not even known he was there. He never stopped to check on those that he attacked, he just knew that even if they were not dead, they were no longer a threat to him so he wasted no more time and energy on them.

Chamley, still mounted and staring caught the eyes of the remainder of Toker's men, his men now, and headed through the throng to Danyard, not a mad rush this time, he did not want the man to see him coming in a mad death or glory charge as Toker had done.

Ahead Danyard's remaining bodyguards also tried to head for him, to give him some protection on his flanks, although at this stage, he did not seem to need it. There were about nine of them that he could see, and still the good looking one led them. Chamley made him out just ahead, the man was skilled with a sabre but distracted by constantly trying to search out his Lord.

Chamley knew, he would only get one chance at this so he scabbarded his sword and reached back to pull his chain mace from a saddle pouch, securing it in his right hand he spurred his horse forward and swung the weapon at the back of the man's head, even though the noise and chaos of the battle he heard the sickening crunch of bone through the man's helm as the heavy spiked ball smacked into bone underneath, the man shot forward in his saddle dropping his sabre and reins as he did and slipped from his horse. He was dragged for a short distance as one foot was stuck in the stirrup and then it worked free and he lay there, eyes glazed over staring up at the stars above, blood and spittle frothing from his nose and mouth, he tried to move but only managed to roll onto his side as a Branvere Destrier ridden by a knight charged over and did what it was trained to do, it stamped on his head, forcing his already damaged skull into the soft earth. Chamley was stunned for a while, staring at the scene. The knight on the destrier laughed out loud and continued to look for further targets, seemingly unaffected by the horror of it and merrily swing his mighty broadsword at the few men hardy enough to try and unhorse him.

Chamley shook himself out of his reverie and looked about for his men, but too late, one of the other bodyguards was already upon him, as he went to block the thrust he realised he was still holding his mace and not his sword and he was too late and watched as the dragoon sabre was thrust cleanly through his chainmail and into his chest, near enough up to the hilt, he felt every inch of it make its way through him and snag on his chainmail out of his back, The dragoon wrenched back on the sabre trying to free it but it was stuck in his ribs and every time he pulled it waves of pain wracked through him. Chamley tried to scream but could not find the air, the dragoon let go his reins and pulled with both hands but still could not free the weapon. They looked into each other's eyes and Chamley saw the fear there, to be on a field of battle without a weapon, he almost felt sorry for the man, then the man looked down at Chamley's hand and saw his chain mace, he reached down and almost gently took it from him, simply sliding Chamley's hand from it. The Dragoon looked like he was going to swing it at him but then, again quite gently, simply pushed him from his saddle. He landed next to the dragoon commander he had struck with his mace, face towards him as they both lay there in the mud. Unbelievably the dragoon was still breathing, a huge gash the shape of a horseshoe covered the side of his face but blood continued to froth at his mouth. Chamley tried to speak to him as he lay there on the field facing him but found yet again, he had no air in his lungs to form the words.

Twenty-Seven
And Let Slip

Jaskin looked on as Hergg turned and ran, he shouted again for the others to stand their ground but he could see the fear in their faces now, the earlier elation at their success quickly fled from them.

"We need to stand together even more now, they fear us in numbers, not individuals." He shouted but as he looked back at his little militia, he knew he was fighting a losing battle, they were scared and with good reason. Then came another almighty roar as the giant Stalker stretched out his massive chest and gave vent to its rage, and Jaskin's men scattered, he knew then that they were lost, so he turned on his heels and ran after them.

The fear for being ran down by a creature was with him as he ran, he quickly saw a house ahead with a small window open, high up about two paces from the ground, if he could reach it he should be safe inside, he may have to barricade the door but that should be easy enough, at least he could fight them as he did before, not be cut down on the street like a fleeing dog.

He ran for the window and leapt at it, forcing his hand inside and shoving it fully open, he struggled through, snagging his sword belt as he did, his legs were still outside kicking so in his panic he released the sword belt at the buckle and heaved himself through, just grabbing his sword belt and pulling it through with him as he landed hard on the floor of the room he found himself in.

He lay there for a few moments getting his breath back, winded but otherwise unhurt, eventually he sat up and looked around him. It was then that he noticed he was not alone in the room; a young woman lay upon the bed. At first, he thought she was dead, so shallow was her breath, but as he got closer, he could feel the heat emanating from her and the sheen of sweat that covered her. He stared fascinated for a while until a howl from outside brought him back to reality. He immediately reached up and secured the open window, although she obviously needed the fresh air the risk of them scenting her was too great. They may come through this house anyway, he thought, but yet again I will make the bastards work for it.

He pushed open the bedroom door to the main house to see what he could use to defend it, he had his broadsword but he was an old soldier, and soldiers can never have too many weapons, especially as his broadsword was a bit unwieldy in a close environment like a house. The first thing he noticed was the build quality, stone walls a foot thick, solid oak beams, as a carpenter himself he had rarely seen such a well-built house, most houses, even good ones started as a shack and got built up from there, this person had started from the ground up and had builders spend a quality amount of time and materials. The door was a thing of beauty and from a glance it looked wooden, but he had seen one like before, it was solid iron, with wooden panelling to give the effect of wood. As well as a main lock it had three deadbolts that could only be operated from the inside, well that's one place the fuckers will not be coming in.

He headed up stairs and found what he hoped would be the case, a solid wood ceiling, only the most expensive houses had such a luxury, most upper floors looked directly into the roof rafters. The upper hallway had a small roof hatch to give access to the roof space, it looked tiny to him but he estimated it to be about a two-foot square, enough for a small human to get through but not a Dark Stalker. A plan began to form in his mind. He headed back downstairs to check for other windows, the only one he had seen on the ground floor was the one he had climbed through and he hoped this to be the case, it was the case but not what made him smile more than he had at any other point that day, for then he discovered a small cupboard with a sliding door open a few inches, he slid it back and could not believe what stared back at him.

Jeldin sat in his high perch on the edge of the tree line, he was completely hidden from view although he commanded an excellent view of what lay before him. He had followed the small company of men as far as he could and observed them, and he had decided that indeed they were here for one purpose, and that was to kill Danyard, and his fears had been confirmed when battle had joined and they had suddenly and at great speed ridden from the wood towards the leading edge of the battle. He had grabbed for his bow but only managed to hit one of them, knocking the man from his horse as they rapidly charged away.

Then he had sat and wondered what he could do now, he could hardly join the battle on foot and his horse was probably back in the stable by now and his brother dragoons were engaged in a fierce fight they could not seem to break out of. He hated himself for the predicament he was in, once again not in the action, and once again just through following orders, but this time he could do something about it, this time he knew what he could do and he was probably the only man who could do it.

Commander Damerall paced and swore and paced, she was ready, the crews were ready, the fucking trebuchets, after five long years, were ready. She waited for a signal, a signal that she knew would not come for she, with her spyglass, had seen Danyard cut from his horse. At this distance she could not even be sure it was him, and although not a soldier herself, she knew enough about war to know an unhorsed horseman did not last long, but then, the last time he had been unhorsed a legend had been born. But the longer she waited, the slimmer the chance the order would come. She thought back to his last words to her.

"You will not release your machines until I, or Lord Gemmell, give the order, is that understood Commander?"

"Yes Sire, but what if, if you fall in the battle?"

"I will give orders to my runners, to signal you by flags, you may take those orders or from a relay sent by me, or Lord Gemmell."

"So, I can shoot by relay Sire?"

"Yes, you can, carry on Commander."

"Yes Sire."

She could clearly see from her position on the battlements with her spyglass what was happening and she was constantly doing calculations in her head, weight, trajectory, distance as the battle ebbed and flowed. Right now she could see the dragoons being herded away from the main battle, a master stroke by the enemy, thousands of foot soldier surrounded them and they did not even have to fully engage them, just keep them away from the main battle, where the Kino'le Army were struggling to hold the line against the monstrous destriers battering their ranks. This is what her trebuchets were for, she could give the order herself but she had Danyard's orders rattling around her head, he was quite rightly scared that the loads would land short, which is why he only wanted them used in a dire emergency, but she considered this to be such. Tears of frustration coursed down her face as she watched the battle, she knew by not letting her shoot, he was taking the responsibility upon himself, which he always did, he simply would not put the lives of that many soldiers in the hands of another.

Being one of only a handful of women, not only in Kino'le but in the entire known world, to hold the rank of Commander she was fiercely loyal to Danyard, but she knew how stubborn he was on issues of safety and could not bring herself to disobey him. She looked at the battle again, training her spyglass for a glimpse of any kind of signal, she did not see anything but as she took it from her eye and turned towards her crews she saw a single dragoon having a heated discussion with her crew captain, she ran towards them as fast as she could.

Lord Gemmell, who had been at the rear of the formations of dragoons to help with command and control now tried to rally what he could of his forces. He was trying to get enough men together to form a small company so they could break out, but every time he got close, they were surrounded again and forced away from each other. He was actually very impressed by their tactics, they had obviously been ordered to only hold them back, they only really attacked when they tried to break out. And then he realised why, if the remains of the Branvere Cavalry spent much more time in the ranks of the Kino'le Infantry then all was lost. He had seen half the Branvere Army quick marching around the battle, he was stuck in and he knew where they were headed. If the Branvere Infantry reached the Kino'le Infantry with the heavy horse in support then there was nothing he could do to save them. He had about sixty dragoons with him by his reckoning but they were being pushed, no not even pushed he realised with frustration, they were being herded like cattle away from the city and more importantly the battle raging behind him. He screamed with rage as the columns of Branvere, only a few hundred paces from him, continued their speed march towards the battle.

He held his sword high and waved it around, his one remaining bugler blew for his life and the dragoons within sight and hearing started to converge on him, a lot of the foot soldiers now letting them through unhindered as they were getting further and further away from the city. He realised with a sudden understanding that most, if not all foot soldiers, held a natural fear of a horse in battle, hardly surprising when you had to train with the Branvere Destrier. But to an infantryman, a horse was a horse and they did not know the temperament of these horses were different to those of their homegrown horses. Gemmell knew he could use this to his advantage, he just had to create a bit of space. He waited and waited as more men trickled in, and when he had about a hundred, he caused his horse to rear up suddenly, the surrounding soldiers who had relaxed their guard were taken by surprise and involuntarily stepped back as he did so, the dragoons around him did the same and within a few heartbeats there was suddenly clear ground before them, the exertion on the horses caused them to snort and stamp in the same manner a Branvere horse did and this created a small panic among the enemy soldiers, as his horses forelegs hit the ground, he dug in his spurs and urged his horse forward, each dragoon doing the same. Gemmell screamed and shouted for all his men and they hit the surrounding lines like a landslide, each man knowing instinctively what to do, the enemy pike men trying to wield their massive long pikes towards the threat but most being too late, and being trampled underfoot as others dived for their lives. Each dragoon knowing that this was their one and only chance, and they had to keep up, either fight and ride, or die trying.

Commander Damerall charged up to the Crew Captain and tried to speak, but was breathless, partly from the exertion of her run over but mostly from the excitement of what she may be doing. For the first time in her life, she was going to use her babies in action here in Kino'le city, where her father had first built them.

"Commander!" spoke the Captain "What are your orders?"

"The dragoon…what did he say?"

"He claims to be Commander Jeldin of the Survival and Tracking School, but I have never met the man, he seems a bit slight for a dragoon. Especially a Dragoon Commander"

"That is Commander Jeldin, I know him personally, from the Commander's Guild. Do not be taken in by his slight frame, you would not want to fight him."

"As you say Commander."

"Jeldin my friend, what say you?" she shouted over to him as he saw her and started a fast walk over to her.

"You must now release your wrath upon the enemy, our forces are in dire need."

"Have these orders come from Danyard?"

"If I say no will you shoot?"

"I promised Danyard I would not."

"Then yes, this is a direct order from the Lord Danyard, you are hereby ordered to use the Southern and Western trebuchet to shoot on the enemy forces at whatever targets you see fit and you are to continue to do so until you have no more enemy or no more shot. Do you understand these orders?"

"Yes, Commander Jeldin, I understand my orders." She said with a sudden dizzy spell as the weight of responsibility fell on her shoulders, lobbing rocks at errant ships in Kardon harbour would pale into insignificance compared to this.

"Captain Tonis, wind her up and send a runner to West, get her wound up as well, our first target is that formation of infantry speed marching around the battle, the current load will be fine for the first shot and use that to get your range, I will make the adjustments and kick out the trigger when I am seated. We will need every able body we have to reload the baskets, whoever we can get, man, woman or child."

"Yes Commander."

General Carmak looked down at his work from the small hillock that he had made his command camp, he had set no tent, much to the disappointment of the few nobles he had with him, insisting that they remained on or near their horses unless he called for their advice and only then were they invited to come to his table, where again he had no chairs so they were forced to stand to give their opinions.

Overall he was pleased, the remaining dragoons were gradually being herded away from the battle and the city and soon his infantry would be joining the main battle, he thought he had caught a flash of Toker's distinctive uniform near where Danyard had joined battle and so even had a hope that the cursed man was already dead. The damn longbowmen had given him a fright early on but now his headache was gone so he could see and think clearly. The Branvere spy network had not known about the longbowmen but so far had been proved right about his other big worry, the giant trebuchets had stood silent and not even as much as a pebble had issued forth from them.

Time to get bloodied, he thought to himself, he nodded to his groom to check his horses tack was tight and correctly fitted and then he mounted up, pulling on his gauntlets as he cantered his command group down the hill, he looked over at the city smiling, but suddenly his smile was wiped from his face and his blood ran cold.

Kathreel, although tiring, was still fighting with his men, the Branvere infantry were only a hundred paces away from the main battle, he was tempted to fight towards them but knew, it would be a folly, the rear ranks of the Kino'le infantry were largely unaware of the threat advancing to their rear and he saw no reason to give them advance notice of it. No order or discipline existed where he fought at that moment, it was every man for himself in a huge and bloody melee. Swords, axes and maces of every shape, size and weight flashed and clanged against armour and took life and limb, the field itself was a quagmire of mud and blood and bodies and parts of bodies.

Life is good he thought to himself, but death is fucking awesome and he is on his way to you Kingdom of Light, and he is going to take every fucking one of you, after we take in slaves what we want first.

He looked up from the bloody field at the army again, paces away now, no more than twenty, he could see the elite of the foot soldiers now, eager to join what they knew would be a slaughter. The men were drawn up in regiments of one thousand, one hundred long and ten deep, each regiment supposed to be one hundred paces from the next but he knew they would not be now, he knew they would be closing the gaps, each formation getting closer and closer to the one in front, the commanders urging them on to glory, a glory that could have no other possible outcome right now.

Then he suddenly had to blink, a tremor went through the ground frightening his mount, and something happened to the front three or four ranks, they were on the ground, fallen over and ripped apart, parts of bodies flying through the air, their comrades to the rear tripping over them in their haste to get to the front, and then he heard it, a sound which could only be described as THHRRRUUUUUUUUUMMM, not very loud but somehow deafening, even in the chaotic noise of a battle. A low menacing whistle came from over his head causing him to duck down involuntarily, he looked up at the rocks and boulders screaming over his head, each about half the size of a man, but what seemed like hundreds of them. They hit the rear ranks of the battle he was in, ripping men asunder and bouncing to cause further carnage, the ground shook and a massive hole appeared in the Branvere lines, the men who had been so keen to get to the slaughter suddenly having a change of heart and backing away.

He sat on his horse completely dumbfounded, how, how could they do this, the one thing he had been assured of was that those catapults had not been even looked at in five years, let alone serviced or used, surely, they could not work.

He had to do something, he had to keep the attack moving, if they lost the momentum now, they would never get it back again. He spurred his mount from the battle to get a better picture of the state of the lines and he realised as he shot through just how close he had come to being hit himself. The first of the boulders were no more than thirty paces from where he had been and the devastation, they had caused sent a shudder through him. From his mounted position, he could see the cone shape they had landed in, two distinct attacks from different angles, two of the four had shot, obviously the other two were out of range, that meant he had a short amount of time before they reloaded and were ready to shoot again, he nudged his horse around and headed for the rear, and so far, unaffected formations.

Commander Damerall screamed with joy, jumped up and down and pumped her fists in the air and screamed again. The basket of South, really just a huge rope net, was still swinging when she had watched the first load from her baby hit the enemy, exactly where she wanted it, utterly destroying the formation that had been about to join battle. She held her breath as West loosed, she watched its high arc, and she knew straight away that something was wrong, it was too low in the sky, too shallow, her elation turned to horror as the load landed short, hitting the battle itself, where their own forces were heavily engaged. She wanted to turn way from watching but she knew she could not, she knew, she had to watch, for it may not have been her fault but it was her responsibility. The beams may be weak the ropes frayed, or any number of other things.

"Captain Tonis, keep up what you are doing, shoot as much and as rapidly as you can, there is something wrong with West, South is all yours until I return."

"Your Command," he replied but she was already running for her horse.

Daskin could see Curan up ahead and he raced for him, like all dragoons he knew this was their only chance, they either made it out now or they were truly lost. Strangely he felt no fear, not like the anticipation of sat waiting for that first charge, his heart had been beating so much he had broken out into a sweat in the cold night air and nearly went into a panic attack, and they he had felt a hand on his shoulder and once again Curan was there, just to one side of him reaching over and he had been reassured, truly you are the brother I never had Curan, you saw my fear but did not criticise me or make me feel ashamed, you laid a calming hand upon me and I knew, I was where I belong.

Curan was about thirty horse lengths ahead and seemed to be racing for Lord Gemmell, the tall silver haired warrior was cutting a swath through the enemy infantry, and so Daskin followed, as other dragoons followed him. His sabre was held high and dripped blood, it dripped and splattered over his saddle pommel and down his arm, soaking through the supple leather of his riding gloves, so much of it there was.

Suddenly he saw Curan's horse stumble, Curan tried to keep its balance but he could see it was hopeless, the beast fell as its forelegs collapsed under it and Curan was thrown head first into a group of startled infantry who had been scrambling to get out of the way. Curan, although dazed, leapt to his feet and looked around desperately for his sabre, it had fallen from his grasp during the fall. He could not catch sight of it but then quickly spied an abandoned broadsword in the bloody mess of the field and he dived for it as the Branvere soldiers closed in on him. Daskin, knowing that he should not for he would be left behind pulled his own mount up and swung his sabre down clean through the shoulder of the first and boldest of the men, he withdrew the blade with a struggle as it stuck in the man's clavicle and then started swinging wildly at anyone coming near Curan or himself, at the same time rearing his mount up to stop any getting a good strike at them both. Curan leapt to his feet and also started swing his new broadsword for all he was worth, he took a moment to look up at the still mounted Daskin, who was screaming for him to jump up behind him. Curan looked about him as he cleanly sank his sword into the side of an oncoming man, seeing his gap he was about to leap for Daskin's horse when Daskin was suddenly thrown from his saddle by an enemy who had taken a running leap at him, they both tumbled to the earth with Daskin taking the brunt of the fall as he was beneath the other man. Curan heard the groan as Daskin's breath was forced out of him by the fall and he feared the worst, he aimed his armoured foot at the man's head and kicked with all his might, the soldiers head snapped backwards in a spray of blood and teeth and he fell from Daskin's prone form, but from Daskin there was no movement.

Captain Elthrick of the Imperial Guard stood on the wall and stared at the battle, he could see the Dragoons were in trouble, if they did not break out, as they seemed to be attempting to do, then they were lost, and if they were lost then the city probably was too. He had not seen Commander Jain for some time now and assumed the worst for the man would not abandon the wall, not at a time like this. Jain and he had served in the Dragoons together but neither of them wanted to go higher than atrop leader but once they joined the Imperials Jain had suddenly found his calling and was promoted quickly. He was happy to serve under him because Jain just seemed to have a flair for administration that bored Elthrick to tears, he had no wish to spend his days form filling, tallying accounts and calculating city patrol rosters.

Like everyone, he had had a moment of elation when the first trebuchet had hit the Branvere lines, but then the terrible despair when the second shot had fell short, killing their own men. He knew Commander Damerall would be on her way there now to find out what had gone wrong and he pitied the Crew Captain if he was at fault, she was an unforgiving mistress when it came to those machines. Her father had built those machines and she was stubbornly proud of him and them, although he did not want to think that human error had played a part but he knew her enough to also know that if a mistake had been made by her or her father it would drive her to her grave.

He had about two hundred men manning the walls but dared not let any go back into the city, they were the last line of defence now and he could not spare any to help the citizens with the Dark Stalkers and it weighed heavily upon him.

He shuddered every time he heard one of the inhuman howls and as he looked along the wall it seemed as if every other man there did too. Most men stole furtive glances his way but he could not give the order. The battle could turn against them at any moment and he had to defend the wall and the hurriedly constructed gate. Each man had hundreds of arrows in baskets and barrels along the inner ramparts but he was still unsure if it would be enough, there were just so bloody many of them. He even had a dozen or so longbowmen to swell the ranks and inspire the men but still he knew, if the battle was lost then so was the city.

He had been getting intermittent reports of a group of citizens hunting the Dark Stalkers and being quite successful at killing them but he had not really paid much attention to it but he had hoped that the screams he was hearing were the dying breaths of the foul creatures. There was a sudden and much louder howl, that did not come from anything that was anywhere near dying he thought to himself and he made a decision. He walked along the wall until he found atrop leader Harken.

"Take two atrops, you in overall command, to the northern quarter by all accounts, and find this militia I keep hearing about and do what you can to assist them, if the battle turns sixteen men will make no difference to the wall but I will die happier knowing we did what we could to destroy all those fucking creatures, I don't want them coming up behind us. You may strip down to light armour for mobility reasons, each man must have his bow and as many arrows as he can carry, kill those things at as much distance as possible."

"Your Command Captain."

Princess Amyeen ran through the palace, she had been running since the barracks but felt no fatigue, she was not even sweating or breathing heavily. She knew that Blood's newfound strength was flowing through her. She did not know for sure where her sister was but she was being pulled towards the strongroom on the lower floor, that would make sense, Buldor would want her where she was safest and the walls were nearly two paces thick protected by a solid iron door. A few startled servants saw her but she ignored them, those not working at an aid station would be too busy with other essential chores, but then she realised that there were no Palace patrols and that was unusual. Buldor would have had soldiers in the Palace to watch for assassins, unless they were already here. The thought struck her like a lightning bolt and she realised that it would make perfect sense that they were, for Lorgane would have let them in, too cowardly to do the dirty deed himself. She quickened her pace as the sudden sounds of melee drifted down from one of the upper floors.

She reached the entrance to the main room of the court and stopped so suddenly she almost lost her balance, to her left were the stairs down to the strong room, where undoubtedly her sister lay and the pull on her was an almost physical thing, but to her right and up was the unmistakable sounds of close quarter battle, steel on steel, steel on armour and the sickening thud of steel on flesh with the associated screams of pain.

She was torn, she knew she had to get to her sister but she also knew she could save the lives of Kino'le soldiers and maybe even kill any assassins before they even got close to her sister. The very same paradox Buldor and Nartan had faced a few moments before, she turned right and ran up the stairs. As she reached the second landing, she saw two men with bloody swords in their hands and a number of bodies at their feet, three Palace guards and a young serving girl. The men seemed to be standing guard at a door where beyond another fight was obviously taking place, they had been placed there to stop any reinforcements from joining the fight, neither had a mark upon them and she realised, they were no ordinary foot soldiers, but highly trained and expert swordsmen. They were about twenty paces from her, they looked over at her together and then one spoke.

"A fucking dragoon, always wanted to kill me a fucking dragoon, fifty pieces of silver for a dragoon sabre is what the King promised to anyone who brought one back, with the dragoon's hand still attached to it obviously."

"A fucking coward dragoon at that," spoke the other one.

"What is it you lot call each other, brother is it? Where are your brothers now dragoon? Dying by the hundred while you hide in here?"

"I am not a dragoon, and I have no brothers but I do have a sister, and this is not a dragoon sabre," she replied as one man stepped forward and one stepped back.

"Woah, only one person I know uses a sword like that, one woman anyway, it's her, it's that fucking hunter woman."

"Don't be fucking soft, what the fuck would she be doing here, in the midst of all this, ain't no fucking bounties here."

"Listen to your friend, or do not, it matters not to me for I am going to kill the pair of you, so shut the fuck up and make your move, either run towards me or turn and run into the room behind you, either way you are already dead."

"Come on, we can take her, if it is her, we will be heroes, she ain't even got that fucking sword drawn."

The first man suddenly ran and lunged at her, sword high and screaming as he stepped forward, he was not the first to make that mistake, there was flash of movement and he was suddenly looking up at her from the floor where he lay on his back, his neck open and pumping out blood. Her sword was now drawn and pointing downward, the blade dripping blood as it ran down the blood channel and dripped on the floor next to him where it pooled on the polished wooden floor. He looked up at her as his eyes dimmed, he thought she looked at him like a hungry man stares at a hot meal, saliva dripped from the side of her mouth and she seemed transfixed by his blood, then she looked into his eyes and wiped the drool away, his colleague made his mad dash for her too, he wanted to tell him, you are right, it is her, run away, but he could not find the strength, his heart stopped beating as his friends body landed with a thump on top of his.

"What the fuck do you mean you didn't weight it?" Commander Damerall screamed at the Crew Captain, she had arrived at West and immediately called the crew to her. "Isn't that the very fucking essence of what we do! The very last thing you do before you wind her back, if you have no tally sheet with the weights on you weigh the whole fucking thing, so you know how much to tension her!" She could not believe what she was hearing, the man stood before her with his eyes down staring at his boots so ashamed was he. "Did you see the men die out there, our own fucking men, dragoons, horses, foot soldiers, archers, all killed by your fucking incompetence. When your wife is dragged off to be a slave for some bloody Branvere soldier it will be your fault, remember that when Danyard hangs you. Look at me, look me in the eyes right now!" As he looked up her fist slammed into his face, knocking him backwards, quickly followed by a kick to the groin as she caught up with his stagger, the man fell to the floor groaning.

"Drag this cunt to the dungeon," she shouted at the nearest men. "I will be down to sign the authority when I have her shooting straight again."

Daskin was dazed, he lay on his front and coughed up some blood and snot as he managed to get himself to a kneeling position, he tried to take a deep breath but pain shot through his chest as he did so, hoping he had only bruised his ribs and not broken any. He staggered to a stand grabbing his sabre from the quagmire of ground as he did so. Curan was near to him, swinging an almighty broadsword for all he was worth, men came at Curan and he cleaved away at them giving no ground, but the man was tiring quickly under the weight of that huge weapon.

He had stood over Daskin and protected his fallen friend from harm, the thought brought tears to his eyes and suddenly he was angry at what his new friend had been forced to do for him, how dare they come here, how fucking dare they try to take what was theirs, the rage built in him with an urgency that frightened him and then he did not feel the pain anymore, he did not feel anything anymore, except for an all-consuming red mist descending on him and he exploded at the men surrounding Curan, his strength returned and coursed through his shattered muscles. He grabbed the nearest enemy and delivered a violent headbutt to him, the man wore no helm unlike Daskin and his skull cracked from the impact and as Daskin let him fall he swung around and sank his sabre into the unprotected side of another man's ribcage, slicing as he did so to prevent the blade sticking between ribs. And the men attacking Curan suddenly fell back, most seeing for the first time the danger that was presented by a berserker, a man in so much battle lust he could not stop himself unless he was cut down. Curan did not know what had happened but all of a sudden, the men who were about to overwhelm him fell back and he saw now at least he had a slim chance to escape.

Kathreel thundered his horse to the untouched regiments, looking for the commanders as he rode, they were still in formation but he knew now that it would not last. The survivors from the trebuchet attack had retreated and joined the formations to the rear, but they had gone to the rear of those formations and the fear from what they had witnessed was evident on their faces, which was affecting the moral of the reinforcements. The bloodlust that had been so evident earlier was now dissipated and fear was rife, he needed to get these men moving forward as soon as possible while he still could. He saw a group of officers moving among the men and was thankful, at least they seemed to know what they were doing, distracting the men with firm and clear precise orders, getting them ready to march forward, not letting their minds dwell on what had happened.

He pulled up at the one who seemed in overall command, shouting as he did so.

"Shuffle the regiments sideways, about one hundred paces or they will be marching through the last impact area and they do not need to see that mess, then march them forward, as quickly as possible."

"Yes Sire" the man replied. He then looked back at the battle area, it was still too difficult to call, but one thing he did know was he that if those damn catapults shot again it could turn the tide, but the machines were not fool proof, they had landed short once and could do so again, and that could turn the battle in their favour, so it seemed that it was now down to fate, and he did not trust that fickle bastard.

He looked over at them, he could see the top of the structures now for the clouds had cleared to reveal a bright moonlit night and not only that, they were lit up by the men loading them. He turned back to the regiments, they were at least now on the move again but the battle was shifting away from them so they had more ground to cover, he was tempted to order a charge right now but he knew that was the greatest moment of control loss, when some men ran faster than others and found themselves surrounded, and at the other end of the spectrum the cowards would find a moment to hide or play dead to avoid the fighting. It was how the Branvere army worked, direct control, every man watched for the slightest hesitation or cowardice, every man under suspicion of betrayal, it kept them in their place, an atmosphere of fear and intimidation ruled the Branvere Army so they would rather face the enemy than the punishments doled out by their own side.

Lady Sarah and the newly wed Lady Nyston stood either side of the bed where the Princess lay, they mopped her brow and tended to her as best they could. She was starting to go into a fever but they did not know whether this was a good sign or not. Although not yet thrashing about she was hot to the touch and a light sheen of perspiration was upon her, their worst fear was of her pulling out some of the many stitches. Buldor and Nartan had been gone for a while now but the fourteen other bodyguards were still there with them. They thought they could hear sounds of a skirmish through the heavy iron door but could not be sure, so thick was it.

They all waited for the coded knock that would signify the return of the Commander but it did not come and Sarah was starting to fret, the surly hulking presence of Buldor gave her a sense of safety that just could not be replicated by the other men. The man in command in the absence of the two men was Captain Carthey, he and all the other men were known to Sarah and it pained her to see them so downcast, defeat to these men was a dirty word and surrender was simply not in their creed. And yet here they were, already defeated once and locked inside a palace strongroom like naughty children while men outside fought and died. It was a fate worse than death for men like these.

She tried to occupy their minds and pass the time by asking them to carry out simple tasks, fetching water and preparing simple foods that were available in the small alcove kitchen but still they were restless and angry. She could do no more for them, or for Victarny if she was honest with herself. Each man was itching for to fight and each man was armed with an array of weapons for the strongroom they occupied was also one of the many armouries.

She was about to approach and speak with Captain Carthey when they all heard a sound from the other side of the door, someone was out there, the sound was momentarily smothered by the sound of a dozen swords flying from scabbards and two crossbows being tensioned, then all was silence again as Carthey silently stepped closer to the door. For a while, the only sound was that of the Princess's breathing as it was starting to become laboured. Sarah and Nyston went to the head of the bed and stood behind the headboard, as they had been ordered to do in situations like this so they could duck down behind it for protection. The shuffling outside the door continued for a moment and then stopped as suddenly as it had started, then Captain Carthey spoke the last words that he ever would.

"I think I heard someone strike a tinder box," and their world exploded in a dazzlingly bright door-shaped flame.

Jaskin could hear the beasts outside the house, they had tried and tried to batter the door down but it was the most well-constructed house he had ever seen. Whoever owned this house was a warrior, and a damn well paid one at that for the weapons in the small strongroom were also of the finest workmanship he had ever seen. They were from all over the known world, the spear he currently held would cost near as damn it the same as his house and the swords took his breath away. There seemed to be one of every type of weapon he could think of, mace and chain mace, spear, short sword, broadsword and even a dragoon sabre, and he knew the only way to get one of those was to earn it or take from a dead dragoon. The broadsword was a thing of beauty, he had held it and marvelled at the blade, shining in the lamplight, but in the end he had discarded it in favour of his own, he had handled it with honour for the last thirty years and it had never let him down, especially on this darkest of dark nights where it was still stained with the blood of the Dark Stalkers it had slain.

He leant the spear against the wall and then he strung and then tested the pull on the short bow he had found. It was an eastern horned hunting bow and very rare, he had heard tales of these sending arrows with more power than a longbow and it was rumoured that Danyard had modelled the Dragoon War bow on this very weapon. He did not know if it was true about the power but he intended to find out, he also found a quiver of twenty bone head arrows, they were known as killer arrows because they would eventually poison a man to death for the carved and shaped heads were designed to smash into dozens of pieces on impact, tearing through muscle tissue and damn near impossible to find every fragment. He had never actually seen one and shuddered at the thought of so many together, for they were the weapon of an assassin, not an ordinary warrior. A chill went through him as he realised who may actually own this house, for it was said she owned a safe house in every major city. He put the thought from his mind, he had to live through this night before he worried about anything else.

He pulled back on the string of the horned bow and brought it to his eye, it pulled smoothly and was easy on his arms, he was surprised how easy in fact, he released the tension on the bow and slung it over his shoulder, tying the quiver of boneheads to his belt. He looked up at the ceiling, he could hear them up there, they would be through the thatch in a short time but the ceiling would hold them for a while. What he had to do was plan where they would come through, the obvious place being the roof hatch. He grabbed as many weapons as he could and arrayed them around the upper room where he stood ready with the spear underneath the hatch and once again, he planted his feet and made his stand against the Dark Stalkers of Dalstock Forest.

Commander Damerall watched the loading of West from the corner of her eye but kept her main focus on the battle, she too was glad of the bright moonlit night reflecting from the snow making it nearly as bright as day. Even at the further distance she was from the battle at West's location she could still see the ebb and flow. She knew she had to hit the infantry companies again, very soon and very hard. She was begrudgingly impressed by their discipline; they had suffered a catastrophic loss but had regrouped and re-organised very quickly. Then in a master stroke they had sidestepped around the carnage of the first impact areas and were again making their way forward.

This gave her some time but not much, she was expecting south to shoot again any moment, and she hoped at the right target. She focused on the lines and formations and saw a single rider to their front, screaming orders as he charged about the front lines. Very brave she thought to herself, making yourself a target like that, obviously he needed to show his own men who was in command and there was nothing to fear. She took this as a personal challenge that could make a massive difference if South could hit him and the foremost regiment, make that entire area a killing zone, make every man who comes close fear what will descend upon them.

A sudden noise filled the air as South released her load, she had ordered oil lamps to be placed in amongst the rocks so they could see the load flying, to help judge the windage and elevation and these she fixed her sight on, and it would not hurt to set a few fires among the enemy ranks either. She watched what to her was a slow lazy arc but to the men on the ground must be a terrifying sight. The load reached its apex and then started to fall and she involuntarily held onto the rampart as it did, it struck the centre of the rearmost regiment, she felt the ground shake as it landed and then the distant screams of the men it had torn asunder. She felt no pity, only satisfaction in her father's pride and joy, doing what they were made to do. Good shooting Captain Tonis she thought to herself, not the target I wanted but good enough.

She walked over to West, she was loaded now, the newly appointed Crew Captain handed her the tally sheet and she checked it over, he looked nervous but eager to please and looked at her with a new found respect.

"I will be shooting her, are the lamps in yet?" she asked.

"No Commander, we did not know when you would shoot and we did not want to leave them in there." he replied.

"Get them in now and I will calculate the tally sheet for windage and elevation as I go, I have a particular target in mind."

"Do you not want the range and weight tables, I have them here."

"I wrote the fucking things, now please wind her up and count down the last ten notches for me."

"Your Command"

She walked over to the battlements once more and looked at the battle again, and again she caught sight of the Knight in command, he was still there, riding around in a fifty-pace circle, to and fro, presumably shouting orders at officers and men. She turned and headed back to West, taking a quick glance the high mounted oil brazier to gauge the wind direction and speed. She ordered the base rotated three points eastwards and she sat herself in the trigger chair that was inside its own protective cage, to protect the trigger man in case of collapse. She stared at the trigger, a wooden lever near her right foot, and she looked up at the massive oak structure above her that her father had designed and built, and she heard his voice carry on the wind.

"Now my little girl, Now! I am so proud of you."

She kicked the release out and listened to its sweet song, she did not need to watch, she knew exactly where it would land.

Amyeen pushed open the door and stared at the seven men still standing, two of which were Buldor and Nartan. The room was littered with bodies, the ones taken down by Buldor obvious, heads and limbs shattered beyond recognition, the hard wood floor was slippery with their blood. Nartan was bleeding heavily from a wound somewhere on his chest, blood oozing from beneath his mail and dripping onto his boots, but he still had his sword in his hand and his usual scowl of contempt on his face. Buldor, although not bleeding as much was not in much better shape, three crossbow bolts protruded from his chest like some kind of big ugly pincushion. Both were pale and sweating as the five Branvere men closed in on them, all armed with big broadswords, obviously warned by Lorgane about keeping their distance from the commander of the Royal Bodyguard. The five were unaware of her presence, so intent on the two men facing them. Sensing they were closing for the kill and as much as she hated to admit it, in the state Buldor and Nartan were in they may actually take them down.

She kicked the door shut behind her and the men spun around at the sudden noise, Buldor and Nartan reacted instantly, Nartan's sword shot forward and speared one of them through the side but aimed in a rising thrust to the heart, the same time Buldor swung his hammer at the head of the nearest man to him, although wearing a helm it did little to protect him from the heavy leaden head, the sound of metal on metal and then the sickening crunch of the man's skull folding in on itself filled the room as the last three looked back behind them in panic.

Realising they were now equally numbered they froze, one ducked and tried to roll away but Buldor stepped towards him and his hammer struck the man on the side of the chest, he collapsed writhing around and everybody in that room knew he would not last long. The two remaining men ran at Amyeen but one slipped on the bloody floor before he reached her and Nartan's blade easily stabbed through his back as he scrambled to rise. The last man knew, he was dead before Amyeen's sword sliced clean through his chain mail and opened up his chest. As his body hit the floor with a dull thud there was an almighty explosion that rocked the palace, the three of them looked at each other in concern for they all knew where the noise had originated from, the strong room six floors below.

Curan saw the change in his young friend, he had never seen it before but he had heard tales of it, the battlefield berserker, a man who knew no fear, no reason, no mercy, hardly any conscious thought at all as he tried to kill everyone in his path regardless of the danger to himself. Curan looked around and saw what he was looking for, a few scattered dragoons still mounted, as he tried to make his way to them the pressing ranks around him seemed to open up in front of him in a spray of blood, and Danyard stepped clear. His long hair matted and red with blood, his dragoon light armour dripping, his eyes frantic but not yet in a panic as he took in the scene before him.

"Well, don't just fucking stand there gawping Curan." he shouted over "Follow that fucking berserker!"

Lord Gemmell and his surviving dragoons burst from the battle like a hundred bats from hell, behind them they left the formations in chaos, bodies of trampled men and those who had been hacked out of their path. He drove his horse hard until they were a good two hundred paces from the battle, he pulled up and let his men surround him and then he shouted for a bugler and a dragoon pushed his way through to him.

"Sound for archers, up and down the ranks, you will have to sound for archers to withdraw for I need them out of that melee and reforming into cohesive units. Each of you will have to find as many as you can and ferry them to a holding point where they can be safe but close enough to get into a position they can loose from easily, once you have one then go back for more. I need others of you to get arrows and spare bows to them, Go Now!"

The men surrounding him shot off whilst his commanders waited where they were, he had seven men of atrop leader rank plus himself.

"Listen to me my brothers, we leave no man behind, that is our creed, we still have dragoons in there, but we have one dragoon in there we must get to at all costs. I saw the body of his horse, Spike, as we made our escape, of Danyard I saw nothing but there was a trail of bodies leading away from it, if we follow that trail, we will find him. Alive or dead we will bring him out for if he is slain then we cannot let the enemy show off his body to their troops, it would inspire them to fight harder, and that we cannot afford. Are you with me my brothers?"

"Lord Gemmell, there are thousands of infantry in there, in close formation, we only just escaped with nigh on a hundred men, and you want us eight alone to go back in there to find one man we do not even know the location of, for a Lord you ask some stupid fucking questions sometimes. Of course, we are with you, our brother is in there."

"You told me those trebuchets could not be used, you told me they had been left to rot for five years, the ironwork rusted away, the wood warped and bent and cracked, the ropes tattered and frayed, you and your useless spy network assured me that I could take this city without having my army smashed to pieces, and now look, look around you. Does this look like the work of a machine left to rot? You can see the individual bodies, and parts of bodies from here, you can fucking smell the bodies from here. Anything you want to say to me?" General Carmak looked down at his Chief of Intelligence, Lord Tromell. The man was on foot and visibly shaking and he stumbled for words, he summed up what courage he could muster and looked directly up at Carmak.

"General, you have my sincere apologies for this, oversight, for that is all it is, an oversight. I am sure his Most Gracious Majesty will see how we were deceived, and that this cannot possibly be laid at my door, it is a grievous tragedy that wounds me that those men and horses died, but how could I have known, such a magnificent deception," he replied. Carmak stiffened at mention of the King, for he knew that the slimy worm was probably right, the King would never go against another nobleman, not against him, a common soldier who had risen through the ranks.

He had had enough bad news in the last few moments, just after he watched the massacre of the first trebuchet load hit his forces a minor noble named Jonoak had ridden at him like a madman, typical noble he thought at first, always the demand with them, but he had been pleasantly surprised by the man's manners and demeanour. But once again, his blood had run cold with the tale Jonoak had told. The harbour destroyed, the incoming ships being tricked into rocky shoals that would probably sink them. No more supplies other than what was on the road, no more reinforcements other than what was on the road. And still no word of his brother. He knew that they had to win this fight today, they could not afford a drawn-out siege in enemy territory without a supply chain.

"You have seen the dead, now look at the living Lord Tromell," he said sternly to the man before him. "You see that man on that white destrier out there, charging around giving orders to officers, reorganising my formations, right now he is the only man I can rely on, no actually, not the only man, the only fucking nobleman I can rely on. He alone turned this disaster around for us, he alone re-organised this mess and made the plan that saved us, look at him, and you seem to be trying your best to make his job even fucking harder... LOOK AT HIM NOW!" Tromell looked around at the horseman charging along the ranks, as they looked, they all suddenly heard the sound they were dreading, the monstrous TTHHRRUUUUUUUUUUUMMMMMMM as once again one of the giant trebuchets loosed its load and they watched in frustrating horror as the load hit the ground where Kathreel had been riding. The ground thundered in anger. Blood, mud and bodies flew into the air, men screamed and once again the newly formed regiments were thrown into chaos and disarray. They all stood in silent and dreadful anticipation, of Lord Kathreel on his pure white destrier there was no sign, Carmak looked down at Lord Tromell and spoke.

"Take this cunt to the nearest tree and hang him," and men rushed to do his bidding.

Atrop Leader Harken of the Imperial Guard tried his best to calm the man who had identified himself as Hergg, he kept on rambling about a giant monster, twice the size of the others. Harken had managed to ascertain that an ex-soldier, now a carpenter, named Jaskin, had organised the militia they had heard tale of and they had killed a few of the Stalkers, but then a giant one had appeared and they had all run off in different directions. Apart from the man Jaskin, who had apparently stood his ground. Shame you did not you gibbering fool he thought to himself, thinking he would rather have the what appeared to be the level headed Jaskin here right now than this idiot.

"And where is this monster of yours?" he asked.

"Northern Quarter, heading for the North gate, the whole bloody lot of 'em going in that general direction, not sure what street we first saw him, think it might have been Street of Sunflowers," Hergg replied.

"Good, you can show us the way."

"I ain't going back there, with those fucking things ripping apart all and sundry, and that big bastard; you will never kill the fucking thing, size of a damn house man."

"Oh I see, suddenly craven are we now, I suppose you were brave enough with Jaskin at the fore were you, with him attacking and killing and you just finishing off." Hergg looked downward shamefully and Harken knew, he had hit the nail on the head. "Well you have a choice now don't you, come with us now and end up a hero or I will drag you to the fucking dungeons myself, and remember how much the Lord Danyard loves a coward, especially when others are spilling their blood so you can live free."

Even Shapley was shocked the explosion he had caused, he had followed the instructions to the letter, and then thought he knew better and added half as much again to the dark foul-smelling powder he had been given to blow the strongroom door off. He himself now lay on his back, coughing and choking on the dense acrid smoke that lingered in the corridor. Shards of wood and small sharp pieces of metal were stuck in his mail and armour. He had been given loose powder as well as measured packages to fix around the edges, he had also been given a small tin of resin to use as a fixative. He had placed them where he calculated the locks, bolts and hinges to be and then he had connected them by fine, twisted, quick burning paper which in turn he connected to the main pile at the base of the door. He had then lit the paper, turned and ran, only to underestimate how little time he given himself and had been blown from his feet to the end of the corridor where he now lay.

He struggled to his feet and was relieved to find no major injuries, his sword was still in its scabbard at his waist and this he drew as he advanced to the smoking hole that had once held a door. The door itself lay twisted and broken just beyond, smoke still coming from it. He was struck by another coughing fit as he approached the smouldering gap and the smoke became denser. He looked back out and up hoping to see at least a couple of his hand-picked men, the prime of the Branvere Army. They would have come running down when they heard the explosion, but so far nothing or no one. He had watched a short while before when the two men had run past his hiding place and he had been close enough to reach out and touch them, but he had just sniggered as they had run past, knowing they were heading into a trap with most of his men ready to take them down. But if they somehow did survive, he knew they would be down here very shortly, he turned and headed for the smoky doorway, slipping on charred pieces of wood as he did so.

The Dark Stalker twitched a few times and then was still, its blood dripped from the ceiling and sprays of it adorned the walls. It had taken the obvious route that Jaskin knew it would, through the ceiling hatch and he had been ready for it with the spear, first sticking the spear blade through its throat as it thrust its ugly head down, and then in its side after it had tried again to reach down through the hatch before committing to dropping through, by which time it was so weak from blood loss it had struggled to rise from the floor as it fell and

Jaskin had not even put any strength into the thrust that had pierced its dark and vile heart.

He had left his broadsword downstairs and armed himself with the dragoon sabre, a short sword, and a small but heavy hand axe, with the horned bow on the floor by his feet. He could hear more of them up there and he realised that they must be desperate for food now, he knew most of this street was deserted by its occupants and so the scent of two fresh bodies in here was driving them to take risks that they did not need to take earlier. Maybe they need to help feed the big one he thought and he suddenly knew that was the absolute truth of it, the energy it must have taken to form that beast had exhausted them all and the creature was weak and vulnerable at that moment, until it fed and built its strength, just like a caterpillar gorging before building its cocoon and transforming into a butterfly.

The others knew the fate of the first one to go through the hatch and they were being very cautious, sticking their heads through for a brief look around and then quickly withdrawing them. He put the spear down and picked up the bow, he knocked one of the bonehead arrows and drew back, waiting for the next head to peer down through the gap, as it did he loosed the arrow from the corner of the room and he watched with satisfaction as it smashed through the creature's cheek, protruding from the other side but minus the bone head, which had done its job and shattered inside the wound. The creature screamed and tried to get its wounded head back inside the hatch but the arrow caught on the hatch edge and it caused it to scream even more as pain ripped through the creature's head. It started to thrash about, panicking to get its head back to safety, and without even thinking about it, Jaskin was there with his hand axe and he smashed it into the centre of its skull, cracking it open and spilling dark grey brain matter to the floor. The creature became still and then fell through landing on the floor with a heavy thud. He heard scratching from above and knew that they would not try the hatch again, not in its current state anyway. He saw a monstrous claw grab the edge of the hatch and ripped the nearest plank away. Oh fuck, they are making it bigger, they will come through as a group next time, he thought to himself, time for a tactical withdrawal, he grabbed his weapons and ran for the stairs down to the ground floor.

He had already placed the remaining weapons from the strongroom here, laid them where he thought would be able to grab them quickly if he lost his other weapons. The first thing he did was nock another bone head arrow to the bow and wait at the bottom of the staircase, and he waited, and waited.

They had got clever after he had killed the first two, he could hear them ripping planks from the ceiling and then the thuds as three of them landed heavily on the floor above him, but they were not yet charging down the stairs, he could hear snorts and low pitch growls coming from them and he thought they are actually bloody planning how to do this, and he had a sinking feeling now that they were on a higher purpose. This was not like it was before, individual hunger and rage, this was for the big fucker outside and they would sacrifice themselves to feed it. He looked at the puny looking arrow nocked to the bow and it suddenly felt like a child's toy, if they came at him in a charge all at once then it would not even slow them down, and he may still kill one of them with a sword through the guts but the others would still tear him apart. He could not run, not with the young woman still in the other room comatose, he could not lift her and undo all the bolts on the door without them knowing and coming straight down for him, and he was unsure he could outrun them on his own, let alone with a maiden over his shoulder.

He let the arrow fall and dropped the bow, reaching once again for the spear he said to himself, "I am well and truly fucked now."

Although Buldor had never been in her service, or indeed even been in her company, he recognised her immediately from the portraits that adorned the palace walls. After her fight with Lorgane she had not put her hair back up into its usual topknot and she looked every inch identical to one portrait in particular, a picture of her and Danyard in dragoon light armour, what she appeared to be wearing right at that moment, with a few minor alterations. He looked over at her, noticed her sword, an exact copy of Danyard's, which also told him who she was, was held in her right hand and still dripping blood. But when he looked up a chill went through him that he had never experienced in his whole life, her eyes dark black pools that seems to just suck the soul from those she stared at. She looked down at the blood pooling at her feet and a drop of saliva fell from the corner of her mouth and Buldor shuddered. Like a bloodhound with a haunch of venison he thought to himself.

"Your Highness, you have returned to us," he spoke "I am…"

"I know who you are, Commander of Royal Bodyguard Buldor, Hammer of Kino'le, and this must be your friend, Nartan Swiftblade. My Sister, she is in the strongroom?"

"Yes Highness."

"Well, stop babbling and bleeding all over my floor and let's get down there and find out what that fucking noise was."

"I will just pull these quarrels out of my chest first if that is okay and I will be right with you, they smart a bit when I move."

Garvak and Geel ran, not their usual fast paced gait that they could keep up for hours, days even, but a sprint from building to building. They did not feel this place of stone and cut wood as they could in their homeland. In Dalstock they could feel every living thing around them, every freeborn creature nesting, every worm and mole burrowing, every insect and rodent scurrying from place to place. Here, where slabs of stone stopped the ground from oozing up as it should do, his feet could not feel the life force of those creatures around him, he could not rely on his instincts to tell him where he was, it was like they had lost one of their senses but the others were not compensating for the loss. This place had no soul, no spirit, and although named the Kingdom of Light by the dwellers of stone that inhabited it, for Garvak and Geel it held no light whatsoever. How people who called themselves civilised could live in such a place was inconceivable to them both. How could you live in a place where you could not feel the life around you through the soles of your feet?

It had been easy enough to fool the stone dwellers that guarded the place they called the North Gate. His people had simply walked from the wood and stood waiting, the men clad in metal suits had shouted and then loosed some arrows at them that his people had easily dodged while he and Geel ran at the wall and scaled its height, about twice the height of a man, no problem for people who lived in Dalstock, where they sometimes hunted Dark Stalkers by running branch to branch. And now they ran, to where they knew their ancient enemy to be, where they also knew, for they could feel the hate coming from it, that the enemy had fed and joined to create the shared conscious.

It took six freshly fed and bloodied Stalkers to create the Beast and such opportunities rarely occurred, for that many Stalkers to feed was rare indeed, which was why he had ordered the slaughter of the settlers all those years ago, for when the Beast was created it was terrible to behold. It had the combined strength and weight of the six that created it but the thought and senses of all those around it, that then worked as one to feed and guard it, for once it was fed and gorged on flesh it had the strength to carry out its purpose, which was to find a new woodland and lay down and die, and from its corpse would emerge the next generation of Dark Stalkers, taking over the new land the way a wasp or ant nest does. The sacred mission of the Tree folk Of Dalstock was to prevent that from happening, at all costs.

They did not want to kill it for that reason alone, for they cared not for the stone dwellers or their affairs that brought war and misery wherever they settled, they wanted to kill it because it would leave the remainder in a weakened state and then they could be eliminated, for as far as his people knew, the Dalstock nest was the last nest in the known world. The Tree Folk of Dalstock may at last be able to live in peace and safe in the knowledge that their children would no longer be taken in the night, even if it cost the lives of their leader and his brother. And so the brothers ran towards their date with destiny, they had no fear, just a grim determination to do what they could for their people.

The King of Branvere, Cathal the Silver, and his most trusted advisor, Lord Balstore, sat at a table in the centre of a birch wood. The tables had been brought with them in their supply wagons with all the silverware that now adorned the table. Both men were now armoured in full plate, and both sets of armour the finest in the known world, hand made by Balstore personally. Balstore's armour was deliberately darker and with less shine than that of the King and that was by design, he did not want to outshine the King's vanity and he thought it made him less of a target, some lessons he had picked up from Danyard. The King's helm was embossed in gold with the pattern of his crown so all would know he was the King on a field of battle. Not that he would ever go into battle, unlike his noblemen who regularly took patrols out and fought skirmishes on the border Cathal was a complete coward and had avoided all forms of danger his whole life, but this suited Balstore for it made him remarkably easy to manipulate.

All the other men in the convoy were also now fully armoured and were stationed close to the table, two other men sat with them, the Commander of the Royal Bodyguard and the Trade Commissioner, he in particular looked very worried and jumped at every sound.

"What ails you Commissioner?" asked Balstore "You look like a startled rabbit, jumping at every sound."

"Nothing really My Lord, I er, am concerned that we may be found by a dragoon patrol, I have seen them train and they are most fierce," He replied trying to put on an air of nonchalance.

"Oh we will be found by a dragoon patrol, I am counting on it, but maybe your real concern is the life you led here, are you going to miss it, all these years you have lived here with your staff, maybe you think His Most Gracious Majesty was wrong to invade this land?"

"No of course I do not, Your Majesty, it was a stroke of genius, the whole plan, and I am looking forward to returning to my homeland."

Balstore watched the man squirm and smiled, he enjoyed teasing him, like all diplomats, slimy bastards he would not trust with a single coin but they had their uses, and this particular slimy bastard had managed to keep the entire plan a secret so maybe he was not so bad after all. Balstore stared at him a bit longer and turned to the Guard Commander.

"When is your first rider due back Commander?"

"Soon my Lord, his orders were only to get a feel for the battle and return immediately, he is dressed as a Kino'le soldier so he should not be stopped."

"Send another one, if the battle turns against us, we can make a fast run to the harbour, and our ship home, we cannot afford to be trapped here the wrong side of the city so I need a constant commentary to plan for our next move."

"But my Lord we have less than thirty men here, after we ambushed our Imperial escort, they fought like devils, everyone was once a dragoon, every man I send away now weakens us."

"You also are scared of a few dragoons; maybe I should make you a fucking diplomat, soldiering seems to scare you."

"I am just letting you know the situation my Lord."

"And I am fully aware of the situation, it is of all my design you ignorant oaf, now do what you are ordered to or I will hang you myself from that fucking tree!"

"Yes, my Lord."

The Master Surgeon looked down at the man laid on the pallet, boy really he thought, but it was the nature of old men to send young men to war. The man obviously had a broken nose, and broken more than once in the last day if he had to guess, but that was not the wound that interested him. The wound on his side from which the man had lost a lot of blood the surgeon had only seen once before, and before today he had never seen a wound like it. A perfectly neat entry wound and a much larger and messier exit wound, but what had caused it he had no idea, something had travelled through his body at such a speed that it had exited the other side taking bits of muscle tissue with it. He knew of sling shots that could stun a man, even put him unconscious, crossbows and other strung weapons but rarely, and very rarely did the projectiles from these weapons travel completely through a body. The amount of power needed to propel even something small and light with that much force was beyond his comprehension and it gave him a headache thinking about it.

He was working at the main aid station just inside the wall behind the Dragoon Mess, apparently the man had approached the station stumbling and collapsed. The Imperial Guard Commander had seen him and considered him to not be a threat as he was not dressed as an enemy combatant, hoping he might have been a survivor from one of the villages on the southern road he had sent a party with a litter to get him into the aid station. He looked at the man's clothes and agreed he was not dressed as a combatant, heavy cotton shirt and Branvere Browns, but half the world wore a version of Branvere Browns so that was no clue in itself. He wore a sword belt but no sword, he had been in some kind of fight but he had not been near the actual battle, more like a tavern brawl, apart from the mysterious wound in his side, but again that could have been made at a distance, if the projectile travelled that fast then the weapon that propelled it could have been hundreds of paces away, he suddenly had an idea of how the Princess had been injured.

Two assistants stood by waiting for his instructions and wondering what was so special about the man. He once again put his finger inside the wound and wiggled it about, before removing it and washing the blood from it.

"Stitch him up, the large wound on his back first and then the small front one, make sure there is no clothing trapped inside him, then reset his nose. But I want him kept under guard, once the sleeping draft wears off and he is awake, I have a feeling Lord Danyard will want to question this man personally."

"You are dressed as Kino'le Infantryman, yet you ride a horse, and a fucking good one at that, anything you want to tell me at this point?" Enquired Captain

Gromm the younger, leader of the Eastern Dragoon Patrol. The man they had captured was sat on the ground, his hands tied behind him and uncomfortably leant against a tree, and at this moment still looking arrogant and defiant, despite his immediate prospects looking extremely grim, which was apt for that was the name given by his men to Captain Gromm, Gromm the Grim.

He had a very subtle manner, and when speaking normally he spoke almost like he was drunk, a slight slur to his words, but when angered he would change in an instant and explode with violence that shocked even those who knew him well, putting the fear of the Grim Reaper into them, hence the name. The rider's pale horse was a dozen paces away, a number of broad head arrows protruding from its steaming carcass.

The patrol had been hearing strange things from travellers on the road and rumours of an actual invasion. So Gromm had ordered an immediate return to the city when the man had ridden like a lunatic around the corner of the wood, they had been harboured up in. Gromm had quickly and instinctively given the order 'Stop him' and an atrop had charged after him, loosing arrows as they rode, all aimed at the big bulk of the horse for the order was stop him not kill him. The broadhead arrow was designed to kill a large animal quickly, especially if it was running, a thick but razor-sharp barbed head four fingers wide designed to sever arteries and veins so the creature would bleed out and weaken quickly. The dragoons were all keen horsemen and hated to kill such a fine beast but they had no other way of stopping the man before he got away from them.

"Also, that is a very fine sword you have there, the mark of Balstore the great on the hilt, I could not afford such a fine weapon and I'm a fucking Captain of Dragoons, don't think an average infantryman would have one. And your horse, a fine white stallion, only one group of people ride horses like that. Branvere Royal Bodyguard of King Cathal all ride around on those fine white beasts, feel free to join in the conversation at any point," Gromm drew his sabre slowly and lets its slow hissing noise sink into the man as it came free of its scabbard. A few of Gromm's men took an involuntary step backwards for they knew what was about to happen. The sword suddenly swung at the man's head and he only just ducked in time as it embedded itself into the tree where his head had been a heartbeat before. "Are you going to fucking tell me anything you CUNT OR SHALL I FUCKING HANG YOU HERE!" Gromm screamed at the man, whose face went white as he tried to turn away from Gromm but all he could see was the sabre embedded into the tree trunk less than a finger width from where his head now was, but then he seemed to find his courage and reply.

"You cannot hang me, it would be an act of war, executing a Royal Guardsman from a neighbouring state, it would cause a diplomatic incident that you can ill afford, not with our King still on your soil," he suddenly realised what he had said and sweat broke out on his forehead.

"So you now admit you are a Royal Bodyguard?" replied Gromm, reverting to his usual slightly drunken sounding drawl. "Now you have a choice, live or die, because I can indeed hang you for you are dressed as a Kino'le Infantryman and that makes you a fucking spy, and I have every right and even a signed Royal Warrant in my saddle panniers to do exactly that to any spy that I find. Not your fucking day is it?"

"I always thought that when the time came for me, I would face my fate with dignity and honour, remain true to my King and Country, but I really do not want to hang. My orders were to ride to the city and then report back to Balstore as to how the battle goes."

"And where is the slimy bastard?"

"About a quarter of a league east of here, harboured up in a wood, with the King and what remains of the Royal Bodyguard."

"There are many woods on the Eastern Road, which one?"

"It is mainly birch trees, the King's vanity again; he thought a silver wood a good place to wait to hear of his victory."

"So, it is true, you fuckers have invaded, how did you manage this? If you had moved an army across the land, we would have known weeks ago, fuck me we would have seen you ourselves, that is one reason we patrol."

"The main force was by sea, cavalry, infantry, supply chain, all by sea, huge trade ships designed by Balstore."

"The main force? What other force was there then?"

"We had a small number of men cross by land so they would not be noticed."

"How many men?"

"Ten men."

"Why? For what purpose, ten is not an invasion or even an advance party, what can ten men do that an army cannot?"

"They can kill a Princess," the dragoons stood listening gasped in shock at this.

"How? How are these ten men going to kill a Princess?"

"Not all of them, just one, the others are his escort."

"Again, I say how?"

"A special weapon, again designed by Balstore, like a crossbow but with a long tubular device instead of a bolt rail and string. It is about a pace long, shoots a small metal ball at great distances, up to eight hundred paces with the man who uses it. Does devastating damage to a body."

"So, this has already happened, our Princess is dead?"

"We do not know this for sure, but the light of Kino'le is extinguished, your kingdom, or your city at least, is in darkness."

"How did you get out of the city without an escort of Imperials?"

"We had an escort; they…er…are no longer with us."

"You ambushed your own escort, you know that if you had been attacked by bandits or raiders on the road those men would have died to protect you, fought alongside you, and you stabbed them in the back, I assume quite literally. Do you remember the Commander's name?"

"Yes, it was Commander Gromm."

"As is my name, for he was my brother, and when I gave you the choice to live or die, I lied."

The Longbowmen of Kino'le stood in a few ragged lines of not quite one hundred and waited. More and more men were being ferried by the dragoons and the numbers were slowly swelling, every man brought could make the difference they needed and each man who dismounted from his dragoon rider was greeted warmly. Many were blood stained and carried wounds that they tried to shrug off. Most still had their stave bows with them, mostly unstrung but all carried spare strings in linen cloth waxed pouches to keep them dry. Those who had lost their staves had been given new ones by the dragoons who were buzzing around the battlefield like flies, the new ones would not be as accurate as the ones they had used for years but they would be sufficient for today. Although waiting for orders they were not idle, they strung their bows and tested the draw of them, and they shoved arrows wherever they could carry them, when their quivers were full, they stuck them in belts and down shirts. They were far enough away from the battle near the wood-line to not draw attention to themselves.

Now they were away from the battle itself the archers could see the terrible damage the trebuchets had caused to the enemy ranks; the battle was clearly visible to the spotters on the castle walls because of the exceptionally bright moonlit night and the snow c o v e r e d field. Whenever a group of enemy formed a column or any kind of large formation they were targeted, one enterprising young officer had tried to use the cover of the woods to flank around to the rear of the battle, but they had been spotted and West's load had scored a direct hit on them as they moved through the trees and the destruction caused had been terrible. Men had seen the load coming and tried to take cover behind trees, but the place they thought would save them had been their doom, for in the tightly packed woodland the heavy rocks had caused an almost explosive effect, trees shattered and were uprooted, rocks and branches rained down and large splinters of wood impaled men who had nowhere left to run. The screams of these crushed and wounded men rang in the ears of the Longbowmen as they were only a few hundred paces from them, some wanted to go and put them out of their misery but they could not break rank now, the time had nearly come for these hugely muscled men to yet again go and do what they did best, keeping the grim reaper hard at work.

"We need to withdraw the men from the rear of the battle, they cannot get to the fore end of it, we must get them back and reorganised with any reinforcements that we have, sound the withdrawal for the rear most units and get them out of range of those fucking machines," spoke General Carmak "Once we have them re-organised we will do what we did with the horseman, strip them down to light order and get them across the killing ground in a fast charge." He looked to his commanding officers, each man a good and decent officer in his own right but at that moment to scared to offer decent advice, especially as they could see from the corner of their eyes the violent twitching of Lord Tromell as he was slowly strangled to death at the end of a rope.

"Yes General." Said the first of his officers as he turned his horse and galloped away to the bugle team.

"General Carmak," spoke Jonoak "Was that really wise? Hanging a Nobleman, I admit I had no love for the man, slimy fucker like all spies and their masters, but still a nobleman, will the King forgive such an act?"

"If we lose this war because of those damn catapults then it will be irrelevant anyway, if Danyard doesn't hang us Cathal will, but if we win…that is another matter, we will return the conquering heroes, led by the peasant general who defeated the Kingdom of Light. The common man will worship me and the King will be forced to forgive me my moment of battle rage, for that is all it was, obviously. The King will also be forced to raise me to the nobility, not that I really give a fuck about that but you see my point, he will have no choice, his pride would not stand it, a peasant winning a war, and he cannot punish a Lord without the approval of the Council of Elders. And those money grabbing bastards will be too grateful when the riches of Kino'le start to flood into Branvere."

"A gamble then, but a well thought out one."

"You could say that, by the way you did well back there. If what you told me is true, not only to escape the ambush at the harbour but also the men who set it, and they must have been dragoons, to plan and set an ambush of that quality that quickly. As you seem to be a man who can be relied upon there is something that I need you to do for me. There is a company of men on that road, I had orders that they were only to be used in an emergency, I now consider it so. They are one hundred strong and dressed identical, I have need of their services. Get them here as soon as you can by whatever means you deem necessary. I am aware there are other companies forming at the rear but these one hundred are needed at the front line as soon as humanly possible. Commandeer wagons or horses or whatever else you need but get them here, as a complete unit."

"Yes General, I assume you mean the Gunne Company?"

"Yes, I do, what do you know of them?"

"I passed them on route here, I know nothing about them as their commanding officer would tell me nothing, but I do know what they look like and whereabouts they are likely to be."

"Then that is all you need to know, go and fetch them for me."

"Yes General."

Jonoak could not help but smile, he had found what he was looking for quite quickly, then had charged about looking for wagons to ferry them to the battle. He had instructed Huxton to order the company to run ahead until wagons could be found that would pass them and collect them on the way. He had no trouble with Huxton which surprised him, he had thought the man troublesome previously but this time he acted like he was not only expecting the order but welcoming it, and he stated that his men were trained to run for hours at a time in full battle array. Fearsome and fearless looking men they were too, but still Jonoak did not know what a fucking Gunne actually was!

The wagon drivers had been another matter, the first group of three wagons he encountered were not even moving, they had gathered in a small clearing and were sharing a pipe, three wagons and six drivers just sitting around when there was a battle raging just a quarter league away. He had shouted at them.

"Start unloading your wagons, immediately, they are needed to ferry men to the battle." They looked at him and a couple of them started to laugh, one man stepped towards him with a loaded crossbow held down at his side and spoke.

"We ain't going near no fucking battle, not after what we heard was let loose in that city, I ain't getting ripped apart by no fucking great monster."

"You ignorant peasant, are you really that fucking stupid, you really think they will be wandering the battlefield attacking our own men?"

"They may well be soon, no stopping 'em when they get the scent and the taste of flesh and blood," he started to slowly raise his crossbow but Jonoak was expecting him to, in a flash his sword was drawn and had slashed across the man's throat, the man staggered back gasping as blood and air frothed at the gaping hole that had been his throat. He dropped the crossbow and the string released, sending the bolt into the leg of a man sneaking up behind Jonoak with a hammer, he spun and assessed the threat from him, the man was screaming and grabbing at the quarrel haft and Jonoak knew he was out of the fight. He spun back to face the remaining drivers, three of the four were frozen in indecision but one leapt for another crossbow leant against a wagon, again Jonoak was too quick for him and sent a kick from his armoured boot clean into the man's face. His head shot back spraying blood and teeth as he went down, hollering and holding onto his shattered jaw. His friends took a step back and reassessed their options, Jonoak's bloody sword was still in his hand and now there was half of them than there was a moment ago.

"Anyone else not going to war today?" Jonoak asked.

"No Lord," replied one man "I know where the big wagons that brought the creatures from Dalstock are, they are now empty my lord. They can carry a lot of your men and have a good strong team of horses to get them there quick, they are harboured up close to here, I shall lead you to them."

"Good, that will be quicker than unloading your wagons, if you had spoken up immediately your friend would be alive and that silly cunt would still have his teeth."

"Yes Lord."

And now Jonoak rode at the head of the convoy of big dark wagons and smiled even more as he saw General Carmak turn his mount and ride towards him.

Lord Gemmell swung his sabre at the man to his front, aiming for his exposed neck but the man was fast, one of the fastest he had ever seen, he ducked under the sweep and feinted to his left as Gemmell's blade hissed above his head, and then he felt the man's mace hit him full in the chest, his breastplate absorbed much of the impact but the blow still knocked the wind from him and he staggered backwards, struggling to stay on his feet. Through the man's half face helm he could see him smiling, thinking he had him on the retreat he brought the heavy headed mace around again for the killing blow to Gemmell's head, but this time he was ready for him and as the man brought down his arm Gemmell's sabre sliced upwards, using the man's strength and momentum against him the blade took the man's hand off at the wrist and blood exploded from the stump, spraying across Gemmell's face, but it did not slow him down, after all these years following Danyard he gave the man no more thought and pressed his attack on toward the next man. He had five of the original commanders he had brought back in with him and they followed him in a rag tag line as best they could.

The men that surrounded them were not the elite of the Branvere infantry but they had still given a good account of themselves and they had not lasted long mounted, the horses being attacked before the men they carried. He had been expecting to be unhorsed quickly but he had found the trail he had been looking for first. They were now all on foot but he was sure they were within twenty or so paces of Danyard and whoever else was with him. The trail of wounded men twisted and turned through the throng, not many actually being killed in the short fight they had with Danyard but a lot bleeding out afterwards. He also knew they were close to breaking out of the throng as well, and he hoped that was what Danyard was heading for, the edge of the battle.

He also knew that they were heading into further danger for they were between what had become two battles, separated by the killing ground that had been created by Commander Damerall and her babies. And if her spotters were not on the ball then they risked being killed by their own side, but if they stayed in this melee they risked being killed anyway.

He was startled by a sudden and almost inhuman scream to his front as his own sabre slipped from the guts of the latest man to attack him, he was about to raise his blade again to hack at the exposed neck of a man who for some reason had his back to him, before he could strike him the man fell and a clearing opened up before him, with a bloodied Danyard at its centre and two other dragoons who were hacking and slashing. He recognised one as Curan, as careful and methodical as always, but the other one he did not know, and if he did, he would not have recognised him, for the man was a picture of blood, gore and rage. Screaming like a demented banshee, his sabre in his hand was chipped and the tip broken off about a hand width from the end, but it did not stop him, men fell to him as he moved to them, most too terrified to defend themselves properly at the sight of this demon in human form, the broken blade causing hideous stab wounds on the men who did fall before him.

Two men fell to him as Gemmell stood dumbfounded and watched, one man with his guts torn out and the second to a flying head butt that sounded like it caved the poor man's skull in. Men seemed to move back from the small group as Gemmell and his small band joined them, officers screamed at men to attack but they were reluctant to move forward, as were the officers themselves, all knowing who now stood before them. The rumours and legends about Danyard's prowess in battle completely satisfied by the dead and dying laying around them. There was the body of an officer at Gemmell's feet and he had the strange premonition that he may have been killed by his own men.

Danyard looked unconcerned by any of the carnage that surrounded him, or indeed the desperate situation he now found himself in. Gemmell stepped forward to stand at Danyard's side, knowing they could not hope to break free of this many men. He was grateful that they had given them some room to die together, the small group closed in back to back and Curan grabbed hold of the berserker, as one would a friendly dog gone rabid. They looked at each other and saw the mood of the enemy shift from the cowardice they had shown to a new steely determination, men tightened buckles on armour and wiped sweat from their hands, and waited for the order. Some men pushed themselves to the fore, looking for glory and others let them, looking to survive.

There was a sudden loud bugle blast, and every man on the field froze, quickly followed by two short blasts and an almost imperceptible cheer went through the men of Branvere as they turned and scattered, tripping over themselves to get back to the rear lines and away from the killing zones.

As they fled the field Curan fell to his knees, exhausted and dropping his broadsword in the blood, muck and mire that the battlefield had become. Daskin slipped from his grasp and tried to chase the men as they ran, stopping and screaming at them as they ran and waving his broken sabre, the bloodlust still strong in him. Danyard spoke.

"Well you took your fucking time Gemmell, do you remember young Daskin? Damn fine dragoon, if a bit of an angry bastard at times, seems to keep breaking his sword too, but doesn't seem to bother him, or even slow him down. Time to leave this party I think, just hope Dammers has got some fucking good spotters out."

Hergg grumbled and moaned his way through the streets, Harken was starting to regret bring the gibbering fool now as the constant moaning and tales of a giant monster were grating on him and his men, it was starting to affect the moral of his men and that is something that no commander will put up with for long.

"Citizen Hergg, that dungeon is getting closer to you by the minute," he stated.

"No, it's not, it's in the castle, in completely the other direction," he replied without an ounce of sarcasm.

"Oh no! It is right in the direction you are heading if you do not keep that fucking mouth of yours shut, if you have some golden piece of advice that will help us kill whatever is in the Northern Quarter, then please speak up and enlighten us, if not keep your fucking mouth shut."

"Ain't killing that bloody great thing, it's the thing that will be doing the killing."

"That's it, one more word and I will have you restrained and gagged, do you understand, don't say anything, just nod," Hergg nodded and then an almighty roar rent the night air.

"I think we may have found your beast Hergg, nock arrows and prepare your weapons, and Hergg, if you run you had better hope the fucking thing kills me for if it does not, I will personally track you down and kill you." Hergg looked at him and once again nodded his pale and sweating head. He had lived and worked in Kino'le long enough to know that you never underestimate a man of the Imperial Guard, for they did not make idle threats, they made promises.

General Carmak sat on his horse and surveyed the situation. Despite the remainder of the Branvere Cavalry being in amongst the Kino'le army in the fore battle he could see that they were being pushed back and they were in danger of being surrounded as the lines began to envelope his forces. He needed to get his men forward but he could get them past the killing ground that the trebuchets had created. The men were very reluctant to cross that now clearly marked area, and they could not do it quickly or in formation for the entire area was littered with rocks of all shapes and sizes, and the bodies of men and horses. The rough torn up ground actually had a red tint to it as so much blood had been spilt on it. Men staggered and crawled around it in a daze, awful wounds on them, their minds and bodies in shock, many missing limbs, and his own men too scared to go forward and help their comrades. Even his old soldiers who had thought they had seen it all turned away so they would not have to look upon it, and hopefully somehow dissuade their guilt at leaving other men in to die there.

He had reluctantly ordered the withdrawal of the rear units, effectively sparing the life of any Kino'le soldier that was there but it was a command that he did not regret, he only hoped that Danyard had been slain before his men withdrew. He had the one chance with Kathreel, but then the man and his horse had been lost, again due to those damn catapults. He could see their outline now, safe beyond the castle wall and was dumbfounded as to how Danyard had kept their maintenance secret, their commander, some blond woman according to Tromell, the daughter of their original designer, had been seen walking around them occasionally but always looking sad, apparently knowing they would never be used, yet another trap he had been led in to.

Yet again, his new hope lay with another nobleman, the young Jonoak, he had ridden away some time ago in search of the Gunne Company, his only hope now was to blast a hole in the lines of the Kino'le forces for his men to charge through. They would need to see something extraordinary to get their courage back up to cross the killing ground in range of the trebuchets. He looked to the rear one more time and elation suddenly filled him, for a dozen large black wagons and a few single riders were heading at speed across the plain towards him. He turned his horse and galloped out to meet them, leaving his advisors dumbfounded as they turned their mounts and struggled to catch up with him.

Commander Damerall strained her eyes at the rear battle, even with her spyglass she could not make out exactly what was happening, when large formations moved around it was blatantly obvious, but small skirmishes and individuals running about were a problem. She thought there was some kind of melee going on at the rear of the fore battle, a divide that she had created to stop the battle being reinforced by creating a huge open killing ground that no man would want to cross, it was one thing to die in the actual battle, sword in hand trying to push forwards, but completely another to be crushed to death while marching toward the battle.

There seemed to be some kind of melee going at the Kino'le end of the fore battle, she could not be sure but had the feeling it had to be Danyard, or maybe a small group of dragoons fighting their way out, she also got a strange feeling that some of the enemy had turned on their commanders but again could not be sure. Her men were tired but exultant, as they had loaded and shot with an accuracy that surprised even her, her babies had performed so well after being idle for years, and her second fear that she would not perform had now vanished. It was like she had never been away from them, her load and ranging orders seemed to come as second nature to her. South and West were both now loaded and ready to shoot again, she was just waiting for the right target, and that was her problem now, so effective had she been that she had no targets, a few columns had made charges across but each one had been met by a barrage and the formations had been obliterated. She was glad she was not too close, for even she could make out the red tint of the bloody ground ion the bright snow-covered field from her position on the ramparts.

As she continued to stare her eyes at the scene to her front, scanning for targets of opportunity she heard the feint sound of a bugle, and the enemy ranks of the entire rear battle suddenly turned and ran. This was not an organised withdrawal, this was a stampede, as men scared witless by the power of her trebuchets, the men who had felt the ground underneath them shake each time a load had landed, finally got the order they had been praying for, and they did not hang around waiting for the order to be confirmed by their officers, they ran for their lives.

As they ran, she could make out a small group of men, maybe a dozen or so, some dropping to their knees, as the enemy fled back to their own lines. She thought that she could make out the distinctive look of Danyard and even the tall slender form of Gemmell but maybe it was just wishful thinking. But what could he do now, another terrible battle still raged between him and the safety of the city, and that was irrelevant anyway, for he would not stop fighting until he had no one left to fight. If the enemy commanders saw him where he was now they would order a quick attack, probably with whatever horsemen they had left, but if he stayed where he was then the enemy would re-organise and attack anyway, and if there was enough of them she would not be able to stop them all, even with both trebuchets simultaneously, unless she tried to destroy them now. The range to the rear where the new formation was forming up was huge, far greater than she knew the safe range to be. The strain on her babies would be horrendous but she could stop this war right now, the lives she could save. Her mind made up she walked back to her babies, and her men.

"Someone go find the Master Carpenter and the Master Smith, right now, we have work to do."

Garvak and Geel readied their spears and stared at the elongated leaf shape heads, each a foot and a half long of razor-sharp blackened steel, the sharp edge ran the length of the blade on both sides, from the tip to where it was fixed to the haft. They were the finest spears known to man, or would be if they were known to normal men, which they were not, they were only known to these men, and for that matter, women, for all adults of the Tree Dwellers of Dalstock carried one.

Each and every tree dweller had their own spear made for them by their father, or nearest relative if their father had already been taken by the Dark Stalkers. The maker would labour for a day and a night at the forest forge, located in a cave known only to the tribe. The Shaman of the tribe would instruct the maker on its construction and then an armful of blood from each would be drained into a rectangular bowl and the heated and shaped head would be dropped into it, the blood of the father and the Shaman would literally be burnt into the steel forever. The haft would be made by the next most important adult in the child's life, usually the mother but again any adult relative could perform this duty if the mother was no longer alive. The weapon was then presented to the child in his tenth year and it never left his side until it was used in anger, creating a bond between person and weapon that was truly an extension of themselves.

The head is specifically designed to cut clean through flesh, to sever arteries and veins and cut muscle tissue to shreds, for that is the only way to stop a Dark Stalker. Even if the spear does not stop the Stalker immediately it

297

was designed to have caused such a grievous wound that it would bleed out as it escaped, so it could be tracked from its blood trail and finished.

Garvak thought back to when Amyeen stone dweller had come to Dalstock with the settlers, despite his harsh words to her that day and the more recent time she had come back, he still regretted having to kill them all. He did not like to kill any living creature and even the death of the Stalkers saddened him, but his people came first and the settlers were a threat he could not tolerate. If the Stalkers had taken them, alive or dead, then they would have been turned or even made the shared conscious and another nest would have appeared somewhere and his people would have been overrun. The one secret he kept from Amyeen to this day was before he had buried them, he had severed every head, for the Stalkers could necromance a fresh body, but not one without a head. But still the act weighed heavily upon him.

He had tried to scare them off at first, stealing their supplies and disrupting their logging operation, but it had not worked for she had organised them, taught them about defences and guarding, about patrols and secure structures instead of little shacks, palisades and barriers, and most importantly, how to fight. So, the little logging camp had eventually become a fort, a high wall all around, one way in or out, completely closed in the hours of darkness.

But it had not stopped the Dark Stalkers and he knew it would not stop his people if he decided so. And he had been forced to make that decision, because of her, they all died because of her. If she had not been there they would have left, but because of her passion and he had to admit, skill at arms, she had inspired them to stay and fight, and because of their child like belief in some mythical entity they believed was the source of the Light of the Kino'le they fought to the death. To be fair to her she did not abandon them, she was quite willing to die there with them, but she had not.

She had killed more than a dozen of his people with that damn war bow of hers, the arrows a pace long of perfectly shaped hardwood with a sharp but surprisingly heavy steel head. At the short range she was using it men had been knocked clean from their feet and pinned to trees, she was the only person he had ever seen as fast with a weapon as his own people, and he had stood and watched her almost mesmerised by the way she moved.

Every single action was thought out, no energy wasted, every step placed in an exact manner to maximise her strengths. He had thought her surely gone when one of his men had gotten inside her arrow range and ran at her, his spear thrust nearing her chest as he leapt at her, but she had not even blinked as she had dropped under the spear, letting go of the bow and drawing her sword in one fluid movement, slicing through the front of the man's femurs in a single stoke as he went past her, and then she had simply picked up her bow and once again looked for targets, knowing the man would no longer be a threat to her for he would bleed out in a matter of heartbeats. Three others, all three close relatives of the man, had watched in horror as he went down, the blood from the twin wounds unstoppable, and then they had charged her, and as good as he knew her to be he did not think she would survive the assault so he had made a quick decision and launched his own spear, she had not seen it coming as she turned to face the new threat and it struck her head in a glancing blow that sliced her face open from skull to jaw and knocked her to the wall so she was no longer a danger to them.

"Stand Fast!" he had shouted at them and they had obeyed instantly, leaving her bleeding on the wooden floor of the fort. He had walked over and retrieved his spear, then looked down at her.

"You will not be as you once were but you will live, if the Stalkers don't get you," he spoke to her unconscious form and then he turned back to his people and started giving orders for burial pits to be dug. His own people that she had slain were carried back to their families.

But now his brother and him faced the greatest challenge of their lives, a challenge that they never thought they would ever face, a chance to eradicate the threat from their lives forever, for his peoples number to grow, instead of being raided and having their children dragged off and killed, or even worse, turned. They both knew that whatever the outcome of this battle today it would probably mean death to both of them, but a death they always knew would come, as long as he could remember no Tree Dweller of Dalstock had died of anything other than at the hand of a Dark Stalker.

They took refuge in an alley between two houses, knowing they could not be seen but still feeling clumsy in an environment that was so alien to them. They knew the creatures were coming their way, even through the stone cobbles of the street they could feel the strength of the one, moving slowly and cautiously through the maze of streets. Despite its obvious strength they knew it was vulnerable until it had fed properly, but the more it fed the stronger and more resilient it would become.

"There is another person near, one who can commune with the land as we do, but she is near death through exhaustion and will be of no help to us." Spoke Geel.

"Yes, I can feel her spirit, greatly weakened, she must have helped many of the wounded, or one greatly wounded, it is of no concern to us for as you say she cannot aid us," replied Garvak "But Stone Dwellers approach and they can do, for there is only one reason they come this way, to fight the creatures and the one, we will wait for their attack and we will make our strike when it is distracted, for its protectors will not let us get near it any other way."

"Yes, my brother"

"Who of you is senior here?" Asked the mounted dragoon "Will one of you step forward and take command?"

"Aye, that'll be me," spoke a young but huge man, as most of them were. He was a bit over six foot but seemed to the dragoon he was as wide as he was tall, shoulders like an ox. He was blood splattered and held what remained of his war-hammer in one hand, his bow in the other. "Name's Truvall, been a Longbowman since the beginning, was one of the first, I hold no rank but I am well respected among the men they will follow me right enough."

"Well you are hereby promoted to the rank of Commander, with all rights and privileges. And this is your first order as Commander, get your men ready and form a line abreast, march towards the battle, do not enter the battle, that is most important, do you understand?"

"Yes, I understand the order but I do not understand the why? What are we to do when we get there?"

"Selective targeting, each man pick and mark a target, as individuals, until you see a large formation anywhere, then engage them. It will be hard work, not hitting our own, especially when they are engaged in combat, but do what you can, and whatever happens, stay in your formation, it is where your strength lies."

"As you say it will be a hard task, and a few of our own may fall to our arrows, you understand that?"

"It is war, these things happen, but this is where you are needed, not slogging your way through a bloody melee with your war hammers, now form your line and make a difference."

"Right you are Dragoon."

"Then carry on Commander Truvall, and the correct reply is 'Your Command."

"But you ain't a Commander and apparently I am, so fuck off on your fancy horse and hack some Branvere cunt's head off."

"Your Command," said the dragoon smiling as he heeled his horse around and thundered away.

Master Carpenter Jonns looked at Commander Damerall with the full look of horror showing on his face, Master Smith Bains did a better job of hiding his dismay but did not hold back about voicing his concerns.

"You cannot do this Dammers, the strain they are under already after five long years sat rotting, I cannot guarantee the ironwork will hold, and if that goes so does the woodwork. Look at Master Jonns, the man is positively pale with worry."

"I understand your concerns, but we must try to hold them off, they will eventually get around my killing ground and once their reinforcements are in the battle my babies will effectively be useless again. We cannot let them get through the wood-line."

"You hit that wood-line once and you can do it again, and again if you have to, until they realise that they cannot get around it."

"If we see them, they could be sending small groups through there right now for all we know, we cannot waste shot on the chance they are when we cannot see them because we will not be ready if they suddenly charge. I am telling you that we have to wind them back now as far as they will go and hit those rear lines."

"And what if they collapse? Not to mention the potential for hitting our own men if they fail towards the end of the cycle, a fall short would be catastrophic for our forces."

"I will take full responsibility for all actions; we will use a lighter load that will travel further."

"Damn it Dammers you designed the bloody things, you know the stress points and weak spots better than anyone alive, you understand the physical elements at play here, it is not the load, it is how far back we wind them, the strain on the crossbeams, into the ropes, the iron cogs, it only takes one to fail and the whole bloody thing could collapse. The ropes alone here could cut a man in half if they broke, so much pressure is on them."

"You think I do not know these things, but we could end this battle and therefore this war right now, instead of wasting time arguing."

"We are Civil Guild Masters, appointed by Danyard, and in every way of equal rank to a Military Commander, we are effectively the same rank as you, and we forbid this."

"You are of course correct, we are indeed the same rank, but you forget one vital thing, this is not a civil decision, it is a military one, and as the ranking Military Commander I am giving this order to my teams on West, and one other thing, I am a woman, and if you fuck me over on this I will nail your nuts to the floor."

"I was afraid you were going to say both of those things."

"You have a few moments to do what you need to with your wood and metal, and then I am winding West back to her full extension."

"Your Command"

Ladies Sarah and Nyston tried to stand, Sarah was on her knees and Nyston was on her back, both coughing and trying to breathe through the thick acrid smoke that filled the strongroom, the very nature of the room now working against them as once it had protected them. No windows or ventilation of any kind apart from the small chimney that served the alcove kitchen. They had been behind the large headboard of the ornate bed where Victarny still lay, it had saved their lives as they had instinctively ducked down behind it as the mighty steel door had exploded from its hinges taking a foot or so of stonework from the doorframe with it.

The door itself lay across the room, twisted beyond recognition, stone, mortar and rock strewn all over. Those bodyguards not already dead were dying, some loudly, some not. The explosion had sent shards of wood, metal and rock in all directions wiping out the men who had stood ready to face whatever came through the doorway, none of them expecting the door itself to come flying through the doorway.

Sarah coughed up a large lump of black phlegm, which she choked on before managing to spit it from her mouth to the floor. She managed to get herself to a standing position by using the headboard to pull herself upright, suddenly pulling her hands away as the smouldering wood burnt her fingers. As her thoughts cleared as slowly as the thick smoke her first thoughts were for the Princess, she did not see how she could have survived the blast, fourteen of the strongest and fittest men she had ever known lay bent and broken around her, their wounds awful, limbs missing and some burnt beyond all recognition. She finally stood and groped her way around the bed. The heavy woollen blanket had been blown across the Princess, obscuring her face. She grabbed the edge of it and pulled it back to reveal the Princess still breathing, light and shallow but still alive. As the bed had been placed against the same wall as the door but thirty paces or so away it had survived the blast, but as she took her first breath without the blanket covering her face, she went into a violent coughing fit that frightened Sarah. She realised immediately that the blanket must be filtering the foul air, she replaced the blanket over her face, covering her nose and mouth. Then she turned her attention back to Nyston, who had managed to get herself to her knees. Still coughing badly, she knew she had to get her to the fresh air outside but she could not leave the Princess.

"Get a blanket, put it over your face, it helps." She shouted at her, knowing that most of the damage was already done to her lungs.

"A fucking blanket ain't going to help you now bitch." Spoke a dark rasping voice as a spray of blood exploded from Nyston's chest and a sword blade protruded from it, as quickly as it had appeared the blade was withdrawn and Nyston slumped to the floor, a gasping breath escaped her and air sucked in around the hideous wound. A Branvere soldier stepped from the darkness and smoke, face blackened and bloody sword in hand, but smiling like the devil himself.

"You continue to surprise me Lord Jonoak," spoke Carmak "the men are ready and you got them here, well done. And I did not think, I would be saying that to anyone today, let alone a fucking nobleman."

"Thank you General," he replied.

"And Huxton, how are the er, weapons? They function, plenty of shot and powder?"

"Yes General, they function superbly, after all, I built them."

"Really? It was my understanding that Balstore and Callan actually made them, you just, polished the final product."

"Well, I had a hand in the design My Lord…er General… I am sorry."

"You will be fucking sorry you call me a fucking Lord again."

"Yes General, once again my apologies, is there news of my friend Callan, do you know if he survived the journey, has he made contact yet?"

"I have heard from none of that party, and remember that my own brother was leading it so I have as much interest in seeing them safe as you do, but they must have got Namtu here and he was obviously successful, owing to the fact that the Kingdom of Light is not currently in light."

"Yes General, of course."

"I would assume they are currently laying up somewhere safe until they can reach us safely."

"I would like to speak with Callan or Namtu, professional curiosity of course, find out how the first batch of ten Gunnes faired with the travel, and of course, Namtu's Gunne, how it performed, at what range."

"Yes, so would we all, but we have more important things to deal with first."

"Of course, what is your command?" As Huxton spoke there was a shout from one of the Branvere spotters, who was galloping his horse to where they stood, they all turned to him as he arrived.

"General," he gasped "Trebuchet, the one on the western wall, it collapsed, its load did not even make it over the outer wall, its main beam went and then it just collapsed in on itself, bits of it every bloody where…now they have only one!"

"To me now, everyone, the gods of fate have given us one chance, and we must exploit it. Get the men regrouped, the reinforcements to the front, the battle weary behind, and you Huxton, your men in the centre of both formations. In front of those already bloodied but behind the fresh men, in two lines of fifty, with you commanding to one side. We need to be ready, we advance in moments, get to your men."

"They still have one trebuchet General." Spoke one of the commanders.

"That is right, they do, and how long will it take them to reload that one trebuchet? Long enough I think."

Master Smith Bains looked at the wreckage around him, his lifelong friend Master Carpenter Jonns lay impaled and crushed, ripped near clean in half at the foot of the mighty swivel base upon which the remains of trebuchet West lay. The pair of them had pleaded and reasoned with Commander Damerall not to wind her back as much as she did but she had been determined that she could end the battle with this one big risk, when they had realised that she was not going to listen to them they had done what they could to the wood and metal they had crafted and then retired to the relative safety of the covered walkway to watch, and say a silent prayer.

To her credit she had done what was expected of her and ordered every person back to safety, apart from the team of heavily muscled ex longbowmen who turned the wheel, each loud click of the safety ratchet sending a shudder through the two Guild Masters. She was in the trigger seat, the only place of safety near the entire structure, for her father had known one day she would take command of the mighty machines and he wanted to keep her safe, so he had built a wood and iron cage around it. He never actually knew if she had realised this, Jonns and him had suddenly discovered it one day when they had spent a day studying the design, it was so well built that the area of safety was very well hidden, strategic struts and beams that would deflect debris away from the seat.

As she sat herself down Jonns had shouted a warning as he saw the main crossbeam start to buckle, and as she kicked the release out it had given way with an almighty crack that froze everyone to the spot and sent a chill through them. The huge net, known as the bucket, had tried to fly through its intended arc but had not enough kinetic energy to get passed its own apex and had descended straight down. The rest of the machine had collapsed in on itself as wood, iron and rope exploded outward. The crank team had tried to run but two of the four were crushed as they ran. Commander Damerall had been resigned to her fate, and sat there, as her whole world literally crashed down around her, still sat in the trigger chair, the shock of what she had done clear on her face even from where she sat.

As the men had run from the debris his friend Jonns had run towards it, Bains had reached for him but he had sprinted away so fast he had fell on his face as his friend escaped his grasp. He had screamed for him but knew it was too late as he saw the bucket empty from a near on vertical drop, rocks, bits of old iron and timber, and anything else they could find with a substantial weight had been loaded into it, and it had all rained down. He did not know what his friend had hoped to achieve, as he ran the damn machine was falling apart, he would not have been able to save it no matter what but still he ran to his death.

And then he suddenly knew why as he stepped towards his body and his line of sight took his eyes towards where she had started to move out of the trigger seat, not a mark upon her. Bains had suddenly realised that he had not been running to the trebuchet, he had been running to her. He had always had a soft spot for her but he did not know just quite how much the man had actually loved her. All those days and weeks they had worked together, going over plans in detail, what could be done and what could not, design and construction, test loads and trials, heady nights in the taverns after a success, and then the big plan, to effectively abandon them, for the world, the part of it watching the Kingdom closely anyway, to see them rot away into disuse. Jonns had always kept himself single, always refusing the advances of the tavern's wenches who would have loved to have snared a wealthy craftsman like him and now he knew why. For the whole time he had been in love with one woman, and that woman being the deadly serious Commander of Trebuchet Damerall, and he had never told a living soul, not even his friend Bains, and that was the saddest thing of all.

She was pale faced and tear streaked as she pulled herself from the seat, the weight of her failure heavy on her. She walked in an almost fugue state, not seeming to notice the debris around her as her body automatically sidestepped it all, until she reached the broken body of Master Carpenter Jonns, his limbs at an awkward angle and pooled in blood. She looked down at him and took in a series of gasping breaths that she could not seem to let go, a sudden constant taking of breath that she seemed to have no control over. Bains grabbed her by the shoulders and turned her towards him, they looked into each other's eyes and she finally let it go, huge sobs wracked her body as he held her close to him and he let her ride them out, each sob worse than the last as she finally let go her emotions.

She cried for what seemed to him to be an eternity until the sobbing came under enough control for her to speak properly.

"He loved me and I knew it, I never let on I knew it," she stammered "All this time we worked together and he never even tried to kiss me, or tell me, but I knew. Sometimes I would catch him staring at me with those puppy dog eyes and I knew, but I was so wrapped up in our work, I thought I could never get involved with anyone, and now he is gone, and I killed him, with my cursed pride and arrogance, I fucking killed him and I should have just fucked him."

"Dammers, we have known each other a long time, nearly as long as you two had, I cannot deny that it was your order that led to his death, but it was what he lived for, working with you, he would have gladly died for you at any time, he did not have to die here, and if in fact he had obeyed your last order he would still be alive, but he did not, he died running to you for he believed that you were going to die, and the only place he wanted to be then was with you.

"Yes, he died here, but these giant machines built by your father and you and him may have saved the Kingdom, and do you know why? Not because you are the world's best engineer, and not because your father was, as much as you don't want to hear that. It's because he built these machines with as much love as he could muster, every beam, every strut, every single piece of wood and iron he put into that machine he built for you, not because he was paid to by the Kingdom, for it was the best way he could show his love for you, and he handed that responsibility down to Jonns, without even knowing it. When I look back it is all so clear now. Every monthly inspection in the early hours, when nobody could see us, he would be like a child waiting for a secret meeting, for he knew he was going to see you again, he would drag out the maintenance and insist on replacing parts that could wait so he could spend more time with you. The more I think about it the more it makes sense, if it was not for his love for you these machines would never have worked after five long years idle. I know you call them your babies, but they were his and your babies, born from love and sustained by it." She looked at him and knew he spoke the truth, her steely resolve returned to her and she spoke as she wiped the tears and snot from her face.

"Help with the wounded, I am going to South. You have every reason to hate me but you do not, you have shown me compassion that I do not deserve, Thank you. I will never forgive myself for what I did here today but the fact that you do not blame me helps."

"Jonns loved you, and he was my friend, he would not want us to be at each other's throats."

Danyard watched as the end formations of Kino'le infantry swung around the enemy lines of the battle to his front, the half army of Branvere was now completely surrounded and no succour would be coming from the reinforcements to the rear for a while yet. He could see the lines being formed by the Branvere army when he looked back, but he knew they would be in no hurry to rush forward into the killing ground again.

It was now a matter of time before his men slaughtered the enemy they had surrounded, duty weighed heavily upon him times like these, some of these men would want to surrender but to leave them alive was to invite defeat, he had nowhere to hold those who would surrender, and no way to secure them against further attack on his forces, and no spare men to guard them if he did.

A mounted dragoon had seen him and his party and had ridden to him immediately, offering him his horse, he had declined as once again it would have made him a target, a single rider among a dozen men walking. He had questioned the man as they made a temporary camp in a small hillock with a few trees. He could not see from where they were but he was then told of the fate of Trebuchet West. He had no other details other that it had actually collapsed in on itself and the load he had seen come down on top of it. Danyard shuddered at the losses it may have caused but it did not surprise him, it had been a gamble all along but an educated one, gambling on the dedication of Commander Damerall and the love that Master Jonns had for her, knowing he would always do his best in her presence, without letting her know of course, the fact that Danyard knew was testament to how well he knew his people.

He sent the dragoon off with messages and instructions, and congratulated Gemmell on his plan to extract the remaining longbowmen from the battle. He looked toward the wood-line and saw them forming a new line, the distinctive size of their longbow staves marking them out even at this distance.

The day was not yet done, and he knew the outcome could still go either way, but he knew it would be decided today, both sides had lost too many men to have this drag out much longer. Another great battle awaited them and he did not know how many reinforcements the enemy could bring to bear, bloody thousands it looked like at that moment. But to his relief he saw only a few horsemen among them, for he knew his forces would not stand another mounted charge, not with only a hundred or so longbowmen to try and stop it. Also unknown to him at this time was the fate of the Princess, by a miracle according to the Royal Surgeon, was still alive when he left, but he did not if she still drew breath.

His fear of an assassin gaining entry to the Palace a big concern to him, but he could only rely on the men he had trained for such an eventuality. The only thing he was sure of was that they would have a hell of a time getting past the worlds angriest man armed with a warhammer. He had a random thought that sabotage had brought down West but he put it from his mind, for if it was there was nothing he could do about it now. And if they managed to get to South and bring her down as well then so be it.

The sound of steel on steel was gradually being replaced by the sound of men in pain, as Gemmell approached. "Your orders?" he enquired.

"We need to get through to the city wall, get the men reorganised, regrouped and re-armed, no point going around this battle, we may as well go through, it sounds as if our men have prevailed so far, and we can issue new orders as we go."

"I know why you want to do this Danyard, it is an honourable thing, but at this stage too risky, we cannot leave them alive."

"Leave who alive?"

"Those who would surrender to us?"

"Maybe that is not my intention."

"Damn it Danyard, we have known each other too long and spilt too much blood together to play fucking games, just give me the fucking order if that is what you require of me."

"I have no intention yet, of anything other than reaching the city and on the way I wish to speak to those who have fought and bled today, and those who will carry the wounds of today for the rest of their lives, and I always value your counsel which is why you are Lord Dragoon, so stop second guessing me and let us go."

"Your Command."

As a group they turned and walked towards the battle area, the fighting had largely stopped now and groups of men stood around and waited for orders to reform. Wounded enemy were being put to the sword and other men helped their wounded comrades to the rear and the aid stations. The ranks parted as Danyard and his remaining command element moved through them. Hushed voices whispered to each other as they saw him, awe struck not just at the sight of him so close but because he was as bloody as any man there. His famous two-handed broadsword back in its scabbard on his hip and his Dragoon Light Armour battered and dented with obvious sword slashes upon it, his helm once again lost to him and his long-matted hair with a bloody red tinge to it.

The men stared at him and his companions as they walked past, the tall dragoon Curan, a figure well known from the taverns and ale houses, a young and exhausted looking dragoon with a mad look in his eye and a broken sabre, a few other dragoons and then the tall slender and stately Lord of Dragoons Gemmell. Eleven men only had emerged from the rear battle and now they walked through the front battle, men began to kneel as they passed and Danyard went to speak but Gemmell stopped him before he could.

"I know you hate the whole bowing thing, especially to you, but just let them do it this once to show how much you mean to them, let them pay tribute to you, for once," he said.

"But I... I guess...you are right this time, they have earned the right, at this moment to do what the fuck they want. I will just never understand the idea, I send them into war, a war where they may not come back from or gain a wound that will cripple them for life and still, they worship me, it makes me...uncomfortable."

"You did not send them to die, they are not fighting for you, they are fighting for their homes and families and way of life, you have given them the training and equipment to fight for what is theirs, and more than that, you yourself have fought and bled for them and their families too, how many men here know about you and Lady Sarah, one in a thousand? Yet here you stand, with the blood of them who would take from them what is theirs still dripping from you, when you could have stayed in the castle safe behind its walls, that is why they worship you Danyard, anyone can command, it takes a special man to lead."

"Alright, alright, shut the fuck up, you are embarrassing me."

They walked on through the parted and kneeling men, Danyard and Gemmell nodding at and speaking with any men they knew, until they came to a group of men with weapons drawn, Danyard pushed through until he found a commander, and then he saw why.

The surrendered enemy sat on the floor, in rows but pushed up close together, Danyard looked and estimated them to be about three hundred, many carried wounds and some of the more able bodied attended to them, trying to stem blood flow and stitch limbs. A huge pile of weapons lay to one side, a deadly mix of mainly melee weapons, swords and axes prevalent but with a few maces and chain maces among them, with the odd projectile weapon scattered on top.

Danyard eyed the commander, his emotions conflicted, he had dreaded this one thing, a mass surrender with only one real choice to be made, and made by him alone. The Commander approached, it was Lord Calston the Younger, his father was nowhere to be seen.

"Lord Calston, what happened here?" he enquired.

"Surrender My Lord, pretty much as a man, they threw down their arms." He replied.

"And you let them surrender and live? How do you expect to guard this many men? When their comrades in arms come screaming back across the field, or do you intend to leave them here to attack our rear ranks?"

"I intend no such thing My Lord, I was a child under the guidance of my father when you became Lord Protector, even though he was considerably older than you he always looked up to you, said you inspired him. You had a nobility of spirit not found in any nobleman, and I have always followed my father's advice. He would be ashamed of me if I gave the order to slay these men, if this is however your order then please tell me and I will see the dark deed done, but the command will not come from me."

"You father will be proud of you, if he lives that is, have you seen him?"

"Not since battle was joined My Lord, he was ahead of me, obviously I am eager to catch sight of him."

"You are not alone in that; I could use his wise counsel right now."

"You are generous with your praise My Lord."

"As you are then, strip them of their armour, everything, chainmail, jerkins, helms, the lot, and search every one of them for any hidden weapons, strip them down to undershirts and leggings, and most important their boots, every man here can walk from this battlefield on three conditions, he does it northward, unarmed and barefoot."

"There are two nobles among them, and you know what us bloody nobles are like with our family swords, they wish to surrender but ask if they may keep their swords. Their armour and everything else they will surrender but not their swords."

"Then they have already made their choice, as have I. They can walk from here unarmed and barefoot or not walk from here, they get no other chance from me. If they do not like it then kill them here and now with their swords in their hands, but they will no longer be noblemen in Branvere regardless of the outcome after surrendering, so their swords and lands would be forfeit anyway. Let our men have the pick of the surrendered weapons and armour and have the remainder delivered to Trebuchet South. I imagine Commander Damerall will have a use for a huge load of heavy and sharp objects."

"Your command My Lord."

Twenty-Eight

The Dogs of War

Commander Damerall stood at south and looked up at her, her emotions conflicted. She still had immense pride in what stood before her, the mighty construction of wood, rope and iron that could cause such devastation on an enemy, but also on her own ideas she had proven with her own recklessness and arrogance in her own abilities. A single tear started to well in one eye and she angrily wiped it away, focus, she thought to herself, you are not the only one who lost someone today.

She walked to the ramparts and stared out on the bright moonlit night towards the enemy formations, even at this distance she could see them rapidly forming into new lines, as were the Kino'le army. A large group of soldiers were walking away from the rear of the battle and it made her heart skip for a beat. Then she realised that none carried weapons, and although not sure she thought they may also be barefoot. She put them from her mind as a sudden bugle note wrought the air and the Branvere army suddenly surged forward.

"Standby South!" she shouted as they rushed headlong towards the waiting Kino'le army. She looked on astonished at the speed they were moving at, after watching them charge and retreat all night they seemed to be moving at an incredible speed. They must be attempting to get across the killing ground before she could shoot. She was suddenly gripped by a fear that she would be too late. "NOW NOW NOW!" she screamed at the crew. They were ready and hanging on her command and she felt the massive machine start to move as the trigger was kicked out, she watched with satisfaction as the massive load flew over her head and in her opinion, right on target.

Carmak watched as his men ran as fast as they could towards the Kino'le lines, the front lines were the youngest and fittest of his men had been stripped of everything that would slow them. All their armour, helms and mail awaited them at the rear, they carried only light swords and they were only for show, for these men would not be fighting yet, they were only to draw out the remaining trebuchet to shoot and he smiled as he watched the trap he had set sprung so well. It is not only you that is a master of war Danyard as he saw the load at the apex of its trajectory, he gave the nod to a bugler and immediately five others joined. The lead formation split instantly down the centre and the men sprinted for the flanks, then headed back down the side of the rear formation and headed for the Gunne Company.

The rear formation that had been marching at normal pace behind the runners instantly stopped and the Gunne Company knelt and raised their Gunnes to their shoulders as they waited for the earth shattering feel of the trebuchet load to hit the ground in front of them. The load hit and as one man the Company paused and counted to five, as the dust was about to clear there was another earth shattering noise as one hundred Gunnes fired simultaneously into the front ranks of the Kino'le Army, stood waiting three hundred paces away. Although that was a huge distance for an accurate shot it did not matter for the ranks of infantry facing them were shoulder to shoulder.

The lead balls tore into flesh and bone throwing men from their feet and into their comrades behind, even those with pieces of plate armour fell as the highly powered balls smashed clean through. Those behind and to the sides stared in wonder at what could have happened as they looked around for an enemy that was not there. And then they saw the terrible wounds on their friends and looked for arrows and crossbow bolts, but saw none.

An eerie and deathly silence settled over the field as both sides stood and faced each other, and then the terrible noise came again as the Gunne Company unleashed their second deadly volley into the unsuspecting and unprepared Kino'le Army. This time from only two hundred and twenty paces as they had reloaded on the march. One more thing happened that day that had never happened before in the history of the Kingdom, part of the Kino'le Army panicked, broke and ran.

Danyard heard the first thunderous shot and looked around in surprise, they had been expecting the bugle blast and paid it no heed, they knew that the army of Branvere would once again advance on them, what he did not know was that he had been led into a trap, for he was at the rear of the army trying to plan his next moves. He had sent orders forward that the Kino'le army was to stand fast and let Branvere throw themselves at his lines and he had also watched as South's load had soared overhead. He had felt the load land and been slightly concerned when he had heard no screams of wounded and dying men, but he did not know if he would have heard it from where he was. But then he had heard a noise, a noise he had never heard before, and that was followed by screams of men in pain. Then about thirty heartbeats later he heard the noise gain and he knew something was terribly wrong, for the rear lines of the army surged back towards him. There were more screams and this time the sound of panic as well as pain.

"Gemmell, what the fuck is that and what the fuck is it doing to our men!" He said as an awful realisation hit him, a memory of a giant man on a beach, a giant man with a half destroyed shoulder and a hole in his back the size of a fist, and a Princess thrown clean out of her carriage with a similar exit wound and his blood ran cold.

"I need a horse now, right fucking now, and so do the rest of you!"

Damerall stared in horror at the scene before her, it was a trap that she had been drawn into and battle would soon be joined and her remaining baby would be rendered redundant, of no use in a close fought melee. And even with both crews working for South only, she still could not get it loaded in time to make a difference. She walked to her small office and strapped on her sword belt; her men were waiting for her as she walked out.

"Time to get bloody my friends, gather whatever weapons and armour you have and follow me, we go join the fight."

Harken stood open mouthed and gawped at the sight before him, the beast stood exactly as Hergg had said, as tall as a two storey house and bulging muscle rippling underneath its dark fur. It was not moving very quickly but it did not have to, another dozen or so of the creatures protected its flanks as it took each lumbering step down the street. His men looked uncertain, even hardened ex dragoons had never faced anything quite like this.

His men with bows had them drawn and arrows nocked, just waiting for his order, the remainder of his men stood white faced with swords drawn and stood their ground. He studied the beast, it took a couple of steps and stopped, sniffed the air and moved again, it was not looking their way and did not even seem aware of his men's presence. However, the outer guard of Dark Stalkers did know they were there and made it obvious they knew, as they hissed and growled at them through their dark red mouths, massive red tongues the colour of bright arterial blood lolled about and tasted the air, sniffing out human flesh.

"They's looking for easier pray, that's what Jaskin said," spoke Hergg.

"Said that once you put up a fight, they learn that you ain't easy to kill and your armour don't taste quite the same as flesh, so they will give you a fight, but they would rather chase down some screaming maiden. But with that big fucker there, I think they will die to protect it. And looking at it now I think as big and fucking ugly as it is, it's like a new-born babe, not quite steady on its feet, but once he's been fed, that'll be another fucking matter."

"That all makes good sense, and I am pleasantly surprised that you are still with us, not running screaming down the street."

"I fucking well ran once, abandoned all my friends and neighbours, be fucked if I am going to do it again, if it's my time then so be it, least I can do for Jaskin is kill at least one more of these evil bastards."

"So, what do you think? How should we go about this?"

"No point attacking the big fucker, you got to kill its escort first. You try to get near big boy and they'll be on you like hounds. I may not be the bravest man around here, but I killed a few of these and you gets to notice a few things about a creature when you have run the fucker through and seen its life escaping it, and I am telling you that big bastard may look the part but he's as weak as a day old hoglet looking for a teat, that's why the others is looking out for it. We got here just in time, cause it ain't fed yet and we need to stop that from happening. Kill its escort Harken and then you will be able to kill it."

"ARCHERS! Target the smaller ones first, lose at will!"

Danyard dug in his spurs and urged the horse faster; Lord Gemmell was close behind, followed by Curan and then Daskin, who had just had the battle of his life trying to fight off an irresistible urge to sleep. Four other dragoons followed them. A fifth had been dispatched to find the hundred or so archers that had been pulled from the battle earlier and get them to the fore end of the battle as soon as humanly possible. The horses that rode had been from what remained of a dragoon unit looking for Lord Gemmell for orders, they had arrived in the nick of time. Those men now on foot were making their way through the ranks to try and instil some order and courage back into the lines.

They thundered along the wood line to the side of the formation, even from where he was, he could smell the acrid smoke as it drifted across the field, the slight taste of pig dung, it stung his nose and stuck to his tongue. Up ahead he could see clouds of it dissipating in the wind. He also saw that the gap between the two armies was shrinking, smoke obscured a lot of what he wanted to see but he caught the odd glimpse and it was enough. In the fore of the Branvere army stood a small unit of a hundred or so men the like of which he had never seen outside of his own disciplined forces.

The first thing he noted was that they wore a uniform, and he knew from experience this was not something Branvere expended gold on often. The second was their total discipline, they walked forward with a slow methodical purpose, each man carrying out an identical action as they did so, which Danyard soon realised they were reloading whatever strange weapon they carried. After a certain number of steps, the formation stopped as one and the front rank went down on one knee and both ranks pointed and aimed their weapon forward and an almighty bang and flash occurred and then the thick cloying smoke and screams from his own men that sent a chill down his spine.

He drew his sword and held it aloft so his men could see it and they all followed suit, each man knowing that they were unlikely to survive what they were about to do, but each also knowing they had no choice, for if they did not then this small but highly disciplined company would rout the entire Kino'le forces. And once an army was on the run it was no longer an army, it was a group of individuals waiting to be hunted down and killed.

They rounded the front of their own formation to a high cheer as the men recognised their long-haired leader. He hung on as best he could at a full gallop across the bloody churned up ground with one hand only, the other still with his precious sword raised for all to see. He sighted the company ahead and he looked for their commander, for he was the man he would try to kill first. But the man could not be seen through the thick smoke that obscured half of the two lines. One end of the lines suddenly turned to face him, run you bastards he thought to himself, like any normal group of soldiers would when facing down a charging group of horsemen. But they were not normal men, and they did not run, they knelt down and pointed their strange looking weapons at him.

Master Archer Brodick had never been so scared in his entire, long, and battle filled life. He had been a dragoon with Danyard during the Mar'thak invasion and had been a founder member of the mounted archers that had been proved so effective against the Mar'thak formations. He had moved onto the Dragoon Training School with the title of Master Archer with the honorary rank of Commander but he had still gone out on patrol at every opportunity he had got, which to his mind was not enough. His wife on the other hand had different ideas now that their children were gone, their son a dragoon himself and their daughter married to the owner of the most prestigious fletcher workshop in the kingdom. She wanted to spend some quality time with him now, not waiting for him to return from patrolling the far-flung corners of the kingdom constantly. And so, as was his right, he transferred to the Imperial Guard after Danyard reminded him he did not have to go on patrol, he could go home every night to his dear wife and do what the crown paid him to do, which was teach dragoon war bow to new dragoons, but he likened this to a man who liked a drink living in a tavern, he had to remove himself from the temptation completely.

He kept his honorary rank of Commander but he did not have anyone to teach in the Imperial Guard, as after a minimum of twenty years of Dragoon service each and every man was already an accomplished archer. They did what they thought was the right thing to do and gave him the title of Master Archer. Yet here he was now, after all the war and horror he had witnessed, after all the men he had killed, seen killed and had tried to kill him he was suddenly terrified of what was before him.

He had always been afraid of the tales of the Dark Stalkers, who rip children from their beds at night, so the stories his grandfather had taught him went. And now it turned out they were completely fucking true, except it was not just children they ripped from their beds, it was anyone and they ripped them to pieces and feasted on their soft insides.

He loosed two arrows from his curved horn hunting bow, the only one of its kind and made for him by his son in law, who was hoping to be named Master Fletcher next year, but both arrows missed as his strength fled him at the point of release. He could count on the fingers of one hand how many times he had missed what he had aimed for, he had never missed a second time, ever, until now. He looked again at the creature tearing at the roof, it was no more than thirty paces away across the street, and yes, it was at an elevated angle, and yes it was moving furiously, but he had hit smaller, and quicker targets than this many times and at greater ranges. He knew it was the fear, turning his muscles to jelly, for in his heart he knew he could kill this beast, his bow was twice the strength of a normal bow, the curved shape giving it strength only possessed by the Dragoon War bow, of which it was copied from, but the fear inside him said if you do not kill it, it will stop doing what it is doing and come for you instead, like it did in all of his childhood nightmares.

He drew his bow again, sighted down the pace long piece of ash to the cold steel head, and watched again as first the arrowhead blurred and then the arrow itself. He released the tension on the bow and un-nocked the arrow from the string, he placed them both on the floor and stood up, stretching his taught muscles and taking a number of deep breaths. Around him the sounds of skirmish slowly faded into background as he calmed his breathing, letting the cold night air wash away the sweat of his body and he once again picked up his bow and then the arrow, he turned sideways on and nocked the arrow to the string, with an almighty heave he drew the string to his face and simultaneously sighted the creature still on the roof of the house, the arrow sang through the darkness and impaled the creature through its abdomen with such force that it protruded from its back, the creature flung itself upright screaming and Brodick's second arrow went straight into the gaping maw of its mouth, again protruding from the creatures back but this time high up on the back of its neck. And that's how we deal with fear, he smiled to himself and looked for another target.

Harken tried to take stock of his surroundings, try to get some kind of order from the chaos, when they had arrived there had been about a dozen of the smaller, or normal sized creatures and now they were down to four, but his men, including a few other citizens who had joined them on the way, were down to nearly half, at this rate there would be no one left alive to fight the colossus, that, when you actually watched for a time, did look weak. It was unstable on its feet and constantly weary of being attacked, it looked truly terrifying but he really did think that Hergg had a point, so it was imperative that they did not let it feed.

The man himself had suddenly seemed to dig deep within and had found his courage. He was currently working with one of his men who was keeping a creature at bay with a spear while Hergg took mad swings at it with his sword, the tactic was working well and the creature was bleeding heavily and getting slower by the moment. While he watched the creature took a sudden mad lunge for the Imperial who dodged it swiftly and Hergg ran his sword into its side and swiftly withdrew it, dark blood spurting from the gash and it slipped on its own blood as they both hacked it to the cobbled street. The rest of his men were all similarly engaged, working in small groups in a kind of slow running battle, apart from his archers who were stood apart from the men loosing harassing arrows out of reach of the creature's talons.

"Brodick, get the men to switch, target the big fucker now, by the time the small ones are dead I want that big cunt looking like a fucking pin cushion."

"We are nearly out of arrows." He replied.

"Then retrieve what you can from the bodies, work in pairs, cover each other."

"Okay, we are on it." They all suddenly stopped and looked as an inhuman scream rent the cold night air. The giant creature had lifted a woman from inside a house, smashing out a window and its frame in one move. They watched in a mix of horror and morbid fascination as its huge gaping maw clamped down on the woman's head and half her torso, it then pulled and ripped her in half with seemingly no effort. He chewed for a bit, still holding on to what remained of her bottom half, innards dropping onto the street with a wet thud. It looked around, seemingly uninterested in the men trying to kill it, and then it took another bite. Harken was still stock still in gasping horror when he noticed a sudden mad scream from Hergg as he grabbed the spear from the Imperial and ran at the creature. This shook everyone from their inaction and the archers loosed the arrows they had nocked. Hergg's spear struck the beast high in the upper thigh and Harken thought well done, go for that big muscle in the leg. The creature did not even seem to slow down, it simply looked down at Hergg who still held onto the spear and backhanded him across the street, wrenching the weapon from his leg as he did so. It looked down at the wound that was now pouring blood and straightened itself to its full and bone meltingly scary height. Two things now happened at the same time, firstly, the arrows struck it and bounced right off, and secondly the leg wound started to close itself up as the foul black blood slowed to a trickle before it even got to its knee. Harken stopped and stared in disbelief and thought to himself, now we really are in fucking trouble.

"It is time brother," spoke Garvak "he is strong now but most of his escort are down, the stone dwellers weapons will have no effect on him, which I think they are just coming to understand, ready yourself, the fate of our people is in our hands."

"Where you go, I follow my brother; it has always been as such," they both stood from the thatched roof they had been laid upon and hefted their spears. Garvak stared at the deep black elongated leaf of the razor-sharp blade and thought to himself that he was about to discover if it was worth the arm full of blood it had cost their father. They slowly stepped backwards until their heels were touching the edge of the roof. And then without another word between them they ran up the slope of the roof and launched themselves into the darkness.

Commander Gromm the younger studied the scene in front of him, that fucking mad bastard Cathal was sat at a fully laid table in his best plate armour like some kind of tournament knight, shining like a giant fucking diamond for all the world to see. Next to him sat Balstore, also in full plate armour, but not as bright as his King's. His armour even seemed to have a few dents that had been beaten out of it. Even the wealthiest of Knights did not have the dents repaired completely, they liked to show them off, like duelling scars, just repaired enough to make them strong again but leaving the evidence of their valour for all the world to see. King Cathal's armour was spotless and smooth, not a scratch upon it.

They had a full service on the table, with plates and goblets and even cutlery, even though they should have been hiding their presence they even had candles lit, two huge candles in elaborate stands at each end of the table, about half a pace in. Something nagged at Gromm, why were they so relaxed, why were they here instead of riding hard for the border and why were they advertising their presence so blatantly. Every fibre of his being shouted trap at him but he knew these lands like the back of his hands and there were no hidden warriors in the surrounding woods, there were no trip wires or pit traps. He was a graduate of the Tracker School and could spot these things instantly, especially ones that had been laid as quickly as these would have needed to be. He had done a quick count of the bodyguards Cathal had with him, less than thirty, whereas he had forty-eight including himself. What the fuck are you playing at Cathal, or Balstore, for it was common knowledge Cathal could not think himself out of a cloth sack.

He worked his way back, as low and slow as he could, still on his belly, the only thing that would give him away now was movement, a few hand widths at a time, then stop and look and listen again, slowly slowly. He cleared the wood edge and raised himself to a crouch, then moved back further until he was far enough away to raise himself upright. He walked back to his men in the next wood, two hundred paces away. His atrop commanders were waiting for him.

"That mad King and his pet brain are sat at table like they are guests of honour at a fucking wedding feast, apart from the fact that they are fully plate armoured as are all of their men. A few other nobles are sat at the table with them, probably that slimy trade commissioner and his few hangers on, but they are not attempting to hide in any way, could be seen by any passing patrol, any thoughts?"

"We are the only passing patrol, that fucker Balstore would know that, he would know every patrol we put out and when it was due back, this has to be a trap, he must know we would find him." Spoke the second in command, Vanmere.

"I cannot disagree with you, it looks like a trap, smells like a trap, it has to be a fucking trap, but I cannot see one, and as you all know I have sniffed out a trap before when no one else has."

"Then maybe you should have waited before splitting that man's head open, they cannot talk with their brains falling down their tunics."

"Point noted, but your cousins are with the southern patrol aren't they? The invasion came from the South. What would you have done?"

"It wasn't a fucking criticism Grim, I would've done exactly the fucking same as you, but it don't help us now do it?"

"No, it does not, but we cannot let that cunt ride from here, or his halfwit king, we must stop them both. I dread to think of that vindictive bastard on the throne of Kino'le. Get to your men and prepare for battle. We outnumber then but that are all in plate armour, their horses are in mail coats only and corralled off to one side with their wagons so they are not planning on a fast getaway. Each atrop will have half its men with bows drawn, bodkin heads, and we will approach and demand their surrender, there will be no discussion, they get one chance and then we attack, I will not be getting into a long drawn out conversation with Balstore or another fucker at that table. If it goes to shit your men are to attack on my order with no quarter given, the King is the only one from whom a surrender will be accepted, but not Balstore, he is just too damn dangerous and too damn clever to leave alive. The table is in the centre of the wood so we will surround it in a circle and slowly draw in closer so they are completely surrounded, we will remain mounted to give us the height advantage of a horse and the obvious threat of us trampling them. If any try to bolt get them with an arrow but do to give chase, do not break the circle formation under any circumstances. Be on the track mounted as soon as you are ready."

"Commissioner, you still look scared" spoke Balstore "I assure you we are quite safe from that dragoon patrol, and you will continue to be safe from them when they arrive."

"When? What do you mean when?" he replied "When! Not if! Bloody when?"

"One of them has already been spying on us, I have a kind of sense of these things, when unwanted eyes are upon me. He was over there, not fifty paces away, he was very good actually. A normal man would not have noticed him, as seems to have been proved by the fact our own men did not see him. He has gone now; I expect they will all be here shortly."

"Have you ever seen these dragoons in a battle Lord Balstore. They are fierce men, brutal in battle and thoroughly unforgiving, they will spare no one here, especially us at this table. They will slaughter us where we sit."

"My dear Commissioner, I do not intend to sit anywhere where a simple Kino'le soldier who happens to be good on a horse can get close to killing me, for that is all a dragoon is, a simple common soldier on a fine horse. Not like our own good knights, everyone a nobleman, from an ancient house and a horse that is the envy of the known world, these dragoons do not frighten me."

"They bloody well should Lord Balstore" came a loud shout from the wood line as the dragoon circle closed in. Balstore looked up and smiled.

"Commander Gromm, of the Northern Patrol, we have been waiting for you, will you dismount and join my King and myself. We have much to discuss."

"There will be no discussion here Balstore, surrender your arms and your King immediately, you are outnumbered two to one and your last runner is already dead, now order your men to lay down their arms."

"You are right about one thing only Commander, there will be no further discussion," replied Balstore as he knocked the candle nearest to him from the table, and the man on the far end did the same to the candle in front of him. Instantly there was trail of flame surrounding the circle of Dragoons and a heartbeat later an almighty series of explosions rent the night air as the sacks that the Royal Bodyguard had laid over the previous days exploded with a force that tore men from their horses and ripped the lightly armoured soldiers limb from limb.

Jaskin stared at the creatures and knew it was all over, strangely he was no longer afraid, just a dull anger resided in him, mixed with some pride at what he had achieved. He had rallied his neighbours and killed numerous Dark Stalkers, and he knew that no matter outcome of today when men mentioned Dark Stalkers again, they would also mention the humble carpenter, father of a dragoon, who chose to fight instead of die.

The three of them had rushed down the stairs at once exactly as he thought they would, he had launched the spear from the bottom of the stairs at the mass of dark fur hurtling towards him and turned before it struck home. He heard a scream as he ran to the far wall, grabbing the dragoon sabre from the table as he went past it. Two creatures lurched into the room from the stairs and they looked at him, they did not seem to be in a hurry now, knowing they had him, and he had a sudden awful feeling that they wanted him alive, and only for one reason, to be fed alive to the big bastard.

He swung the sabre around in front of him in desperation but he knew it was pointless, he would not be able to kill them both. One of them then threw himself against the door to the street, it rattled in its frame and he did it again, he seemed to have no concern for his own safety, just to get the door open. The frame splintered and he dug his claws into it and started to pull on the door itself. Jaskin leapt at the other one and swung the sabre at its neck, cleaving down into it, dark blood sprayed out and the creature fell to its knees but by then the first one had ripped the door frame away and the door swung open, the way to the street clear. Jaskin pulled on the sabre but could not free it from the creature's collar bone, he turned in time to feel a huge claw grab him by the head and throw him bodily through the doorway.

Darkness surrounded Commander Gromm, he could hear horses neighing far off but could not see them in his semi-conscious state. He thought he had burns on his body but could not be sure, every inch of him hurt and smoke was surrounding him, a tang of pig shit hung in the air that seemed to stick to his nostrils. He knelt up and retched violently and then vomited. He stayed where he was for a moment and waited for his head to clear, the birch wood was a scene of devastation, the sliver trees lay with his men, broken, twisted, burnt and utterly destroyed.

He stood and tried to take stock of what had happened, but he could not comprehend it, the nearest he could come to was, when he and his brother had snuck out of their small cottage as children when a storm had been raging, and they had witnessed lightning strike a tree, that tree looked like all of these did now, a smouldering stump. He had no idea what could have caused such an explosion, but he knew that Balstore had planned it and they had been in their full plate to protect themselves from it. That Balstore was one calculating bastard. He knew that if they had caught them on the road then he would have probably been captured, so he had laid a trap, and he had fallen right into it.

He was too numb and shocked to feel a specific pain from one area so he checked himself over as best he could, every muscle hurt and although he had a few minor grazes he was sure he had not sustained a major injury. He looked around and saw what remained of his horse, a dozen paces away. The poor beast had been ripped in two, the two pieces lay apart from each other connected by nothing but steaming entrails, the smell suddenly hitting his dazed senses. Whatever had caused one of the explosions must have been directly underneath him, the horse taking the full force of the blast and throwing him clear. That's why he survived and his men had not.

His men, he took a few moments and walked among them, looking for signs of life and as he did, he saw what a carefully laid ambush this had been, more like an execution than a trap. His men had not stood a chance and he had led them right into it. What could he do now, he could not return to Kino'le the only survivor of this ambush, his own pride would not allow it. He did the only thing he could, he checked his weapons. He could not find his own sabre, for it had been in his hand when he had ridden in, but not far away was one of his archers and he could see the man's sabre still in its scabbard. He took it and the man's war bow and a full quiver of arrows. He looked back at what remained of his patrol and before he slid deeper into his very own pit of despair, he jogged from the wood and followed the tracks made by the enemy King and his convoy.

The lead balls cracked past Danyard's head as he charged, but he had no knowledge of it as the surge of adrenaline hit him, oblivious of his surroundings he was focused solely on the men in the formation to his front. The man to his right fell suddenly as his horse went down, Danyard was only a dozen paces away from the front line of men and he raised his sword into a high attack stroke, bringing it down perfectly into the neck of a man in the front row as his horse careened into the second row. Gemmell, who had filled the place to his right but slightly behind hit the formation at full gallop and sent six men from both rows flying into their comrades, the remaining dragoons did exactly the same thing further down the line, men scattered and ran to avoid the angry beasts and small number of madmen who had charged a formation of one hundred highly trained soldiers.

Danyard's horse burst from the rear line and he immediately swung it around to attack again, Gemmell and the few dragoons were trying to trample men and cause general chaos in the lines to try to completely break the formation and discipline, rearing their horses and crashing them back down again. As Danyard charged he saw one man step back from his line and take aim at Gemmell, there was a flash and a bang and smoke filled the air as Gemmell's sword arm exploded at the shoulder, his sabre, midway through a strike was flung from his hand and he was nearly flung from his horse. He looked across and stared in a mix of wonder and horror at the wound. The ball had torn clean through his mail and shoulder guard leaving his right arm hanging useless at his side. Danyard charged his horse towards him, using the power and force of the horse to shove men aside and swung his own razor-s h a r p sword at any that came close to his friend. He rammed his horse into the flank of Gemmell's and pushed him to the edge, his meaning clear, get out now while you still can. Gemmell looked up at him with a look that said it all, I cannot abandon you now, even with one arm and in no fit state to fight he could not ride away. And then Danyard's horses head exploded in a spray of blood and bone and he tumbled to the field, once again he was unhorsed and surrounded by enemies.

The remaining men of the Gunne Company scattered before him as he rolled away from his fallen horse and came up swinging his sword, the first man within reach lost an arm still clutching his Gunne as he tried to step backwards, the spray of blood from that wound hit the men behind him and the man to his side and they tried to turn away as Danyard's sword took another man's head and buried itself in another man's shoulder, sticking in his shoulder blade Danyard tried to pull it free but it was stuck fast, he raised his leg as the man fell to get some leverage on it when his femur muscle seemed to explode in front of him, he felt no pain as he watched the blood spray out, taking with it small parts of muscle tissue. For the second time that day he felt a helpless fear as he realized, he could no longer stand and he fell to the muddy ground on his hands and knees, he looked up into the eyes of a man smiling at him through the clearing smoke of his Gunne.

And so the mighty Danyard falls thought Huxton, as he watched Danyard fall onto his face and slip into unconsciousness.

The trade commissioner was white faced and in shock, he had seen men die before, he had ordered men to die before, nobody of importance in King Cathal's Kingdom became important through being pleasant to others, but what he had just witnessed and sickened him to his core. The men, the dragoons he had come to respect so much during his years in Kino'le blown to pieces like, well like nothing he could think of, because he had never seen the power of Balstore's latest invention.

As he had ridden in, he had not even noticed the dark green sacks full of powder that had been secreted here a few days prior. The dragoon that Balstore had told him had been watching them had not come close enough to notice them either. He had seen some the links of rolled up paper obviously filled with the damn stuff too but he had paid them no mind, being too busy attending to the King. He had heard tale of it from the men of the Royal bodyguard but even he had not suspected it could be used as such, had he not seen it for himself.

He should have known when the men all donned their armour and he had been ordered to do the same, a task he had not been required to do for over twenty years and up until that point, a set of purely ceremonial armour. But he had been glad of it when the sacks exploded, Balstore had filled them with nails and rivets and other small pieces of metal to cause maximum damage, and it had done so. The lightly armoured dragoons quite literally torn to shreds in front of his eyes, even those not hit by a blast had quickly bled out from multiple wounds.

As Balstore had knocked the candle from the table, he had also snapped shut his own visor and reached across to snap shut the Trade Commissioners, and then the blast had come and nearly knocked him from his seated position, quickly followed by the sound and shock of hundreds of nails and rivets bouncing from their armour. The aftershock of the blast hit him hard too, it seemed to literally suck the air from his lungs as it burnt the very air around them and as soon as he did get a breath it was a breath of foul-smelling acrid smoke. He had eventually opened his eyes and his visor and the Bodyguards casually started to remove their armour, and so, with nothing to say he had followed suit and started to unbuckle his now battered and dented armour.

He realised just how naive he had been, Balstore had planned this whole bloody thing with cold calculating detail. The escort north, the ambush of that escort, and now this, the execution of a whole bloody patrol. He knew, they would now skirt south, around the city, and head for the temporary harbour, where the cowardly King could claim credit for everything from the safety of his own galleon, while men old and young fought and died for him.

They were still in heavy woodland and so not risking a gallop, just a gentle cantor so the wagons could keep up. The wagons had a small escort but he heard the orders from Balstore, if in doubt, abandon the wagons, even with the King's and all the other armour their priority was to get away, the fact that most of the Bodyguards had spent over a year's salary on their own armour did not bother Balstore, he had always had a fear of being captured. Perhaps Balstore is right, he mused to himself, maybe he had spent too long in a Kingdom where people were treated with respect had affected him, as a pose to a Kingdom run by a madman, or a madman and his pet dog to be exact.

Balstore was up ahead with the leading men while the King was in the centre, as usual, protected on all sides. The one flaw in Balstore's plan had been the need to travel north from the city at first which put them further into enemy territory. The trade commissioner had argued to leave earlier and meet with the invasion force but Balstore had rightly pointed out that this would have caused too much suspicion and Danyard would have insisted on a much larger escort as well as probably having them tailed by a number of dragoon patrols. Once again, the King's vanity had won through, invading a country while being a guest of that country, things like that amused the little prick.

Balstore suddenly gave the order to go faster which they all knew meant abandoning their precious armour and they did not like it but they could do nothing about it, even the Guard Commander did not like to contradict Balstore. The men looked back at the wagons, only four outriders remained with the wagons, and the four drivers armed with crossbows, to protect a prize that would make any band of thieves rich for life.

The Dragoon War bow was a masterpiece of medieval engineering, little bigger than a standard bow it could loose an arrow at an accurate range of about one hundred and fifty paces, while the best longbowman could manage about two hundred and fifty while most standard bows would be hard pushed to hit anything above seventy.

It achieved this by clever design of the right wood and a curious shape, the famous yew tree that formed the stave of all longbows was used for its strength and flexibility but with a forward facing curve in its shape that allowed more power to be achieved with a shorter length, very useful for a man on a horse. They were very distinctive but only allowed to be handled by another dragoon, punishment of expulsion from service was an order direct from Danyard if a dragoon ever handed one over to a non-dragoon. If an enemy was ever hit by an arrow from one then the standing order was also, they died by that arrow, no enemy should ever be able to walk away and tell tales of the Dragoon War bow. They were of a design Danyard had once seen as a child and they were completely unique to Kino'le and the dragoons for Danyard was paranoid about the technology being copied. All of which was completely unknown to the two outriders at the rear of the Branvere two wagon convoy.

Both were young, twenty-four and twenty-two respectively, the younger was from a minor noble house and the older was not, but despite the difference in class they had become firm friends having been accepted for training in the Branvere Royal Guard at the same time. As per the requirement both were accomplished horsemen at the start of their training. The Royal house having no time to train a man to ride a horse to the standard that would be required for the ceremonial part of the job.

The horses themselves were all bred from the same bloodlines for the last two centuries, all pale geldings, easier to control than the stallions. The pale shade of them to represent the silver of house Cathal, also the ruling house of Branvere for the last two hundred years. Gromm looked down at their bodies as he walked past; not even noticing the valuable sword one of them wore. The first arrow he had loosed from less than eighty paces behind had punched clean through the man's helm, through the rear of his skull and out of the front before breaking on the front of his helm. The second man had been too shocked to react and all he had managed to do was turn his horse in terror when the second arrow had smashed clean through his mail surcoat, torn his heart open and punched out of his back, not being able to break out of the chain mail it had stuck there, metal head pushing the sheet of linked iron rings away from his back.

In any normal situation, Gromm would have searched the bodies for any item of value or interest for his patrol report later, but this was not a normal situation and he no longer had a patrol to make a report for. Once again, he glanced at what was obviously a nobleman's sword, knowing it should have a significance but he could not put a coherent thought in his head, he just had an overwhelming need to push forward, to follow and destroy those who had destroyed his men.

A crossbow bolt suddenly thudded into the tree beside his head, again normally he would have dived for cover but he did not, he calmly nocked an arrow and drew the bow, taking a natural aim at the wagon driver who had just noticed him from fifty paces to his front, he loosed the arrow and watched as it hit the man in the shoulder, spinning him around and making him fall from his wagon. His co-driver did not wait around to take his chances and cracked the whip on the horse team and the wagon jolted forward, shouting a warning to the other wagon and outriders as he did so.

Both wagons moved off at speed as the two remaining outriders turned their mounts and galloped towards Gromm. The first one died in the saddle as an arrow took him through his Adam's apple and then severed his spinal column as it exited his back, the arrow so far embedded that the fletchings were sticking out from his throat. The second man managed to draw his sword before his horse careened into his now out of control colleagues horse, he looked over and saw what had happened to his friend and tried to turn away and run for it when another arrow took him in the side of the face through his jaw, knocking teeth clean out as it travelled through. The force of the blow knocked him from his horse and he landed heavily on the cold ground. He lay there supine, struggling to breath and looked up into the cold dead eyes of a man whose soul appear to have died, he tried to speak but could not form any words through his shattered jaw, just a pathetic gurgling noise came from him. He closed his eyes for a second and opened them in time to see the flash of a dragoon sabre.

Harken watched in horror as his men's arrows simply bounced from the creature, not even bloody scratching it, he returned his sword to its scabbard and grabbed a fallen spear, it's now or never he thought to himself, I have to inspire the men or they will flee, once again the privilege of command.

He hefted the spear in both hands and ran at the creature, screaming at the top of his lungs as he did so, he was within a few paces of it and was preparing to thrust his spear into its abdomen when two men suddenly appeared in what seemed to be mid-flight in a massive leap from the roof of the house. Harken came to shuddering halt and stopped stock still, dumbstruck by what he was seeing. They wore no armour, no protection whatsoever, just a one-piece green tunic made of a rough cloth, both with long matted hair and both were barefoot. They were armed with only a spear each, but a spear the like of which he had never seen before. Normal looking wooden haft, but the metal head was a foot and a half long and leaf shaped. As he stood and watched the creature backhanded him across the street, just like he had done with Hergg and he was flung backwards and he thought he felt some ribs break as he landed against the far wall, despite the pain he could not take his eyes from the men in the tunics as a sense of unreality settled on him.

The first man, higher in the air, aimed his spear for the giant creature's neck, he was in mid-air with his spear held two handed over his head, thrusting his body forward to get as much power into the thrust as he could. The second man was lower down and further back, trying to get his spear into the creatures back which was side on to his colleague. At the last instant the creature knew something was up and turned towards the first man, as his spear dug into the flesh and bone of the creature it turned and slapped him clean out of the air, sending him sprawling to the cobbled street.

Thick dark blood exploded from the creature's neck wound spraying the few men brave enough to still be close to him.

The second man's spear missed completely as the creature twisted away and he flew past, he was fully prepared for the fall and let go of his spear as he hit the ground and rolled away, dispersing the built-up kinetic energy that would have killed a less well prepared man. He sprang to his feet in an instant and lunged for his precious weapon, a dozen paces away. The creature, although wounded and bleeding seemed to be no weaker and took two massive steps towards it, seeming to know what a danger this special weapon was to him. He put one massive taloned foot on the haft and ripped the head from it, throwing it down the street as far as he could, then grabbed the man who it belonged to and ripped his head clean from his shoulders, throwing his head down the street where it landed near the spear. It then lifted the body to its huge vile mouth and bit away the shoulders and then squeezed the man's soft insides into its mouth. Harken, who had watched the whole thing from the place where he had landed was suddenly galvanised into action, the sheer horror he had just witnessed forcing him from his immobility. He looked around desperately for the first man, and more importantly his weapon, he saw the man lying motionless against a wall, but he could not see the man's spear. He stood and tried to run as pain from his broken ribs shot through him and he slipped on the blood covering the street, he stumbled towards the man, the creature saw him and aimed a giant kick at him, had it connected it would have killed him but as he did so an arrow struck the massive open wound in its neck and it screamed in pain and stumbled forward, off balance. Harken looked up and saw Brodick smile at him, already another arrow nocked and ready to loose and smiling like the devil himself.

Harken reached the man and rolled him over, relief flooding through him as he saw the man was close to his spear, the head of it anyway, with about three foot of haft still attached. It must have snapped when it hit the ground he thought, sorry I do not have time to check you for injury my friend, but I need your fucking spear, we all need it, it is quite literally our only hope.

He looked at the creature; it was trying to get to Brodick, across the street on a flat roof. He was causing much consternation to the beast, loosing an arrow at the open wound and moving quickly, so quick and accurate was he that the creature could not get near him, but did not stop trying. Harken silently thanked Brodick, it created the perfect distraction for the rest of them.

As he watched, he suddenly realised that the wound was closing, Brodick's arrows were causing it pain but the wound was definitely smaller now than it had been, and it was confirmed when he saw a number of Brodick's arrows on the street, he hasn't missed that many times he thought. He then made the connection he needed, he realised what he had to do, he needed to get the spear in and stuck, it had to stay in to keep the wound open. That's why they had gone for its back and neck, to get a chance of their spears penetrating deeply into its body. Do not run out of arrows yet Brodick, just a little longer.

He took the haft of the spear and felt the weight of its strange-shaped head, it would be off balance now with only half of the haft so its use as a projectile weapon of no use to him. He turned and faced the diabolical beast, this is it, do or die trying. He took a two-handed grip on the weapon and looked up at it as he ran from the side, he must try for the abdomen or lower ribcage, wedge the fucking thing in there and try to knock some air from its lungs at the same time. He went through a strong moment of doubt, the two men who had brought these weapons had probably trained with them their whole fucking lives, and yet they had failed, what hope did he have? But right at that moment what choice did he have? Two paces away he prepared for his leap upwards just as it caught scent of him and it swung its massive bulk in an amazing turn of speed to face him, bringing one huge taloned claw down on his head.

Lord of Dragoons, Lord Gemmell, saw Danyard fall and tried to turn his horse towards him, but it was proving difficult as pain shot through him with every movement and men hemmed him in on all sides. His arm hung uselessly at his side with the occasional twinge but he did not think this was a good sign, for he did not expect to see the day out anyway. He looked around desperately, looking for some hope that he could save Danyard only to watch in horror as the last two mounted dragoons, Curan and his mad young friend Daskin were dragged from their horses and beaten to the ground with the wide ends of the enemy's strange looking weapons. Feeling nothing but contempt for himself, he tried to turn his mount away in a vain attempt to escape, but to no avail, a man grabbed for him and he found he no longer had the strength to fight the man off because of the amount of blood he had already lost and he also was dragged from his horse and beaten into the bloody field.

Twenty-Nine

The Princesses

Lady Sarah stared at the man before her, he looked in a terrible state but there was no disguising the look of triumph in his eyes. She turned and ran, slipping on the bloody floor as she did so. She had no immediate plan other than to get away from him. Then she realised that she needed to try and distract him, keep him away from the Princess, barely alive in the bed that she now ran from.

He stared at her from the wide bed where she lay, covered by blankets and only taking very shallow breaths, he had not yet noticed her. Sarah looked around frantically for a weapon and her eyes settled on a crossbow, but it was not drawn, the string forward. She knew, she would not have time to grab it, draw it and load a bolt before he was on her. A sword, she thought, I need a sword, and then she remembered Danyard's kukri in her waistband at the small of her back, she also remembered her basic lessons in combat but also some of the other lessons Danyard had spoken of, which did not make sense at the time but did now, do not let the enemy know what you have, always have a deception plan. She knew, if she pulled the kukri now, he would simply knock it from her hand with his much longer sword, she needed to get him closer but keep him thinking she was just a weak and simple woman.

He raised his own sword and pointed it at her, it was still stained by her friend's blood and she shuddered at the sight of it but also felt the anger rise in her. He spoke.

"Well bitch, you gonna come here or are we gonna dance around this fucking room all night, see your friends' blood on my blade, yours will be joining it soon enough, but my, you are a pretty one. And look at those fucking great tits, think I will have some fun with you first, you want to come over here and I will be gentler on you."

"You think a pathetic little man like you can take me do you, I'll eat you for breakfast, I'll wager you can't even get it up," she replied.

"Oh I am gonna fucking show you now bitch," he said as he suddenly lunged for her, exactly as she was expecting him to do, she took few steps backwards reaching behind for the kukri as his eyes fell on her heaving bosom and they changed from a look of anger into one of lust. She started to breath heavier to accentuate her cleavage and she watched as his eyes were drawn to them as he slowly walked forward towards her, as if he had no control over his own eyes or movement. You stupid fucking men she thought, all the bloody same, so easy when it comes to it. His right arm let his sword relax and the blade tip scraped on the floor, and his left arm reached out and grabbed her breasts as she stepped away from the bedside and looked up into his eyes and smiled, then with a savagery that she did not know she possessed she stepped backwards and to one side, drew the kukri and brought it down with all her might into his wrist. The heavy axe like blade cleaved clean through the bone and sinew of his wrist and he screamed as his hand fell away and a fountain of blood exploded from the stump. His scream was suddenly cut short as Buldor's Warhammer came down onto the crown of his head from behind, crumpling his skull and causing his body to collapse, dead before he hit the ground. Buldor stared at Sarah and smiled, the pride of what she had done evident on his face as he lifted his hammer from what remained of Shapley's head.

"Buldor… I…have never been so pleased to see a man so ugly in my entire life," she said as she collapsed into his arms sobbing with relief and dropping the bloody kukri to the floor as she did so.

"Don't know why, seems you had it all under control, don't need no big ugly fucker like me with you around," he replied.

"But there is still a war going on, we need to move the Princess to a safer place, she lives still?"

"Y… Yes, under the blankets, I do not think we can move her yet, she is too weak, who is that dragoon, I…recognise him…her…oh my… Princes Amyeen…is that really you?"

They both stared at Amyeen, as she and Nartan approached the bed, she seemed to be in some kind of trance as she reached out to lift the blankets from her sister's face, and as she did, for the second time that day, Sarah was blinded by an explosive light and thrown across the room, as were Buldor and Nartan.

Jaskin was thrown bodily across the street by the beast that had dragged him out of the house by his head. Despite the pain from all over his body, he could feel an awful pressure in his head and he knew his skull may be cracked, his thoughts were becoming more and more incoherent by the moment. He landed at the foot of the giant creature that had scared his militia away previously, just as an Imperial Guardsman was thrown across the street by his head, dropping a strange looking spear as he flew backwards. There was a sickening crunch as he hit the wall of the house across the street and he slumped down still.

Jaskin looked about him, trying to make sense of the world, he could not seem to think straight anymore, pain pulsed in his head and he beat at it with his fists, he knew where he was but not how he came to be here, he knew he was in mortal danger but he could think why, even when the creature reached down for him he could not make the connection. Its huge claw grabbed him and lifted him up to its monstrous gaping maw and he suddenly remembered everything, he screamed what he knew would be his last breath, its mouth opened wider and its breath washed over him and made him retch. He closed his eyes and waited for the pain and darkness.

But then, all of a sudden it was light, he noticed the difference through closed eyelids. The dark changed to light so rapidly that it made him jump even in the absolute terror that he was in. The creature had still had him in its grip but he was no closer to its mouth and he felt its grip on him loosen, he kicked and struggled and loosened himself, he looked down at the street and did not relish the fall but it was a better alternative than what awaited him if he did not. He struggled more as the creatures hold on him weakened further and then he flung himself to the ground, landing off balance and heavily and the pain that only a broken ankle can cause shot through him and he cursed all the gods in creation.

As he hobbled away, he saw the spear, with the half haft, the matt black razor-sharp head still dripping the gloopy blood of the creature and he knew, it suddenly made perfect sense to him. Jaskin the Carpenter, father of Daskin the berserker dragoon, of the Kingdom of Light, picked up the spear of the Tree Folk of Dalstock as the creature turned away from him, and with all his remaining strength he rammed it as hard as he could into the massive femur muscle of the giant Dark Stalker. He was expecting a scream, a roar and a fountain of dark blood but he did not get it, the blood oozed out down the leaf shaped blade and dripped heavily from the broken haft, thick and gloopy it slid from the creature. He pulled the weapon out and rammed it in another spot and the same thing happened except this time the beast fell to the cobbled street and tried to crawl away, getting slower and slower.

The words of his own father came to him, from the stories of the Dark Stalkers, they cannot function in light, their blood thickens and their entire metabolism goes into a sluggish hibernation. He pulled the spear from the second wound and limped after the creature, it was getting slower and slower as it lost more blood and the blood it did have got thicker and thicker, Jaskin caught up with it as it fell to its front and stood watching for a moment, and then without warning thrust the spear into its back, severing its spine cleanly until he felt the spear tip strike the cobbles of the street and there he left it and he collapsed as the light rapidly spreading outwards from the palace bathed him in its familiar warmth.

Huxton looked down at the four enemy now held by his men, all four were on their knees apart from Danyard who was still unconscious, sprawled out to their front. The remainder of the Gunne Company waited for his orders.

"Lord Gemmell, Lord of Dragoons, my most Gracious King Cathal the Silver of Branvere will be more than happy with your head, and that also of the supposed legend currently squirming around in the mud at my feet, but I think I will keep you both alive for now, until my King lets me know his pleasure. These other two will make excellent target practice for my men, for the new trainees I will need to swell and expand the Company. You and your little band of horsemen did quite a number on my men with that charge, as you can see there are only about three dozen of us left standing, that's sixty odd you managed to kill, very impressive, but you will never be a match for even a half trained man with a Gunne, you and your kind are finished now, you will soon be a thing of the past." spoke Huxton.

"There is nothing gracious about your King, you pig's rectum, make all the plans you want, you will never make it out of Kino'le alive, not with Danyard and myself hostage." Spat back Gemmell.

"Oh, how quaint, you think you can still win. I have no intention of ever leaving Kino'le, I will take your house to live in and your wife as my bed slave, you gibbering fool."

"You have not won yet." Spoke Gemmell as he looked up at his captor he noticed the Branvere men looking towards the city, in a mix of fear and awe, and before he knew what was happening, he was bathed in warm light, a light so bright initially it hurt his eyes, he squinted up at the men to his front and as if a dream come true they were suddenly struck by powerful pace long arrows, knocking them clean from their feet, he shuffled around, wisely staying on his knees, knowing to raise himself to standing was to invite death from what could only be the Longbowmen of Kino'le. As enemy fell around him, he saw them through the gaps, about a hundred of them, doing what they did best, he watched as the light reached them and he thought he had never seen such a fine thing in all his life. They switched targets, starting to reign arrows down onto the Branvere formations. The combination of this new assault and the sudden return of the light had a startling effect on the enemy, Men stood around not knowing what was happening, and then before the light reached them, they panicked thinking it would burn them, so they ran. Lord Gemmell finally stood with the help of Curan and Daskin, his shoulder now a dull ache, a small trickle of blood coming from it and the pain bearable, from that he knew he had no broken bones.

The three of them looked at the army of Branvere in full retreat and each could not suppress a smile, until that was, they looked down at the prone from of Danyard, still in the mud. A terrible fear settled on Gemmell as he ordered Curan and Daskin to lift him up, he had spent many an hour in combat with the man and never seen him downed, never beaten. He looked up again, the Branvere army continued to flee the field, he could not at this stage say if they would reorganise and reform but the Longbowmen were giving methodical chase. Nocking and loosing as they went, picking off targets of opportunity as and when they arose.

"Curan and Daskin, I must ask one more thing of you this day, take what infantry and dragoons you can muster and pursue them, harry them wherever they go, they must not be given the chance to regroup, chase them to the sea if you have to, if they wish to negotiate a surrender they may do so, but not with any arms, even the nobles, no one walks from our Kingdom armed. And most important, if you see Balstore, the Lord Bastard himself, he does not leave these lands. The King is irrelevant, he is just puppet anyway. Now go and find yourselves a horse before I collapse."

Carmak looked on and he knew it was over; the Princess lived and lived strong by the look of the light that now enveloped the Palace, city and most of the battlefield. Even though, it had no physical effect other than a bit of warmth it carried a huge significance for the defenders. It reminded them of why they were fighting, for their homes and their values, and also that the enemy had failed, despite all the resources available to them, to kill the Princess. And to his men it represented something they did not understand and therefore something they could not defeat.

He had done what he believed no one else could have done, he had rallied his troops after defeat and re-rallied them when he thought all had been lost, but he knew he would not manage it again, not with the light and those damn longbows, outranging everything he had, and to be honest even the Gunne Company, for accuracy from a standing position was limited to about one hundred paces, whereas the longbows were still hitting his men at over two hundred. And he had seen for himself the decimation of the Gunne Company and he knew they were lost. Some of the men were now running with the rest of them, he did not see Huxton among them and hoped the slimy fucker was dead, he never did like him, too much like his master.

A shiver ran down his back as he his thoughts turned to Balstore, the man's vengeance upon him would be terrible, he would not have him killed, he was far too malicious to give in to such a simple option. He may kill him eventually but not before forfeiting his lands and titles, putting his family out of their home and probably burning the whole fucking place to the ground. Unless, I kill the fucker first he thought to himself with a wry smile. He turned his horse and led his entourage away from the light.

"General!" spoke Jonoak "Where do we head? What direction? We cannot really be seen leading the retreat, can we?"

"No, we cannot, but by now the King and his party will be heading for the beachhead, unbeknown to him it no longer exists, he would be grateful for this information I would imagine. We head east, away from the city but we will attempt to rendezvous with His Majesty, then think of a plan from there."

"Of course, general."

Gromm urged his horse faster, it was one of the silver Geldings of the Branvere Royal Guard and it was a fast beast. He had taken it from one of the outriders he had killed and he originally approached it with the utmost caution, knowing the reputation of the Branvere horses. But he had found it to have a gentle soul and it seemed glad to be in the company of a human again, and it was still saddled. It had let him take the reins and it had even nuzzled his head down to his.

He had already overtaken both of the supply wagons not even slowing down to engage them, and dodging the few hastily aimed crossbow bolts that had come his way, him knowing that the wagon drivers would have no interest in getting into a real fight with him, the man who had single-handedly killed their escort. He himself had no interest in what was within these wagons, although the various sets of plate armour within could have made him a wealthy man for the rest of his life many times over. What he wanted now more than anything had no financial value, although one man was going to pay dearly for it.

The trail was easy enough for him to follow, the horse's hooves churning up the ground as they had fled. His war bow was slung on his back and he had a dozen or so arrows for it. His dragoon sabre was in its hip scabbard, he knew he could easily ride into a trap but he was past caring, his only thought was for the death of Balstore, for his brother probably dead on the southern road, and for his men, his other brothers, blown to pieces by some evil device of Balstore's invention.

He was suddenly aware of light spreading out from the area of the city, the light did not usually extend this far, encompassing the Palace and City but not much beyond, but now it seemed to be extending much further outwards. He smiled for the first time in a whole day, this could only be good for him and bad for those he hunted.

Balstore could feel the light as he urged his horse faster, he did not need to look over his right-hand side to see it coming towards him, he just knew it was. He was riding so hard. he had nearly caught up with the two scouts he had sent ahead to check for ambush and the King himself was struggling to keep up with him. He could hear the breath of the King's horse behind him and the shouts of the all but useless trade commissioner way behind. The man had never been a decent horseman and stood no chance of making back with them, and he felt no regrets leaving him to the mercy of the Kino'le forces. A surrendering soldier was one thing, a man who had lived among his enemy for years and been fully aware of the plans to invade quite another, there was a word for a man like that and that word was spy, and spies did not last long in the hands of an enemy.

He still did not know why he had to avoid the light but the force driving him to do so was a living thing inside him that absolutely could not be disobeyed. He had to outrun it, but he knew he could not, still he did not look at it, but he could still feel it creeping up on him. The rage started in him and before he could control it he was screaming in anger, the need for him to get away was all consuming, and being a man used to getting exactly what he wanted the frustration in him was beyond his control, and one more emotion he was not used to, not for a long long time, fear.

Suddenly, the light covered him and he screamed in anticipation of the burn that he knew was coming, but it did not. He felt the warmth from the light and the shock of it caused him to fall from his horse. He landed heavily, and tried to roll away from the light under the cover of a tree, but it was so bright that the shadow it created was too shallow and a heavy thumping started in his head. At first, a slow but constant pulse building up and up, he could feel his veins expanding with the pressure. He had moments of black out and he knew he was becoming delirious. When he opened his eyes, he saw the Royal Surgeon kneeling over him, trying to calm him and force some strange looking goo into his mouth. The King had dismounted and was looking on, concerned, speaking rapidly with the Surgeon, words that Balstore could hear but had no understanding of as the pounding in his head grew and grew. The trade commissioner pulled up and looked down too.

"What ails him Master Surgeon?" he asked.

"I have no idea, some kind of fit, I have tried to force some sedative into him and he damn near on bit my fucking fingers off, I do not know what we can do with him but we cannot stay here much longer, we will be captured, especially with the noise he is making, we could try to tie him to his horse but I cannot think of anything else," he replied.

"Let us do that then, you men, grab him and tie him to his horse, as fast as you can, knock him unconscious if you have to," two of the bodyguards knelt down and bound his hands together and then dragged him to his feet.

Balstore's head was flying side to side as froth and spittle flew from his mouth as an arrow flew from the woodland and smashed into his forehead, the heavy bodkin arrow split the fore of his skull and due to the pressure built up inside his skull split in two and his brains exploded out covering the two men. One stood dumbstruck as the other dived for cover and Commander Gromm rode from the wood line a hundred paces away, Dragoon War bow in hand and another arrow already nocked. He cantered his horse forward slowly and deliberately, drawing the bow as he did so and loosing another arrow. The arrow struck another of the bodyguards as he dived for the King, impaling him through the shoulder and spinning him to the floor.

The remainder of the bodyguards dragged the King to his horse and forced him into the saddle as another arrow hit another bodyguard. The remaining men ran for their horses and started to mount as another arrow embedded itself in the flank of the Kings horse; it reared up and threw the King from the saddle. He landed heavily on his back, the wind knocked from him as he tried to stand, he got to his knees and looked up into the dead soulless eyes of a now dismounted dragoon walking slowly and purposely towards him, drawing back on an evil looking bow. For a moment he was frozen in fear, he stared at him, knowing he could not avoid the arrow, and remembering what one of these arrows had done to Balstore. As he remained frozen to the spot a flash to his front made him stagger back in fright as a lone horseman crashed through and cleaved the dragoon from his feet, the horseman's sword making a sickening crunch on the dragoon's unprotected head.

The horseman wheeled his horse around and made his way to the stricken King, who was struggling to his feet and still backing away, unsure if he was friend or enemy. The King's bodyguards at last reaching him and forming a protective circle. The horseman drew up twenty paces short and dismounted, sword already back in its scabbard so he did not pose a threat, and he then fell to his knees in front of his King.

"Who are you?" asked King Cathal.

"Jonoak my King, of Shamir Port, my father is Lord Shamir," he replied. "Jonoak, yes I remember your father presenting you to court in my service."

"I also remember the day, but at this moment I have grave news My King, the harbour is no more, attacked and destroyed by a dragoon patrol. Burnt the harbour and my ship, lured all others onto rocks by using false signal fires so we can assume there are no more reinforcements. You cannot head in that direction for you will be trapped against the sea. And the battle for Kino'le, is over, our army is in full retreat, a long story but the use of trebuchet and longbows saw our forces decimated. General Carmak is behind us by half a league or so, with twenty men, he will know more about the situation and can advise us to our best course."

"Very well, we will do as you suggest, as it would appear you saved my life, and I think I will be needing a new counsellor."

They looked down at Balstore, his head almost split in two. What the fuck happened to him thought Jonoak.

The two Princesses of the Kingdom of Light stood in the palace strong room and faced each other holding hands, neither were fully conscious of their actions but were not unconscious. Victarny had risen from the bed like some kind of ghostly wraith, no effort or pain had shown on her face as she had stood and taken her sister's hands. The light surrounded and emanated from them both, a light so bright it would have blinded a normal person.

Sarah and the two bodyguards lay sprawled where they had fallen after hitting the walls, a deep even breathing pattern coming from them in their sleep as their wounds closed up and healed. The sisters had no conscious thought but knew everything going on within the light that continued to spread outwards. They could feel the blood sinking into the land, the pain of those they loved, the pain and fear of those who had come to take from them by force what was theirs, and little areas of darkness where the light would never penetrate. The soul of Lorgane the Wizard trying to escape the burning light, the bodies of the Dark Stalkers turning into dried husks, and what remained of Balstore after he had tried to run for the coast. Of all the enemy in their lands they knew they could not let him escape and again without conscious thought they had sent the light straight into his head and started to boil his brain, it had taken no effort on their part but they had been helped by Commander Gromm.

Danyard and Gemmell bleeding on the field, their wounds closing and blood flow slowing as did all that the light touched. A man from Dalstock, dressed strangely, every breath he took pained him with most of his ribs broken. A young woman of a similar age to the sisters, with a connection to Amyeen, laying on a bed near dead from exhaustion. And Blood, flying like never before in the light and stronger than ever, swooping low over houses and soaring high again and again.

The light continued to spread out over the land and their thoughts pulsed with it, the defeated army on the run, mixed emotions, glad to be alive but scared for the future, both here and on their return to Branvere. Sad for their friends who would never leave this land, men who spilt their blood to serve the vanity of one man, even the normally emotionless Blood Huntress felt their pain through the empathy of her sister.

The soldiers fear increased as the light hit them, some thinking it would burn them and causing them to run from it, but to no avail, it spread over and they slowed down in wonder as it touched them, relief running through them when they did not burst into flames at its touch. The consciousness of the Princess's spread to them with the light and told them what to do, to lay down their arms and the pursuing army would leave them be, as most did, throwing swords, maces, axes spears and crossbows far from them as they could, some also going as far as removing pieces of plate and chainmail, as expensive as it was it was no use to them dead. They slowed, knowing that if the army behind them caught them, they would be safe.

As the light hit Balstore they forced more and more pressure into him, even the compassionate Victarny had a rage about her that was unstoppable, this was his plan, his war, every man woman and child who had suffered had done so at his instigation and they let their full rage build in his head, and then suddenly the pressure released itself and they did not linger to find out why as their minds seemed to be separating.

Slowly they both began to regain control of their own thoughts, a separation of minds occurred as each individual mind fought against the invasion and control of the other. Amyeen, used to sharing her mind with another living being lingered longer until her sister suddenly pushed her out and they both collapsed to the floor, the energy they had expended sending out the healing light suddenly taking its toll on them. They did not awaken for three days.

Epilogue
Four Days Later

General Carmak watched as his wounded were loaded onto the wagons, most wounds miraculously healed but some men still in fever or delirious. In the absence of Balstore and the majority of Branvere's nobility wiped out he found himself the ranking officer apart from the King himself, and Danyard did not trust the King. The retreating army had started their long march home two days ago, but he and the King's entourage had been held prisoner for two more days while Kino'le made its demands for war reparations. But now they were to board wagons to be sent home by ship from Kardon, the plan being they would arrive before the ragged remnants of their army and placate the remaining nobles who had lost sons but more importantly to them, the irreplaceable bloodlines of their destriers.

The final battle had ended and they were being allowed to leave with King Cathal still head of state. Danyard had had most of his discussions with the enemy General and they had formed a mutual respect for each other. Carmak was checking that each man being loaded was actually a Branvere soldier for he did not want a Kino'le spy in his midst.

The Kino'le Royal Surgeon kept a close eye on him as the last man was lifted onto the wagon and then he waved him over.

"We have one more man, I have had him kept under sedation for each time he wakes he starts screaming about bats and giant men and The Blood Huntress of all things. In his lucid moments when he is calm, he remembers being in a battle but cannot remember where or how he came to be wounded. He is wearing Branvere Browns and carrying a sword scabbard bearing the mark of Balstore. Is he one of yours?"

"Oh yes, he is, he is one of ours, and I am glad to see him alive, please have him put on the wagons," he replied as he looked down into the unconscious face of Callen.

About the Author

G. E. Webb lives in a small Hampshire town with his partner of nineteen years. He has had various jobs including soldier, bouncer, printer and warehouse manager. At present, he is serving in the railways.

He also lives with the world's angriest tortoise, the world's most evil cat, and the world's laziest bulldog. This is his first novel and he started it before he had even heard of *Game of Thrones*, all the while battling a serious chocolate hobnob addiction. *The Blood Princess* is the first novel in what will be *The Blood Trilogy*.